Give Me Time

Also by Linnea A. Due

HIGH AND OUTSIDE

Give Me Time

LINNEA A. DUE

WILLIAM MORROW AND COMPANY, INC.
NEW YORK

This is a work of fiction. While there are references to certain public figures, the central characters and other private parties portrayed herein are products of my imagination and are not intended to resemble actual persons.

Library of Congress Cataloging in Publication Data

Due, Linnea A.
Give me time.

I. Title.
PS3554.U314G5 1984 813′.54 84-6677
ISBN 0-688-03926-X

Printed in the United States of America

First Edition

1 2 3 4 5 6 7 8 9 10

BOOK DESIGN BY PATRICE FODERO

For Clyta

ACKNOWLEDGMENTS

I would like to thank Carole Bennett, Elisabeth Cornu, Laura Israel, Tirza Latimer, Susan Matheson, Rochelle Singer, and Sabina Thorne for their support and encouragement; Harvey Ginsberg, my editor, for his skill and patience; and Emily Rosenberg and the Berkeley-Oakland Library System for research assistance.

1968

CHAPTER 1

Six months after Martin Luther King was shot, four months after Bobby, six days after the 1968 Democratic National Convention shook Chicago, upperclassmen at New York's Ridgedale College for Women gathered in the dining hall to participate in an arcane ritual that everyone agreed was not only sexist but delightfully kinky as well.

"I can't believe we actually do this," Portia Bethany said to Natalie Lehmann.

"Believe," Natalie said. Then she remembered. "That's right. You've never done this before. You were on stage last year yourself. . . . Hey, Hadel, this is Portia's first exposure to the Grand Freshman Parade."

"And our last," Hadel Farnon said as she set down her overflowing cup of coffee and moved the books Natalie had used to save her a seat. "It's easy, Porsh. Pretend you're a judge in the Miss America contest, except you're judging nearly everything but beauty."

"What you're really judging is how money-hungry the admissions committee was this year," Megan Franklin said. "For instance, they let in Tracy Baker, who is an utter moron but also an heiress. The broker the school gets, the more they go for people with big bucks."

Natalie winked at Megan. "And you don't have big bucks?"

Megan was not known for being graceful about her up-and-coming trust fund. It was, she told Hadel one loose-tongued evening last year, fit restitution for living with her father the tyrant, who would earmark the money "POP—payment on performance" if he could only rewrite her grandmother's will. Hadel now predicted anger, and that's what Natalie got in return for her attempted ribbing. "I'm talking about *quality*,"

Megan said, a scowl souring her American blond beauty features, made merely pretty by her air of frantic preoccupation. "She'll be a husband-hunter who spends her time leafing through *Town and Country*. Here they come."

The first freshman bounded eagerly across the back of the long dining hall. She was peering around, trying to see everything at once. Hadel shook her head sympathetically. Undisguised interest was a big no-no.

"Cherry Cheerleader," Megan said. "That's what I mean. What the hell is she going to do at Ridgedale?"

Portia screwed up her funny chipmunk face, which she often did before she disagreed with someone. To those who knew her, it meant "no offense." To the cop who bashed her over the head last spring at the Columbia sit-in, it was probably a sneer. Hadel wondered how someone who wanted to direct plays and foment the revolution could be so determinedly courteous. "Not everyone has to be a prima donna," Portia was telling Megan. "This school is so ego-heavy with its artists and dancers and actresses, I'm surprised it doesn't topple into the river. Hey, that one has a good, strong sense of herself."

"I don't know," Natalie said. "She looks a little awkward." As they watched, the woman brushed her hand against the stack of saucers, and one clattered to the floor. They could all see her ears reddening against her shirt collar as she bent to pick it up.

"Training," Portia said. "After all, she's only eighteen."

"You're only nineteen," Hadel said, laughing.

A few more freshmen braved the gauntlet of critical scrutiny. Hadel decided her three friends made a good combination. Theatrical Portia supplied the poise and grace perspective; Natalie, president of everything from junior high on, provided the leadership and ability index, while Megan, their renegade debutante, filled in with brief social sketches. Hadel could have offered her analysis of where the unknowing freshman fit on her one-to-ten scale of lesbian leanings, but instead she kept her mouth firmly shut.

"Hey, check her out!" Megan said.

"Cute," Portia nodded. The tall, slender woman wore overalls over a leotard. She glided across the dark dining hall, her feet never seeming to touch the ground.

Natalie grimaced. "A dancer," she said. "They're too . . . too-too for me."

Megan sighed. "You're right. Neurotic six ways from Sunday."

"'Six ways from Sunday'?" Hadel questioned.

"Stop hassling me," Megan snapped. "You haven't said a damned thing so far."

"Hadel never says anything at the freshman parade," Natalie defended quickly.

"I still think she's cute," Portia said.

Natalie smiled. "You're so loyal, Portia. Of course she's cute. But she's too affected for the likes of us."

"Affected *and* frigid," Megan suggested.

Natalie nodded. "My thoughts exactly. Thank you, Megan."

An undeniable air of excitement hovered around their table, as if their toes were abutting forbidden territory and the guards were out to lunch. "Anyone listening to this would think we were all a bunch of lesbians," Portia said after nearly half the freshmen had paraded past.

Hadel smiled into her coffee. The only thing she liked about this ritual was the outspokenness of straight women looking at other women. Hadel suspected lesbians would be a great deal more shy.

"Jesus!" Megan exclaimed.

Everyone whirled to see. The woman Megan was staring at was short and sprightly, clothed in army fatigue pants, tire-tread sandals and a bikini top. Her long hair, bleached nearly white from the sun, was a splendid counterpoint to her spectacular tan. Her entire upper body was toasted a deep hazel-nut brown. As they watched her survey the cafeteria line, they could all see clearly the one break in the perfect tan—the stark white outline of a crucifix emblazoned on her chest. Written on her flat brown stomach in Magic Marker were the words "Do Unto Others" followed by three dots.

"Migod," Natalie said. "She can do unto me any time she wants!"

This remark was really hopscotching too far into the forbidden territory, so Megan hastened to ask, "Do you think she's a

Christian?" She made "Christian" sound like an offshoot of Hitler Youth.

"Obviously," Natalie said.

Portia had a wide grin on her face. "She's Catholic."

"Catholic . . ." Megan muttered. Silence for a second as they all absorbed this information. Portia and Megan were long-lapsed Episcopalians. Natalie was, as she put it, a nice Jewish girl who believed in absolutely nothing. And Hadel was truly nothing, having grown up in a family hostile to religion in general. Being a Catholic and wearing a crucifix to boot were momentarily overwhelming.

"She's also not a freshman," Portia said, still wearing her silly grin.

"How do you know?" Megan demanded.

"She's my sister's roommate. Her name's Laney Villano, and she's a sophomore transfer, but she was put in with the freshmen. No one knows why."

Everyone wondered why. Then everyone wondered what awful thing they'd said about Portia's sister during her moment on stage at the Freshman Parade. "Don't worry," Portia said. "When I told Toni about the parade, she had a fit and went down to Freddy's for lunch. Laney didn't care. In fact, I think she concocted that outfit to make everybody's eyes pop out of their heads. She looked perfectly normal when she got here."

"Hmph!" Natalie scoffed. "That's not so good then."

"She succeeded," Portia pointed out.

"Admirably," Hadel said, still watching Laney in the cafeteria line. She turned back in time to catch the sharp look Natalie shot her. Hadel locked her gaze to the tabletop and fumbled for her cigarettes, her heart beating loud enough for Portia and Megan to hear. But they were watching Laney, unaware of Hadel's discomfiture and Natalie's questioning eyes. The moment stretched on until Natalie laughed and said, "You did that, Hadel."

"I did what?" Hadel yelped, half hysterically.

Portia and Megan swung back, catching the tension in Hadel's voice.

Natalie spoke slowly, giving Hadel time to recover. "You waltzed in here wearing a black leather jacket, blue jeans, army boots and mirror sunglasses. Remember? Whereas you arrived on campus in a Kimberley knit and a suede pillbox hat."

"I was just getting comfortable," Hadel protested, relieved. "I didn't know this happened."

"I know you didn't. That makes it even stranger."

"Natalie, look at what I'm wearing right now." Natalie peered across the table, then glanced underneath. Hadel was wearing a tee shirt, a black leather jacket, blue jeans and army boots. "The sunglasses were because I was terrified," Hadel explained.

Natalie nodded. "Weren't we all!"

Hadel and Natalie strolled lazily up the long hill to the dorms, place-kicking small rocks in the path. Hadel noticed a few sophomores pointing the two of them out to the freshmen. She suspected they looked intimidating to the new students. Natalie was medium-height and angular, her quick hands always moving, while her deep-brown eyes beneath her long waves of dark hair reflected an amused acceptance of the world. Humor connected the two friends—lines were already etched across Hadel's forehead, caused by years of raising her eyebrows in laughing disbelief. But where Natalie was accepting, Hadel challenged; shorter, stockier, slower to react, with clear blue eyes that pulsed with a disconcerting intensity. They made a good team, had done so all through college. Hadel imagined the sophomores were saying, "The taller one is Natalie Lehmann. She's president of the student body. And the other one is Hadel Farnon. She was campus coordinator last year even though she was a junior. They do everything around here." It was true. Natalie and Hadel had developed into the school's power alliance. The odd thing was neither especially cared. Hadel hadn't even run for office last spring. They were looking ahead, becoming frightened again. The comfortable interlude of a successful college career was nearly over, and neither was naïve enough to imagine that college popularity protected one from the nakedness of real life.

But now Hadel was worried about something more immediate. She needed to cover up for her hysteria in the dining room, lave it over with conversation guaranteed to catch Natalie's interest. She chose a surefire subject: Megan's complete avoidance of anything remotely sexual. "I was surprised Megan showed up today," Hadel began. "She even made that 'frigid' comment."

Natalie grunted, apparently too lost in an internal dialogue to respond. Hadel glanced at her. If Megan didn't get Natalie talking, nothing would. They walked on in silence, reached the dorms and continued past without pausing. When they came to the jungly area surrounding the long-abandoned apple orchard, Natalie veered off the path and knelt down, poking at an anthill with her finger. Over her shoulder, she called, "You think Laney Villano is cute?"

Hadel's stomach dropped to her feet. Away from the dining room, from the freshman parade, the question took on very different connotations. Hadel stammered out what she hoped was an acceptable answer. "She looks like she might be an interesting person."

Natalie stood up and saw the fear in Hadel's eyes. She didn't press further. They began walking again.

Hadel had always been an enigma to Natalie, from the moment she'd stood behind her in line in their own parade. Natalie was giggling nervously with someone she'd just met, aware that the upperclassmen were staring at all of them. Hadel had turned around and looked up at Natalie from behind mirrored sunglasses, and Natalie had thought, "Whoa! This is someone to stay away from," but then perversely she'd babbled, "I'm from Philadelphia," and Hadel said, "I'm from Berkeley," and they had started talking and hadn't stopped since. Yet though they supposedly told each other everything, Natalie felt Hadel kept a part of herself hidden, and that part was the key to her brooding silences and piercing eyes. Underlying her seriousness, however, was a kind of childlike hope; Hadel always seemed to be searching for something, as if she needed a kind of completion. Natalie had found this confusing. Hadel was so solid, so private—what could she possibly want? It wasn't until junior year that Natalie found herself entertaining the idea that Hadel might be searching for another woman.

She and Hadel had meandered down to the mail room on a beautiful spring morning, a month before the end of term. They picked up their mail and lay down on the grass in the warm May sunlight. A fresh breeze was skittering through the leaves of the elms along the campus road. "What's this?" Hadel asked, separating a small pink envelope from her other mail. Natalie was uninterested. She was enraged that once again her sister had failed to write, even when she had specifically asked for advice about Jeffrey, whose off-again, on-again attitude was making her miserable. She riffled irritably through the pages of *Time* and found her sister's letter stuffed between People and Books. She ripped it open and began devouring it in great gulps. Forgotten, Hadel slowly opened the pink envelope and drew out a single sheet of paper smelling of roses. A bold, defiant hand had written in dark blue ink: "We've been in classes together for three years. I think about you. If you're interested in meeting me, come to the corner of the apple orchard nearest Bendix at eleven this Friday night." The note was unsigned. Hadel read it twice and then poked Natalie away from her sister's letter.

Natalie emerged unwillingly, but she took the pink page and read as directed. When she finished, she furrowed her eyebrows at Hadel. "I don't understand," she said. What she couldn't understand even more was why Hadel was acting so pleased, smug almost. "But this must be from another student." Natalie waved it in emphasis. "Don't you think? It says in classes. And this is a woman's handwriting."

Hadel leaned over and peered at it. "Yeah. Either a junior or a senior. The three years thing," she explained to Natalie's blankness. "That's nice, isn't it? I wonder who she is?"

Natalie was completely disoriented, as if her quietly intellectual mother and staid lawyer father announced over dinner that they'd decided to move to Manhattan and run numbers. She couldn't imagine how she would feel if she had received such a letter. Terrified? Ashamed? Disgusted? Indignant? All of the above, she figured, tending toward the latter. Yet Hadel was undeniably—what?—flattered, though now she was stumbling a bit, groping toward Natalie as if she needed clues. "What will you do?" Natalie asked, a chill spreading inside. She almost expected to hear Hadel say, "Meet her, of course." And then what will *I* say?

But Hadel shrugged. "Nothing. I have to go back now. I've gotta work on my economics paper." She went off clutching the letter, as if it were a precious gift to be savored in private.

Natalie remained on the grass for nearly twenty minutes, her sister's letter lying forgotten next to her. A force flood of memories was raging through her—Hadel's refusal to sleep with any man she liked, instead fucking people she'd met once at a party and never seeing them again, ignoring their frantic phone calls for days on end until they gave up. Sophomore year, at an insane Columbia Law School drunken orgy, Natalie had wandered into a bedroom to get another pack of cigarettes out of her jacket pocket. She had literally stumbled over Hadel blowing a big blond hunk on a pile of coats. Hadel hadn't even noticed; the blond waved Natalie away weakly. In the car going home, Natalie approached the subject obliquely: "You were gone for a while there. I wasn't sure where you were."

Hadel was almost asleep. "I was in the bedroom," she mumbled.

"With that beautiful Swede," Natalie concurred. "He's gorgeous."

"Hmmm . . ." Hadel began nodding out over the dashboard.

Natalie poked her. "What's his name?"

"Whose?"

"That beautiful guy you were with in the bedroom," Natalie said, exasperated. The one with his cock in your mouth, you nitwit.

"Oh, the blond guy? I don't know. He was there when I went in. We didn't exchange names." She giggled. "It was fun."

Natalie discovered she was white-knuckling the steering wheel. She forced herself to calm down. "Hadel, I don't understand. Why won't you sleep with Steve when you really like him?"

"I won't even kiss Steve," Hadel snapped, wide awake.

Natalie knew this too. Steve had once unburdened himself to Natalie, horribly bursting into tears when he came to the no-kissing part.

"I've told you and told you, Natalie!" Hadel wailed. "I couldn't be in love with him. I'd always be . . . distant. He deserves somebody nice who's in love with him too. It'd be mean for me to lead him on when I could never be what he needs."

"But . . ." Natalie sputtered, filled with the image of her friend with the prick of someone she didn't even know down her throat, while Steve, a brilliant medical student, scratched feebly on Hadel's door like an unwanted stray kitten. "But *you're* nice!" Natalie hollered. "You're very nice! Do you think you're bad?"

"What?" Hadel was staring out at the dark night, at the shadowy trees whipping by the thruway. "No. I don't think I'm bad. I love him, but I could never be in love with him, that's all."

Steve had hung on through the first months of junior year, perhaps thinking a summer away would have made Hadel's heart grow fonder. He gave up in November, fading back into med school, though he occasionally called Natalie to ask how Hadel was. Hadel hadn't replaced him with another bright young man. She had been elected campus coordinator of student activities the year before; she threw herself into the job, arguing the jukebox selections with shadowy Mafia types, persuading people on the New York State liquor board to give Ridgedale a liquor license, figuring out an alarm system to warn students if the drug bust people appeared on campus. Steve, listening to all this news resignedly, would finally hang up with a heavy sigh.

Natalie stretched out on the grass, thinking of Hadel's obvious pleasure at the little pink note. Would anyone but a lesbian be thrilled at this proposal to meet in the darkest corner of the apple orchard? Natalie thought not. Lesbian. The word seemed etched in the grass, silhouetted in the shadows, whispered in the breeze. The chill inside her grew until she actually started shivering. How could you think such a thing? she railed at herself, but she had to admit the explanation fit the facts. Hadel could blithely sleep with strangers because it meant nothing more than a few moments of excitement. She couldn't sleep with Steve because he deserved someone who could love him. And the reason Hadel couldn't love him was because she could only love women. And knew it. So why hasn't she said so? Why hasn't she told me she's a lesbian?

And Hadel still hadn't told Natalie, in spite of Natalie's little encouragements, like asking her today if she thought Laney Villano was cute. Natalie glanced over at Hadel trudging along beside her. Hadel hadn't spoken a word since the fear had washed her eyes. She's frightened of telling me, Natalie thought, but she's more frightened of telling herself, even though she already knows. That's probably why she didn't meet the woman in the orchard that night; she hadn't even stayed on campus. It was very confusing, and Natalie was aware she more than halfway hoped Hadel would never bring it up at all.

After her unsettling walk with Natalie, Hadel escaped to her room and pretended to be unpacking her trunk. Natalie had already begun fixing up her room across the hall. She had carried what seemed like hundreds of plants up the two flights of stairs from her car, and now she was suspending them in front of the windows until her room resembled a dark, furry cave. Hadel could hear her singing odd snatches of "Bali Hai." Hadel endured ten more minutes of jungle music before she got up to close her door. Good timing, because just as she reached for the doorknob, she caught a glimpse of Natalie, now attired in her tropical print halter top and white shorts, hauling out her Don Ho records.

Hadel turned to the back of her airmailed edition of the *Berkeley Barb* and began to read the sex ads. One ad requested "an intellectual not afraid to laugh, a cynic not afraid to cry, a sensualist not afraid to love." It turned out to be an ad placed by a couple for "a bisexual woman to join our family, to grow with us and love with us." Hadel scanned the rest of the ads. It seemed half the families in Berkeley were dying for bisexual women. How come they didn't want bisexual men? And were there that many bisexual women to go around? Hadel certainly didn't classify herself as bisexual, though so far she'd only slept with men. No, she was queer, all right, probably a ten on Kinsey's one-to-ten scale. She just hadn't found anyone to be queer with, which, any way you looked at it, was a prerequisite.

Hadel threw the paper on the floor and picked up her latest World War II pulp novel, *Beachhead at Iwo Jima*. The sergeant, a crusty old guy of twenty-four, was trying to get his unit dug in while at the same time finding the kid through scathing rounds of machine gun fire. There was always a kid, and the kid was always lost. Hadel identified more with the sergeant, who would eventually either fall on a grenade to save the kid, or be saved himself by the kid when the kid became a Man. The sergeant had just spotted the kid quivering behind a beached landing craft when someone knocked on her door. "What?" Hadel growled. She didn't want to return to Ridgedale right now, not even for Natalie. The person who barged into her room after another perfunctory knock, however, was Megan, for whom it was definitely not worth leaving Iwo Jima. "*What?*" Hadel's growl turned aggrieved.

"Hi, Hadel," Megan said heartily. This was dangerous; Megan was never hearty unless she wanted something. She ranged over toward Hadel's bed and stared at the *Barb*'s cover photo, which showed several people with very bloody head wounds. The sixty-point type blared, "Cops Go Berserk in Chicago."

"Disgusting," Megan said. Hadel couldn't tell if she meant the blood or the demonstration. "Well!" Megan chirped, dismissing Chicago, "Natalie went to Hawaii again this summer, huh?"

Hadel muttered an assent. She kept her book in front of her face, wishing Megan would take the hint and scram. Unfortunately, Hadel's peace of mind was even less interesting to Megan than Chicago. "Say," she said, "remember that paper on Luther I never did last year?"

Hadel groaned. She now knew why Megan was being so enthusiastic.

"I saw Mr. Crider in the library, and he said he was ignoring it, but he couldn't ignore it much longer and feel good about himself. You know that approach? I told him I'd give it to him tomorrow morning. So I was wondering if you brought those Dexedrine again this year." The spark of tension in her voice could have electrocuted a large man. Every September, Hadel arrived wth a plastic jar filled with five hundred orange tablets, a going-back-to-school present from her doctor father. Hadel ended up taking probably twelve, while Megan accounted for most of the other 488.

Spare me, Hadel begged the heavens. Real life was full of these gray areas of culpability. If she gave Megan the speed, was she responsible for Megan's almost-certain nervous collapse four months down the road? If she didn't give her the speed, was she responsible for Megan's failing the course? She longed to escape back to her book, where the priorities were clear. You tried to save your buddies and save yourself. You didn't have months to brood over the consequences of your actions, because you were either dead or in another life-and-death situation a minute later. "Don't you remember last spring, Megan? You went days without sleeping. You lost twenty pounds. You thought Grace Pearson wanted to kill you."

"Oh, I know. I'm not getting into that again. I just need three for this paper."

Hadel ignored the grays and chose solitude. Megan would never go away without her precious pills. "They're in the bottom drawer of my dresser."

Megan shook out the pills, showed Hadel she had taken only three, and scooted out the door, a crooked smile of triumph on her face. Hadel went back to Iwo Jima, but she couldn't shake the memory of Megan crunched against the dorm wall, pleading with Grace Pearson not to kill her. Equally distracting was the way "Tiny Bubbles" had discovered a way to seep through her closed door. Things were not going swimmingly, and school hadn't even started yet. Hadel decided to avoid the dinner hour by slipping off to the bar downtown for a double cheeseburger.

She had just settled herself in the farthest booth, under cover of Freddy's greasy gloom, when she discovered Laney Villano standing in front of her table, cradling a draft at her side. "You go to Ridgedale, don't you?" Laney asked. Her voice was as beautiful as her face, which was twice as beautiful close up as it had been across the dining hall. Not movie star beautiful, but real beautiful, with life and anger and softness and determination rippling under that expectant half smile. Hadel realized Laney was looking expectant because she was waiting for an answer to her question. "Yeah," Hadel said. Then she waited for Laney either to go away or to sit down.

Laney sat down, plonking her draft on the table between them. "You want some beer?"

"I've got an order coming," Hadel said. On cue, the waitress appeared carrying the cheeseburger, fries, and a Coke. It all looked sickening spread out on the table in front of her.

Laney was watching with hooded eyes, drumming her fingers lightly on the tabletop. Hadel bit into her cheeseburger and discovered she was having trouble chewing, much less swallowing past the constriction in her throat. "You're Hadel Farnon," Laney announced. "You're a bigwig."

Hadel shrugged her shoulders. It was all she was capable of at the moment.

"My name's Laney Villano. I'm a sophomore transfer who got put in the freshman dorms and no one knows why." She rattled off this information as if she'd memorized it for a test.

Hadel said in the same rote monotone: "I'm a senior and I live in Simpson, which is the third floor of the administration building. I know why."

"Why?" Laney asked, putting her fist on the table and her chin on her fist.

"Simpson is the best 'cause there's no one there at night but sixteen students. I got the best dorm because I'm a bigwig." She paused and then smiled at Laney. She could tell it came across as a smile because Laney smiled back.

Laney reached across the table and dragged Hadel's book of matches in front of her with her free hand. She played with it for a moment and then said: "I know why I'm in with the freshmen."

Hadel nodded while she bit into a French fry. She had decided the fries were safer, being smaller and easier to swallow. "You don't have to tell me," she said.

Laney made a face. "It's because my parents are ticked off at me. I applied here as a freshman and didn't get in. I refused to come for the personal interview. I didn't want to go to college. I ended up at NYU, and then I skipped out after my first year. That summer I went to a Wilderness camp—" Hadel waggled a French fry for more information. Laney blinked acknowledgment and edged her fist and her chin an inch closer on the slick brown surface of the table. "Wilderness is like Outward Bound, teaching people to survive in the woods, but it's supposedly more rigorous. I stayed for the summer and qualified for instructor's training that fall. My parents caught up with me by spring. They made me reapply to Ridgedale and dragged me to the interview. This time I got accepted. My parents convinced the administration I was socially immature and should be in with the freshmen. They think I'm immature because I'm not buckling down to college, which they say is the necessary stepping-stone to a career or marriage. If I'm not buckling down to college, by inference I'm not buckling down to life."

All this, Hadel marveled, said from her fist. Laney finally

raised her head to take a brief sip of beer. Then she put her head back down. "Why are you called Hadel?"

"Hester Dale," Hadel answered.

Laney nodded. Then she pointed at Hadel's cheeseburger. "That's getting cold."

"I'm not too hungry."

"Me neither," Laney sighed. "So what do people do around here for fun? How about sports?"

"Sports?" Hadel hadn't thought about sports since she was in junior high, when it became obvious women weren't supposed to play or be interested in sports. At the time this was a severe blow, because Hadel loved basketball. But it was common knowledge at Truman Junior High that the only girls who played sports were queers. The threat of being "found out" was more than enough to make Hadel recoil in terror. That a substantial number of the most popular girls in school were on GAA teams didn't faze her; they could afford to defy the edict, while Hadel couldn't. If *she* played, everyone would know. Hadel looked now at Laney, who was studying her with a quizzical expression, one eyebrow raised. "Sports?" Hadel repeated.

CHAPTER 2

Megan finished her paper for Mr. Crider in less than an hour. She had downed one of the Dexedrine the moment she'd left Hadel's room, and now she popped another as a reward for a job well done. The paper was secondary; her real accomplishment had been assuring herself another year's supply of the triangular orange pills. She had caught Hadel as a fly fisherman plays a trout, jerked the line so the hook was deeply embedded, reeled her in with growing certainty of triumph. As the second pill engaged the first in a clash of superheroes, Megan embellished her own battle with fishy Hadel, judging the tautness of the line, the precise moment for the quick flip of her wrist, allowing Hadel to run free for a giddy second before Megan demonstrated, with another skillful jerk, the exact and decreasing parameters of this cage of life. Finally, tiring of the game, she beached Hadel, yanked her out of the cage to lie gasping on the gravel, then measured off her catch with wide-apart hands, a very big trout indeed.

"What are you doing?" Natalie asked. There wasn't a hint of a smile in her voice.

Megan whipped around in her swiveling desk chair, her hands still outstretched. "Ah . . . ah—"

"Well, come and see my room."

If Natalie had asked Hadel what she was doing, Megan thought resentfully, the dash of acerbity in Natalie's tone would have been far outweighed by the promise of wry laughter, to be released as soon as Natalie heard Hadel's undoubtedly marvelous explanation. Megan's lot was to be treated with suspicious scorn.

"Hadel's gone," Natalie said over her shoulder. She continued wondering aloud what had happened to Hadel, as if they were having a normal conversation, but Megan had grasped the point—she was strictly a substitute room-viewer.

She made appropriate remarks about Natalie's jungle haven, which looked as if furry and repulsive insects would crawl out of the plants the moment Natalie fell asleep, and then she escaped back to her own room before Natalie could mention the freshman parade. Megan didn't want to think about the freshman parade. She had spent hours trying not to think of it. She felt for the reassurance of the third pill in her jeans pocket, and she pulled it out and swallowed it. Then she stood still, consternation coloring her cheeks. She hadn't meant to take the pill; she'd wanted to save it for tomorrow or even the weekend. But how could she be expected to behave sensibly after an entire summer in the company of her iron-fisted father, who demanded a life trail as smooth and clear as glass? It was no wonder she'd taken the third pill or made a fool of herself at the parade.

She pulled on her jacket and dashed down the stairs, her feet moving more slowly than her mind so that she nearly tripped. Would she be besieged by the parade and her father all night? She had to exert control. She tried to think of reeling Hadel in, standing over her as she gasped on the beach. But that didn't work either, because underneath it all she knew there was no joy in tricking Hadel. Hadel ascribed the best motives to everyone, honestly believed she was helping Megan by giving her the pills. Hadel would give Megan the shirt off her back if Megan asked for it. Furthermore, Hadel had not disgraced herself at the freshman parade, had not pronounced someone frigid just to be one of the gang, had a backlog of so much respect she could keep silent for a hundred years and the others would never once press her for a comment. Hadel was above gossip, above sexual bantering. Megan could trick Hadel to the beach, but she couldn't measure her. How could minnow fins encompass a trout?

Megan was walking so fast she almost slammed into a tree in the middle of the apple orchard. She picked her way through the darkness more carefully, found the path and the fork and followed the left turn to the music building. It loomed up before her suddenly, and she sighed with relief at the sight of its brick walls, its black, deserted face, its mute practice rooms. It was all hers, as it almost always was. The front door opened (had they left it unlocked the entire summer?), and Megan strode down the central hall, mistress of the manor, flicking on lights as she passed. She entered the recital room, flooded it by throwing the switch that activated the bank of bulbs mounted high in the ceiling, then threw open the French doors at the back. She sat down at the baby grand and began playing slowly, running her fingers across the keys as if she were strumming a guitar. She added a bass line with her left hand, and then, as the third pill winged in with the second and the first, she went ragtime, became a keysmith in an 1890s Arizona cowboy bar, the guys playing poker behind her, the girls clustered around the piano. She wrapped her lips around a chewed-off cigar, reached for the shot glass when she finished a song. There was no applause; Megan was just doing what she'd been hired to do.

How nice it would be to play invisibly, to be accepted for performing her job, to banish her autocratic father with his unsatisfied expectations. She'd been so glad to get back to Ridgedale, get the hell out of Virginia, but nothing had changed here. Hadel might well give her the shirt off her back, but she had no more respect for her than Natalie did. Hadel and Natalie were a pair unto themselves—Megan had no function in their lives beyond being a petty irritant scrounging speed. One of her fondest memories was the evening she and Hadel had gone out to dinner after Hadel had driven her to a doctor's appointment; Hadel had told Megan over their pork chops that she thought Natalie's boyfriend Jeffrey was an idiot. Megan was so pleased—Hadel had trusted her with keeping a secret from Natalie. But the dinner had never been repeated, and Natalie and Hadel did nearly everything together, occasionally inviting Megan along as an afterthought. Megan fantasized an image of them as full-to-the-brim shopping carts, stuffed with turkeys and oranges and cartons of milk, while she rolled slowly through the night shadows of an abandoned supermarket parking lot, her metal basket cobwebbed and rusty.

She mouthed her cigar, launched into another tune but the parking lot stubbornly refused to budge from her head. *Shopping carts?* She tried to laugh. It didn't work. Her lips wouldn't move. She began to slam her fingers against the keys, her flesh the advance troops of an army of frenzy. She closed her eyes and saw her shopping cart wildly spinning, pointlessly careening in circles on its little rusted wheels. When she opened her eyes again, she felt moisture on her lids, on her cheeks. She brushed away the tears and played even harder. As she pounded away, she watched herself being nuts. She was fascinated with this person driven to insanity by drugs and her father's high-altitude demands. Another part of her was Megan the child looking at Megan the adult. The child was disappointed and bewildered. Megan couldn't stand disappointing anyone. The confusion on the child's face hurt her most of all and finally caused her to stop bludgeoning the piano.

Before Megan stopped, however, her pounding had snared an unwilling audience of one. Hadel had mentioned the old apple orchard to Laney as they'd walked back up from Freddy's; after Laney dropped Hadel off at the administration building, Laney had headed straight for the abandoned orchard, needing quiet to think how to get out of her assigned room with Portia's sister Toni. When the overgrown path Laney was following forked, she took a left and discovered not only the antithesis of quiet, but also that what she had feared most about coming to Ridgedale, her not being able to keep herself apart from the turbulences of those around her, was happening already. She stood underneath the tall windows, chilled by the frenzied quality of the piano playing. Telling herself that the desperation was not her own didn't help. She knew what she should be able to do—shake her head at the person's misfortune and continue her walk. But what she knew and what she told herself only mushroomed her panic, for she was unable to move her feet. The more she struggled to unlock bone and muscle, to force herself to take one step and then two, the more overwhelmed and paralyzed she became. Her own handicap—that of being unable to tell where she ended and another person began—prevented her from separating herself from the craziness of whoever was inside the music building, playing that devil piano. She was mired by the insanity of someone else as surely as if she had stumbled into quicksand.

She realized that her ability to function at all in the face of such a handicap was largely the result of the overseas postings of her diplomat father and translator mother. If she had grown up in the States, her brother Ronald might have gone his own way, oblivious to the affliction of his younger sister. As it was, however, they were often each other's only companion, and Ronald was willing not only to listen but also to help Laney learn to survive in a world she found incomprehensible.

Ronald recognized that Laney saw things differently by the time he was eight, shortly after the family's move from Pakistan to Ecuador. One evening Laney, then four years old, appeared at the dinner table wearing a bandage wrapped around her left hand. Her explanation—that Daddy had stepped on her kitten Patches' paw—struck her parents as cute. Ronald thought otherwise. He waited until until dinner was over, when the two children could escape to the garden. "Dad stepped on Patches, not on you," he told her once they were out of parental earshot.

"So?" she queried. Any insolence in her voice was canceled by the look in her eyes. Laney worshiped her towheaded brother; apart from Patches and a few of her toys, Ronald was the only focus in her life. Her parents were too big to encompass—trying to see them was like straining her neck to take in a whole tree when there was a pretty, bright bird on the limb right in front of her.

"Then why is *your* hand bandaged?"

"Because Daddy hurt me when he stepped on Patches."

"That's impossible," Ronald scoffed. They had reached the south wall of the garden. Ronald led them to a small bench, where they sat down. "You're not Patches, so you can't be hurt when she's hurt."

Laney considered this. "Sometimes I can be Patches," she countered.

Ronald stroked his eyebrow slowly with the tip of his finger, a habit he'd picked up from an embassy guard in Karachi. "Can Patches be you?"

Laney gnawed on her lower lip. Ronald was asking hard questions. "No, I don't think so. Patches is a cat."

"Right!" Ronald said triumphantly. "And you're a person. So you can't be hurt when Patches is hurt, and you can't be Patches either."

Laney didn't want to disagree with Ronald, but she couldn't help it. She shook her head regretfully. "Sometimes I can." She added a moment later, afraid she'd hurt him, "I'm sorry."

"No," he said. "I understand."

Perhaps because he was a child himself, when fantasy and real life flow one to the other, he did understand. And because he was a serious boy who loved his sister, he was worried. He understood that Laney was not "overly sensitive," the tag she quickly acquired. He knew that when she cried out upon seeing a dog hit in the street, her cry was not one of horror, but a gasp of pain. He knew that when Laney dropped a plate and then examined her hand, she was not looking for cuts but for breakage. When Ronald left for college ten years later, he was still worried, though in the interim he had, in effect, "socialized" her, taught her the outer perimeters of experience that could be termed personal. She very rarely made the sort of mistake that would cause others to look at her oddly. Ronald was aware, however, that he had provided her with a constant backdrop of support. He had no idea how she would function without him. All he could do was leave her with a piece of advice: if she could lose her boundaries to something negative, she could also flow into something positive. "Focus on someone strong," he told her, though he knew this could have unhappy consequences. Thinking of those consequences, and regretting now that he had allowed her to pin herself on him so completely, he said, "You have an advantage, really. This is all a game, every bit of it. Those who can stand away from the field occasionally can join back in with a better idea of strategy." He had just glimpsed an important truth: Laney's savior could never be another person, for no one would be capable of providing her with the ordered environment she needed to sustain herself.

Although Ronald was proved right in the long run, he had left Laney equipped to handle the immediate challenges of her life. Far more calculating about what was necessary to her emotional survival than others her age, she went on to a brilliant career at American Students Abroad High School in Madras, joining student activities by the drove—the tennis team, the dramatic society, the debating club. That she was stunningly beautiful and a witty conversationalist didn't hurt her chances either. At the end of her senior year, she had won the crowns of homecoming queen and prom queen and been voted "most popular" and "most likely to succeed." But the senior year glory that she cherished most, and the one that would have shocked

Ronald to the core, was bedding down a startled Lucinda Balforte in the sleeper section of a train bound for Bangalore during a school field trip. While being Miss Teen Dream, Laney had developed an eye for women, and Lucinda was quite a catch, almost as desirable as Laney herself. Best of all, though Lucinda avoided Laney for the remaining weeks of the year, on the last day of school she handed Laney a note in which she had written a veiled but complimentary reference to "the fun we had on the field trip."

When Laney arrived home that day, she found gray-faced parents and a telegram announcing Ronald's death in an automobile accident in New Hampshire. Laney climbed the steps to her room, veered automatically toward her dresser and began to cream off her makeup, staring at herself in the mirror. Then she fell to the floor and kicked and screamed without a sound, biting the heel of her hand to keep quiet, for hadn't Ronald told her over and over again that she couldn't let anyone but him know when she was frightened? Ronald's worry—that no one could give Laney the kind of place she required for survival—began to come true on the day of his death.

Laney surfaced with a snap. She had been standing outside the music building for minutes, foolishly remembering Ronald when she knew Ronald couldn't help her anymore. Her muscles were quivering dangerously; she was as tense as a bird dog on a point. The insane piano playing had continued—in fact, now seemed to be reaching some sort of apex. Laney shuddered. She *had* to get away from here. Focus on someone strong. Ronald's advice had worked in the past. She cast around among the few people she'd met here and realized Hadel was perfect for tonight's task. She was eminently level-headed. She would not be frightened by the chaotic slamming on the keys, not be paralyzed by the turmoil of someone else. And even if she were afraid, as Laney was now, Hadel would keep her head, not fly into hysteria. Hadel was, in fact, a hero type, one of those who chose to be brave when she knew no one would fault caution or even trepidation. And though Laney suspected heroes valued death more than life (why else would they throw themselves in front of trains, or dive into frozen lakes?), sometimes it was calming to think of them, in the same way it was helpful to imagine oneself to be Minnesota Fats when faced with a difficult pool shot. Laney discovered, if she placed herself in Hadel's mind, that she could very easily unstick her feet, walk away from the music building and get back to the freshman dorms.

She stood for a moment at the bottom of the dorm stairwell, waiting for her head to clear. This evening's experience was exactly what had concerned her about coming to Ridgedale; there were too many crazies here, and she could see herself seeping into each and every one of them. Something had to be done, and done quickly. She could create her own structures—her question to Hadel about sports had been the start of that—but more was needed. She decided to stick close to Hadel, avoid the music building and get rid of the roommate. Staying away from the music building was easy, and it was possible both her other goals could be accomplished with one bold stroke. Portia, as Hadel's friend and the roommate's sister, was the key to Laney's plan, hatched hurriedly as she mounted the steps to her floor.

Laney's roommate problem had started that morning, from the moment she'd walked in the door of her new room, carrying her battered suitcase scarred from twenty foreign countries and countless trips by sea, rail and air. Antonia Bethany had looked at Laney's suitcase and sniffed. She had a set of matched luggage, which she was displaying to best advantage by littering both beds with an assortment of makeup cases, hatboxes and five or six varied-shape suitcases.

Portia, who'd been trying to aid her prickly sister, was relieved at Laney's entrance. She shoved Antonia's stuff unceremoniously off the bed next to the window. "Cut it out, Toni," she said to the wail of protest. And to Laney, "I'm Portia Bethany, and this is my sister Toni. What's your name?"

Laney introduced herself and looked around the room in dismay. "Do we all live here?"

Portia laughed. "No, I'm a sophomore. I live over in Bendix Hall."

"I'm a sophomore," Laney said.

"These are the freshman dorms," Toni said nastily. "You must have gotten the wrong room."

"Afraid not," Laney answered. She opened her suitcase and then sat down beside it on the bed. "Boy, I'm tired." She lay back and stared at the ceiling, while Toni rolled her eyes and sighed. A slob for a roommate, just what she'd always wanted. On the other hand, the roommate had an amazing tan. Maybe she had a sun lamp. "Where'd you get the tan?"

Portia grimaced. "Don't be rude," she instructed.

"In Morocco," Laney answered. "My father's in the Foreign Service."

"That's like us, then," Portia said. "Our father's career army—we've been to a million places, mostly ugly, for a year or two at a stretch."

Laney nodded. "That's how it was. It makes for independence, but it's disorienting. New school, new language, new house, new money, no friends."

Toni was pointedly ignoring this conversation. She refused to acknowledge she might have one thing in common with this person who certainly had not been educated at Cathedral, the preparatory school she and Portia had been sent to. Why Portia was even attempting to chat was beyond her. She started rescuing her luggage while Portia described the freshman parade. "You mean they look at people?" Toni said, aghast. "That's really queer! What kind of a weird place is this?"

"It's all in fun. Everybody's interested in the new class. There're less than five hundred students here, so a hundred-some people is a big addition. It's a way of doing what everybody's going to do anyway, and have fun doing it besides."

"Well, they can stare at somebody else," Toni said. "I'm going downtown for lunch."

Portia shrugged and glanced over at Laney, who was lying on her bed apparently not listening. But then Laney caught Portia's eye and winked.

When Laney burst into the room, brimming over with her clever plan, she found Portia and Toni in nearly the same positions as she'd left them that morning. Toni had put away her matched luggage and had now piled posters all over Laney's bed. Portia swept them all off on the floor. "How'd you like the freshman parade?" Portia asked.

"Fascinating," Laney said. "I wouldn't have missed it for the world."

"You were the big star."

Toni looked at them suspiciously and announced she had to wash her hair. The moment she walked out the door, Portia and Laney started talking at once. "Look," Laney overrode, desperate to propose her idea, "are there empty rooms around? Closets? Anything?"

Portia wasn't the least bit surprised. "There's a living room in Bendix. We don't have a TV, so it doesn't get used much. But you'd have to get out if someone wanted to entertain her parents or boyfriend or something. If that happens, you can hang out in my room."

"What are we waiting for?" Laney snapped her suitcase shut and followed Portia out the door.

One week later, Laney organized the Ridgedale Old Girls' Touch Football Team. She did this by putting signs in the dining hall and Freddy's. Four people showed up for the first meeting. Laney went around and collared all the drunks and drug addicts. Fifty people came for the next meeting, mostly for the free wine Laney had advertised. Hadel was one of the four and one of the fifty.

Laney stood up in front of the noisy crowd stuffed in Bendix's living room and drew plays on a blackboard she'd borrowed from the science laboratory. No one paid the least bit of attention except for Hadel, who managed between sips of wine to ask several intelligent and searching questions. Laney assigned everyone tasks. She picked thirty-two players, eight cheerleaders and six officials. This worked out perfectly, since four women had already passed out underneath the couches. Laney announced the first game would take place Wednesday, the very next day, between twelve and two.

During half-time, Laney drew everyone together and changed the name of the team to the Ridgedale Old Girls' Tackle Football Team. Touch was all passing, Laney explained. There was no room for real strategy or brute force on the line. She also intimated that she had challenged several other women's colleges to games. Everyone blustered back onto the field.

When they lined up for the first play, Hadel found herself opposite a big bruiser named Leona Carswell. Leona ran over Hadel and sacked the quarterback. Hadel picked herself up off the ground and looked sorrowfully at Laney, who tapped her clipboard in sympathy. On the next play, Leona elbowed Hadel in the breast and pounded past her. Hadel spun around in pain and happened to grab Leona's flowing shirttail for support.

"Holding!" the referee shouted. "Five yards!" She paced back the distance, and the quarterback looked at Hadel sorrowfully. Laney was now rapping her clipboard, a stormy look on her face. "Third and twenty-two!" the ref screamed to the heavens.

As soon as the ball was snapped, Hadel plowed into Leona and shoved her back. Leona bit her arm, but Hadel kept shoving. Their team completed a thirty-four-yard pass. "Excellent," Laney congratulated Hadel.

Ridgedale won two intercollegiate matches. Bryn Mawr forfeited when not enough people showed up for the game bus. Vassar came, complete with matching Bermuda shorts and a real coach, but left in protest over unnamed indignities on the line. Radcliffe insisted that Ridgedale journey to Cambridge, but the administration refused to fork over the needed funds. The game with Barnard was canceled because of a Vietnam Day March in New York. "Next year!" Laney promised the team. Meanwhile, she still held practice scrimmages until the North Lawn began to resemble a battlefield and the gardener threatened to quit.

CHAPTER 3

Natalie bustled into Hadel's room, shivering and chafing her arms. "It's freezing!" she cried. "Don't they know it's November? Why don't they turn on the heat?"

Hadel raised her head a fraction of an inch, enough to let Natalie see she had noted her presence but wanted to finish this last sentence. She was deeply immersed in writing her current short story, the third of the year. She was, in fact, quite pleased with her production. In spite of Laney's football team, Natalie's constant interruptions and the general hysteria surrounding Humphrey's defeat two days earlier, Hadel had managed to continue writing her strange, surrealistic stories, which one teacher said reminded him of Borges. Heady words. Hadel would be his pal for life. She finished her sentence and looked at Natalie inquiringly.

"It's Megan," Natalie said. "We have to help her."

"Spare me. Go drop a bomb on Washington instead. Better yet, finish, or I should probably say start, that law paper you were supposed to turn in to George last week. What's happened to the future dynamo of the ACLU?" Natalie had decided when she was thirteen she would be a civil rights lawyer, and she had planned her school career accordingly, with her presidencies and committee work. As she'd progressed from secondary school to college, her student offices, which she had always enjoyed more than her studies, demanded increasing amounts of time. She seemed to have taken the time pressures, as well as her early admissions acceptance to Columbia Law School, as license to ignore her senior year assignments entirely.

"I don't have the energy to do it. Besides, who cares about law when the country elects Richard Nixon as President?"

"That's just when you should care. Come on, Natalie. If you

can't work, go call what's-his-face." It was not the thing to say. A flash of real pain darkened Natalie's eyes before she blotted it out with a fake-stricken look. "Alas, Jeffrey is no more."

"Since when?"

"Yesterday. He's fallen in love with some Pembroke poopsie. He met her on the train."

Hadel tapped her pen on her paper. She told herself her creative flow had already been hopelessly damned. "Rotten," she said.

"He said we weren't right for each other. After more than a year!"

"Why didn't you tell me yesterday?"

Natalie pressed her thumbs against her temples. "I've got such a headache. I don't know. I didn't know how to say it."

Hadel got up and rubbed Natalie's shoulders. "I'm sorry you feel bad, but I think his saying you weren't right for each other was the only intelligent thing he ever did. He's dumb, Natalie. *Really* dumb."

Natalie thought about this for a moment. "Sometimes I did have the feeling he wasn't very perceptive. But you have to admit he was gorgeous."

"I'll admit nothing of the sort. He looked like a surfer, even though he's from Rhode Island. Even worse, he *tried* to look like a surfer, which is a good indication of his lack of brains. But the biggest measure was he didn't realize his good luck when you fell in love with him. He took you for granted." Natalie began to cry softly. "Natalie, listen. He was too dippy to see he had the most wonderful person in the world, so why cry over him? Forget him and find someone who appreciates you the way you should be appreciated."

Natalie laughed. "The way you tell it, I should never have a broken heart. If they don't like me, they weren't worth it anyway."

Hadel shrugged. "Seems sensible, doesn't it?"

"I don't know. But I feel . . . I want to do something. And Megan does need doing."

"Oh, Natalie!"

"It's a rescue mission."

"I don't want to rescue anyone!"

"Come off it, Hadel. The whole school knows you could have

saved the *Titanic* with the contents of your sewing kit. You got famous after the last near-suicide."

Hadel had talked a woman out of jumping down a four-story stairwell. She didn't remember what she'd said, but whatever it was had worked. Hadel made follow-up visits for three evenings afterward. The third night, as they were comfortably ensconced on the rug of Deering living room, leaning against the couch seat, the woman asked in a quiet voice if Hadel was a lesbian. Hadel catapulted off the floor, shouted, "No!" and then commanded herself to calm down. "Why would you ask such a thing?" Hadel's voice was steady, but she stuck her hands behind her back, out of sight.

"I thought you were," the woman said. It was a simple, honest statement, with no censure.

"Well, I'm not," Hadel snapped. She'd barely spoken to her since, but at least the woman had elected to continue among the living, thereby strengthening Hadel's reputation as a one-person campus emergency crew.

"Come on, Hadel," Natalie was saying. "You don't even have to walk outside, and it's partly your fault anyway."

"Partly my fault?"

"Your fucking Dexedrine. Megan is so whacked out she's like a roller coaster on no track. She's been in her room playing Clue for thirty-six hours."

"Who with?"

"Herself."

Hadel laughed. "All right. That in itself sounds fascinating."

The two knocked on Megan's door. A long pause preceded an irritated "So come in." Hadel turned the knob and stepped into a cave of cigarette smoke, overflowing ashtrays and sticky diet cola cans. Megan, cross-legged on her bed, staring intently at her Clue game, was hardly visible through the shrouds of wispy smoke. "Christ!" Natalie said, angling past Hadel to the window. "This is disgusting, Megan!" She jammed up the window and flapped her arms around, trying to coax the smoke out the opening.

"Stop it," Megan complained. A faint breath of breeze had scattered one of her folded papers.

"Is that the name of the murderer?" Hadel asked, pointing at the paper.

Megan nodded. Her eyes were so bright Hadel marveled they hadn't burned through the back of her skull. "The murderer, the weapon and the room."

"Uh-huh." Hadel sat down on the bed, jarring the board slightly.

"Watch out!" Although she didn't move, Megan gave Hadel the impression that she had wrapped her arms tight around the board, protecting it with a mother's ferocity.

Natalie was getting tired of flapping her arms. Once she'd seen the actual human devastation involved in her rescue mission, she discovered she had no stomach for it. She wanted to head for healthier surroundings. "Megan, you can't stay in here playing Clue all day and all night."

"I like to," Megan said.

Stymied by the elementary logic of this answer, Natalie went back to flapping.

"Maybe the board is tired, though," Hadel suggested. "It's not used to being played on this much."

"Oh! I never thought about that!"

"You must be tired, too," Hadel continued. "Probably the best plan is for both of you to take a nap, and then when you wake up and start playing again, you'll have better games because you'll both be refreshed."

"Are you sure the board's tired?"

Natalie muttered and fidgeted. Flapping at the window hadn't helped much. The room stank.

"The board looks wilted," Hadel answered. "Think how long it's been played on."

"Hours," Megan said. "Days."

"That's what I mean. It's not used to it."

Natalie strode over to the bed, ignoring Hadel's sharp headshake. "Megan, you're totally exhausted. Now Hadel and I are going to put the board to bed"—grasping one end of the board as Megan clung to the other—"Megan! Give it to me!"

"Wait a minute, Natalie," Hadel said. "Megan probably wants to put it to bed herself."

Megan was still stunned at Natalie's overt action. A solitary tear began to trickle down her cheek. "Hadel? Do you really think the board's tired?"

"Oh, for God's sake!" Natalie grabbed the board out of

Megan's fingers and folded it in half, the pieces and papers still inside.

"No!" Megan hollered. "You're folding Colonel Mustard! You're crushing Mrs. Peacock!" She tried to grab at Natalie, but Natalie spun around with her back toward Megan and stuffed the game in its box. She about-faced and held up the game triumphantly. "See, the board's in bed."

Megan's face crumpled. "You folded Colonel Mustard," she whimpered. "He wasn't the murderer. Mr. Green was."

Hadel glared at Natalie, forcing her to bite back a retort. "Megan, it's O.K., honest. They like to sleep inside. They're in their house."

"But their house is folded—"

"Megan, I wouldn't lie to you. It's really all right. Their house is made to fold. It's like switching off the lights for them. They're fast asleep by now, and you should try to sleep, too, so you'll be all set to play when they wake up."

"But how long do they sleep?"

"Only six hours. So you should get to bed right now so they won't have to wait."

"Oh. O.K., Hadel." She disappeared under her covers. Natalie played at adjusting the window. Within five minutes, Megan was sound asleep.

"Three days she's been awake," Natalie said. "Your Dexedrine."

"You were cruel," Hadel hissed, drawing Natalie outside and shutting the door. "Why'd you grab it?"

Natalie started to argue, but then she stopped herself. "I'm sorry. I'm too upset about Jeffrey."

Hadel's heart went out to her, even though she thought Jeffrey wasn't worth the price of a train ticket to New Haven. "Come on," she said. "My treat at Freddy's."

The stomach-wrenching gloom that invaded the campus following Nixon's election dissipated with the approach of the holidays. The dining room was mobbed on the Tuesday before Thanksgiving. Dozens of people had evidently thought it politic to put in a rare campus appearance so they could be thrown out of their dorm rooms late Wednesday afternoon, thus making it seem as if they'd been around for the preceding months of school. Not that the guards would be impressed, Hadel thought, and they were the ones checking to be sure all the students had left. Hadel sat with her feet propped up on the chair next to her, spearing overdone potato chunks with her fork, listening to Portia and Megan argue about whether it was morally correct or hopelessly out of it to inform partygoers there was hash in the brownies. Portia advocated a small, tastefully hand-lettered sign, while Megan maintained that anyone going to a party should expect not only hash in the brownies but acid in the punch and grass in the spaghetti sauce as well. "Do you want to label everything?" she huffed. Hadel was trying to change the subject when Natalie angled among the tables, armed with a bowl of Jell-O and a cup of tea. She usurped Hadel's footstool. "Do all these women go to school here? I haven't seen half of them since registration."

"What's that?" Hadel asked.

Natalie made a face. "Dinner. I figure if I eat hardly anything for a week, I can eat as much as I want Thanksgiving—" Natalie suddenly threw down her spoon. "Hadel, I forgot to tell you. You can't come home with me this year. We're going to my sister's in Boston, and it's just going to be us. My parents didn't want to do the big thing at home."

Hadel was a study in consternation. "Well—" she began.

"Too late to get a hotel reservation," Megan said dourly.

"Of course it is," Natalie agreed. "But Hadel, it's obvious. Go to Megan's for Thanksgiving. That way both of you can drive down instead of Megan flying."

Megan said nothing, apparently thinking. Hadel kicked Natalie under the table, horrified at the thought of an uncomfortable dinner with Megan's father, whom Megan referred to as Big Daddy Hitler. Portia saw the kick out of the corner of her eye and offered her own family: "They're moving to Fort Ord on Monday, so they're staying in a hotel and eating with friends, but you're welcome to come."

"No," Megan decided. "It will be fine for you to come home with me, Hadel."

So Hadel, who would much rather have crashed with Portia's parents in D.C., found herself, forty-eight hours later, sitting in the dining room of a magnificent Virginia mansion surrounded by the ne'er-do-well brothers, Richard and Robert, the long-suffering mother and the dictatorial father, who began polite dinner conversation by cross-examining Richard about his grades at Yale.

"C'mon, Father," Richard groaned.

"'C'mon,' what?" Mr. Franklin demanded. "Don't they teach you to speak English properly?" He positioned his fork above a piece of turkey and glared at his son. Hadel decided Mr. Franklin really did look intimidating, with his cool brown eyes, his gray moustache and his bloodless lips, which had not cracked a smile since Hadel had been there. In fact, he had even scowled at Hadel's old Galaxie, which did look odd sitting on the elegantly manicured drive next to two no-nonsense Saabs. Hadel recalled that none of the kids was allowed to drive since Richard had "borrowed" a new Mercedes and totaled it ten minutes from the house.

"My grades are fine," Richard mumbled into his plate. Hadel thought the most gullible person on earth wouldn't have believed this statement. Everyone suddenly got very busy eating, except for Mr. Franklin, whose fork was still poised above his turkey.

"B's, Richard," he said and plunged down the fork, stabbing the piece of meat. "B's or no football next year." He chewed pleasantly, told Megan's mother to compliment the cook and then continued with Richard, who had stopped eating and was sitting with his hands on his lap. "I know *they* ask only for a C average. I ask for a B. I assume you're not thinking of football as a career." No answer was required; Richard opened and closed his mouth soundlessly. "You'll need a B average for business school. That's more important than a few more newspaper clippings to pin on your wall. You'll thank me later."

The other people at the table were shoveling down food as if they were to be graded on sheer volume eaten. Megan raised an eyebrow at Hadel.

"Robert," Mr. Franklin said. Robert jumped and looked to Richard for help, but Richard's face was so pale and full of rage that Robert quickly turned back to his father.

"How are your grades?"

"Fine, sir," Robert answered.

"When I called last week, I was told your grades are average. *Average!*"

"I think I'm doing well. I—"

"Do you want to go to another school, Robert? Leave Andover?"

"No, sir."

"Then get busy."

"Yes, sir."

Hadel braced herself, since there was one to go. But first there was a call for seconds, and a round of how delicious everything was. Robert was looking worried, but he was eating. Richard was pushing his food around with his fork. Finally Mr. Franklin said, "So how is Ridgedale, Megan?" Hadel stared at him. His grimace was supposed to be a smile.

"Fine, Daddy, I'm doing quite well. It's a bit boring, since this is my last year, but I'm hanging in there."

Hadel couldn't have imagined a bigger lie. Megan and Natalie were running neck-and-neck for the most papers endlessly postponed, forgotten, never started or never finished. For Natalie it didn't matter so much, since she already had her early admissions, but if Megan had any future educational plans, she was in serious trouble.

"Good," Mr. Franklin said. He was eating his turkey quite placidly now. "Perhaps you'd play something after dinner."

"Certainly."

The conversation turned general, but Hadel was hardly able to eat, waiting for the ax to fall. Perhaps he hadn't called Ridgedale. Of course, Ridgedale would never tell a parent anything. And what was there to tell? Ridgedale didn't give grades. Come to think of it, why had Mr. Franklin allowed Megan to go to Ridgedale at all? It was like sending David Eisenhower to Reed. Hadel was glad when they moved to the sitting room; she hadn't been able to swallow for the past fifteen minutes.

After everybody had been given brandy (except Robert, who had a minuscule glass of sherry), Megan sat at the piano and started playing her familiar medley of Scott Joplin tunes. Hadel sipped at her brandy, relieved. Megan could scarcely botch this—she'd played these songs hundreds of times. But as she went into the second number, Hadel found herself gritting her teeth, for Megan was plonking away like a beginning pianist at a school recital, not hitting any wrong notes but not injecting life into what she played either, striking the keys hurriedly, as if she were rushing to finish. Hadel sneaked a glance at Mr. Franklin, but he had collared Richard again. They were deep in what looked like a man-to-man talk, and Richard's pale face was being subsumed with red from the outside in, so he appeared clownlike, with his neck and ears burning scarlet. When Megan pounded out the final notes, everyone applauded and rose as one to offer pleas of exhaustion. Mr. Franklin was surprised, but he acquiesced. He proposed that he and Mrs. Franklin have a nightcap, and the younger generation escaped.

They mounted the stairs silently, until Richard whirled on Megan. "Lucky you," he said.

"Shut up," Robert told his older brother. Megan was leaning on the rail, her eyes closed.

"Lucky, lucky Megan."

"Shut up, Richard." Robert thrust forward in front of Megan. Hadel thought this was brave, since Richard, though no taller, outweighed stringbean Robert by a good fifty pounds. And Richard was in a dangerous mood, ready to explode at anyone who stepped in his path.

Richard, however, was taken aback at his brother's defense. "You don't think she's lucky?"

"No." He gripped Richard's arm and drew him up the last flight of stairs to the boys' rooms. Hadel and Megan remained on the second landing, Hadel shifting from foot to foot, pretending to be interested in a portrait of some Franklin relative. Megan finally opened her eyes and started walking toward her room. "My father was in a good mood tonight," she said. She wasn't talking to Hadel, but Hadel felt compelled to reassure her. "Yes," she said quickly, "of course he was." Megan entered her room and closed the door.

Hadel vanished into her own room and stared at her suitcase. Inside were her means of making it through the weekend: two new war novels and a book about nine people adrift on a four-man raft. Now, however, she knew she couldn't make it even through breakfast. An escape plan was vital. She woke up with the answer at dawn. She explained to a sleepy Megan that she had developed a terrible toothache from a recurring gum infection. She knew a dentist who would treat her on a holiday. She had to return to New York immediately. Megan did not protest.

CHAPTER 4

Hadel crept up the last flight of stairs and collapsed in her room Friday evening. Driving from Virginia, puzzling about Megan the entire way, had exhausted her. Luckily, the school checked only to be sure the students were gone Wednesday afternoon; they made no restrictions about when anyone could return. The administration building was unlocked, though the reception desk was unmanned. Hadel settled back to wait for Natalie.

She didn't have to stifle her story for long. Oppressed by the way her parents popped out of the woodwork every time she and her sister found a moment to talk, Natalie arrived Saturday morning. She'd seen Hadel's car in the parking lot and bounded up the steps.

"Why're you here? Is Megan back, too?"

"Megan's still there. God, Natalie, Megan's father—"

"He's a real Nazi, huh? What'd he do, scream at her the whole time?"

"No. He screamed at her brothers. He doesn't scream at her. He doesn't even notice her. She's the *girl*."

Natalie narrowed her eyes. "Are you serious? Tell me what happened."

Hadel told while Natalie paced the length of Hadel's room. "All these years of complaining about her father's demands, his unattainable expectations . . . and then he pays no attention to her." Natalie shook her head. "I wonder why she asked you down there. She'd know you would see."

"She didn't ask me down there. You forced her to invite me. Anyway, you know how she is about her money. She might have thought it would look as though she were ashamed to have me meet her family or something. I did feel sort of like a country cousin. But mainly, I think she's convinced herself that her father does expect all this stuff from her. It's so internalized she thought he *would* do it."

"Awful. And you were there to see he doesn't. What's going to happen now?"

"I don't know. She must feel so worthless, a million times more worthless than she says he makes her feel. It's her whole personality, this business with her father, and it's quicksand."

Natalie shuddered. "Maybe she can rationalize your knowing. Maybe she could talk to you. She trusts you."

Hadel shrugged. She looked out her window at two other returnees walking toward the dining hall. And then she noticed a familiar figure tossing a football up and down. "Look! Laney's back already too!"

"Hot damn," Natalie said. But sarcasm was lost on Hadel. She was beaming with pleasure and excitement, Megan forgotten.

Within fifteen minutes, Hadel had manufactured a reason to go outside. She wanted, she told Natalie, to check her oil. Back and forth to Virginia had been a long trip. She wandered past Laney, not looking in her direction. "Hey, Hadel!" Laney called.

"Laney!" Hadel said, feigning surprise. "How come you're back so soon?"

Laney shrugged. "I never left. I hid out downtown when they came by to check, and then I sneaked back in. I *did* eat a turkey sandwich on Thursday, though." She was smiling, as if this tale of holiday deprivation required no sympathy.

Hadel felt compelled to give it anyway. "Oh, that's awful. I wish I'd known."

"It was fun, actually. Would you like to go to Nathan's and get a hot dog?"

Hadel hated hot dogs, but she would have driven Laney to a wrecking yard in Newark if Laney had wanted to go there. They talked very little on the way, wandered around Nathan's in companionable silence and came back the long route by the river, so they could see the shadows of the trees on the water. When Hadel pulled up in the parking lot, Laney jumped out and started toward Simpson. Once they were inside the administration building, Laney vaulted up the carpeted steps two by two, ushered Hadel into her own room and then shut the door behind them. "Now," she said, leaning against the door as if to prevent Hadel's escape, "you didn't really want to go to Nathan's, did you?"

"Sure," Hadel said, examining Laney's face for a sign of what game they were playing.

Laney flounced over to Hadel's bed and sat down. When Hadel continued to stand near the door, Laney patted the bed impatiently. "C'mere," she coaxed.

Hadel crossed the room gingerly, as if she were walking on a freshly waxed floor. She sat a respectable distance away from Laney, who grinned at her and moved closer. "So what do you think about this place?" Laney asked.

Hadel blinked. They were going to sit here on the bed and have a nice, intimate conversation about Ridgedale? Well, what else did you expect? Hadel asked herself. Zero, that's what. "I like it. People leave each other alone."

"Oh, yes," Laney agreed. "Everyone has a healthy respect for everybody else's idiosyncrasies. Too healthy, in fact. Someone could rig up a scaffold on the South Lawn, complete with cardboard cutouts of executioners and priests and sheriffs, hold an opening and hang herself in full view of everyone. People would simply argue about whether it worked as a piece of art."

Hadel laughed. In the middle of the laugh, Laney reached over and unbuttoned the top button of Hadel's shirt. Hadel was too confused to look at her. She forced her gaze to the window and continued the discussion. "There'd be the art *in perpetua* argument. If the artist has to hang herself to make the piece work, it's a happening, not art." Hadel shook her head, distracted by Laney's vision of the public hanging. It really would happen that way. Not one person would tower above the crowd and point out they were witnessing a suicide. Poor taste, my dear, to bespeak the obvious. But while Hadel was thinking about Ridgedale's skewed approach to reality, Laney had completed unbuttoning her shirt and was now cupping Hadel's breasts on the palms of her hands, leaning over to kiss Hadel's nipples delicately. "You have beautiful breasts," she said.

Hadel told herself this wasn't really happening. She'd wanted it for too many years, too many months, too many days, but, on the other hand, it did *seem* to be happening. And when Laney lay her on her back and began kissing and caressing her so gently, so wonderfully, Hadel thought: Migod, it *is*! and walked straight into her own pure happiness, pure passion, found she was soaking wet, knew she'd found the answer to the ultimate question—am I or aren't I?—never have to wonder about that again, and in this space of a few seconds fully recovered herself and turned to Laney. "Let me undress you," she said. "I want to feel you."

It was so beautiful taking Laney's clothes off and turning her so the setting sun glowed on patches of her skin. It began to snow as they danced in Hadel's warm bed; afterward Hadel would remember the utter silence of snow, the heavy blanket of stillness through which her joy cut like a laser of yellow light. She was filled with it, with the singing in her head, with the wonder of Laney, the miracle of finding herself. She stayed awake long after Laney had fallen asleep, watching her head on the pillow, reaching out to touch her long hair, almost as white as corn silk and just as fine, feeling the heat from Laney's body next to hers. Strange, she thought, when the reality is even better than the fantasy. No dream could be this good.

Laney left at nine-forty to go to work in the library, kissing a now sleepy Hadel, telling her she'd be back around one. Hadel tried to sleep again, but the excitement was rampaging through her, so she hopped out of bed, tossed on her robe, and walked across the hall to Natalie's room. "Hi," Hadel said.

Natalie was deeply engrossed in a Strindberg play. "What's happening?" she asked, not even glancing up from the book.

Hadel slumped in Natalie's armchair and waited. Natalie finished the passage she was reading, jotted something in her notebook, put everything aside and looked at Hadel. Then she stared at Hadel, transfixed. Hadel's face was shining bright as a beacon. "What's going on?" Natalie said, smiling in advance. It had to be great to make Hadel, who rarely had more than a sardonic twinkle in her eye, look as if a world government dedicated to peace and human rights had just been ratified by every single nation. "We've stopped the war," Natalie hazarded.

Hadel shook her head impatiently.

"You've sold a short story!"

"No. I'm—I'm in love."

"In love!" No one could look at Hadel's face and not share her happiness. But Natalie knew her moment of truth had come. The hope that Hadel had fallen in love with a man flitted briefly through Natalie's mind, but she banished it. Hadel had come on a mission of explanation to her best friend; Natalie could detect a strain of anxiety under the joy. And since she loved Hadel dearly, this made her angry—Why does Hadel have to be fearful? Does she think I'll reject her? Does she think I'll scream and toss her out of my room? I don't know what I'll do, Natalie realized. She's going to say it, and I have no idea how I'll react.

"Something else happened besides," Hadel was saying. "I—this sounds dumb—but I found myself, too."

"That doesn't sound dumb," Natalie said automatically, then cursed herself. Shut up and let her talk!

"You know how you always got upset about Steve? I wished desperately I'd fall in love with him, but at the same time I hoped I wouldn't, because it would have been a lie. It would have been denying what I already knew about myself, what I've known since I was eleven, or even earlier . . ."

Say it, Natalie thought. Then she decided to make it easier. "Who are you in love with?"

"Laney. I'm in love with Laney."

"Is Laney in love with you?" Natalie asked quickly to give herself time.

"I don't know. We didn't talk about that. But we slept together, so . . ." Though Hadel's voice trailed away, her face was so full of innocence and naked hope that Natalie almost groaned aloud. Damnit, if Laney hurts Hadel I'll strangle her. . . . Why am I thinking that? The whole world is going to hurt Hadel! Can I strangle the whole world?

"Do you think it's wise?" When in doubt, Natalie tended to revert to her lawyer father's belief that any problem in life can be solved by asking difficult questions. The answers to these questions created precedents to respond to more questions until finally everything could be answered.

"Do I think it's wise to be in love with Laney?"

"No. Do you think it's wise to sleep with a woman?"

Hadel looked confused. "Well, if I'm gay, I should sleep with women."

Ah, ha! Natalie thought triumphantly, still thinking of the necessity of personally strangling the entire world. Hadel said "if," not "since." She's unsure. "What I mean is, it may not be wise to *be* gay."

Hadel's face cleared. "Oh, I see what you're getting at. But I am or I'm not. I wasn't offered a choice. Do you think it'd be wise to be miserable all my life with a man I couldn't love? But that's no longer an issue, Natalie. After last night—I was so turned on I couldn't believe it. I was fainting with happiness just lying next to her. I've never felt anything remotely like that. Never. It was even better than I imagined it would be. It was soft and wonderful and—" Hadel's face was glowing again, as if she were transported to the most romantic place on earth with her lover—with Laney, Natalie reminded herself. Instead of looking dark and furtive with Steve. "See," Hadel finished, "I had to stop the Ping-Pong game in my head and listen to what my body said. I have to be me. Don't you understand?"

Natalie couldn't go on being judicious with Hadel's eyes so worried and her voice close to breaking. She hopped off her bed and hugged Hadel tightly. "Of course you have to be you, baby. There's no point in being alive otherwise." As Hadel sighed with relief, Natalie thought: well, now I do have to strangle the whole world. But wasn't that what I was planning anyway?

It wasn't until the second week of December that Portia realized she was missing out on all the gossip. Too involved, she lamented, in casting her student project, Jean Genet's *The Maids*. It should have been easy, considering there were only three parts, but that, of course, made it much harder. One or even two rotten people might sink into the background in another play, but *The Maids* had to have three accomplished actresses, commodities Portia was having trouble finding in spite of Ridgedale's reputation for theater arts. She was too critical, several rejected actresses said, but Portia was the only sophomore chosen to direct a play this year, and she was going to reward Mr. Wellington, the head of the drama department, with the best production she could muster, even at the expense of keeping up with the lives of her friends.

First there was the demise of Natalie's Jeffrey, which Portia had sensed before Thanksgiving but hadn't had corroborated until yesterday. But the big news was completely unexpected.

Natalie had asked her over to offer suggestions to Natalie and Hadel's revision of the parietal laws, rules the school hadn't enforced for several years. Portia gathered she was supposed to add the "what the underclassmen really want" perspective. Since she was in violation of the rules every time Charley stayed in her room, Portia was glad to help. She and Natalie read through the revisions, armed with red pencils. At one juncture (after the whole story of Jeffrey came tumbling out), Portia wanted Hadel to settle a minor disagreement. She started across the hall, but Natalie rose out of her chair like a Valkyrie and sputtered, "No, no, they are, uh, *engagé*!"

"*They?*" Portia questioned, and then the small bewilderments of two weeks fell into place, such as why Hadel was so joyful, why she suddenly had so much energy, and why, above all, Laney had abandoned the Bendix living room. "Oh," Portia said. There was no point in pretending she had already known. The curse of the chipmunk face, Portia called it. She had a nearly impossible time hiding the slightest emotion.

"Neither one told you? That's odd." Natalie described Hadel's visit of explanation, while Portia was swamped with a wash of hurt and irritation at Laney, who was supposed to be her very good friend.

That was yesterday. Now, walking over to Natalie's to check on the next revision, Portia decided that Laney hadn't told her because she hadn't thought it was important. Laney could be blasé about being a lesbian because she never seemed to care what anyone thought of her. At times, in fact, Portia was astounded by Laney's sense of self-possession. Who else could come to a school like Ridgedale and start a football team when football, to nine tenths of the student body, meant a bunch of fascist flag-wavers cheering on their side in a miniature war? A voodoo society or an Ayn Rand study group would have been easier ventures. Laney's certainty had made the team work; *she* saw nothing wrong with playing football and, after a short two weeks, neither did anyone else. And yet wasn't there something odd about Laney? How *could* she be so sure of herself at the age of twenty? Wasn't there something disconnected about her way of reacting to the world? The existence of the team itself had been the important thing to Laney, not the game or its players.

Hadel was a lot easier to understand. Now that Portia was

finally noticing, she saw that Hadel's energy had increased monumentally, as if a huge dam had been unleashed inside and Hadel were surfing on top of the rushing water, filled with strength and peace. Not one whit of intensity had left her eyes; if anything, happiness made her eyes deeper, bluer, more challenging. Natalie said she thought Hadel had more to defend now that she was whole.

One thing worried Portia. Hadel was as excited about Laney as she was about finding herself. Although Laney liked and respected Hadel and even seemed to depend on her, there was a way in which Laney looked past Hadel the person and saw something about Hadel she needed. Hadel knew it too, Portia remembered; several times Portia had seen Hadel blink at Laney quizzically, and once at dinner, when Laney had proposed a parachute jump as a wonderful weekend activity, expecting Hadel not only to be enthusiastic but also to make all the arrangements, Hadel had asked the table at large, "Who does she think I am?"

"King Kong," Natalie had replied, winking at Portia; they both knew Hadel was afraid of heights.

"Mothra," Laney laughed, and the moment passed, but Hadel's question had been genuine.

Now Portia doubted that Laney was in love with Hadel, either with the real Hadel or with whatever Laney's image of Hadel was. Surely Laney, no matter how self-contained and eccentric in her vision of the world around her, would classify falling in love as news important enough to relay to her closest friend.

Portia mounted the second flight of stairs and was nearly bowled over at the top by Megan, who rushed by, carrying a load of library books. "Hi," she hollered, disappearing down the stairs. "Too busy to stop."

"What's with Megan?" Portia asked when she got to Natalie's room. She nodded at Hadel, who was hunched over Natalie's desk, leafing through the penciled revisions. "She's gone nuts," Natalie said.

"Good if you went so nuts," Hadel observed.

"I've got one Jewish mother already, Hadel." Natalie threw a Xerox copy of the proposal at Portia. "Remember Hadel went home for Thanksgiving with Megan?"

Portia nodded, already scanning the changes. She noticed, however, Hadel's quick warning glance at Natalie. Something was going to be left out of this story, probably what happened at Megan's. "Well, Hadel came back early, and Megan came back late as usual. Except that Megan suddenly started doing every single thing she'd put off for two years, all her old papers and stuff."

"I even saw her in the science lab, doing lab reports from last year," Hadel said from the desk.

"She hasn't talked to anybody since she's been back," Natalie continued. "She's either shut up in her room or in the library."

"Maybe she realized she was starting her last semester soon," Portia suggested.

"Or maybe she decided she wants to go to graduate school," Hadel said.

"Maybe," Natalie said in a voice that meant "not very likely." "Anyhow, I'm going to take this to the dean tomorrow morning, so let's hash this stuff out."

Three hours later, Portia emerged from the meeting war-torn, recalling her weariness with all the discussions last spring during the gym crisis at Columbia. What early this afternoon had seemed a simple matter of crossing out the parietal laws turned out to be a controversial issue. Portia hadn't realized that more than half the students didn't want the rules changed. Unenforced parietal laws, Hadel had explained, was akin to having your cake and eating it too: amorous swains, no matter how insistent, could be switched off at midnight with no hard feelings, or could, on the other hand, be safely spirited into bed. Halfway to Bendix, Portia paused for a moment to smile at a monstrous snow animal, which could have been a dog or a bear. The late-afternoon chill had halted the melting process, leaving the animal in a sort of exhausted slump, a posture that matched Portia's feelings exactly. Any alteration in the status quo, she realized, was bound to be subject to the pull and tug of different factions. The Morningside Park business was a good example. Her decision in that case to protest the actions of the shakers and the movers—the builders—had earned her a head-cracking and a bumpy trip down a flight of stairs at the hands of New York's finest. Columbia had contracted to build a double-decker gym in Morningside Park, the bottom gym for the surrounding community, the upper half for Columbia students. The university pointed to the playing field and tennis courts in the same park as successful, university-built, shared recreation areas. The proposed gyms, however, were separate facilities with separate entrances, lending credence to the rallying cry, "Gym Crow." When conceived in the fifties, the plan had seemed an instance of one hand washing the other: the community gained a gym, land-starved Columbia received the airspace above the community's gym at low rent for their own structure. By the sixties, however, the connotations were very different. Apart from the charge of deliberate segregation, Columbia's possible expansion plans, never publicly explained, exerted a shadowy menace over the surrounding area. Portia remembered the flyers: "Do you want a bulldozer knocking down your building?" The prospect of losing a rent-controlled apartment to university expansion was devastating. And now, Portia reflected, Columbia's board had decided to reconsider the Morningside Park site after shelving the idea after last spring's strikes and sit-ins. Portia had been asked to leaflet on Tuesday. The dog-bear seemed to gaze at her reproachfully as she decided she couldn't spare the time. She still hadn't found the right Claire, and if she didn't cast the part soon, she was going to have to start reinterviewing people, which would create so much resentment she might as well not put the play on at all.

By the time she'd reached Bendix, however, she was whistling. The falling temperature and the walk through the squeaky white snow had refreshed her. Everything would work out. Columbia's board would give up on the gym, not wanting a repeat of last spring. Ridgedale students would simply have to take responsibility for their own rejections rather than hiding behind a paper law. Hadel and Laney's affair might not last the month, but meanwhile Hadel was coasting on funds of good cheer; after the long meeting, Hadel had galloped down the stairs ahead of Portia, pulling on her jacket, shouting over her shoulder that she was meeting Laney for a drink downtown. And a Claire would surface. Portia smiled as she yanked hard on Bendix's sticky front door.

CHAPTER 5

Megan surfaced from her paper-writing at one in the morning. She had two sections left of the last paper, and she'd used up the six pills she'd sneaked out of Hadel's bottle during lunch on Wednesday, when she'd felt exhaustion chipping away at her resolve. Megan paced the hall for a couple of minutes and then pounded on Hadel's door. Hopefully, Hadel had gone away, or even left for Christmas break. Megan didn't want to talk to her. She didn't want to talk to anyone until she'd finished everything, all the stuff she'd meant to do for ages. . . .

When no answer came, Megan opened the door and stepped inside. A great struggle seemed to be going on under Hadel's blankets. When Hadel finally lifted her head, her face was flushed, her eyes unfocused. "What?" she growled. Laney sat up next to her, throwing a length of sheet off her face. She put her arm around Hadel's bare shoulders. "What's happening, Megan?"

"Uh . . . sorry. I need a pill, Hadel. Can you give me a pill?"

Hadel didn't answer. She was having a lot of trouble breathing. Laney took over. "Hadel, where're the pills Megan wants?"

"Bottom drawer," Hadel muttered. She turned her face in Laney's neck.

"Take several," Laney suggested.

"No, no," Megan said. "One's fine. I've gotta stop, see. Have to stop taking these pills . . ." Her voice died as she concentrated on getting one out of the bottle. It was hard because her hands were shaking.

"Take the bottle," Laney said.

"No! One's plenty. Then I'll stop. I just need one. Sorry!" She dashed out the door, slamming it behind her.

Hadel sighed against Laney's neck. "You know how you seem to slide into coming? I was—"

"Shut up," Laney commanded. She slipped her hand down until her fingers touched Hadel's wetness, and a moment later, Hadel was gasping again.

The last person Hadel expected to see beckoning her at lunch was President Pattison. The two had despised each other since they'd met, early in Hadel's freshman year. Even stranger, Pattison was smiling crookedly, as if he knew his smile was inappropriate and he was trying to mold it into a frown.

"Hester," he said, after Hadel had woven through a pack of students. "Would you mind stepping outside for a moment?"

I certainly would, Hadel thought. This couldn't be about the proposal; Natalie had delivered it to the dean only that morning.

Once outside on the snowy path, Pattison spent a bit of time playing with his pipe and adjusting his neck scarf. While he fussed, he leaned one hand on his cane.

Both of them avoided looking at each other, Pattison preferring his pipe, Hadel the snow and the yellowed moss on the stone wall of the dining room. "Hester, the dean and I have spent the last hour debating options."

So he was talking about the proposal. But why was he smiling like that? "Options?"

"Yes. Of what we're going to do with you." Hadel shot an irritated glance at him, and he continued on smoothly, his smile now openly broad, "*now that we know.*"

The world collapsed behind Hadel's eyes, but she didn't even blink. She watched disappointment at her lack of reaction wipe out his smile, and he abruptly became hurried. She was glad he was going to press on to the end; if she had to respond, she thought she might faint.

"We were told about you," he said, "but not the name of your 'partner.' If you cared to give us that information—"

He paused, waiting. She was thinking that if she cried in front of this man, she would hate herself forever.

"I thought not. The dean made this suggestion: you would live off campus, continue on as a student here, but be under a"—he shrugged—"code of silence? Meaning you would leave campus immediately after your classes, not speak to any student while on campus and not entertain any students of this college in your apartment in town."

Hadel retreated way into herself. If she walled off every approach, she could keep standing here for hours. But as she traveled deeper, she found anger and her voice. "I will not be treated as a leper," she said. She was surprised at how clearly she spoke.

Pattison's eyes widened. "Then you'll have to leave. You'll graduate from here; register as a visiting student at any acceptable university and send the grades to us. Officially you're taking a senior semester away, rather than, say, a junior year abroad."

Hadel said nothing.

"Today's Friday. I'd say a couple of days should do it, hmmm? I presume you're all caught up on your work for this semester? You've always done quite well academically." He had recovered his smile. "See the dean for the specifics. Good day." He turned uphill and walked away, tapping his cane at intervals.

Hadel remained on the path while the last group of eaters departed the dining room and flowed around her, glancing at her curiously. Once she was able to move, she walked quickly up to the dorm, darted past the administration level and emerged on the third floor with the knowledge that something too terrible to think about had just happened, so it was better not to think.

A note from Megan was pinned on her door. "Finished everything, have to split for Virginia right away. Good luck. See bathroom." Hadel walked into the bathroom she shared with Natalie and Megan. A box of chocolates sat on the bathtub rim. "Condolences" was printed on the lid in raised gold lettering. How had Megan known? Pattison surely hadn't told her, nor had the dean. Hadel remembered Megan's early-morning pill foray. She told herself not to think again, but there was no escaping the conclusion that Megan could have known only one way—by being the person who had told. Hadel picked up the box and sank onto the toilet seat. Natalie found her there a few minutes later, holding the chocolates on her lap. "Hadel?

Hadel?" She pulled the box away from Hadel's white fingers. "Hadel? Did somebody die?"

Hadel started crying.

Megan had been one of the first at breakfast that morning. She consumed a piece of dry toast and a soft-boiled egg. It was only seven-thirty, far too early. By the time the hands of the clock clicked agonizingly to eight-fifty, she'd nursed only three cups of coffee, a record low for the past two weeks. She left the dining hall and walked quickly up the ice-slick paths to Simpson. She nodded to the woman on the reception desk and began climbing the carpeted flight of stairs. No harm there, she was simply going to her room. Except at the first landing she would turn right, toward the dean's office, instead of continuing on up the stairs. She started her turn, but something stopped her: hurrying feet in the dorm hall above her head. Natalie rocketed past her, carrying a sheaf of photocopied pages. "Hiya, Megan!"

"Hi," Megan echoed, watching Natalie give one short knock on the dean's door and disappear inside. How many times, Megan wondered, had she seen Natalie and Hadel pop casually into the offices of the school's administrators? How many times had she answered the dorm phone and discovered she was speaking to the chairman of the board, who had called for one of her two friends? School officials invited the pair to fund-raising parties, sought them out for opinions on school policy, let them have a free hand in student affairs. Megan had talked to the dean exactly once in her school career—last year she had been summoned to the dean's office to account for the two missing papers she'd promised her English literature professor the semester before. It had been a thoroughly humiliating experience.

Natalie burst out of the dean's office as fast as she'd entered. She smiled at Megan. "Got a class!" And she was gone, pounding down the steps to the reception area below.

Megan hesitated a moment longer. She wished she hadn't thought of those lit papers. Did the dean tackle Natalie about each and every one of *her* missing papers? Did the dean ask Natalie if a family problem were at fault? Megan gritted her teeth. Forget Natalie, forget past embarrassments. Hadel was the point. Megan idolized Hadel—no, not idolized—respected her and, at the same time, knew she was jealous of the respect that others accorded to Hadel so quickly. Now Hadel had shown she was unworthy of *anyone's* respect. The school administrators who invited Hadel to parties should know that the student they valued so highly was morally maimed, a pervert. Megan would be congratulated for her loyalty to the school.

Fifteen minutes later, however, after listening to Megan's stumbling story, the dean was making it clear that Megan should have kept her information to herself. "But don't you see," the dean explained, "now that you've told me, I'm required to tell President Pattison."

Megan's instinctive reaction to this statement was a shrug, but she couldn't complete such a heartless gesture while the dean was literally trembling with anguish. She muttered an insincere "I'm sorry," not knowing why she was apologizing. Of course the dean would have to relay the news to Pattison; Megan had assumed that, just as she'd assumed Hadel would be told to leave. It was all very unfortunate, but Hadel had, after all, committed the crime and should, therefore, suffer the consequences. Megan realized, however, that she had seriously misjudged her reception. Perhaps if she had known the dean better, she would not have erred.

The dean reinforced Megan's fears by asking her if she were angry at Hadel. Hearing the clipped tone of dislike in the dean's voice, Megan decided her only hope for survival was sticking to the truth. She shook her head, not trusting herself to speak. She *wasn't* angry at Hadel, though she was beginning to resent this sure-to-lose position Hadel had placed her in. The dean suggested that Megan had misunderstood what she'd seen in Hadel's bed. She detailed an escape route: "Sometimes we think we see what isn't there. If a possibility exists . . ." But Megan spurned escape, having already committed herself to the truth. Perhaps the dean would respect her if she were honest. "I'm not mistaken," she said slowly. She answered the dean's questions. She was absolutely certain Hadel was having a relationship with another student. Her name? That was a shock—it was Hadel they were concerned with, wasn't it? Hadel was the one everybody doted on. Laney was a nothing, worse than a nothing, a temptress. Just look how she had flaunted herself at the freshman parade! "I don't know her name," Megan said. The dean didn't press. She drummed her fingers on the desk while Megan, sitting upright as a rod in her chair, decided to gamble. "Ask Hadel. If she denies it, I'll forget it ever happened."

Megan's offered out was a test. The dean could have said, "After what you just told me, I don't know that I would trust her answer," or even, "I'm not sure which of you I'd believe." Instead they stared at each other, and Megan frowned, for she saw hopelessness in the dean's eyes. The dean had believed her all along, and Megan's revelation had not erased one chalk-mark of respect from Hadel's over-full blackboard. The dean also understood that Megan's gesture had no value; both of them knew that Hadel would never lie. Megan slid back in her chair, feeling nauseated. The dean folded her hands carefully.

"I think it would be best, Megan, if you were to take a senior semester away. It's your decision, but you might be more comfortable elsewhere." The dean paused. "Thank you," she added, and Megan saw it had taken the self-control of a lifetime in school administration to force those words past her lips. These half-bitten syllables were Megan's congratulations for sacrificing herself for the good of the college. And though the dean's eyes were now guarded, the wash of hopelessness and pain had been overridden by an unmistakable glaze of hate, directed, Megan realized with a queasy thump, at her. Hadel had triumphed again, even when she had been exposed as morally bankrupt. Megan got up to leave. "I brought Hadel home with me for Thanksgiving," she blurted, oppressed by the weight of a thousand stones. "I'm not angry at her." She paused at the door. "I simply thought it was best to tell you."

Ridgedale, determinedly unique, had an unusual application form. It asked none of the usual questions, beyond name and address. It didn't inquire about student activities, volunteer work, or even grades. Instead, it instructed the applicant to answer a series of essay questions, one of which was "Whom do you most admire?"

"No one," Hadel had written. "Everybody starts with a different set of circumstances and abilities. I think the point of life is to try to make myself into the best person I can. Trying to be like other people, even in so minor a fashion as admiring them, is evading the challenge of my own life." Seventeen-year-old Hadel spent forty minutes worrying about this answer. It sounded pompous. What she'd written, however, was true for her, and Ridgedale's director of admissions had sent a cover letter telling the applicants to be open and honest. "Ridgedale's creative style will not appeal to everyone," the letter said. "Your honesty will help us determine if you are one who would benefit most from a Ridgedale education." Hadel took this statement at face value. If they didn't like who she was, better to know immediately and apply at another college where she would be accepted as herself. She mailed the application the next day and received an early admissions within a month.

Hadel had now stopped crying and was trying to explain all this to Natalie. They had moved from the bathroom to Hadel's room. Natalie was unable to understand the significance of the application form. "You didn't write on there you were a lesbian," she pointed out impatiently. She was anxious to *do* something.

"I know! But does that one fact obliterate every other aspect of me? Part of the way I am is because I've known about myself for years. They like the inner turmoil but not the outward manifestation?"

"Hadel!" Natalie snapped. "We've got to have a plan. Did you admit anything to Pattison?"

Hadel shook her head.

"Well, then you can deny it. Say you're so naïve you didn't understand what he was talking about. Tell them Megan's a speed freak, that she's hallucinated things in the past. Any number of people will testify to that."

"No. Why should I lie?" She thought for a moment. "I guess this *is* such an enormous thing it obliterates everything else. Why would I have fought it for so long otherwise? But now that I've come into myself, I can't just turn around and walk away."

"I don't mean deny it to you. Deny it to them!"

"I feel . . . complete. Scared but complete. Denying it would be going backward. Besides, that dignity to stand by who I am is all I have left."

Natalie could tell Hadel was going to start crying again. She didn't want to watch. She couldn't remember Hadel crying before, and the prospect of witnessing Hadel sobbing twice in one day was frightening. "I'm going to talk to the dean," she announced. She left the room at a trot.

Instead of crying, Hadel started packing. There was no reason to prolong the agony by delaying her departure until Monday. She thought about going back to Berkeley. She loved Berkeley. She thought about seeing her parents. She loved her parents. But she didn't want to go back home while she was hanging in emotional tatters. She wanted to return on her own, as a whole, proud person. So that's what I have to do, she told herself. I'm just not going to have any help doing it. She continued packing until Natalie said behind her, "The dean wants to see you." Natalie's eyes were bloodshot. She lifted her shoulders in the air when Hadel looked a question at her. "Pattison is adamant. He's always wanted to get you, and this gave him an excuse."

Hadel went off to see the dean. The dean cried. Hadel didn't. She was finished crying.

Portia heard about Hadel at dinner from Laney, who leaned over to whisper the news and then dashed away. Dazed, Portia turned back to her new Claire. "I really respect you, Portia," the Claire said, nodding her head twice to make sure Portia understood her sincerity. "I'm a sophomore too, and I didn't expect to get a good role until next year." She nodded again. It was the most she'd moved all afternoon, during which she'd given a reading with all the warmth and activity of a block of ice. Perversely, Portia wished she'd heard about Hadel before she'd chosen this woman, so she could at least point to distraction as an excuse. The woman's only qualification was she looked the way Portia pictured Claire. "I have to leave now," Portia interrupted. "We'll start rehearsing right after Christmas break. Learn your lines. Move around." She exited before Claire could go into another spate of nodding.

The atmosphere on the third floor of the administration building was grim. Hadel had packed everything but her bedding; the blank spaces on her walls, where her posters had hung, looked like wounds. Hadel lay on her bed, trying, through exhaustion and shock, to be intermittently entertaining. Natalie had started an obscure argument with Laney about macrobiotic diets. Although Laney mouthed appropriate comebacks, her heart wasn't in it; she seemed frightened, pulling into herself as a turtle hides in its shell. She sat shivering on the floor in the coldest part of the room, the corner under the windows. When Hadel suggested she move to a warmer spot, she shook her head.

Portia tried to assess the situation the way she'd been taught in the Left: the misery here was turning inward, unfocused anger was changing to depression, helplessness, bickering. Her job was to mobilize the anger, direct it toward the proper source. She began to feel excited. They could beat this thing. They could make demands. But was homosexuality a revolutionary issue? It had to do with sex, not poverty or racial inequality or institutional power. Of course, women were beginning to identify discrimination based on gender, but wasn't that a side issue? After the revolution—Portia realized she was getting off the track. Natalie further confused her by holding out a box of chocolates. "Did you see these?"

Portia examined them. *Condolences?* "What's this?"

"Megan's parting shot."

Portia looked at Hadel. Hadel shrugged, as if the chocolates were irrelevant. Natalie was more forthcoming. "Megan left them in the bathroom."

"*Megan* told?"

Natalie nodded. "Trotted on down there and blabbed. Then she left for Virginia."

"She's nuts," Hadel offered in Megan's defense.

"She might well be nuts," Natalie shot back, "but her reason for telling is she's Day-Glo green with jealousy."

"Oh, Nat—" Hadel began.

"It's true. You're so endlessly loyal you don't see it. She's envious of you, all right, just as she is of me. But you get the brunt of it because she actually matters to you, and she knows it. Paradoxical, huh?"

Hadel couldn't, or wouldn't, respond to Natalie's charge. She stared at her hat rack standing near the door. "I thought you might want the hat rack, Portia. I don't have room for it in my car."

Natalie continued as if Hadel hadn't spoken. "You're always ready to believe the best of someone when often the worst is closer to the truth." She paused, looking at the box of chocolates. "I haven't decided yet what I'm going to do to Megan when she comes back." The way she said this, very matter-of-factly, was much more ominous than a threat.

"I don't think she's coming back," Hadel said slowly. "The dean told me she'd set up this senior semester away thing for someone else this morning. I assume she meant Megan. Anyway, that's not the point."

Portia had been waiting for this moment. While Megan was unquestionably the traitor, energy was wasted on her. "Exactly," she said. "We have to do something. Tomorrow morning—"

"I'm leaving tomorrow morning."

"Instead of you leaving, we distribute a flyer telling what's going on here. That's what we do tonight, write it. Tomorrow morning, we make copies and pass them out. We call for a general student strike—"

Laney nodded vigorously from her corner.

"No," Hadel said. "It wouldn't help. Besides, I shouldn't have to fight it. There shouldn't be anything to fight. I'm the same person who's been here all along."

"Damn it, Hadel!" Natalie was quivering with frustration. "Things are not perfect in this world. You demand perfection or you withdraw."

Portia thought Natalie should have substituted the word "surrender" for "withdraw." Knowing Hadel's obsession with war novels, the idea that she was surrendering might have galvanized her to fight back. It might also, Portia realized, have sent her into a funk from which she would never emerge.

"I'm not a political issue," Hadel insisted. "There're no pros and cons to debate. I'm just me."

It occurred to Portia that Hadel might not want it blasted all over school that she was a lesbian. "We can do something undercover. Set off a bomb in Pattison's office. Send a communiqué with an ultimatum."

"That's a great idea," Laney said, except Portia had the feeling Laney would think blowing up the Statue of Liberty or flying to Paris was also a great idea. It was disconcerting to see Laney, whom Portia thought of as strong and vital, sit around shivering. It made Portia uncomfortable, reminding her of some of the actresses she'd interviewed for Claire. Half of them were so eager for the part they would have let Portia shave their heads if she'd decided Claire should be played bald.

"Swell," Hadel said. "The old bastard would die of a heart attack. And even if he did, it still wouldn't help. I tell you, they will not change their minds."

Portia sighed. Hadel was probably right. Nothing would help, and the pain of a hopeless fight would be overwhelming for all of them. But what was the matter with Laney? Why didn't she think of something, instead of looking scared? Is she so afraid of losing Hadel? Portia tried to detect a closeness between Hadel and Laney, apart from their being friends. But they hadn't been lovers long, only two weeks. Portia imagined how she would have felt if the parietal laws had actually been brought to bear on Charley, if he'd been discovered in her room after two weeks, and she was getting kicked out of school. Would she run to him? Probably not. She would be too freaked, everything would be too new, the price she was paying would be greater than the emotion between them, at least at that early stage. And it was worse in Hadel and Laney's case, because everything had to be hidden, as if their love didn't exist—that is, Portia reminded herself, if Laney loved Hadel, which she still doubted. Laney's fear was rooted in something other than loss of love.

The night ground on. No one wanted to leave the room, sensing, perhaps, that it would be a betrayal of Hadel. Hadel fell asleep around two, while Laney stayed in her corner, upright on the bare floor, as if she were performing a penance. Natalie and Portia talked fitfully and then watched the approaching dawn.

Hadel awoke at six. She stripped the bed and packed the sheets and blankets in her trunk. Everyone watched. She went into the bathroom and everyone waited. When she came out, she said, "I might be able to make Lexington tonight if I leave right now."

Natalie cleared her throat. Laney rose from the floor. Portia wondered if Hadel would be able to drive with such blank eyes. The only other time Portia had seen such eyes was when she was fifteen, during a migrant workers' demonstration in Texas. Portia had heard about the demonstration from some young soldiers at her father's army base; she hitchhiked to the site in an old rackety pickup truck. Workers had chained themselves to a gate entering a partially harvested field. The town fire truck had come, and the sheriff's men sprayed the people on the gate with water from high-pressure hoses. When the water was shut off and everybody pressed forward to see, the workers' eyes looked just like Hadel's.

The four of them walked down the stairs, walked down the path, Portia and Natalie in front with the trunk, Hadel and Laney behind, each carrying a suitcase. As they loaded the car, Natalie started crying. Hadel hugged each of them quickly, kissed Laney and got in her car. She didn't warm it up. She drove to the corner, gave three loud honks on her horn and was gone.

Three hours out of New York, Hadel tried to entertain herself with hero fantasies. She conjured up a racehorse-stealing story in honor of Kentucky, where she planned to make her first overnight stop. Her mind began to wander halfway through the horsenapping scene, so she turned to saving people from rip tides along the Southern California coast. That failed miserably, too. It was hard to imagine being heroic when every single highway sign reminded her she was going home in disgrace.

But disgrace implied she was ashamed. She didn't feel shame. If being gay was so despicable, well, then she supposed she was despicable too. Being gay was not inseparable from the larger her. But in spite of everyone telling her she was despicable, she didn't have to feel it inside.

Had she failed herself in some other way? She hadn't broken down in front of Pattison. She hadn't denied the charge. She hadn't whined to the dean. She had headed off Portia's leafletting suggestion. Hadel intensely disliked the idea of crowds rallying to her cause. She wasn't a cause. And being someone else's project meant linking her own growth to the efforts of others. That smacked of weakness. Yet, she reminded herself, hadn't she unwittingly become Pattison's project? He had told her to leave, and here she was, already two hundred miles away.

She gritted her teeth. All right, so she hadn't disgraced herself. She had departed with honor and dignity. But she still had to withstand the effects of that enforced leaving. She already missed Natalie. She missed Laney. She missed Ridgedale. She had been ripped away from her lover and her closest friend and her home.

Buck up, Hadel, she told herself. No matter how honorable you are in battle, perishing of shell shock in the aftermath is ultimately a defeat. And this was just an opening skirmish. Natalie's "Is it wise to be gay?" question made a lot of sense. Of course it wasn't wise to be gay; it was also suicidal to deny it if you were. Between the suicide of her own soul and an unwise course, Hadel would choose foolishness every time. What she had to guard against, she saw, was that the consequent blows to her soul didn't make her see herself as others would see her. In the past two weeks she had changed from an intelligent, sensitive student to a person beyond the pale, a species of subhuman the rest of the population righteously shunned. She would never again, in her entire life, have the freedom of being seen as herself. Her lesbianism would always take precedence, mark her as an outcast. Ridgedale's administrators could legitimately chuck her out—with tears, perhaps, but with no question of the moral rectitude of their decision.

So what does it all mean, Hadel? she asked herself with a touch of irony. Can I live with honor and dignity, try to become the best person I can and protect my soul from the millions of people who think I'm a dangerous pervert all at the same time? Can I be both human and a freak? She remembered her own pronouncement about not evading the challenge of her own life. Now that she fully understood the challenge, evasion sounded pretty damn smart. She laughed out loud, the first break in twenty-four hours of gloom, and headed off the next exit to find a place for lunch.

1969

CHAPTER 6

Natalie dug the toe of her left shoe into the deep red carpet as if she were a bull about to charge. A mad kamikaze attack into the depths of the hotel ballroom would have netted her several dozen alumnae, three waiters and a few trays of champagne. Only a couple hundred points, she thought. Not even worth the scowl on my face.

Normally Natalie enjoyed these events. A twenty-minute fund-raising speech was a small price to pay for a plane ticket and a hotel room. Tonight, however, was not normal, because Hadel had not been around to arrange the entire expedition.

Hadel, for instance, would not have blocked the whole thing out of her mind. Natalie's memory had been jogged five hours earlier by an imperious voice on the telephone demanding to know when her flight arrived so someone could be dispatched to the airport to pick her up. "Oh, well . . ." Natalie stammered and then named a time at random.

"My!" the woman huffed. "I certainly hope we don't have traffic problems. By the way, I've reserved one room with a double bed and a single. I trust that will be sufficient. A cot is extra."

Natalie's head was swimming. A cot? What on earth was she talking about? "Perfect," she said. "See you soon." It was only after she'd hung up the phone that she remembered she was supposed to appear at the Boston Alumnae Association's annual fund-raiser with a freshman and a transfer student in tow. The transfer student was easy. Natalie had returned from Christmas vacation to find Laney still ensconced in Hadel's room. She had, in fact, been meaning to speak to Laney, since Laney could not continue living at Simpson. The seniors down the hall had friends planning to move into Hadel's and Megan's rooms.

Natalie racked her brains for freshmen. In spite of being president, and supposedly representing the entire student body, she finally admitted she didn't know a single freshman. Luckily, Portia phoned, listened to Natalie's hysteria and volunteered her sister Toni. "Now, don't hang up, Natalie," she continued, her voice angry as she remembered her reason for calling. "I need help, too. This creep has been crashing in Bendix." His name was Si Akers, Portia explained, and he had arrived just after Christmas. In the postholiday confusion, everyone thought he was someone else's friend. "By the time we realized he was a crasher, he had hooked up with Betsy Andrews. He's living in her room. He's dealing drugs all over the dorm, and he steals stuff out of the refrigerator constantly." Natalie kept glancing at her watch while Portia explained what had *really* raised her ire. Si Akers had interrupted a rehearsal of *The Maids,* which Portia was holding in the living room. He had waltzed in like a crown prince and begun strumming on his guitar just as the Claire had started to *move.* "Now she's paralyzed again!"

Natalie tried to keep the impatience out of her voice. "That's a problem, Portia. Before he was a trespasser, but since he moved into Betsy's room, he's a boyfriend. I can't go to the dean and ask her to invoke the parietal laws when we're advocating repealing them." Portia didn't answer. Natalie hoped she was thinking of the larger issues and not of how to draw and quarter her unwanted dorm resident or, for that matter, her unhelpful student body president. Then she remembered the Boston trip and her missing freshman. She had heard that Portia's sister was a bitch. "Would you mind asking Toni for me?" she pleaded. She was overwhelmed by the flood of things she had to do: write a speech, wash her hair, call Ridgedale's accountant to requisition money. She had no time to call a bitch too.

Although Natalie and Toni were suffering from the frantic pace—they had arrived at the hotel in Boston with fifteen minutes to register and change into their fund-raising clothes—Laney was quite at ease. Natalie watched her drift through the ballroom in a simple raw silk dress, creating much the same effect she had in the dining room the day of the freshman parade. Conversations dwindled, eyes snapped open and drinks remained untasted in the wake of Laney's passage.

"Forthright," a man said over Natalie's shoulder. "She's got that charisma thing. Makes you think she's honest. She oughta be a politician's wife."

Natalie looked at the ceiling and suggested that perhaps Laney should go into politics herself.

The man slapped his thigh. "Hey, good, good!" he brayed. "You girls are comers, all right!"

Though Natalie knew she was fund-raising, she was incapable of laughing at what the man found so hilarious. He stopped guffawing when he noticed her stony face. A minute later he excused himself for a drink, and Natalie figured her not laughing had just halved whatever amount the man had planned to give Ridgedale. She leaned against the wall and sighed. Perhaps ACLU lawyers were not required to be charming on command.

She meandered toward the hors d'oeuvres table, lost in one of her reveries about her life as a lawyer: the brilliant argument that wins the impossible case; the lost piece of information found at the last minute; the skillful manipulation of the jury, keeping the honorable solution in the forefront of their minds at all times—a combination, she thought with amusement, of Perry Mason and Rachel Carson.

If it was so much fun pretending she was a lawyer, then why was she so dreading law school that she could hardly complete her work at Ridgedale, knowing the finish of one meant the start of the other? This was one of what her father would call his hard questions. He generally answered his hard questions with an exhaustive, oblique illustration from a precedent-setting case, which was supposed to illuminate the pros and cons of the issue in dispute. With this sort of personal quandary, Natalie preferred her sister's method. Ever since Natalie could remember, her sister, three years older, had caught Natalie by the wrists and singsonged: "Natalie, do you really, really and truly, do you really *WANT TO*?" Since her sister chose her occasions carefully, Natalie's answer was an earsplitting, "Yes, I really WANT TO!"

Natalie picked up a shrimp by its tail and stared at it blindly before she bit it delicately in half. After years of listening to her father, she realized with dawning horror, she believed law to be stuffy and mechanical, a transparent overlay with arrows indicating the one right way through the maze, when the human affairs it strove to map were not only three-dimensional but also full of switchbacks and detours. She munched on another shrimp as she listened to her sister's voice: "Natalie, do you really, really and truly, do you really WANT TO?" Oh, my God, she thought, what have I done?

"Natalie," Laney said.

Natalie emerged from her vocational nightmare to discover a blunder of a more visible nature: she had downed nearly the whole tray of shrimp, shrimp purchased, she knew, by the school to loosen purse strings, not to feed student ambassadors. "Who speaks first?" Laney was asking.

Natalie considered. Laney would probably be the most amusing and should go last, but being student body president gave Natalie some privileges. "Toni goes first, then you, then me," she decided. "Don't be scared. These people will be thrilled with just about anything—"

Laney flashed her a smile so brilliant it stopped Natalie in midsentence. "Save it for Toni," she said. "I feel fine."

But in the middle of Laney's impromptu round of jokes about adjusting to Ridgedale's eccentricities, Ann Bailor walked into the ballroom and sat down in a folding chair at the back. Since everyone's attention was focused on Laney, only Laney noticed her. What she saw was a woman in her midtwenties, about five-seven, with close-cropped hair and a thin, mobile face. She wore a gray suit and blouse, and she held herself in a manner that invited no interference, her shoulders well back, her head high. Laney thought she would have looked imposing, even intimidating, except for a hint of uncertainty as she glanced around her, as if she weren't quite sure what she'd stumbled into but she'd make a good show of it anyway. Laney had never met Ann Bailor. But because Laney's brother Ronald had spent years teaching her the boundaries of her own person, she was acutely sensitive to the clues presented by the external behavior of someone else. The woman who had sat down in the back was projecting a style, a mood so like Ronald's own mix of dignity and confusion that Laney could hardly contain her excitement. Laney watched the woman lift her index finger and stroke a line across her eyebrow, exactly as Ronald had done since he was a young child. The resemblance was uncanny. When Ronald had told her to find someone strong, Laney thought, he had meant someone like this woman, whose manner was at once compelling and achingly familiar.

Meanwhile, she realized, the audience was beginning to stare at her fixedly and Natalie, front row center, was shifting in her chair. "I guess you can tell I'm not a public speaker," Laney told the assembled donors. "In fact, I've forgotten what I was just talking about. Now, I didn't come up here to demonstrate what a fool I am. I came for a very selfish reason: I discovered a month ago I'd transferred into a school on the verge of bankruptcy. The trauma of changing schools was worth it for just one year at Ridgedale. But believe me when I tell you I'd rather have two more. Thank you." Thunderous applause. Natalie saw the man she wouldn't smile at clapping his hand on his thigh in appreciation, his pudgy face split wide with a grin. Score one for Laney and her corny honesty.

After Natalie's speech, which dealt with facts and figures, Laney drifted to the back so that she could meet the woman in the gray suit, but Natalie had beaten her to it. She and the woman were hugging. "Laney," Natalie said, "this is Ann Bailor. She was a senior when Hadel and I were freshmen. We were all good friends. It's wonderful to see you, Ann. I'd never expect you would turn up at something like this."

"I wouldn't, except I figured you'd be here. Let's go get a drink in the hotel bar."

As they started off down the hall, Natalie remembered Toni, who was standing off to one side waiting to be noticed. She waved her along with them. The four bustled into the bar and sat down at a table. While Laney skated over the I.D. problem with the waitress ("Oh, we left our purses in our room. We're with the Ridgedale alumnae group."), Natalie recalled with a start that three years ago she had decided Ann was gay. Ann and her roommate Karen Parker had lived together since their sophomore year. Once she had heard a couple of seniors gossiping about Ann. "Dyke City," one of them said with a laugh. Clothed in her liberal splendor, Natalie spent even more time with Ann after that. But neither of them had ever talked about it.

In answer to Natalie's "How's life?" opener, Ann launched into a long description of her job as a reporter, the stories she'd covered, the eccentricities of her boss. Toni, after experiencing a momentary shock that a Ridgedale grad could do something so prosaic as work, seemed to decide to go along with the joke and listen politely. Laney, Natalie noticed, was staring at Ann fixedly, evidently making Ann uncomfortable, because she began directing her conversation solely to Natalie. "How's Hadel?" Ann asked. Silence. "Well, she's fine," Natalie said slowly, and then she told Ann the same lie she'd told her parents, that Hadel had wanted to take some undergraduate courses that weren't offered at Ridgedale. Ann asked if Toni and Laney knew Hadel; Laney allowed that Hadel had been on her football team, and Toni, going along with the spirit of the cover-up, denied knowing Hadel at all. "How's Karen?" Natalie asked. "Fine," Ann said and then switched the conversation back to work. Natalie figured Ann and Karen had broken up, or were at least having serious problems.

Natalie imagined how differently the conversation would have gone if Ann and Laney were straight. Though Ridgedale women imagined themselves too sophisticated to have steadies, or acknowledge a date as a date, the fact that Laney had been lovers with an old pal of Ann's would have emerged quickly once his name had been mentioned. This would have given Ann and Laney a common ground, a link, lightening the atmosphere and encouraging Ann to treat them to a blow-by-blow account of her disaster with Peter, her lover since college. Instead they were gliding carefully around the edge of the lake, steering clear of the thin ice in the center.

And did Ann and Laney even know they had a link? Natalie had read in a book that homosexuals could recognize each other by some sort of sixth sense. If so, Ann and Laney hadn't developed this faculty; Natalie was sure neither knew the other was gay. Should I have said something? "Hi, Ann, this is Laney. She's as queer as you are." Lovely. Would it be like this for Hadel and Ann and Laney all their lives? Unable to talk about what was important for them, pretending about everything, since almost everything, with the exception of a job, was related in some way to being gay or straight—your living situation, your romantic dreams, your relationships, children, family, friends—even something so minor as who you'd bring to a Christmas party or your high school reunion. God! Natalie felt bowled over by the sheer immensity of the alienation. When she had asked Hadel if this course was wise, she'd been more sensible than she'd realized. How could anyone bear it? And meanwhile, here at the table, Ann was watching her curiously, Toni's brief fling with politeness had been abandoned for her normal sulk, and Laney was leaning back in the booth, still staring at Ann.

"I'm sorry," Natalie said. "I'm exhausted. I think I'll go up now. I've got your address, Ann. I'll write."

She and Ann stood up and hugged quickly, while Toni struggled out of the booth around Laney, who hadn't moved a muscle. "Think I'll have another," Laney said. "I've got my own key."

Natalie nodded. Ann looked confused but sat back down in the booth while Laney signaled the waitress. As Natalie and Toni walked through the lounge and across the lobby, Natalie was aware she was angry—maybe they do have a sixth sense, and now they'll talk.

Instead, Ann was finding the potted palm in the corner absolutely fascinating once Natalie was gone. When the waitress brought the drinks, Ann began sipping hers rapidly, wondering why she'd stayed with this disturbing young woman. Courtesy? A lack of another place to go?

"You won't look at me," Laney said.

Ann shook her head, though she couldn't have explained what she was denying.

"You're very beautiful," Laney continued.

Ann almost upset her drink. In her confusion, she babbled: "Me? Why, that's ridiculous. I'm not beautiful. You—you're stunning. You're the one who's beautiful."

"So that's why you won't look at me?"

Ann looked at Laney. She had to. Their eyes locked, and they both disappeared in the joining of Ann's smoke gray and Laney's blue, in the mix of colors and the absence of fear. Ann drew away, finally, to discover her hand clenched into a fist, and the fear tight in her throat. She wanted to bolt from her chair, but an equal fear of seeming foolish stopped her; Laney was young, a child, too naïve to understand what was happening. She was playing games; to Laney, this falling into each other probably meant the vibes were good.

Except Laney now said: "I know it's too early to propose, but the minute you walked into that room, I knew you were the woman I'd marry." Ann did spill her drink. She thought she might drown in the sea of Laney's eyes. "Though Karen is a complication," Laney continued. "She is more than a roommate?"

Ann's drink seeped into the carpet, forgotten. Laney propped her chin on her fist, a gesture that made Ann think she might expire in the next couple of seconds. "Yes," Ann heard herself say. "I mean, no. We—we broke up five months ago."

Laney nodded. "My complication recently got uncomplicated, too. Would you like to show me Boston tomorrow?"

"Yes," Ann said. "Yes."

"Come on, I'll walk you to your car."

"Car?"

"Sure. Did you think this was a line?" Laney laughed. "Thank God you'll know me better soon. Especially now that you're looking at me."

They walked out silently and stood next to Ann's car. "Pick me up at nine," Laney said. She kissed Ann chastely on the cheek and walked back into the hotel.

CHAPTER 7

A few days after the Boston trip, Hadel received a phone call from Natalie. "Are you unhappy?" Natalie began. Hadel thought there was little likelihood of her being happy. Not only had she lost her closest friend and her lover and her school, but also her mother had decided not to speak to her, and her father was walking around looking as if he were being brave in the face of mortal injury. Receiving no answer to her question, Natalie launched into a blow-by-blow account of her self-analysis during the one-woman shrimp feed. "Don't do anything drastic," Hadel counseled. "You can finish Ridgedale and still not go on to law school. Take one thing at a time."

"I don't know," Natalie sighed. "I realized my only reason for carrying on the law fantasy as long as I have was I never thought I'd actually have to do it. It was supposed to be something to shake my head over while the air raid sirens were blaring."

Where have I heard that before? Hadel asked herself. Only from everyone she knew. Her generation was the first in history to assume as children that the total annihilation of the earth was just around the corner. "That's why everybody's parents are so flipped out," Hadel said. "We grew up thinking each day was our last, never planning for the future. Our parents did nothing *but* plan for the future, since their present was so dismal. It's philosophies in collision."

Instead of continuing in pleasant abstractions, Natalie drove straight for the jugular. "Are *your* parents still flipped out?"

Hadel didn't want to talk about it. "Yes," she said tightly. The same day she'd arrived home, a letter had come in the mail telling her parents she was having "an unnatural relationship" with another student. That was when her mother stopped speaking to her and her father started being brave.

"Still?" Natalie had spent a half hour on the phone with Hadel New Year's Eve, predicting family reconciliation within the week.

"I'm looking for an apartment," Hadel said now. "I'll call you when I have my new number."

"Sure," Natalie said, and then zoomed ahead to what later became obvious was the real reason for her phone call. "By the way, Laney met Ann Bailor in Boston."

Hadel's stomach somersaulted. She had thought Natalie wasn't going to mention Laney. If her stomach insisted on doing gymnastics when Laney's name was spoken, Hadel hoped the news was more interesting than Laney meeting Ann at the fund-raiser.

"How's Ann?" Hadel asked, trying to make her voice less tense. Who cared about Ann? Hadel hadn't seen her for years. The important person was Laney.

"Fine," Natalie said. She paused. She seemed to be choosing ways to say whatever was coming next. "Portia tells me Ann and Laney are going to get married. To each other, I mean," she added, in case that part wasn't clear.

"Huh," Hadel said. She wondered if she would faint. In spite of the fact that Laney had not called or written, Hadel spent hours each day planning her future with an attentive and loving Laney. Her Laney fantasies were about the only thing keeping her alive. Shell shock was advancing rapidly, and now she had nothing to hold it at bay. Unfortunately, thinking about fainting usually precluded the real act.

"Still there?" Natalie asked softly. "Well, look, even if your parents are being drags, can you rest?" This question could be understood only in the context of Natalie's trips to Hawaii, where she "rested" from whatever assailed her—tiring student body offices, the press of unfinished schoolwork, broken love affairs.

"Natalie," Hadel said, unable to erase entirely her tone of hopelessness, "no one ever did, ever has, or ever will come to Berkeley to rest."

Both of Ann's parents were lawyers. She had never once considered following in her parents' footsteps. A certain distrust for the spoken word had been bred into her at birth. She was taking Laney with so much salt she was going to have to start hauling it away by the truckload soon. Laney didn't seem to mind, though Ann was frank about it.

Laney disarmed Ann twenty times during that day in Boston. "You don't believe a word I've said, do you?" Laney would laugh delightedly and press Ann's forearm with her thumb. "That's O.K. You'll see I'm serious soon."

It became a challenge not to believe, to avoid contact with this seductive woman whose eyes lit up at the sight of a ship, a cobblestoned street, the half smile on Ann's face. As the challenge became greater, Ann submerged her doubts and found herself staring at Laney more often. A miracle. A wizard. A witch. She was beginning to forget she was too frightened to fall in love.

Over a lobster dinner, Laney said she could probably change her plane ticket to the following evening. Would Ann care to go to a movie and then drop her off at a friend's dorm at Boston University? They could spend Sunday together, if Ann didn't mind.

Ann didn't mind in the least. She remembered nothing about the movie but Laney's hand tightly folded in her own. Once inside her apartment, however, reality intruded. Karen was furious: were they splitting groceries or not? Now that it was snowing, shopping tomorrow would be twice as hard. "I can't go shopping tomorrow," Ann said. "I'm going out. I—met someone. At the alumnae party."

Karen looked up from her shopping list, her big, dark eyes momentarily sharp. "Great. Keep it in the family."

Ann sat down at the table. "She's not an alumna. She's a student."

Karen's lips twitched with the beginnings of a smile. She wiggled her fingers for more information.

"A sophomore," Ann admitted. She couldn't remember ever feeling so ridiculous.

Karen giggled. Since it was the first happy sound out of her in months, Ann felt especially betrayed. She escaped to her room and upbraided herself. Laney had a good line. Knew she'd marry me from the moment she saw me! It wasn't very complimentary. And what makes her think I want to marry her? But why dwell on it? She probably wouldn't show up at the coffeehouse tomorrow in Cambridge, and Ann could come home and go grocery shopping with Karen, snowing or not. A dismal prospect, but it was safe and predictable.

Laney was at the coffeehouse, with sandwiches and a bottle of wine for a picnic.

"It's the dead of winter," Ann protested, thinking Laney was more beautiful than yesterday. She made herself draw inward, even if it took not looking at Laney.

"A car picnic," Laney explained. "It's easy."

They took off to find a crag overlooking the ocean, where they ate the sandwiches and talked. Ann felt her defenses breaking down, and just as rapidly, she shored them up again. She fully expected never to see Laney again after today—Laney would go back to New York and tell someone else she was going to marry her. She'd already said twice that she wasn't interested in a college romance, coming up to see Ann every weekend. So what could this be but a charming interlude?

But then what was the point of the marriage proposal? It certainly wasn't a device for seduction. Every time they'd slip from vertical to leaning to lying, Laney would carefully untangle herself and suggest a topic. Drugs? Was Ann into drugs? That was one time too many. Ann was taken aback by the rejection; she didn't consider herself forward. She moved away from Laney and described her first acid trip in glowing detail.

After Ann's acid trip, Laney told her about Hadel.

"You and Hadel were lovers?"

"In the sense that we made love, yes. I wasn't in love with her."

"Then why—"

"Because that's what she wanted. I wanted what she wanted. But we weren't in love."

"You both weren't?"

Laney paused to think about it. Why hadn't the possibility that Hadel loved her occurred to her before? "I don't know. I hope she wasn't in love with me. We didn't talk about love. We didn't talk about commitment."

Ann remembered Hadel well enough to know she would assume love, mentioned or not. In spite of her forbearance with other people, Hadel dealt in absolutes when it came to herself.

She wouldn't understand grays or fine points. "Isn't that sort of cold?" Ann asked, her own voice chilly.

Laney either didn't hear her tone, or didn't react. "No. No, it wasn't. She wanted to be lovers, and it was fine with me. But even if she hadn't gotten kicked out, I would have ended it, now that I've met you. If it had gone on after this weekend, *that* would have been cold."

"Who started it?" Ann was sure Hadel hadn't.

"What?"

"Who made the first move?"

"I did, I guess. But it was there all along. It didn't matter who started it."

Ann knew it mattered to Hadel. How could Laney not see that? But even through the stirrings of horror, knowing Hadel and Laney had been lovers made Laney seem more real to Ann, more than a beautiful fantasy who had appeared out of nowhere. Hadel, above all, was eminently sensible. She would not have been interested in an illusion, even though she must now think their being lovers had been unreal. If she ever wanted proof, however, she could look to her current residence in California.

They drove back slowly, and by then it was time for Laney's trip to New York. Over protests, Ann brought Laney to the airport. Laney said nothing about seeing her again. She kissed her good-bye and got on the plane. Watching the plane taxi out to the runway, Ann figured this was one of those experiences she would laugh about in a few years, after she'd forgotten the feel of Laney's hair, or the tilt of her head. It was a good story, she decided. By the time she pulled up in front of her apartment, she knew it was more than that. Laney's visit had demonstrated to Ann how desperately lonely she was.

It was taking hours to get back to Ridgedale. So many hours, in fact, that the two-cab taxi office at the Ridgedale train station was pitch black, closed for the night. Laney sighed, hoisted on her backpack, and began the mile-long walk uphill through softly falling snow.

By the time she reached the traffic circle, about a quarter of the way, she was enjoying the hike up to the college. The snow deadened sounds, so all she heard was the squeaking of her feet treading through the snow, the rustling of the pack as it shifted across her shoulders, and her own even breathing. Her feet were warm and dry, thanks to the good boots she'd bought last year for Wilderness.

Walking on, able to see only a couple yards in front, less behind, for the lights of the train station had faded, Laney felt protected, enclosed in her own moving pocket, safe from the terrors of the world. Yet she was aware her sense of safety was temporary. She had seeped into the snow the same way she seeped into others. Her flowing—sliding into the reality of those around her—meant she was only a mirror; her being was fluid, reflecting disturbances and joys, almost as the tides rise and fall with the journey of the moon.

Moon child. She smiled to herself. Well, that's what she was, a Cancer, a homebody. When Ronald died, she never thought she would find a home again.

She might have stayed on in India, but she felt safer adhering to the spirit of Ronald's plan for her, going to school in the States, than she did drifting off into an unknown future. Besides, she'd read the U.S. magazines, knew about sororities and beer busts and cramming for exams. With football weekends and all-night gossip sessions, college seemed no more than a live-in version of high school.

Within a week she realized she'd been misled by the magazines. No one was wearing cute separates in maroon and navy. "Sorority" was a dirty word. NYU didn't have a football team. It was 1966, and Laney had not been in the United States for eleven years. She had never heard of strobe lights. She'd listened to a Bob Dylan record only once. Psychedelics sounded like something a psychiatrist would prescribe. If her parents said the war in Vietnam was necessary to protect our interests in Southeast Asia, they were probably right. The other students' strident voices, the demonstrations, the hostility toward anything conventional terrified her. She was ignored, pegged as naïve and deluded. Even her beauty was suspect, a fatal flaw in this anonymous army of soldiers who fought not for leaders but for principles. Laney felt like a ragtag British steamer wallowing through monumental waves, each succeeding day afloat an amazement, yet for what? An earlier storm had wiped England from the face of the map. She could perhaps put in at temporary harbors, but how could she ever find another England? Ronald was lost to her forever.

Her first temporary harbor was a student named Janice, a poor choice. She was one of the dissidents, the loudest and most fervent in their dormitory. Janice took it upon herself to teach Laney the ills of American corporate and military might. It developed that Janice thought Laney's father was more important than he was, that convincing the daughter might influence the father. But Laney had already understood by then that she had mistaken Janice's passion for strength, her conviction for stability. In many ways, Janice was no more grounded than Laney, though Janice's ills seemed to eat at her from inside, more aligned with depression and anger than Laney's fear. By the close of the school year, Laney was spending days shut in her dormitory room, clutching her pillow, dreading the sound of the laughter and the voices from the rooms around hers, those voices that seemed about to slip over to madness or mayhem.

At least, Laney thought, pausing as the road began its climb up to the campus, she had learned some lessons. Hadel was a far better harbor than Janice, though Laney had always been aware, even with Hadel, that she had dropped anchor in Djibouti when Portsmouth was what she'd had in mind. And now? Laney wondered what Ann was thinking on this dark night. Was she awed at the unfolding of a miracle? Did she realize that if Laney hadn't been in the right place at the right time, hadn't gone to Boston as the transfer student, they might never have met? Laney shook her head. No, they would have met, for they were meant to be together, but better sooner than later. Ann wasn't thinking about any of that, though; she wouldn't recognize the existence of a miracle until it affected her life, and Ann had not given Laney enough credence to know that Laney would change her life forever. Laney would have taken bets that Ann was mulling over their conversation about Hadel, probably thinking Laney was heartless. It had been a risk to bring Hadel up, but Laney had had to—better for Ann to hear it from her than from someone else, and being Hadel's lover had increased Laney's credibility an important notch. What luck, Laney realized suddenly, that the school had removed Hadel from the scene just as Laney met her partner for life. She had no stomach for teary scenes.

She had reached the downhill gate, the one near the dining hall. Now the stretch to Bendix. The snow was even deeper on the campus, and she foundered a couple of times, but her stumbling only added to her exhilaration. Several times on her slippery course up to the dorm she touched her backpack, as if to reassure herself that it still contained the train schedules and maps she'd gathered at Grand Central. When she pulled within sight of Bendix, she couldn't resist throwing back her head and yelping a wolf cry of happiness. She had found Ann, and Ann would soon see she was serious.

Laney walked into the *Register* offices, looking as if she knew what she was doing. No one stopped her. No one seemed to notice her. A hidden camera, however, strategically placed in a light fixture, would have recorded the following: the men caught each other's eyes and winked, and the three women watched the men, then raised their eyebrows and grimaced. Men! the receptionist thought. Show them a cute ass and they'll take off like hounds on a scent. The other two women, both typists, comforted themselves with the thought that Laney was prevented from being a true beauty by the sheer energy in her face and eyes; American standards of beauty, even in these tolerant sixties, demanded a certain vacuousness for a woman to be called truly beautiful.

Laney smiled as she waited for the elevator. She knew exactly what the women were thinking. Her flowing into those around her made her a master of the external, a wizard at presenting herself to others. One day at lunch during high school, she deliberately sat next to a girl she knew she intimidated. The girl had never before so much as glanced in Laney's direction. Laney settled down next to her, noted the girl's involuntary intake of breath, and then, pushing the flaxen hair from her eyes, she began to look like a cow. She tried to be a cow as hard as she could for perhaps ten minutes before the girl turned to her and said, "You really are a nice person, Laney. I never realized before." Laney had to clamp her teeth hard to hold back her triumphant laugh. As penance for her experiment, she invited the girl to every one of her parties for the rest of high school.

She stepped inside the elevator, faced front, and grinned

broadly at the receptionist, who recoiled before the closing elevator door cut off Laney's view. Laney punched a button and thought about Ann as the car began to rise slowly. Laney's mastery of the externals ranged beyond herself. Her ability to type personalities by the way they acted had come a long way since her mistake with Janice. Laney was certain she knew more about Ann after two days together than Ann knew about herself. Like Ronald, Ann was serious and almost painfully shy, yet she had told Laney her dream was to go into television newscasting. Ronald's plans were equally ill suited: he had chosen banking, when teaching or medicine would have been more compatible with his interests. It was as if the two would have been dissatisfied with success gained at something appropriate. They had to handicap themselves and then plunge ahead with blind determination. Further, once a path had been chosen, including the disposition of living situations and relationships, deviations from that path would happen very rarely unless a push was applied, which was what Laney intended to do to Ann this afternoon. The drive to prove oneself through work was an effective foil against the push and tug of more personal needs. But in spite of all of this, the part most important to Laney was that Ann was actually inner-directed, possessing a serenity she had hidden from herself. If Ann would let her, Laney could use that serenity as a foundation for the home she planned to build for both of them.

The elevator let her off in front of a closed door, sparely marked "Editorial." Laney patted the pocket that held the keys to the house she'd rented yesterday for reassurance and luck. Then she pushed open the door of the crowded newsroom, picked out the editor and walked up to his desk. She saw he was far too sharp to appreciate her cow look. "I'd like to see Ann Bailor," she announced.

"How the hell did you get up here? Never mind. I know how. . . . Whaddya wanna do, claim responsibility for the bombing at the depot yesterday?"

Laney shook her head. "No. Ann's a friend of mine."

"So see her after hours."

"I can't. I have to catch the four-thirty train. Anyway, it'll just take a couple of minutes."

"A couple of minutes to hand her the latest manifesto? How

come you guys always pick on Ann? She just started here two years ago, but every deadbeat who knows how to join two sticks of dynamite wants to tell Ann Bailor how he did it. What's she got, revolutionary magnetism or something?" Laney was tapping her fingers on the desk, a slight smile lighting her eyes. "I'm John Farbus, by the way," he said suddenly, holding out his hand.

Laney grasped his hand and let her smile get wider. "Laney Villano. But I'm not—"

"That's what they all say. Don't think you're any different. Some guy last month stopped me on the street and asked if I'd give Ann a message. Turned out to be a kid from Madison, thinking he was some radical public-relations rep assigned to the East. . . ." Farbus rambled on, though he knew Laney wasn't a revolutionary. He wanted time to check her out, time to exercise his sense of responsibility to his most promising reporter. Farbus had recognized Ann as somebody special the day she started work. He knew she wouldn't stay at the *Register* long; she wanted television, and she'd get it. She was an excellent reporter, and he wanted to make her even better because he was disgusted at the level of reporting on most television news shows. He also liked her personally and had soon figured out, through omissions in conversation, that she was a lesbian. Farbus had divined she had broken up with her girlfriend some months back, but her cloud of gloom had been replaced by bemusement in the past few days. Farbus suspected the woman sitting opposite him was the cause of that bemusement. There were similarities, he saw. Laney meant to get what she wanted as much as Ann wanted television. And Laney meant to get Ann. Ann, with her focus on her career, was too naïve and confused about her personal life to match wits with a determined suitor.

"I hate to disillusion you," Laney was saying, "but I really didn't come to deliver any great political statements."

He sighed. He wanted to tell her to make Ann happy. Instead he directed her to the second-level basement. "The morgue," he said. "But this morgue doesn't have bodies."

Ann was surrounded by heaps of newsprint, microfilm strips and notebooks with large, scrawled writing in pencil. She was exhausted and frustrated. Farbus had assigned her a story, then assigned her the background, then the background for a piece of the background. She'd been in the morgue for two days straight—this last stretch was thirteen hours. She hadn't eaten in nine. She had read enough about timber rights, chemical spraying and ski resort conglomerates to drive her into a coma. She had been about to burst out crying when Laney walked in.

"Oh, dear!" Laney said. "You're so tired!"

Ann did start crying then. Laney was the last person on earth she'd expected to see, and it wasn't until she'd seen her that she realized how badly she'd wanted to. Laney offered hope and affection, two emotions Ann hadn't experienced with Karen since they'd graduated from Ridgedale. It was as if life outside the school had crushed Karen, leaving her an empty shell, and Ann spent every moment away from work endlessly trying to fill her up. She cried harder, furious that she was breaking down in front of this strange person who said she loved her.

"Is anyone here?" Laney asked.

Ann shook her head, and Laney began kissing her cheeks and her hands, rubbing her shoulders, until Ann made tiny noises that had nothing to do with weeping. Laney stifled these with her mouth, until Ann was nearly lying down in her chair, Laney looming over her. Ann was astounded by her own transformation: one moment she was devastated by exhaustion and the emptiness of her existence, the next so consumed by need that she doubted she could stop if Farbus himself came into the morgue.

It was Laney who stopped, drawing away from Ann and sitting on a chair a long foot away. She was breathing hard. "Jesus Christ, I want you, Ann."

The rush that vaulted through Ann's body rocked her; she had to grab onto Laney's quickly offered hand for support. "I didn't know it was possible to be this turned on," Ann said.

Laney took a deep breath to steady herself. "I found us a house. It's in Woodsmere. That's an hour away for you, a couple of hours for me. I only have to be at Ridgedale three days a week, so it's fair."

"A house?" Ann echoed. "A house?"

Laney nodded. "It's beautiful, and it's only two hundred fifty a month. You can afford a hundred twenty-five, can't you? If you can't, I can. I can get more money from my parents." Maybe, she added silently to herself. She had decided to sell her old Afghanistani prayer rug, which would bring in a couple of hundred. Unfortunately, it was with her parents in Morocco; it would take time to ship and sell it. She also needed to arrange two library shifts at Ridgedale to make up the rest of the rent and pay for her train rides.

Ann was shaking her head. She couldn't make a connection between this raging inside her and a *thing,* a house.

"It's our house," Laney explained carefully. "For us to live in. I got it right away because I knew we couldn't wait. I need you."

"But, but . . ." Ann realized there was nothing in her head, so she shut her mouth.

"I want to be married to you. I told you I don't want to have a college affair, with you in Boston and me at Ridgedale. I want to marry you and live with you. For that we need a house."

"Ahh . . ." It was finally coming clear. "I see. You found the house. And we'll live in the house and commute." Now that she'd figured out the point of all this, Ann waited for the reaction to hit. She sat blankly, and then she thought: this is insane. Laney wasn't joining her for a weekend of fun in Boston. Laney was asking her to *act.* "What if it doesn't work out? You decide we should get married and live in a house. What if next week you decide we should get a divorce?" Her question unleashed such a flood of fear that Ann shrank away from Laney, dropping her hand as if Laney might squeeze too hard and crush her.

Laney didn't rush to comfort her. "I know I sound crazy to you. We meet and I tell you you're the woman I'm going to marry. We spend two days together, and I get us a house. O.K., I'm nuts. But sometimes I see things. I see us together, married, for years, 'til death do us part. What I always forget is other people don't see things, or they don't see the things I see. We'll wait. I'll cancel the house."

Ann listened to Laney's words, but she was thinking about the fear that had suddenly overwhelmed her. It meant at least part of her was taking Laney seriously. Part of her thought it would be wonderful and exciting to run off with this stunning woman. Part of her wanted to be married and this time wanted the marriage to work. But that was frightening too. She had wanted it to work with Karen, had desperately tried to make it work for the past two years before everything collapsed. She felt angry for a moment. If she had never met Laney, she could have gone on for a whole lifetime never knowing how miserable she was. And this is what I'm angry about? That Laney might save me from a life of misery?

No, she had to get off this track. People don't save other people. People save themselves. And this plunge into Laney's world is exactly what I need to save me; with work as my priority and my human need for companionship, I will never leave that apartment. Even if it lasts only a month with Laney, it will get me away from Karen's silences. She looked at Laney, who was beginning to smile. "O.K.," she said.

Laney bit her lower lip and shook her head. "Thank God. We can move early Saturday morning. Do you have a lot of furniture? Should we get a U-Haul?"

Ann laughed. How could she think about furniture when she was free? Leave the dinette set and the couch and chairs with Karen. It was the middle of the month, but two weeks was ample notice in their neighborhood. Karen would have no trouble renting the room by February.

"No, I hardly have anything but a bed. We can tie the box springs and the mattress on top of the car. Well, I do have some kitchen stuff and clothes. But do you want to come all the way here? Maybe I should meet you at the house."

Laney shook her head. "I want to help carry things. I'll be there around nine."

The moment Laney left, Ann bounded up to the newsroom, bursting with energy. "My, my," Farbus said. "I should assign you to the morgue all the time. You seem to thrive on it."

Ann flung herself down in the chair opposite his desk. "I didn't quite finish on Taylor, but I was wondering if I could go home now. I've been here since—"

"I know, I know," he said, waving her off. "You took a nap and came in during the wee hours of the morning."

"I'm going to move," Ann said.

"I figured."

"You did?"

"Your friend came up here first to find out where you were."

"Oh. Well, I have to tell my roommate."

Farbus nodded. "Good idea." He sat back in his chair and smiled at her. He wanted to offer congratulations, but he said nothing. After a moment, Ann smiled back at him. "Thank you," she said, as if he had spoken.

Ann strode into the kitchen to find Karen eating a dried-out hunk of hamburger from Zippo Burgers. "Ugh! Why do you eat that stuff? Why won't you cook?"

Karen shrugged, her shoulders lifting a bare half inch from their characteristic depressed slump. Ann watched her for a minute. Just say it, she told herself. "Karen, I'm moving out."

No response, not even a jerk of comprehension.

"On Saturday," Ann expanded. "I'm moving to Woodsmere."

"With your sophomore?"

"With my sophomore." Ann waited for anger, for tears, for an acknowledgment that the four years they had spent together were ending. Minutes ticked by. Ann watched, exasperated, as Karen took another bite of her hamburger and chewed it slowly. It hadn't occurred to her until now that she didn't have to share Karen's moods or tiptoe gently around them. "Are you on some kind of drugs or something? You're so—"

"Bland? Tranquil?" Karen rummaged in her purse and drew out a bottle of pills. "Tranquilizers," she said. "I'm not bland, I'm tranquil. Maybe they have blandilizers. Then I could be bland *and* tranquil."

Ann left the room and began to pack. Three hours later, on her way to the bathroom, she glanced in the kitchen. Karen was sitting in exactly the same position, staring into space, the crumpled pieces of hamburger wrap clustered around her like offerings.

CHAPTER 8

February 20 at last. Backstage was a futuristic dream and a present nightmare. Huge concrete columns supported a large, windowless, rectangular space, now littered with clothes, books and pieces of furniture. In the pursuit of clean lines, the designers of the performance hall had eliminated hooks, closets and shelves. The clutter one play spawned frazzled Portia; she felt she was swimming through an ocean of mess. She stumbled over a chair, slammed a huge cardboard crate on its side. "*Where,*" she demanded finally, "is the fur cape?"

Solange narrowed her eyes with agony. "My God."

Portia whirled to face her. "You forgot."

"I have so much to remember. The long speech, not to trip when I go out to the balcony, to light the cigarette awkwardly. I haven't lit a cigarette awkwardly since I was eleven. . . ."

"You forgot!"

"Where is it?" Jackie asked, ever-faithful Jackie, who studied American history and knew all there was to know about Shaker joinery and Amish quilts.

"We are borrowing Tina Michaels'."

"I'll get it, You need it for the first act?"

"*The Maids* only *has* one act. But we don't need it at the start. Come in through the rear door."

Jackie darted away.

"You better get out there," Portia warned. Solange and the Claire departed for the stage, while Madame remained, doing deep-breathing exercises, gripping a chair back with straining hands. "Make sure your face is dry," Portia told her. She went to the left of the stage, where she could watch without being seen. The lights dimmed. The audience quieted. The footlights came up.

Twenty minutes later, Jackie tapped her shoulder. She was holding the fur cape. Portia jerked her head toward Madame and sank back into the play. After weeks of frustration and endless explanation, it was magnificent. Solange knew her lines, the Claire was actually light on her feet, quick with wide gestures. When Madame entered, the whole theater seemed to chill. Solange didn't trip on the balcony. She remembered her speech. She carried the tea faultlessly, her mouth moving in silent protest. The audience exploded. It was over, three months' work in little more than an hour.

"You were so hard," Solange told her afterward at the cast party. She sipped at the school's cheap sherry. "You became another person."

Jackie nodded vigorously as people eddied around, congratulating the actresses. "You became a tyrant, a strength."

"You banished doubt," the Claire said.

Portia laughed. Portia of the chipmunk face, the child carted from army base to army base, the house president who got roughed up by the cops at Columbia, the sophomore who alienated nearly every actress at Ridgedale, had triumphed beyond even her own expectations. Mr. Wellington, the head of the drama department, raised his glass in congratulation. Before she could respond, Natalie cleaved through the crowd and hugged her. "It was wonderful!"

"Were you there? I didn't see you."

"I was standing along the wall."

"Natalie, Hadel sent me a telegram: 'Happy play. All well in Berserkeley.' "

Natalie nodded. "God, I miss her. Have you talked to Charley yet?"

Portia, about to head toward Mr. Wellington, turned back, startled. But Natalie had already joined another knot of people, and they were laughing at whatever she was saying. Natalie must just assume Charley is here, Portia thought. When Charley had come by two days earlier for his regular Tuesday evening visit, they had parted with no good-byes, and certainly no promise of his attending the play. Worse, they had not fallen into bed for one of their Après-Charley's-Shrink-Appointment Flying Fucks. Instead of F.F. Forty-nine, Charley had announced he had decided to become an architect, and Portia had made the grievous error of laughing. Charley's blowing up buildings seemed more likely than his designing them. She had met him while he was being trampled by a horse during a Washington peace march. Besides, he would dwarf a drafting table.

Portia's laughter killed off any chance of Flying Fucks. Charley was hurt; when Portia discovered he'd been thinking about architecture for months and had been examining graduate school catalogs, she too was upset. Why had he not told her before? When he began assuring her that architects had a role in the revolution, designing low-cost, efficient urban housing, Portia exploded. "Architecture is the most bourgeois occupation I can think of! Building playthings for the rich! Plundering the earth's resources to scatter monstrosities all over the landscape! Do you know how many people live in a single room in most of the world?"

"You imagine people *like* living ten to a room?" Charley countered. "You think it's a badge of revolutionary integrity? It's a symbol of poverty and oppression! Look at our generation. We're the biggest in the history of the world. What's going to happen when we start having babies?"

"I'm certainly not going to have babies," Portia declared stoutly. Charley left in a huff, and they hadn't spoken since.

Portia had nearly made it to Mr. Wellington's side when she spotted Charley, wearing his air force jacket and woolen mittens, leaning against a post near the entrance. Portia wove past bodies as hands reached out to touch her shoulders and people praised her. Charley smiled. He had trimmed his beard, and it looked motheaten. She reached up and stroked his chin. He followed her outside, into the February slush.

"You'll catch cold." They clung together, Portia crushed against the warm leather. He smelled wonderful.

"I had to come. It was brilliant, Porsh. You should be proud. You even got that stiff one to move. How'd you do it?"

Portia laughed again. She couldn't think of answers. "Will houses make you feel this way?" she asked suddenly. The words tumbled past her lips, and she longed to pick them out of the chill air, erase their sting. He would think she was being sarcastic, when she only wanted to know.

But he smiled easily. "Yes, they will."

"I was thinking, Charley. . . . I was thinking you didn't tell me because you knew I'd react the way I did. I realized what upset me most is that you're planning a career at all. It reminded me of my parents, always asking what I'm going to do after college. I hadn't known before their questions bothered me so much." Portia's parents were never satisfied with vague answers about the Peace Corps or serving on watchdog committees, in spite of her long interest in political activism, beginning with the agricultural workers' strike in Texas. Since then she'd pamphleted, stuffed envelopes, attended conferences, gotten bashed on the head at Columbia and ignored the jeers of S.D.S. acquaintances when she worked for Humphrey. Her parents, however, wanted assurances of a Real Career, which Portia saw as synonymous with turning her back on the ills of the world.

"I know," Charley said. "I told you badly, anyway. I was afraid to tell you because we *are* so close."

Portia hugged him again. They would have to talk more, but the hostilities were over. They stood under the arch of the walk, kissing and laughing, until Natalie hrumphed from the top of the steps. "Mr. Wellington's wondering where his greatest student director is," she apologized.

"I've gotta go anyway," Charley said. He caught Portia's hand, squeezed it hard, and took off over the grassy knoll to the train station downtown.

Mr. Wellington was almost effusive. Effusive for Mr. Wellington meant growling words of praise into either his moustache or his pipe stem, but that was more than anyone had gotten out of him since a group of graduate students put on *The Ghost Story* in the fall of Portia's first year. The circle of well-wishers grew by the minute. The free sherry had probably drawn more than a few—among them, Portia noted with displeasure, Si Akers, her unwanted dorm resident. He was gulping sherry and chattering a mile a minute about his plans to homestead in Alaska. "Take nothin' with me but an ax, an old dog and an old lady," he told a gaping freshman. The closest he'll ever get to Alaska, Portia thought sourly, was to kick a husky on his way across Central Park.

The gathering was dwindling by the time Tina showed up to collect her fur cape. Jackie and Natalie had already gone, pleading a headache and studying, respectively. Si had scrounged enough free sherry. Only the hard-core drunks were left, cursing the rotgut sweet stuff while they checked bottles to make sure they'd siphoned off every drop. Portia waved at them and went out the side door. On the way to Bendix she began to come down, and her thoughts turned to disappointments. She didn't like the way everything had changed. There would be no after-play drink with the old crowd. The four who had sat together at the freshman parade had splintered apart months ahead of time. Hadel was in Berkeley. Megan, they had discovered, was at Anna Parkins College in Virginia. And Natalie and Portia could not seem to get together without the added chemistry of the missing two members.

And Laney, at whom the old crowd had gawked that first day, was too involved with her new life even to bother to come to the play. Portia hadn't believed it when Laney told her about the place in Woodsmere. *"You rented a house?"*

"Of course. If Ann and I are going to get married, we need a house, right?"

"Laney—" Portia temporized.

But Laney wasn't listening. "That's what Ann said when I told her. 'A house? A house?' I reminded her I didn't want a college romance. It's a great place, Porsh."

"But what did Ann say?"

"'Yes,' " Laney reported smugly. "She said 'yes.'"

Portia decided then and there this Ann person was as nuts as Laney. Who would meet someone three days earlier and agree to move in with her?

It became more understandable when Portia met Ann at the wedding. Laney had insisted Portia and Charley appear in Woodsmere to witness the nuptial vows. Portia hadn't wanted to go, but Laney wouldn't take "no" for an answer. "How often are you going to come to my wedding, huh?" There was no getting out of it, and Charley was surprisingly eager, pooh-poohing Portia's trepidations.

One thing Laney was right about: the house was great. It was an old two-story stone structure that the owners used as a summer house. Ann and Laney had to vacate from June 15 to September 1. Because of this and the fact that the second floor was off-limits, the house rented for only $250 a month.

"It's fantastic!" Charley enthused. He and Laney rushed off

to explore, leaving Ann and Portia sitting on the only furnishing in the living room, the rug, smiling self-consciously at each other. Ann was attractive, Portia saw, with character in her face and a reserve that might be hiding shyness. "It's chilly in here," Portia said. It was actually closer to freezing.

"It is," Ann agreed. "There's no heat. Laney said she thought we'd be warm enough, but I don't see how." In another era, she would have wrung her hands. She suddenly seemed very vulnerable and confused, and no wonder—she had been transported to an icy house in the middle of winter by a woman she barely knew. "You must think this is totally crazy," Ann said. "I suppose it is. . . . I'm not the kind of person who does impetuous things. I can't quite believe it myself. I was very unhappy where I was. I didn't even realize it until Laney showed up. For the past year I've thought of nothing but work."

She continued talking while they built a fire. The physical effort of carrying in the logs seemed to loosen her tongue. She was most sure of herself when she talked about her job. Throughout Ann's monologue, Portia formed a picture of a woman who had existed in solitary confinement for months, imprisoned by Karen's withdrawal from life. Ann was one of those people who are only truly at ease in their careers, where both the goals and the strategies necessary to attain those goals are known quantities. The same people were often least capable of managing their personal lives, unable to see they were trapped in a draining relationship. Since Ann couldn't discern the problem, work became the solution. Then Laney had opened up the prison gates, offering escape and enlightenment at the same time.

As the fire began to take the chill off the living room, Portia understood that the two women were really opposites. Ann was competent at one facet of her life, and she truly cared about it, while Laney was competent at everything and cared about almost nothing. It was an interesting combination, and, appearances aside, more in Ann's favor. Laney caring was a major commitment. Ann was sliding along, using Laney's energy as a springboard to another reality; she would find it difficult to perceive Laney as anything but a savior or a wonder who had magically appeared to brighten her workaday existence. Despite Ann's moving in with Laney, marrying her, Laney was going to have to wait longer for the real joining, for the time when Ann was able to see Laney as a person.

"I'm a little concerned about this wedding," Portia admitted as they stretched in front of the fire. "I'm afraid of being a captive audience, I think."

Ann shook her head. "It will be very simple. We're going to exchange rings." She smiled. "Laney went out yesterday and bought the rings and the carpet. I guess she realized people might want something to sit on." She patted the surface of the rug, as if she needed to reassure herself that the rug was still in place, covering the cold stone floor.

"Jitters?" Portia asked.

Ann laughed. "Yes. If I let myself think about it, I'd probably run screaming out the door. It's all so fast. But I've never felt so . . . complete with someone. I don't want to let her go."

Portia nodded, then wondered aloud what had happened to Laney and Charley. Before Ann could respond, the missing pair arrived with beer and chips. The chicken would be ready soon, Laney said. Charley bubbled about hand-hewn boards and nails fashioned one by one. The upstairs, he said, had been added later. Ann had quieted after her long talk, and Portia was content to listen to Laney and Charley fantasize about the history of the house.

They ate by the light of the fire, and then Laney went into the bedroom and returned with two small cardboard boxes. She sat in front of Ann, and Portia moved closer to Charley, reaching for his hand. A log shifted in the fire, first disturbing and then intensifying the silence. Laney handed one of the boxes to Ann, and they opened them to reveal two plain gold bands. The firelight played on Laney's silky hair, and Ann was solemn, her gray eyes intent. They took out the rings and fitted them on each other's hands. Then they kissed. Portia knew she would remember that moment years later. The fire outlined their bodies, colors were absent in the dark, their skin glowed warm and their kiss was tender and soft. When they separated, Charley and Portia let out the breaths they'd been unconsciously holding. Charley left the warmth of the living room for the ice-cold entry hall, coming back with the bottle of champagne he'd hidden in his overnight bag. The cork popped clear up to the rafters. "Cheers!" he cried, and all four drank from the bottle, laughing with delight.

Portia shook her head, symbolically clearing away the cobwebs. If she continued meandering around the campus this way, lost in her thoughts, she'd freeze to death. She regretted not spiriting Natalie off to Freddy's, even if they couldn't talk. Had Hadel connected them all? If only everything hadn't changed! Who would have predicted the power brokers would really have no power, that the four of them, so tightly knit, would unravel in a matter of months?

Had it all been Laney's fault? Of course it hadn't. Laney wasn't responsible for Megan's telling nor for the administration's hysteria. At most, Laney had been an unwilling catalyst. But she certainly hadn't spent much time mourning Hadel's absence and, judging by a conversation she and Portia had had a few weeks ago, her view of Hadel was inexcusably callous. Laney had asked how Portia had liked the wedding, and Portia had answered honestly, telling her it had affected her more than she expected, but she still found it hard to grasp Laney's quick dismissal of Hadel. "I think I've been difficult about Ann because I feel I didn't help Hadel enough. Since I was a rotten friend, I want all her other friends to be twice as wonderful to make up for my own failure. Your getting married to Ann a month later isn't my idea of twice as wonderful."

Laney laughed. "You've been analyzing this into the ground, haven't you? Hadel's fine. She's been noble and heroic and stoic, the stuff of all her fantasies."

"Fantasies?"

"Sure. Hadel, the hero. Natalie's the politico. Didn't you ever notice that Hadel's basically uninterested in politics or manipulating people? She serves out of duty. Being asked to leave Ridgedale gave her something to be heroic about. It fits right in with her life plan."

Portia stared at Laney. Was this how Laney dealt with her own guilt, acting as if Fate were somehow being satisfied? How could Laney presume to know Hadel's life plan? "What am I?" Portia challenged. "A hero or a politico?"

Laney smiled lazily. "Neither. You're interested in politics, but you're uninterested in power, making you hard to corrupt. A very dangerous combination."

Portia recalled now that she had not liked Laney's smile, nor her own rush of pleasure at Laney's assessment. She continued her trek toward Bendix, wishing that Laney had found it in her heart to give up two hours of her library shift so she could come to the play. But Laney was frantic for money now, what with the costs of firewood and the train fares back and forth to Woodsmere.

Her sister had no excuse beyond her new boyfriend, who supposedly had a family home on Martha's Vineyard. Dear Toni, who couldn't bear Portia's triumphs. Portia was house president? A job for small minds. Portia was pals with the power brokers? Look how Hadel's power helped her. Portia was in love with Charley? Toni was dating wealth, good-looking wealth at that. The theater? Was Portia planning to be an *entertainer*? And worse, of course, was the Portia that meant the most, the political Portia, who made Toni's eyes blur in instant boredom. Toni, you are such a fake, though I wish I had your face instead of mine. Well, did it matter? Did she care that she thought her sister was a pretty fool? It hurt, she knew that much. They'd been thrown together all their lives, the new kids on the base, the major's children. At Cathedral, Portia and Toni, the army brats. Toni thrived at Cathedral. She thought she'd thrive at Ridgedale. Portia had tried to tell her, but Toni would never listen. Ridgedale was too kooky, at once too demanding and too undemanding—insisting she make her own way in a school with high expectations and no structure. Poor Toni, floundering and drawing farther away from Portia every day. Of course she wouldn't come to see Portia's success.

Portia mounted the dorm steps, turned the doorknob and then bashed her shoulder against the swollen wood. She nearly fell into Si Akers, who was standing in the narrow entryway, waving his fingers in front of his eyes like fronds of seaweed in a lazy current. He was, Portia saw, staring fixedly at the snow, using his fingers as homegrown strobe lights. Cheap sherry and bad acid, a winning combination. As she pushed past him, he turned with her, still wiggling his fingers, though now he hunched over a bit so he could sight directly at her face. Portia was about to snap at him when he lost interest in her and moved off down the hall toward the kitchenette, probably to slaver someone's peanut butter on someone else's bread.

Portia headed for the living room, wanting to share both her triumph and Si's latest small assault with Laney. Laney usually stayed overnight on Thursdays; her library shift didn't end until eleven. But the room was dark. Portia switched on the overhead light and sank down on the couch, sticking her foot underneath to touch Laney's sleeping bag. She felt suddenly empty. The play was over, all the planning and rehearsing, and the high of success. Success was ephemeral at Ridgedale; there were too many talents for one to be lauded for more than a couple of days. Besides, Si was enough to bring anyone down to earth. But since when had success become so important to her? It wasn't: what was important was escaping her own questions for a while, throwing herself into a project that worked. Go to bed, Porsh, she chided. Forget Charley and Laney and Hadel and Toni for now.

She left the living room and walked down the hall. Betsy Andrews' door was standing wide open, ready for Si's grand entrance, and Betsy was lying naked on her bed, stoned out of her mind. Her eyes were slits, and she was singing quietly while her hands moved across her breasts, tweaking her nipples as she sang. Portia stood outside, finding her simmering irritability at Si escalating to full-blown anger. She remembered Betsy's last music department performance, a blend of Betsy's high, reedy voice with her own piano compositions. When Portia had left the hall, she hadn't joined her friends at the inevitable sherry party. Instead, she'd wandered off into the darkness of the apple orchard, humming lean melodies, wondering how someone nineteen years old knew enough to be simple. So even on her way to bed, she was confronted by issues. Her community values told her that whatever Betsy wanted to cram into her mouth was her own business, that the only sin was laying one's values on someone else. Wasn't that part of the lesson of Vietnam? But Portia couldn't deny that her hands were shaking with rage.

Si emerged from the bathrom, a crooked grin on his face. "Hi ya, baby. How come you don't like me?"

It was the "baby" that did it. Portia put her questions on the back burner and became the consummate house president, "Si, I'm afraid you'll have to leave."

"Huh?"

Dumb. God, he was dumb. "Pack up your dope and split."

His face got ugly. "Who says?"

"I do."

He laughed. "Don't mess with me, Miss House Prez. Don't even think about it. Go back to your room and stick a banana up your snatch."

Betsy was blinking rapidly on the bed, trying to come down to planet earth. Si brushed by Portia and turned up Betsy's stereo. Jimi Hendrix blasted through the dorm. Si smiled at her. He reminded her of a cornered rat. She walked into Betsy's room and switched off the stereo. Behind her, at the door, she felt the presence of other people, Jackie, Marsha, Adelaide. Portia moved toward Si, watching him fight the urge to backtrack. "Get out of here," she told him. "You're a misery-maker."

"You think you can make me leave?" His hands fluttered around as if they were birds searching for a place to land.

"No one wants you here," Portia said quietly. "You're garbage."

He flew at her, pinned her to the wall and started pounding her head, her shoulders, her back against it. Betsy's posters fluttered to the floor one by one. His hands had slowly edged up until they were around her throat, and Portia couldn't breathe. She tried to pry him off, but he'd gone into overdrive, unreachable. He wasn't even looking at her. No one moved. Portia could see her friends standing there, ringing the door, watching intently, the ultimate television crime drama. Portia's eyes began to dim. White light was shutting everything out. The white began turning to gray. Her throat and tongue were doing something funny. Then she breathed. She breathed and fell to the floor, retching because it hurt so much. She started crying, coughing, on her hands and knees on the floor. Someone was kicking something, an inert heap of jumbled clothes off to her left. Si. Laney was kicking Si, who was screaming thinly, the wail of a tortured cat. Portia grabbed her head as the sound came pouring in, Si screaming, Laney hollering, not at Si but at everyone crowded at the door: "What the fuck is the matter with you? Were you just going to stand there and let him kill her?" Portia was still sobbing, still on her knees. Laney helped her up. "Throw that bastard outside," she told Marsha.

"Oh!" Marsha squawked. "Oh, but—"

"Throw him outside! Now! And all of his shit. All of it!"

Everyone started moving at once. Laney turned her back on them and half-dragged Portia to her room. Laney got a washcloth from the bathroom and wiped Portia's face. Portia had fits of trembling that left her limp and exhausted, too weak to resist when the next fit shook her. "He was killing me," she said. It hurt to talk. "No one did anything. They watched." She grabbed Laney's hands. "Why did they just watch? *Why?*"

"I don't know. Because they think it's uncool to do anything? Because whatever happens happens?"

"But couldn't they see I was *dying*?"

Laney shook her head. "Maybe we don't do anything. Instead we yell about what someone else has done."

"They're my friends."

"They *are* your friends. I don't really understand. . . ." She stopped, thinking of how she'd had to shove them aside to get in the room. They hadn't resisted her pushing; their bodies were malleable, lifeless. Laney remembered the times that fear had paralyzed her own body, made it impossible for her to move. But Jackie and the others hadn't been frightened, hadn't been rigid or stiff. Something other than fear had prevented them from acting. "I think," Laney said slowly, "they didn't know they *could* stop him. They were incapable of doing anything because they didn't know they could."

"It scares me, Laney. The way they acted scares me more than Si's trying to kill me." Her face was blank, incredulous. She started when Jackie poked her head in to report that Si had gone. "Why didn't you help me?" Portia asked her.

"I—I don't know. I didn't know what to do. But it happened so quickly, I didn't have time to think!"

"It didn't happen quickly!" Portia shouted. "It happened slowly! It took forever! And you all just stood there until I couldn't even see you anymore!" She threw her hands in front of her face.

"You don't understand," Jackie pleaded. She started to add more and then shook her head helplessly.

She still wouldn't know what to do, Portia thought. She

watched Laney and she still doesn't know. "Please, both of you, get out of here. I need to be by myself."

Jackie tried to speak again, but Laney gripped her arm and drew her outside, shutting the door softly behind them. Portia paced around for a few moments and then threw herself on her bed, burying her face in the pillow. I didn't know what to do. That was the answer? The answer for anyone who watched someone else dying?

She stood up and walked around again, a tower of rage until a tiny voice accused, What have you done lately? Then her steps slowed, and she sat down on her bed. Aren't I watching while American bombs kill people halfway around the world? Don't I truly think I'm powerless, in spite of my marching and my letters and phone calls? I don't even do anything when it's happening to one of my friends! She had suggested organizing a protest in Hadel's defense. She had mentioned placing a small bomb in the administration offices, but she herself hadn't taken the idea seriously, figuring it wouldn't help. Now her doubt seemed no more than an excuse to do nothing. A bomb would have scared the shit out of the president and the dean. It would have made them realize they couldn't send the students off like lambs to slaughter. They had killed part of Hadel, and she and Natalie and Laney had watched just as Jackie and Marsha had watched Si. She was sickened at the memory of her relief when Hadel had rejected her offer of help, at her own decision that discrimination against homosexuals wasn't important, as if that had ever been the issue! Life was the issue! Will I sit here forever waiting for the revolution, paying lip service to my belief in self-determination for the oppressed of the world? While the war goes on, while my country kills hundreds daily? I'm no better than any of those who watch. I must become a person who acts.

Portia stood up and looked in the mirror. Big red blotches contrasted with the paleness of her throat. She knew they would turn into bruises. She smiled at herself, saw strength in her brown eyes. That little accusatory voice inside had saved her from the sin of complacency, started her on a new path. She would try to meet some people who had committed themselves to action. She couldn't just watch any longer.

CHAPTER 9

In May Berkeley was at its best. The sun glittered white-yellow in a span of ice-blue, the air was fresh and sweet, the hills behind the campus were still green from the winter rains. A visitor to town, strolling along crowded Telegraph Avenue, his hair ruffled by the light morning breeze, could be excused for thinking all was right with the world—that is, Hadel added to herself, if the visitor didn't mind being besieged by panhandlers and dope dealers ("Taba acid, buddy?" "Joint? Just a buck, man.") every other step of his walk, and *every* step in this neck of the woods, the block between Dwight and Haste, the haven of the street people. The few actual tourists Hadel could see through the windows of the Mediterranean Cafe, smack in the middle of the block in question, had more sense than her theoretical visitor. They were speeding along the avenue, grim looks on their faces, heading toward their cars or buses.

What was causing the tourists to hurry to their cars was directly behind Hadel's back, separated from the cafe by an alley. It was a strip of earth that ran between Dwight and Haste and extended from the rear of the shops lining the alley to the street above.

This empty, nearly block-square stretch of land had been claimed as a park by street people, neighbors, students and anyone else who wanted it. Renamed People's Park, it had been groomed and petted until it had turned as green as the hills behind it. Vegetable gardens, trees and flowers were planted. A playground was constructed. Barbeque pits were dug, benches built. All this had taken less than a month and was a nice instance of the community banding together without institutional urging or approval to create a needed open space in the south campus area. The approval part, however, was the problem.

The university owned the land, and the university wanted to make the area into a parking lot. This morning, at dawn, the police had sneaked out and put up an eight-foot-high fence around the stretch of green. They were now standing guard, waiting to defend their fence. It was, as usual, a case of Right vs. Might. Throwing up a fence, Hadel thought, sipping her cappuccino, was unnecessarily provocative, a gesture akin to dropping a ton of bombs on a country that had offended by not honoring a trade agreement. It seemed as if the powers that be were itching for a fight.

They wouldn't have to wait much longer. The three men at the next table, for instance, had entered the cafe muttering quietly. It had taken them just ten minutes to talk themselves into a rage. Hadel smiled as she remembered Natalie's admonition to rest. Resting was not an indigenous art form. Spacing out probably came the closest in appearance, but the two were derived from entirely different schools: resting was doing *something,* while spacing out was falling into nothing from doing too much something, be it drugs or politics or, God help us, studying.

No one was studying today, at least not at the Med. No one was even doing drugs, which was so strange any late-departing tourists might have thought they were in another city entirely. Until, of course, they listened to the rhetoric, far dearer to Berkeley's heart than drugs, sprouting from the mouths of most of the people in the coffeehouse. Drugs came and went, even the political issues came and went, but the requisite long faces and windy speeches those issues spawned remained the same. Hadel could tell, however, that People's Park was not going to be solved by a few shouted speeches. The three men at the next table had already left to gather others for a run at the fence.

Hadel thought perhaps she should start her walk across campus before the fun started, but she was curious. Since she'd come back from Ridgedale, she'd been remarkably disconnected from the white water of Berkeley political action. Instead, she was devoting all her attention to learning the mores of another country. She hadn't needed a passport or a visa. Two names from her mother's hairdresser were all it took. Finding the bars had been the easy part. Becoming a citizen, though, was proving to be next to impossible.

As soon as she had moved into her apartment on the campus's north side, she began visiting the larger of the two lesbian bars, deep in the heart of East Oakland. When she walked in wearing her work shirt and her jeans and her long hair, no one said a word. The bartender served her reluctantly. Hadel glanced around at the staring faces. They reminded her of those in a hostile freshman parade. The bar's regulars wore sweat shirts, slacks and either short or ratted hair. Someone bumped her elbow, knocking the beer out of her hand. Someone else said, "Go back to Russia."

Hey, Hadel thought. Hey, I've got a goddamned Purple Heart. I got kicked out of school for this. I've had enough shit slung at me already. Don't sling any more, not in my country.

"You wanta throw rocks, throw 'em in Berkeley."

"You live in Berkeley, doll? Why don't you stay there?"

She kept returning to the bar, night after night, Saturday, Sunday, afternoons. She figured they must admire her persistence if nothing else. She liked watching women dance together. No one ever asked her to dance. Finally one woman talked to her. Hadel suspected she'd been egged on by the loud group at the bar, but she didn't care. It was her big chance to prove she was a citizen.

"What are you?" the woman asked, setting down her beer and then herself.

"I'm a student," Hadel answered. She knew "student" was a bad word, but she'd decided long ago she wasn't going to lie. She needed these women too much to lie to them.

"No, that's not what I mean. What are you?"

Astrological sign? Heritage? Social class? Political persuasion? Religion? By this time her interrogator was laughing. "Come on," she said, "what are you, really? Everyone wants to know."

Hadel was pleased that she'd made the woman laugh. But she was mystified. She wanted desperately to answer the question. If everyone wanted to know, it must be important. Maybe they would like her if she answered the question.

"You're gay, aren't you?"

Was that the question? Did they just want her to acknowledge she was a lesbian? "Oh, yes," she said.

"Well?" The woman prompted her with curling fingers. "Are you a butch or a femme?"

Hadel was stricken with disappointment. "Oh, that," she said. All this fuss for something that made no difference! Her thoughts showed on her face. The two of them stared at each other, the woman's eyes equally transparent. To her, it made all the difference in the world. Hadel couldn't pretend it mattered. They might all be citizens of the same country, but that country existed in two universes.

She was now marginally accepted. No one talked to her much, beyond introducing themselves at the start of a pool game, but beer wasn't regularly dumped in her lap either. She was, she thought, unhappily alienated from everything, from the straight community, the gay community, the political community. No one lived in her universe but her.

The level of shouting outside had increased. Half the Med's customers fought to get out the door. It seemed a mob of students had marched down Telegraph from the university. Hadel told herself to get up and go home. It would be a demonstration like every other demonstration. The crowd would surge up toward the park, screaming at the cops, who always stood ramrod straight, with deadpan faces, as if an expression of anger or sympathy or even glee would open the floodgates to hell. The crowd would flow forward several times, and the cops would arrest a few at the front. They would hit a number of people with clubs and finally blanket the whole area with tear gas. End of demonstration, at least for the day.

O.K., she told herself. You know what'll happen. Now go see it anyway. Don't separate yourself forever. She picked up her notebook and joined the crowd on the street.

She was instantly struck by three unusual things about this demonstration. The first was the composition of the crowd. The street people and political types had been joined by others who had helped with the park—the neighbors and the run-of-the-mill students, plus even the fraternity-sorority crowd, clothed in their George Brooks and Joseph Magnin spring fashions. The park had merged five usually disparate groups. Woe to the university.

The second oddity was the composition of the cops. They expected a holy war, judging by the conglomeration of forces present at the scene, all in their different uniforms. There were campus cops, Berkeley cops, the Highway Patrol, and the Alameda County sheriff's deputies, the hated Blue Meanies, dressed in their baby blue uniforms, tear gas masks already affixed, so their faces were invisible, hidden behind big black snouts. The third and strangest sight was that these defenders of the fence were carrying shotguns. Didn't they know this was a demonstration, King's X?

A funny sort of moan went up from the crowd as the cops raised their guns. The shouting grew in volume. Hadel edged forward, trying to see. She smelled fear as well as excitement. People were packed together, facing the pointing guns. And suddenly the cops started shooting. They were shooting at the rooftops, shooting from their hips above this motley group of people who wanted to tear down the fence. No one moved for two very long seconds, and then everyone did something at the same time, only they were different things. Some people threw themselves to the ground, to be stepped on by the mob in front, backpedaling frantically away from the shooting. Some people bent low at the waist and bolted to the right or to the left, to the cover of stores or awnings. Hadel stood stock-still, staring with disbelief at the red-yellow puffs belching out of the guns. They can't do this, she thought, and then a hippie in a filthy poncho grabbed her hard by the wrist and yanked her out of the street. "Wait," she protested. "They're not supposed to—Wait!"

"Sorry," he mumbled on the sidewalk, letting go of her. He shrugged and shook his head apologetically, the whites of his eyes huge. He kept shaking his head.

"But—" Hadel started. She was confused. The cops were now wading through with clubs, gas masks clinging to their faces like elephant trunks. A man staggered by her, holding his hand over his forehead. Blood dripped between his fingers. She realized she was still carrying her notebook. She looked at it hanging down by her side. She couldn't think. She had to get away.

By the time she reached the university proper, she was trembling so hard she could barely walk. Her knees were weak. What on earth was I doing? Why was I standing there like a big bull's-eye, like a target in an arcade game? Did I honestly think they would stop because I was standing there thinking they should? She couldn't remember ever doing anything so crazy before. On the peace march from Berkeley to Oakland, when Hell's Angels had joined the Oakland cops on the Oakland/Berkeley line and had sat straddling their hogs with their chains wrapped around their fists, Hadel had taken one look and disappeared down the fastest route available.

Today was dumb. Dumb and dangerous. She searched for a reason. Why had they shot? That didn't matter. What mattered was that she had stood there. Had her self-esteem plummeted that much from being kicked out of school? Was this a manifestation of the worrisome shell shock? Or has being a lesbian made me so alienated I think I'm impervious to everything around me? This last, nuts as it sounded, had the ring of truth.

She was thinking so hard she didn't hear the helicopter until it was right over her head. She looked up at the grinning faces inside the big bird as they shoveled two tear gas canisters out the bay door. She was inundated by the cloud of gas; gasping and crying, she ran blindly ahead, smacked hard into a tree and fell, her notebook flying out of her hand. She abandoned the notebook and crawled forward until she reached the outer edge of the cloud, where she collapsed on the grass, her stomach heaving. Someone shouted over the whoosh-whoosh of the blades. Hadel wondered if the pilot planned to land on top of her. Her war-novel reading had given her one advantage: she knew the limits of the weapons of war. The helicopter couldn't land if it didn't have enough clearance. She crawled back into the cloud until she ran up against the tree again. She buried her face in the roots, trying to use the dirt to filter the air she was breathing. She heard the person shout again, and the helicopter veered off to the left and disappeared.

As soon as she was sure the helicopter was gone, she staggered a few steps forward and took stock. Her notebook was hopeless, its pages scattered over a fifty-yard radius. Her clothes stank of tear gas. Her nose was running like a faucet, and her eyes felt as if they'd been doused with a bottle of onion juice. She wanted nothing more than to go home.

She felt so overwhelmed by a wave of desolation she nearly fell to the ground. Where was this home? No longer at Ridgedale, no longer at her parents', who regarded her with a sort of loving fear that curdled her insides. Certainly not at the bar in East Oakland, with its ritualized two-step of appropriate behaviors. And also not at her apartment, toward which she was now heading. Her apartment was one of twenty-six tiny studios crammed into a three-story building on Euclid. Twenty-two of those apartments were rented either to Arabian students or to low-level drug dealers. The four women who lived in the building scuttled to their rooms with nerves tensed, listening for footsteps behind, watching for doors opening ahead. The trick was pretending to be blissfully unaware of running a gauntlet, since visible fear only drew the men faster. A marvelous feat of playacting, Hadel thought as she climbed the steps. She supposed women the world over were equally skilled.

Inside her apartment, the door locked behind her, she sat down on her bed and thought about the past few years. First they kill off our leaders, then they beat us, then they kill us. It had started in 1963 with J.F.K. and had run through a hundred peace demonstrations, culminating, at least in the public eye, at the Democratic National Convention in Chicago. And now they had started something new. Shoot with shotguns. Land helicopters on anyone carrying a book. At least the succession of events had a kind of logic.

She took off her grimy clothes and lay full length on the sheets. Her eyes were still tearing. Looking at her pack of cigarettes made her retch. She thought about Portia getting smashed on the head during that sit-in at Columbia. What had the cop felt like who hit her? Portia had such a funny, sweet face, the most loyal, basically *good* human being Hadel could imagine. Why, then, had the cop hit her, and that other crazy guy at Ridgedale tried to strangle her?

For that matter, why had Megan run and ratted to the dean? Because Hadel knew her father didn't care beans about her? Because Megan was left out, jealous of Hadel and Natalie? Megan was the debutante, the one with the money, the important family. By rights, they, the California doctor's daughter, the Philadelphia lawyer's daughter, should have been buzzing around Megan's circle. What were they, anyway? Newly upper-middle class. Natalie's mother was an *immigrant,* for God's sake. All of Hadel's grandparents were immigrants. Ridgedale was made for Megan, and Hadel and Natalie were running it. Was that why she told?

Nothing made sense. The cops with their shotguns, the helicopter, Portia nearly getting strangled, Megan telling, none of it was sensible. But then it wasn't sensible that she was still alive. She'd been young when President Kennedy was killed; she was still young now. But she'd never expected to reach twenty-one. Never. If someone had told her when she was thirteen that she would celebrate her twenty-first birthday, she would have laughed in the liar's face. Sardonically, of course. Everyone's sardonic when they're thirteen. Maybe that was the problem. They'd laughed at death too soon. There was a certain innocence to that brand of bitterness. They'd laughed so soon their laughter had dried up by the time they were seventeen. Well, they were all living on borrowed time, Hadel had no doubt about that. The past eight years felt like an unexpected gift from the heavens. If the helicopter didn't land on her tomorrow, or the earth didn't blow up under her feet, she wasn't sure what she would do. She had lived with the imminence of her own death for so long, it had become an old friend. As she remembered what she'd written on her application to Ridgedale, she wrapped the sheet around her and laughed. What's all this stuff about becoming the best person I can be? Hmmm? It was just like Natalie and her lawyer fantasies. Hadel had never once suspected she might actually have to do it.

The next evening's newscast was full of questions. No one knew who had given the order to fire, or who, among the various law-enforcement agencies present, had actually shot. Several people were seriously injured, one critically. Governor Reagan announced that the students were looking for an excuse to riot. He called up the National Guard and slapped a curfew on the city.

"Martial law in Berkeley?" the newscaster asked. Were bars supposed to close at nine-thirty so customers could get home by ten? Were classes canceled? No one knew. Tanks rumbled up and down Telegraph, and soldiers stood guard in front of the bookstores and the coffeehouses. The general consensus of the news shows seemed to be that Reagen was overreacting to duck the real issue: who had authorized the shooting? They ran the clip of him giving the finger to a crowd of protesters.

Natalie called the next morning. "Hadel! Are you all right? I've been so busy I didn't even hear about it until Harrison told me today."

Hadel described the shotguns and the helicopter, leaving out her own version of Custer's last stand. No need to worry Natalie, who wouldn't understand alienation running that deep. Natalie was most interested in the helicopter. "You were just walking?" she asked skeptically.

"What do you think? I was firing at them with my antiaircraft gun? I was going home! There was no one else around."

"That's amazing. Bastards. Why a curfew on the whole city?" Natalie had been to the Bay Area with her parents when she was twelve. She knew the campus comprised a very small part of Berkeley.

"Divide the enemy. Tell the Black Panthers on Shattuck they can't go out after ten because street people on Telegraph want to have a park." Pause. "Who's Harrison?"

"That's why I've been so busy. Harrison Forbes. I met him at Fillmore East. He's at Columbia Law, and he's wonderful!"

"That's nice, Natalie. Better than Jeffrey, I hope."

"Much. A million times. I met him at the end of April. It's so exciting, Hadel."

"Good. How are Laney and Ann?"

"Who knows? I never see anyone except Portia. Are you coming back for graduation?"

Hadel had thought about it, but the only person she wanted to see was Natalie. There was the expense to consider. "I doubt it. Do you think Megan will come?"

"I'm pretty sure she won't. No one's heard a word. Hadel, be careful, O.K.?"

"I'll try my damnedest." She hung up and wondered if going back would be good for her. She could see Natalie and meet Harrison, who hopefully was better than Jeffrey. It would finish Ridgedale for her, or maybe it wouldn't. Maybe it would bring up a whole load of grief she was trying to squelch under the weight of other miseries.

She held onto the possibility of going as if it were a lucky piece during the next two weeks while furor raged around her. One of the injured died, the ACLU sought an injunction against Reagan's "state of emergency" laws, the cops launched a tear-gas attack over a ten-block area and 482 people were arrested in one sweep, including outraged shoppers and a mailman. When Hadel threw away the lucky piece a few days before graduation, asking Ridgedale to mail her diploma, she felt she had chopped the last rope that held her anchored, that she was now afloat on a sea without end. She dredged deep inside and came up with a spark of life. Get a job, the spark told her. Stop feeling so dismal. But she sensed she was holding tight against surrender. She was getting very tired. Natalie was right. She needed to rest.

CHAPTER 10

Megan watched a bead of sweat inch over the eroded crevices of President Thayer's forehead. The president's bushy gray eyebrow foiled the law of gravity. The bead disappeared in the springy gray hairs as if it had fallen on the Mojave. Another shiny pearl appeared, this one welling from the bare area around his left temple. Instead of plunging down his jaw, it too became caught in the twisted channels of his forehead, traveling a good four inches before it was sucked up by his other eyebrow. Megan was so mesmerized by the vanishing sweat that she almost forgot what she was doing, which was nothing less than cutting out a pattern for the rest of her life. She would provide the pattern, the cloth and the scissors. Before work could begin, however, President Thayer, head of Anna Parkins College, Megan's senior semester escape route from Ridgedale, had to initial the design.

Megan had conceptualized the pattern five weeks earlier while lolling in her private bathtub (Anna Parkins had distinct advantages over nearly bankrupt Ridgedale), brooding about her future. Graduate school was definitely out, despite her straight A's this semester. Ridgedale's no-grade policy was a smoke screen; when graduate schools demanded a grade point average, Ridgedale complied, extrapolating grades from the four- or five-line evaluation reports issued to students by their professors each semester. Megan knew that she had too long been classified as a malcontent and a procrastinator to fare well under such a secret and subjective process.

Ridgedale's secrecy, however, had its good points. Megan had arrived at Anna Parkins with a clean slate, both academically and socially. After an initial period of confusion, she had realized she was regarded with a flattering degree of awe in her new surroundings. She was invited to every dinner and every party. Her advice was sought on matters as diverse as boyfriends, seating protocol, abortions and the relative dangers of various drugs. Her status, she knew, had nothing to do with her family or her money. Plenty of other women at Anna Parkins had these advantages. Ironically, Megan's edge was Ridgedale, with its sophisticated, kook-school image. The only wonder was why she had left such a paradise. Megan immediately invented an undefined, malingering disease for her mother. She had left Ridgedale to be closer to home. This quick fabrication had tripled her net worth: not only was she beautiful, intelligent and forged by the white-hot heat of Ridgedale, alma mater of any number of successful and creative geniuses, she was also a dutiful daughter. The infusion of success and creativity had not made her into a dread stuck-up, or blinded her to the important things in life, which (spoken with the hushed reverence of hypocrisy) were not a successful marriage or a successful career but a willingness to sacrifice these earthly goals for the good of Another, particularly Family.

Megan had discovered, not unexpectedly, that she far preferred being a superstar at Anna Parkins to being considered lazy and, to the students at least, half crazy at Ridgedale. If only, she sighed, wiggling her toes in the warm water of her bathtub, I could find a way to stay here.

And that was when Missy Langford, who was a bit of a bubblehead, knocked politely on the bathroom door and then entered the steamy room (Megan modestly draped a towel over the tub) to complain that Mrs. Rogers, the assistant director of admissions, was pregnant and therefore resigning, which was a terrible blow because her sister (whom Megan gathered was even more of a bubblehead) was applying to Anna Parkins next year, and how could she get in if Mrs. Rogers wasn't here? Apparently Sparkle (Sparkle! Megan moaned to herself) hadn't done well at Miss Pringle's and had, in fact, had to have hours of private tutoring, after which she'd still done poorly, but Mrs. Rogers owed Daddy Langford a favor (undisclosed), and now what were they to do? Megan paraded a stream of options before a gratefully nodding Missy, but meanwhile her mind was occupied with one thought: how to obtain the position vacated by the pregnant Mrs. Rogers.

And now here she was, five weeks later, all the groundwork completed, sitting in front of President Thayer, watching the sweat vanish into his spongy eyebrows. Seemingly unaware of his important role in her future, Thayer was skip-jumping from one pleasantry to another. "Quite warm today. Summer in a few weeks. Fruit trees were lovely this year. You've done brilliantly. Truly an honor to have you at Anna Parkins." He was, Megan thought, timing his sentences to the revolutions of the ceiling fan over his desk.

"It was my pleasure, sir. These four short months have meant more to me than I could ever have imagined." She spoke slowly, not wanting the conversation to be over before it had begun. Surely some of the hints she'd dropped had reached his ears.

"When is your graduation at Ridgedale?"

"Tomorrow." Megan didn't add that she had no intention of attending the ceremony. She wasn't going to squander her new feelings of competence and independence on a formality; seeing Natalie or Hadel could return her to the hopelessness she'd left behind.

"Do you plan to go on with school?" Thayer asked. This was not an appropriate question for the man who was supposed to initial her pattern. She decided he needed a clue.

"I've thought a great deal about college administration," she said, casting her bread upon the waters. "Columbia has a good program, though they've had so much trouble lately . . ." She let her voice trail away as Thayer came alive to cluck-cluck over his counterpart's inability to control its rampaging students. "Cordier's being blackmailed," he said, grinning wolfishly at his choice of words. Megan smiled back with the right touch of reticence, letting him know that she sympathized but was certainly not going to participate in racist jokes. Over his slightly embarrassed "Hrumph," she reminded him: "And then, of course, there is my mother to consider."

"Ah, yes. Not well. Don't want to be too far away." He looked at the fan as if he were seeking guidance. "An idea was brought to my attention the other day. Of course, I doubt that you would consider it, we're a small college, though our reputation is good . . ." His face was growing red through the unaccustomed flood of words. He's actually ashamed, Megan thought. "As you may know, our assistant director of admissions is leaving us at the end of this month. It may not be what you have in mind?"

Finally! she exulted. But she couldn't jump at the offer when he was being so apologetic. "What a wonderful opportunity, sir. I would have to think about it and then talk it over with my parents. I wouldn't want to make such an important decision lightly. Could I tell you Monday?"

"No rush. Perhaps this would be a good solution to both our requirements."

"I think it might be," she said gravely. She left him smiling and mopping at his eyebrows with a handkerchief. The bushy hairs had reached their saturation level.

Thayer's secretary was busy typing. The hall was scattered with faculty members. Once she was outside the building, Thayer could see her from the windows of his corner office, and Megan was finding it nearly impossible to maintain her contemplative look and slow, steady pace. She wanted to scream and turn cartwheels. She controlled herself sufficiently to stare at the players on the tennis courts for a long moment before she headed for the trees above the hockey field. Only after she'd climbed the long hill and reached the protective cover of the trees did she allow a restrained whoop to escape her lips. And then, disappointed in the mildness of her shout, she rolled madly on the thick carpet of green, her skirt tangling around her legs, until she grew dizzy with the heat and the bruised-grass smell clogging her nostrils.

She propped herself up on one elbow and surveyed her domain. Much lovelier than Ridgedale, really. Not as high-powered, but the setting was exquisite, and any loss in reputation was amply made up for by Anna Parkins' financial stability. Now that she had her place, her pattern ready for the cloth and the scissors, she could think of Ridgedale and her experiences there with more equanimity. And why not? Megan the failure was gone forever.

A scene flashed in her head of her and Natalie and Hadel baking banana peels in the dorm oven freshman year, Donovan singing "Mellow Yellow" in the background. She laughed. Banana peels! Super drug of the sixties for about two months. Then came hash and speed and acid and mescaline. Hadel,

Berkeley-bred, a dope smoker since junior high, had pooh-poohed the banana experiment from the start. She'd brought back some good dope from the Haight after Thanksgiving, super-clean and dusted with opium. Natalie had gotten hash, but it was Megan who provided the acid, courtesy of one of Richard's friends, windowpane acid, guaranteed pure. Freshman year had been fun, hadn't it? She couldn't remember anymore.

Megan arched her back and pictured herself from the field below, with her cherry blond hair and her long neck and lean, tanned thighs. Beauty queen. Success story. Tomorrow, home for dinner, she would quietly announce her news. Robert would be pleased, Richard envious, her mother neutral, as if any good news for Megan was really meant for someone else and the mistake would be discovered soon. And her father—he was the measure of how much she'd changed. She must have been out of her mind, denigrating him to her friends at Ridgedale. When she'd arrived home in December with a tale of special classes she wanted to take at Anna Parkins, her father accepted her story at face value, but her mother hadn't. "Aren't you home a few days early?" she asked. Megan shrugged, retired to her room and slept for thirty-eight straight hours, arising once during that period for dinner. It was the first time in her memory that she had eaten with her parents without one or both of her brothers present, since their school holidays, both in prep schools and college, coincided with hers. No one spoke for several minutes while they ate. Leaden as she was, Megan could hardly fail to notice her father staring at her, as if he were charged with noting every flaw and blemish on a badly worn but priceless Greek vase. Finally Megan looked up at him. "What have they done at that school to exhaust you so?" he asked softly.

Perhaps it was because his tone was so plaintive. Perhaps it was the hope that her parents would rally round to her side. Whatever the reason, Megan blurted out the whole story. Her father came through like a trooper: as he listened, he puffed up visibly above his roast, his face gradually becoming the color of the rare meat. "How dare they?" he bellowed. "They encourage perverts! And to think she was at our table!"

Her mother merely said, "I thought Hadel was a friend of yours."

Her father ignored her mother's comment. He raged on about speaking to Harry and Joseph and how that cesspool would never see another penny of his, or theirs. Megan heard nothing. She and her mother were staring at each other, and Megan stiffened as she felt a knife entering her heart. With a surgeon's precision, the knife excised that portion of her that loved her mother. Megan sat still a moment, her hands folded in her lap, expecting the wound to be mortal. It wasn't. She smiled at her mother and then turned toward Mr. Franklin, who was blustering like a sail fluttering ineffectually in the wind. He was rather sweet, she thought. She couldn't imagine why she had ever been intimidated by him. "Daddy, honestly, don't bother. I don't want to go back there ever. And if it's that kind of place, why concern ourselves with it? Don't you agree taking my last semester at Anna Parkins will be a good thing?"

It was where he'd wanted her to go in the first place, a sensible school close to home. He nodded at her question, slightly mollified. "Well—"

"It's finished," her mother said. She picked up her fork and began eating. After a moment's hesitation, Megan and her father followed her lead. When they moved into the sitting room for brandy, Mr. Franklin engaged Megan in a long conversation about her future. She hadn't touched the piano that night, nor had he asked her to play for them since. When Richard and Robert arrived home for Christmas, Robert was bewildered by the dinner-table announcement that Megan would be taking courses at Anna Parkins. Richard favored her with a pitying, know-it-all tilt of his head. But when the five of them trooped into the sitting room, and Mr. Franklin separated Megan off again, whispering to her that the boys should never know the real story, Richard stared at the piano and at her, bolted his brandy and dashed upstairs.

Oh, he'd been furious! And he would be so furious tomorrow when he heard about her job. Megan hugged her knees, imagining once more how each would react. Who else could she tell? Her cousin Ellen. The people here. But she'd left out someone important. Of course: Natalie and Hadel. If only she could tell them! They'd be so excited, except she supposed they really wouldn't be. They hated her. They'd like to string her up, or see her plummet headfirst off a twenty-story building. Wouldn't they? She didn't know. She wished she hadn't started thinking about them, not on this day that would begin her new life. No reason to think of Ridgedale either, all memories of which were dominated by the dynamic duo, at least the happy ones. Otherwise she had been hiding in the music room, slamming her hands against the keyboard, tears dripping off her chin. But she'd survived, come to claim this different Megan, gotten away from Hadel's magic pills. She had known as early as November that she couldn't endure another spring like junior year, when she'd actually seen Grace Pierson come at her with a rock, though no one else had.

Now that she thought about it, a lot of her troubles at Ridgedale could be laid at the feet of her two supposed friends. Just as she'd been classified as lazy by the faculty and the administration, the students had her typecast as third wheel to Natalie and Hadel almost from the first day of school. Natalie was so predictably take-charge and Hadel so tiresomely staunch. Between Hadel's morality play and Natalie's upstaging, a normal person had no room to exist. Yet look where Hadel's supposed integrity had led her! And Natalie, whose conception of modern womanhood seemed to consist of hopping into the sack with any boy with whom she fancied herself in love, couldn't be far behind Hadel in their plunge to the lower depths of society. They'd been flying high, all right, but now it was a case of water seeking its own level. Megan laughed at herself. Really, this was a bit Victorian, wasn't it? After all, Hadel had been extremely nice to her on occasion. But then she was nice to everyone, so that hardly counted as a point in her favor.

Water seeking its own level. Though the idea was harsh and antiquated, Megan needed to look no farther than her family to see it in action. Her mother, like Hadel, pretended to subscribe to high moral principles. Yet in spite of performing all wifely duties (with the possible exception of the one that Megan could not imagine, nor wish to imagine), Mrs. Franklin barely acknowledged her husband's existence. Megan had often wondered what her parents did when the three children were off at school: eat dinner in silence, retire to the sitting room and stare at the paintings in silence, climb the steps to their separate bedrooms and then meet again in the morning without a nod? Her poor father! Mrs. Franklin, of course, also despised Megan, and that unmotherly emotion was returned in full by her daughter. But more to the point, her mother treasured Richard, who was the Franklin offspring most undeserving of affection. Megan could have forgiven her mother for doting on Robert (after all, she had her father's special love), but her mother's bad taste in choosing surly, sullen Richard was unconscionable, or, as Megan now suspected, not bad taste at all but an instance of water seeking its own level. Perhaps the noble stance of people like Hadel and her mother was really covering up the rot underneath, the rot that drew them like magnets to Laney's flaunted sexuality or Richard's bad-penny sheen. Megan had simply been too naïve to see it before. Her father, unfortunately, glimpsed none of this. There wasn't much he could do about her mother, Megan admitted, but he contributed to the Richard-worshiping by deluding himself that his first son would go into the business—husband the family's 51 percent of the stock in the lumber company her great-grandfather had started. This plan was so patently absurd Megan laughed aloud. Richard was capable of only one thing: getting into trouble.

She remembered a June evening years ago when she was twelve and Richard was eleven. After dinner, she had gone out on the porch to slump in the big wooden swing. Lulled into near-sleep by dinner and the dripping hot night, she was barely conscious of her father murmuring in his study, though the study window was open right above the swing. His voice invaded her half dreams, becoming louder and angrier. She had begun to rise when she heard the sharp crack of a hand on a cheek and Richard's wail. She vaulted to her feet, her muscles tense for flight. The house waited, silent.

It was the one and only time her father had hit any of them. Something to do, Megan gathered later, with girlie magazines and rubbers, boy things. The Hartfields' kid, Tom, was never allowed to come to the Franklins' again. Her father had been a little rough, but seven years later, Tom had broken his parents' hearts when he got a girl in trouble and had to drop out of college to marry her. He was training as a buyer for a department store chain, not bad but not up to anyone's expectations, either. Her father, it seemed, had been right all along. Hard work and discipline during childhood and adolescence paid off in adulthood.

Shadows had blackened the playing field. Megan rose from the grass and smoothed her skirt. She should be getting back to her dormitory room to pack a few things for the weekend at home. She turned down the path and picked her way through the trees, emerging on a slope overlooking the campus buildings. They were arranged below her so carefully they seemed to be a still life: *Fruit in a Bowl.* Lovely, she thought. My place. My pattern. It was all so perfect she couldn't help feeling perfect within it.

CHAPTER 11

Hidden discreetly behind a hedge, Ann was testing how it felt to lie on a patch of bare ground. A month ago, she had come out of the kitchen of the house at Woodsmere and seen Laney stretched out in the dirt, not behind the hedge, but near the pansies she'd just put in. "Why don't you lie on the lawn?" Ann had cried.

Laney had tilted her head forward and shaded her eyes with her hand. "Dirt's no harder, and there aren't as many ants and bugs. I've seen people sit on wet grass when the ground ten feet away was dry." She laughed and put her head back down.

For some reason that conversation had stuck in Ann's mind. She leaned over and crumbled some of the earth through her fingers. It was soft and warm on this first Saturday in June, Ridgedale graduation day. Laney had finagled a job on campus, seating parents and friends and then helping with the buffet after the ceremony. She wouldn't be back for several hours.

The dirt *was* warmer than the grass, Ann thought judiciously, trying to be fair. The dirt smelled good, too, with a rich mustiness that reminded Ann of mushrooms and fine cheese. But there was no need for her to choose between the dirt and the grass. Two days after that conversation, Ann had arrived home from her commute to find that Laney had built her a bench against the elm tree, a very comfortable bench, with a cushion and a backrest. Ann stood up and crossed to it.

Laney had positioned the bench perfectly, Ann thought, curling up in it and leaning her head against the trunk of the elm. It was in filtered shade, so Ann wouldn't get too hot or too cold. It faced the most beautiful part of the yard, where Laney had worked wonders in only a few short months. She had started dozens of pansy and petunia seeds indoors in flats;

these were now crowding the beds with bright flowers. She had potted up daffodil and tulip bulbs, keeping them in a cold frame until the soil had thawed. But the most spectacular planting was that of the ranunculuses, put in at the same time as the other bulbs. The brilliant orange and yellow flowers, together with the wine-colored tulips, had been enough to send the Woodsmere Garden Society (eight members) through the yard with cameras. Ann was amazed. She wouldn't have known where to begin to tame the mass of overgrown shrubbery and weeds.

Laney had certainly known, just as she had known how to build the bench and install outdoor lighting along the garden path. The first moment it was possible to work outside, Laney had dashed into the yard and uprooted what had seemed like half the vegetation. Ann had watched from the window until the level of destruction, coupled with Laney's ceaseless energy, made Ann's legs shaky. Without ever sowing a seed or pulling a weed, Ann knew she would be the kind of gardener with a yard full of ugly, misplaced plants, all of which were saved because they had a right to live. Laney had no such compunctions. One of the reasons the garden looked so wonderful was Laney's ruthlessness with any plant that showed signs of malingering or, worse, disease. "If they aren't healthy, out they go," Laney had told Ann when she'd come back into the house from that first day in the yard. Ann had nodded weakly. She was remembering how Laney had refused to look at the injured raccoon Ann had discovered by the woodshed in late January, how Laney had clapped her hands over her ears and run for the house when the raccoon squealed in pain.

Ann wriggled on the bench, stretching and recrossing her legs, which had begun to tingle. The sun was now streaming through the bare trunks of the fir trees up the far hill; it was early evening, and Laney would be on the train, coming home. Ann wished they didn't have to vacate for the owners this summer. Laney had already arranged a sublet in Boston, so that was settled, but Ann hated the idea of anyone else living in the stone house. To her own surprise, she had grown to love both the house and the town. She hadn't expected to have much time to meet their neighbors, but the locals had been curious about the two young women braving the winter out on James

Road. Extroverted Laney had ignored the overtures, but Ann had helped with the Easter egg roll, attended town council meetings, gone to dinners. She had even become somewhat of a resident celebrity with her few *Register* columns on life in a small town. Woodsmere and the house had given her an underpinning she hadn't had in Boston, a home base cluttered with holidays and births and deaths, frozen pipes and bright flowers. Not once had she resented the long train ride to Woodsmere (which was nearer to two hours than Laney's optimistic one-hour prediction), even when she'd stayed overtime and was expected back early the next day. Coming home completed a circle of which work was only a part. It was very different from those last months in Boston, when she had lost herself in her job, when unlocking her apartment door meant confronting Karen's depressions.

The other surprise, of course, had been Laney. Ann had lived with Karen so long she had become used to raging fights and bitter silences. Laney was the opposite of moody, always eager for fun. She was undemanding, perfectly content to listen to classical music on the radio while she worked in the garden or cooked dinner for the two of them to eat by the fire in the living room. She seemed to know just when Ann needed to be alone, when Ann was hungry, when an affectionate caress was more valued than a declaration of love. But it was Laney's lovemaking that was truly uncanny: she anticipated what Ann wanted before Ann knew it herself. It was as if Laney were capable of crawling under Ann's skin and seeing all that was inside with more perception than Ann could ever manage. Ann found herself living in a state of sensual astonishment, and she began to wonder if she were being spoiled, to worry that this attention focused on her was as unequal as the love she had lavished on a rejecting Karen.

What did Laney want in return? It became increasingly disconcerting for Ann to have her needs fulfilled when she felt she was unable to pay Laney back in kind. In fact, the more attentive Laney was, the more Ann forgot—even the simplest things, such as Laney being afraid to drive. Ann would often hitch a ride to the train station from the man next door, and she would dash off in the morning, handing Laney a list of things they needed from the store. She would discover later that Laney had left the car in the driveway and walked the mile to town and back, on the return trip carrying a load of groceries. The worst part was that a week later, Ann would forget again, and Laney would repeat the performance. "But why don't you remind me you don't drive?" Ann railed the third time it happened.

Laney shrugged. "I don't mind walking. I enjoy it."

In February? Ann asked herself. With the snow piled up six feet high along the road? Ann retired to the bedroom to berate herself for yelling at Laney, and Laney, of course, recognizing that Ann needed to be alone, stayed in the living room.

Is there such a thing as too much perfection? Ann wondered during her soul-searching in the bedroom. But she admitted a moment later that she was being uncommonly insensitive. Part of it, she knew, was a backlash against Karen. Although Karen had kept Ann's needs at bay, she had expected—and Ann had delivered—a nearly second-sight attention to Karen's roller-coaster mood swings. Ann had often felt oppressed by Karen's unspoken demands and by her own anxious hovering, as if total concentration would convince Karen that Ann loved her. Leaving Karen sitting at the kitchen table, surrounded by the pile of hamburger wrap, had torn the chains from around Ann's neck, and she had resolved not to let anyone claim her so completely. Laney was, unfortunately, dealing with a lover too hungover from her last binge to tie one on again.

But that's not what Laney wants, Ann argued with herself. Yet more and more, she had sensed that Laney *did* want something more, did have some unmet expectation.

Ann didn't discover what it was until she received a summons to Phoenix in the middle of April. It was a job interview at a television station, a response to one of her résumés, mailed out on a schedule of three a month to stations around the country. Ann had received the call at work; the station was willing to pay her plane fare. Ann made reservations for the next day. When she returned home that night and told Laney the news, Laney's face literally darkened, as if a tornado had kindled between her eyebrows. Ann took a step back, startled.

"Phoenix?" Laney questioned.

"It's just an overnight trip," Ann soothed. "They never seem to come to anything, this is about the sixth interview, but I need to keep my name in . . ." She hesitated, suddenly aware that she was explaining away her dreams. "I mean, I *want* it to come to something. I want to be in television news."

"Of course," Laney said. She refused to say anything more, but that night she made love with an edge of frantic despair, as if it were to be the last time. Ann left with mixed feelings, sorry that she had somehow let Laney down but glad to get away from Laney's unsettledness. When she returned, Laney met her at the door. "I don't think I got the job," Ann said, certain that Laney had been waiting in suspense the entire time she'd been gone. "There was a guy my age, and he had a lot of experience. And a woman, too. She was prettier." Ann expected relief, even concealed joy, to flash across Laney's face, but Laney remained solemn, preoccupied, as if she hadn't heard. She led Ann into the living room, where dinner was waiting on two plates placed on the low bench Laney had found at the Salvation Army. They ate without talking, Ann mystified. Karen had often greeted Ann with silence when Ann returned from a job interview, but Laney's refusal to speak was not a punishment. Instead, she seemed to be preparing herself to announce something. When they had finished eating, Laney put the plates aside and said carefully, "I need someone I can depend on."

Ann flew to the defensive. "But when we met, I talked about wanting to be in television news. You've seen me send out the résumés."

Laney shook her head once. "I mean your trip."

Ann was nonplussed. "Going away for a two-day trip makes me undependable?" Good God, how will she react if I ever do really get a job?

"I didn't know you were leaving until the day before."

"But neither did I!" Ann protested. "I told you, they called me at work." She was starting to get angry, and she had to force herself to lower her voice. "Look, they call me to these interviews and I go. That's the way it happens."

Distress clouded Laney's eyes, and Ann reached out to touch her, but Laney jerked back, determined to finish what she had to say. "I know. Now I understand about the interviews. I'm sorry I got mad at you." She picked up the plates and carried them into the kitchen.

Ann remained sitting for a moment. Laney hasn't even thought about what would happen if I landed a job, she realized. Just as Laney didn't make the connection between the résumés and interviews, she hasn't linked interviews with a job offer. What matters is I left her for two days.

Almost unwillingly, Ann followed Laney into the kitchen. Laney was crying as she washed the plates and silverware. "Laney?" Ann stroked the back of her neck. "Why are you crying?"

When Laney turned around, the distress in her eyes had shaded toward fear. "You were angry. I thought you'd leave if you were angry."

Ann didn't know what to say. She reached out for Laney and hugged her.

In a sense I did leave, Ann thought now. The sun had almost set behind the trees, and it had grown chilly. She got up from the bench and walked inside, turning on the garden lights for Laney. Ann stood at the bedroom window, watching gray light fade the colors of the woodshed and the lawn. After the Phoenix trip, after the conversation in front of the fireplace, Ann had shied away, frightened of Laney's needing her. They went on as always, eating dinner, making love, working in the garden, but both knew Laney was waiting and Ann was retreating. Dark circles smeared the underside of Laney's eyes, and Ann wished for the days of late winter, before she'd understood the depth of Laney's dependence. Several times Ann even caught herself wishing for Karen, with whom she knew what was expected.

And that was what was upsetting Ann now, this pining after Karen, even after Ann had finally realized that all Karen wanted was a receptive audience, one who would reward good acting with relief and bad acting with sustained applause. But Ann knew how to be an audience. She was not certain she knew what Laney wanted, and she doubted she could provide it. Laney seemed to need neither attention nor support, but a constancy in thought and deed that came from within. Ann didn't know if she had enough inside herself to give.

She went into the bathroom and turned on the water for a hot bath. As she undressed, she remembered a Sunday a couple weeks earlier when Laney, as usual, was working in the garden. Ann was reading the paper, sitting on her new bench, listening to Laney hum a melody that seemed familiar. Twenty minutes later, she had it—"Alice Blue Gown," a song her mother used to sing when Ann was a child. Ann chimed in with Laney's humming timidly, embarrassed both by her voice, which never had been good, and by the words, which described strolling around downtown, showing off in a dress of the light-blue shade made popular by Alice Roosevelt Longworth, Teddy's daughter. Laney's face brightened at Ann's less than auspicious singing debut, and she left the petunias to give Ann a hug. "You don't sing?" Ann asked quickly, confused by the intense pleasure she felt when she glanced into Laney's eyes, which were dancing for the first time in weeks.

Laney laughed. "Only when no one can hear me."

Ann thought it a reproof: Laney had the good sense not to subject someone else to her singing. But Laney leaned forward and tugged on Ann's elbows, drawing her forward. "But I like to hear you," she said. "I like to hear you happy."

Still perplexed, Ann could only stare at the ground between Laney's feet, and Laney had finally kissed her forehead and gone back to her plants.

And now, as Ann stepped into the bathtub, she knew a resolution of this pining after Karen and pulling back from Laney would never come until she stopped focusing on them and started looking at herself honestly. She was self-conscious almost to the point of stiffness, she admitted, shy and withdrawn, holding herself away from people. The job interviews, flying over two thousand miles to try to sell herself to someone she'd never met, someone who was judging her on her appearance and her manner as well as her qualifications, were pure torture. She often wondered why she did it, why she subjected herself to a process so difficult for her. But she knew instinctively that if she only did what was comfortable, she would end up sitting at home reading all day. She needed to be with people, to draw out others, let them have their say. This action, in turn, drew her out and then gave her her greatest joy, for once she was pulled protesting from her shell, she was smooth and relaxed, questions and conclusions rolling from her tongue as easily as skates sliding on slick ice. She loved that slide, and she would endure a hundred minutes of anxiety for one of smooth competence. Going back to Karen would be akin to shutting herself up for a lifetime read, though, she thought smiling, a great deal less pleasant. And what was this yearning for Karen other than a wish to return to a relationship where she was unchallenged, where she need not reveal anything of herself, be nothing but an audience?

She wondered, lying in the steaming water, if she hadn't exaggerated Laney's dependence. Hadn't it really been Laney's otherworldly perception that had disturbed her? Had she been afraid of what Laney would see or, more to the point, what she would find lacking? This shying away from Laney could become a dangerous habit, could extend to other areas of her life as well. Protecting herself from the needs of other people meant paralysis, imprisonment. She might one day look back on her relationship with Karen, that terrible flawed rationalizing of Karen's every move, and say, "I really did love that woman." My God, Ann despaired, I may as well be in my grave! And she needed Laney then, for she suddenly saw Laney as the embodiment of life, life freely given, while she had turned that gift away again and again, pushing Laney into a limbo of her own, and all because Ann was afraid to reveal, and then to give, of herself.

Laney came home when Ann was out of the tub, the towel wrapped around her middle. "Laney!" Ann shouted when she heard Laney's footsteps in the hall.

Laney came into the bedroom, her face drawn and tired, her loose cotton pants wrinkled from the heat and the long train rides. "Ann?"

Ann held out her arms and Laney stepped forward and let herself be hugged. "I love you, Laney," Ann said.

Laney pulled away. "You do?"

They looked at each other for a moment, and then Laney's eyes danced as they had that day in the garden. She stepped close, pulled Ann's arms around her waist, and the two began gliding around the bedroom, Laney humming in Ann's ear. When Ann's towel began to loosen, she took over the lead, guiding them serenely toward the bed. She was too self-conscious to dance naked in the middle of the room, but she imagined almost anything could change, given enough time and the determination to accept a challenge.

1971–72

CHAPTER 12

Hadel set the phone down and decided to finish her cup of tea. She needed five minutes of quiet before she went on a mad cleaning orgy, vacuuming every square inch of the house, washing a week's worth of dishes, mopping the kitchen floor. Once she'd accomplished all that, she would be able to see what else needed to be done. She sat back with her tea and smiled. Natalie was coming to visit. U.C. Berkeley was paying her way. Hadel hadn't seen Natalie for two and a half years, not since that morning in December when she'd left Ridgedale.

The university was flying Natalie out to attend a memorial showing of her movie *Kent State.* One year ago Natalie had kissed Harrison good-bye, loaded her Japanese-made movie camera and tape recorder into her old Morris Minor and driven to Ohio to spend five days interviewing people who had witnessed the National Guard pump a volley of bullets into a crowd of students. People talked to her because her interest was not in gathering facts for a newspaper or a government investigation but in relaying the horror of the killings. She returned to New York with reels of tape and miles of film, which she spent hours editing, too many hours to continue at Columbia Law School. Both Harrison and Hadel urged her to take a leave of absence, but she dropped out before finals, saying there was no point in pretending she would ever reenroll. After she'd got the sound worked onto the film, she peddled her movie. A few coffeehouses showed it, and then a Greenwich Village theater, and finally she got it on public television, and it won an award. Then everybody wanted to show it.

None of which meant much to Hadel, who loved Natalie for Natalie and didn't care if she was Joan of Arc as long as she was happy. It did mean, however, that Natalie was arriving on Monday afternoon, in less than seventy hours. Hadel had finished her tea. While she changed the vacuum cleaner bag, she began to worry about all the things Natalie might find about her life that were, well, *distasteful.*

There was Hadel's job for instance. For the past year and a half, Hadel had been working as the editor of a porno magazine called *Sexy Seventies.* She did precious little editing; she was actually the writer and production manager for the monthly slick. Anyone who had spent a few weeks in the Bay Area trying to get an editing, writing or proofing job, along with the eighty million other English majors, not to mention all the people with *experience,* knew what a miracle this job was. Natalie, who had so far avoided the job market while becoming a filmmaker and a feminist, wouldn't know. Hadel, a recent feminist herself, realized that her job ranked on a popularity level with herbicides in the newly sown fields of sisterhood. Her only hope was that Natalie would be amused.

Hadel's feminist blundering had been made abundantly clear to her by another portion of Hadel's life Natalie might have trouble adjusting to, namely Hadel's lover, Michelle. Michelle had a lot going for her: she was quite lovely, in a translucent, fragile way; she was extremely intelligent, well-read, left of center on all the correct issues; and she was an ardent feminist. Hadel was overwhelmed by all these qualities when they first met at, strangely, considering Michelle's present attitude, the porno magazine. Michelle had been the receptionist and bookkeeper, something she no longer wished to discuss. After a year with Michelle, Hadel added an erratum sheet to the gilt-edged volume Michelle presented to the world. Missing from page 122, line 13: Michelle is a bitch. Not a whiny, obvious bitch like Portia's sister Toni, but a clever, get-her-own-way bitch. Hadel was not too dismayed by this discovery. Michelle couldn't help being a bitch. She was lovable in many other ways. And most of all, she was Hadel's lover, and that gave her leeway to be a lot of things Hadel would have found reprehensible in a friend.

Then, Hadel thought, unplugging the vacuum cleaner and going off in search of the mop, there was the house. Soon after her graduation from Ridgedale, unable to bear any longer the nerve-wracking, twice-daily trip through the halls of her building on Northside, Hadel had rented the West Berkeley cottage.

It had only one bedroom, and the bathroom was located off the bedroom, at the very back. The living room was in the front. Natalie, bunking in the living room, would have to cross the kitchen and the bedroom to use the john. The house also had no heat and was in a terrible state of disrepair, the landlord uninterested in keeping up his fifth and smallest moneymaker. There was a large hole in the kitchen wall. The window in the faraway bathroom was broken. The living-room walls were half orange and half cream. Hadel made a quick walk-through inspection after she finished mopping. Each eyesore, every evidence of slovenliness and neglect stared out at her.

There was nothing for her to do. Or rather, there was far too much to do. She could drive herself crazy in the sixty-eight remaining hours before Natalie's arrival, or she could work on those defects that had some hope of being repaired. This plan in mind, she spent two days in the vegetable garden, laying in perky lettuces from six-packs, tomato plants with ready-made yellow blossoms, onion sets that would actually poke through the soil during Natalie's visit. She surrounded all these with a thick redwood mulch, on which she sprinkled a liberal amount of sweet-smelling cocoa bean hulls. Michelle watched all this activity from the back porch, which was in danger of toppling off the house. Halfway into the second day she bestirred herself, drove to the hardware store and replaced the frame of broken glass in the bathroom. See, Hadel congratulated herself, nothing's as bad as it seems, even Michelle.

Natalie arrived during Hadel's workday and instead of going to Hadel's house and finding the key under the mat, as they had decided, she took a cab directly to Hadel's office. Hadel looked up from her typewriter and saw her standing in the doorway, striking a pose: "Is this the den of iniquity? Looks like a layout room to me." In the midst of the hugs and the kisses, Hadel noted that she had gained the ten pounds Natalie had lost, that Natalie, as a result, was even more angular, her face slimmed and defined, with high cheekbones and a firm chin. The effect was not hard: Natalie had grown into her own competence. In the world she now lived in, her ability to cut quick to the bottom of issues with humor and bluntness and then to focus instantly on the next item was received with anticipation of great things to come.

She beamed at Hadel, telling her she looked terrific, that her eyes were as outrageously intense as ever, and since she'd gained weight her leather jacket finally fit right. She reached behind Hadel and grabbed a page of the story Hadel was writing, "Yacht Party." "This is why you went to Ridgedale? 'He timed his powerful thrusts to the upsurge of the waves against the hull, penetrating her deeper than he ever had before, and she howled for it, clawing at his shoulders, arching her hips to meet his in a relentless slap, slap that increased in volume as their bodies became slick with sweat.' Oh, Hadel!"

"*Pourquoi pas?*" Hadel asked, laughing, and she couldn't imagine why she had ever worried. They dashed out of the office like two children on a holiday. Natalie loved Hadel's house simply because it was a house. Natalie and Harrison lived in a fourth-floor apartment on the Lower East Side: no yard, no elevator, no heat unless they called the landlord three times a day.

"Do your parents mind your living together?"

"Probably," Natalie said, tearing into the grilled cheese sandwich Hadel set before her. "But we don't want to get married. Did you know that only three people in our class have gotten married?" Natalie had been conned into volunteering for the Ridgedale alumnae committee and had this sort of information at her fingertips. "Three people out of the hundred-twelve women who graduated, and that was two years ago. Amazing, huh?"

They basked in the thought that only three members of their class had fallen into the establishment trap of legalized love, though Hadel had an errant flash that it must be nice for marriage to be a choice. But mostly they basked in each other's company. They trailed around after one another, talking, talking. Natalie loved the vegetable garden. She loved the splintering back porch. So Natalie wouldn't go overboard, Hadel felt compelled to point out the deficiencies she'd seen on her inspection tour. "The living room really bothers you?" Natalie questioned, playing with her dark, curly hair as she looked at the two-color walls.

"Well—" Hadel started, wishing she hadn't brought up the living room. After all, she'd lived here for months without noticing anything extraordinary about it.

"So we paint," Natalie concluded, nodding her head.

"Now?"

"This minute."

They went to the paint store, where Natalie insisted she would buy the paint. She had planned, she said, to take Hadel and Michelle out to dinner, but since Hadel was *so* upset by the living room, Natalie figured that painting would be a more permanent house present. Hadel didn't object. Natalie with an idea was unstoppable.

By unspoken agreement, they talked about everything under the sun but their lovers while they painted. They wanted to be together as individuals, not two halves of two different apples. Love lives could be postponed. The hiatus ended when Michelle walked in just as they were finishing the trim. "My God!" she said. And then she pointed out that she had to leave again in half an hour.

"Shit!" Hadel yelped. "I forgot." Michelle volunteered at the Women's Refuge Monday and Wednesday evenings, and Hadel was supposed to have dinner on the table the moment she stepped in the house.

"We can go get hamburgers," Natalie suggested.

"Ah—bu—" Hadel was about to explain that Michelle didn't eat unhealthy things like hamburgers, but Michelle was nodding yes in a harried, irritable way, meanwhile trying to be cordial to Natalie. "I loved your film. I understand your new film is on alternative jobs for women?"

"Yeah, I oughta film Hadel." Hadel and Natalie laughed, but Michelle didn't. "Let's go," she said. The hamburgers were quick and greasy, and Michelle dropped the other two off at the front door. Hadel felt a sense of relief as the car pulled away from the curb. Neither of them spoke for a moment after they walked in the house. "She's very attractive," Natalie said, pulling the drop cloth off the couch so she could sit down. Hadel slouched in the armchair, knowing Natalie would be unable to stop at a physical description. Natalie looked at the ceiling and said, "Hadel? Do you remember Portia's sister Toni?"

Hadel smiled. "Didn't your mother ever tell you to be tactful?"

"What?" Natalie covered, meanwhile failing to stifle her smirk. "I just asked—"

"Stop it!" Hadel leaned forward and poked her in the ribs. They laughed at the absurdity of Natalie's hopeless stab at subtlety and her equally hopeless deception, and they laughed at the idea of conscientious Hadel hooking up with a twenty-four-karat bitch. Hadel recovered first. "We have good times," she said. "Not as many as at first, but still good. She's had trouble adjusting to living with someone. And she's been sick a lot."

"And you take care of her?"

Hadel nodded.

"Maybe you need someone to take care of you."

Fighting words. Hadel the brave, braver now that she had her compatriot Natalie by her side? Never. But she wanted to explain to Natalie how Michelle had appeared like a vision in the midst of misery, how unhappy she'd been going to the bars and meeting no one she could talk to, how isolated she was. Now she'd met others, but Michelle had been first, and Michelle was her lover. Hadel was afraid Natalie wouldn't understand. Natalie had grown up a citizen in her own country. She was accepted and valued for who she was. All Hadel could do was tell Natalie how she and Michelle had gotten together.

Hadel had been working at the porno magazine for a month when she was drawn out of her office by a huge argument between Michelle and Greg, the Neanderthal publisher. Michelle, who did all the accounting, billing, ordering, typing and telephone answering, was also expected to make the coffee. She had refused from the beginning. "That's why I hired you," Greg thundered.

Hadel proposed that since there were five people in the office, each should have a day. "You expect *me* to make coffee?" Greg screamed. "That's her job!"

Nonetheless, Hadel's suggestion was adopted and worked out well except on Thursdays, when Greg didn't get over his resentment until close to noon. Hadel and Michelle made a pact to go to the cafe down the block every Thursday at ten. It was at the cafe that Hadel tried to light Michelle's cigarette. Michelle dragged Hadel to her C-R group that night. Hadel told the group she was only trying to be polite. It turned out she was stripping women of their power. "But I'm not a man," Hadel protested. She assumed being a woman herself gave her certain privileges. This was incorrect, the group explained. Lighting another woman's cigarette was simply bowing to the old patriarchal customs designed to keep women in their place. Hadel grumbled from the depths of her beanbag pillow. She still thought there was nothing wrong with being courteous.

There were two new women in the group who announced right off that they were lesbians. They said they didn't feel very connected to women's liberation because they had almost nothing to do with men. This statement was greeted with laughter. One woman explained that since men had the power to hire, to fire, to rent and to sell, there was no way to have "almost nothing to do with men." That made sense to Hadel. She stopped grumbling and started listening. The other women told the two lesbians that they should feel *doubly* connected because they were the vanguard of the movement. Most of the women in the room, they explained, wanted to become lesbians so they would not, at least, be voluntarily giving energy to men. "They take so much anyway," one woman said. "Why give them more?" She said that lesbianism had become a political statement. This was news to Hadel, and, judging by the looks on the faces of the other two lesbians, news to them also. Hadel wasn't sure she liked her life being termed a political statement by people she didn't know or trust. She also thought this giving-energy business was a strange bed partner for romance. Would these women force themselves to fall in love with other women? Hadel remembered all the times she had wished she could fall in love with men, with Steve in particular. She hadn't been able to. Why would it be any different for straight women?

Hadel kept on going to the meetings because they made her think, and she enjoyed talking to most of the women. After one meeting, however, almost everyone stopped speaking to her. She had told the group how much she liked her job, how she felt competent and responsible.

"I don't get it," Hadel said to Michelle over a steaming cup of hot chocolate on their next Thursday foray to the cafe. "Why is it O.K. for you to work here and not me?"

"Because I'm a receptionist," Michelle said. "A receptionist's job is shit everywhere, oppressive everywhere. It doesn't matter where I work."

"You mean if I despised my job, if I was miserable and did

horrible things I hated to do plus got low pay, then it would be all right?"

"Exactly," Michelle said, tapping her finger on her head. "You're getting the picture." She had a twinkle in her eye. "Three of those women work at massage parlors. They give blow jobs all day long. But see, they're using men."

"What? How? They give lousy blow jobs?" Hadel couldn't believe it.

"No. They get a lot of money. The men pay twenty-five or thirty bucks. They usually fork over a tip, too. The women make a fortune. They turn in half their salaries to the movement, so men are paying for the movement that's eventually going to strip them of power. See, the women take something where men think they have power, paying for women's bodies, and they turn it around on them."

Hadel nodded. It made a weird sort of sense. The only way for most women to make large amounts of money was sex. If some of those dollars supported the little women-owned papers and businesses springing up, Hadel could see how giving blow jobs could be a revolutionary act.

"We're just starting," Michelle said. "We have to do things now we'll think are horrible later. That's the way it is in war."

Two weeks later, Michelle invited her to dinner. Hadel was surprised, because in spite of the C-R group, they knew little about each other. They left for Michelle's after work, Hadel stopping to pick up a bottle of wine. Michelle's apartment was in an old building on the south side of the campus. "I hate this place," she said. "It's so decrepit." It was a million times nicer than Hadel's old apartment, but Hadel could see what Michelle meant. The carpet in the hall was from the forties and had worn down to rows of twenty-foot-long threads. Michelle had made an effort in her apartment. The walls were covered with very complicated pen-and-ink drawings of forest and pond scenes, with foxes and frogs and birds. "These are beautiful," Hadel said, examining each one intently. "Where'd you get them?"

Michelle was in the tiny kitchen, crushing garlic on the cutting board. "I did them," she called.

"You drew these? They're terrific!"

"I majored in fine arts in college. Big mistake."

"Why?"

"Because it's totally unrelated to what I want to do now, which is work for the movement. But for years I had this big dream of being an artist when I grew up."

Michelle came in with two plates piled high with spaghetti, and a basket of garlic bread. Hadel poured the wine while she talked. "Michelle, you *are* an artist. These are of professional caliber. Isn't the whole point of the movement to free women so we can be who we want to be? That's anything—artist, lawyer, athlete, the President."

"I keep telling you we're just starting," Michelle said morosely. "We won't achieve that for several generations. Our generation's job is to lay the groundwork, fight the legal battles, protest the inequities so the next generation of women will be stronger, less crippled by self-hate."

Hadel disagreed violently, but she wanted to think about it before she said anything more. She was glad when Michelle changed the subject: "Good old *Sexy Seventies* has been running in the red for quite a while now."

Hadel sipped at her wine. "I know. Greg told me we might not get paychecks this month."

"What? We better get paid. Not all of us are independently wealthy."

Hadel finished off the remains of her spaghetti while she considered Michelle's remark. "You're not referring to me, are you?"

"I have the job applications in my desk. I saw you went to Ridgedale."

"That hardly makes me independently wealthy. This job saved—" Michelle was laughing. "What?"

"You're so serious," Michelle said. "I went to Radcliffe with a junior year at R.I.S.D. My great art career, remember? The difference between us and the rich kids is we have to work after our classy educations."

Hadel was startled. Why had Michelle read her job application?

"I had the feeling you would never tell me anything about yourself," Michelle said. "You like talking with me, but it would never have occurred to you to ask me to dinner, even after I took you to the meetings. You would have kept everything on a purely professional level. You never, for instance, would have told me you're a lesbian."

Hadel's tongue was thick in her mouth. She invited me over to dinner so she could attack me! Her stomach clamped painfully around the spaghetti and garlic bread.

"That wasn't on your job application. I heard you telling Greg one day when he asked you about boyfriends. You told him very casually—Greg, the superpig of the Western world! I thought for a while you didn't like me or trust me enough to tell me. Then I realized it was the opposite. You told Greg because you couldn't care less about him. Isn't that a little bass-ackward?"

Hadel said nothing.

"Of course you never asked about me either. You might have to respond in kind. It's safer for you to be open with all the people you couldn't be bothered with. With someone you like, you're a stone wall."

Hadel wondered how she could possibly escape. Michelle got up and went to the kitchen, carrying the plates with her. "I'm making tea," she called through the open doorway. "Aren't you wondering why I've been thinking about all this?" Michelle came back in and stood next to Hadel's chair. "You weren't, were you? You were trying to figure out a polite way to get out of here. Someone really worked you over, didn't they? Hadel, please stop being frightened long enough to hear me. I'm a lesbian too, and I like you a lot. I like the way you are. There's nothing to be scared of."

Hadel stopped listening. She felt her brain breaking up inside, as if it were a big iced-over lake thawing out in sudden spring heat. The explosions of the splitting ice were deafening. Since she'd returned from Ridgedale and discovered she didn't fit in anywhere, she realized she'd abandoned love, even friendship. She had isolated herself, pulling back whenever she liked someone. The power broker felled by life's blows, she thought wryly. But it really wasn't very funny. The difference between the Hadel at Ridgedale and the Hadel of today, content to stay alone in her rented house, was staggering. If Michelle hadn't forced her to see— She glanced up. Michelle was smiling at her encouragingly. Hadel started talking.

* * *

Natalie had stretched out on the couch during this recital. Now she lifted her head. "You were miserable, weren't you? I didn't know how to help. If you had told me more . . ." She nodded, thinking. "All right." They smiled at each other, Hadel relaxing deeper in her chair. She felt light and airy with the gift of Natalie's understanding. Hadel closed her eyes, wanting Natalie to stay forever. The lonely times seemed to drift away from her body, lost out the open window into the night.

Hadel rushed home from work, hoping for a few minutes alone with Natalie, only to find Michelle hovering in the kitchen, checking her watch. "The film's in an hour," she complained, "and it takes twenty minutes to park."

"Natalie's not here?"

Michelle shook her head. "Do you think I should put on the soup?"

"Sure. I'm going to get ready." Hadel allowed herself three minutes under a steaming hot shower, wishing that she hadn't had to work that day. The only time she'd have alone with Natalie now was the short drive to the heliport in the morning.

Natalie arrived as Hadel was dressing, spilling over with apologies: she had discovered a rare-book store on Telegraph Avenue and forgotten all about her film showing. "Can I help with dinner?" she offered, and then she looked at her own watch and squealed. "It's *really* late!" She ran off to shower and change.

She emerged for dinner, smoothing down her wool skirt anxiously. "Is this all right?"

Hadel thought it was fine, but Michelle went into the bedroom to dig out a brown and pink scarf. She looped it under Natalie's collar and examined her critically. "Perfect," she pronounced.

Natalie let out a breath and sank into her chair. "Split pea soup," she said. "Wonderful."

Hadel put a basket heaped with French bread on the table. "Are you nervous?"

"Oh, no," Natalie said, spooning up some soup and blowing on it delicately. "I've done too many of these things. The audience always asks the same questions, anyway." She tasted the soup. "Ah, very good! What's that, wheat germ?"

"Secret ingredient," Michelle smiled.

"Umh-hmm," Natalie said, her attention already elsewhere. "Listen, Hadel, here my trip's almost over and I haven't told you anything about anybody." She began a nonstop news bulletin from Ridgedale. "Portia decided not to run for any student offices, and she's not doing a senior play. She didn't have to, really, because she did *The Maids* sophomore year, but I'm sure Mr. Wellington was disappointed."

"Head of the drama department," Hadel interpreted for Michelle.

"She's been volunteering at Head Start since the beginning of last year," Natalie explained. "It's all she can talk about. Strange, huh?"

Hadel nodded. Portia's interests shifting from theater and radical politics to children was improbable. But Natalie was already full-speed ahead on topic number two. "Ann finally got her big chance," she reported. "An independent television station in Chicago offered her a newscasting job. First research, but they promised they'd work her into on-camera spots."

"Ann is Laney's girlfriend," Hadel said to Michelle.

"She considered not taking the job, because it started in January and Laney had the last semester of her senior year left. But eventually they gave up the house in Woodsmere, and Laney moved into the living room of Portia's dorm. Apparently she's miserable, but she insisted on Ann going because it's what Ann's been working for all these years."

Michelle had been hanging on every word. Now she put down her piece of French bread to say indignantly: "Well, I should hope so! They're the ones who got married, aren't they? I can't understand why *some people* insist on aping the worst patriarchal structures, when lesbianism, by its very nature, is the ultimate revolutionary act."

Hadel had heard Michelle say "some people" in that tone of pitying astonishment before, and she didn't like it at all. "Everybody's vision is different," she interposed mildly, glancing over at Natalie to see how she was taking this lesbian chauvinism.

"Oh, I agree." Natalie gestured wildly with her soup spoon, missing Hadel's comment and her furrowed eyebrows. "Marriage has existed for one purpose only: to legalize oppression."

"Yet people persist in coupling up like obsessed magnets—"

"In sacrificing individual identities for a security that's ephemeral—"

Hadel endured several minutes of this conversational tennis game, thinking Michelle and Natalie were rather blind: weren't both of them involved in committed couple relationships? Finally she cleared her throat. "Doesn't it seem likely that two are less lonely than one, and three or four are more exhausting than two?" They paused, and then they turned to gaze at her. She didn't know what else to say and sat there stony-faced, while they stared at her as if she were a savage at a nineteenth-century high tea, who had unexpectedly said something witty between bites of cake.

Michelle broke the silence. "We have got to leave this second."

"We'll park in the lot," Hadel promised. "We won't drive around looking for a space."

Hadel had already seen the film. This time she listened for the inflections of Natalie's voice, hearing how Natalie had broken through shock to get at the disbelief and horror of her eyewitnesses. The movie was powerful, and the audience in the crowded auditorium appreciated it, giving Natalie a standing ovation. Watching her up on the stage, fielding questions with energy and wit, answering with semaphoring hands, Hadel felt a strange mix of emotions: pride, love and something she didn't want to admit, an underlayer of jealousy. She suspected Michelle, sitting beside her, was comparing the two of them, wondering why Natalie Lehmann was friends with loser Hadel. This was real life. Elements of competition had entered. Natalie had made her beginning, and Hadel was still hunched over a blank typewriter page, wondering what would fill it up. Unhappiness? Failure? Or success, something she cared even less about, or thought she didn't, until tonight. And success in whose eyes? Michelle's? Her parents'? Hadel didn't know enough about where she was heading to separate what would constitute a success from a failure.

As a child, she had hoped for nothing more than life. Later she had hoped for nothing more than to find herself and, once found, she had hoped to find others so she wouldn't be alone. I've put a lot of energy into being a lesbian, she thought. I spent years knowing I was gay, years trying to convince myself I wasn't, years of standing on the sidelines of adolescence, the observer. And after all that turmoil, after I finally become a lesbian, I see that loving women is not an achievement, not an identity, but simply an indication of a sexual choice. No one should care less, even me.

Hadel was quiet on the way home. When they came in, she avoided Natalie's eyes. She went into the kitchen and began washing the dinner dishes. Natalie pretended to get involved in a book until Michelle ran out of things to say and went into the bedroom. Natalie appeared at Hadel's side as Hadel shut off the water. "If you don't tell me what's the matter with you, I'm going to lie on the floor and kick my legs and scream," Natalie threatened.

Hadel said nothing. She would never in a million years tell Natalie she was jealous.

"You're jealous, aren't you? Do you know how many times I've been jealous of you? If this is the first time you've been jealous of me, which I gather it is, since you're acting so guilty about it, I'm terribly insulted."

"What? Why have you been jealous of me?"

"Because I'm flash-in-the-pan, fritter from one thing to another, and you're deep."

"Deep?" Hadel scoffed.

"Come in the living room so we can talk," Natalie urged, glancing at the open bedroom door. They sat down on the couch, which was now piled high with blankets and pillows. "I take the easy way out, and you hang in there battling."

Hadel rolled her eyes. "That's—"

"And you have the good fortune to be gay."

"What?"

"You think I like being straight? Men are a lower form of life. I'm serious. Unfortunately, I happen to like screwing with them."

"Oh, Natalie! You think women are better? Women are idiots!"

"I know women are idiots. Men are scaly idiots."

"Even Harrison?"

Natalie drew a deep breath. "No, not Harrison. He's a jewel."

"I want to see this jewel. Send me a picture."

"I don't need to send it. I have one with me." Natalie rummaged in her purse. "Here."

Hadel examined the photograph. Harrison was good-looking, that was obvious right off. He had dark hair, dark eyes, a tanned, crinkled face. He was wearing a light blue sweater under a gray sports jacket. He looked jaunty but serious, the sort of man who was dependable without being driven. "We can actually talk to each other," Natalie was saying. "We go out dancing on weekends. I'll just be glad when he gets out of law school at the end of the month. He won't be so pressured."

"I'll be glad when Michelle starts law school," Hadel said, meanwhile telling Harrison's smiling face not to hurt her friend. "Maybe she'll stop talking about every stupid dispute at the Women's Refuge twenty-four hours a day."

"Michelle is going to law school? You didn't tell me that."

"Hastings. September." Hadel handed back the picture. "He's handsome, all right. So he's managed to inch up your evolutionary scale?"

"The only one I've found," Natalie avowed. "Hadel, it's law school that's changed Michelle. Even the prospect of it is enough to drive a person mad." She paused, watching Hadel's eyes. "Are you still jealous?"

Hadel considered. "No, though I have no idea why not."

"Good. Come here, give me a hug. We love each other." They held one another for a long moment, and then Hadel kissed Natalie's cheek. "I don't want you to leave," she confessed.

"I know," Natalie said. "Somehow I never thought we'd live away from each other."

"I know." Hadel patted Natalie's arm and went off to bed.

Hadel woke at two-thirty in the morning. Michelle lay beside her, breathing evenly. Hadel turned on her back and stared at the ceiling. She was hot, and she carefully edged the blanket toward Michelle. Two minutes later she was freezing cold, and she quietly drew the blanket back.

She thought about her conversation with Natalie. What they'd said was true. She would never live with Natalie again, never share the minutiae of Natalie's life in the same easy way they had for three and a half years at Ridgedale. The closest she would come would be occasions like this, visits back and forth, the only times she would see Natalie sleepy, or Natalie waiting for something to happen, or Natalie reading. Whenever they saw each other from now on, the seeing itself would be the event. Living their lives would not coexist with living with each other.

They had, alas, become adults, and their priorities had shifted. Natalie had her own life with Harrison, and Hadel her own with Michelle. They had houses, careers, mates, responsibilities. Hadel almost started crying: never had adulthood seemed so oppressive. Where had she ever gotten the idea that adults were supposed to be free? Kids, in their rigid, constrained environments of classrooms and dormitories, could be much freer.

Hadel moved closer to Michelle, who woke slightly. "What's wrong?" she mumbled, throwing her arm across Hadel's shoulders. "Can't you sleep?"

Hadel didn't answer. She pressed against Michelle, pulled the blanket up tight to her chin and closed her eyes.

CHAPTER 13

Monday afternoon, six days after the film showing, Hadel opened a letter addressed in Natalie's spidery handwriting. "Hot Flash from Ridgedale!" was splayed across the top in the largest and boldest letters Natalie could bring herself to form. "Imagine my surprise," Natalie wrote, "when I ran into Portia after attending a horrible alumnae board meeting. Remember I told you Laney's living at Ridgedale, pining away for Ann? Nothing could be farther from the truth. In late February, in a misguided effort to cheer Laney up, Portia invited her along on a dinner date with Charley and dormmate Jackie and Jackie's boyfriend Bob. Result? Laney moved in with Bob the next day, and they've been living happily ever after. Portia's run out of excuses for Ann, who calls a couple of times a week, asking for Laney. End flash. Pretty damned incredible, isn't it? Harrison's dying to meet you and says *he's* jealous I have such a wonderful friend. Love you, sweetie."

Hadel carefully reinserted the letter back into its envelope and began to prepare her after-work cup of tea. While she waited for the water to boil, she glanced several times at the letter, sitting on the kitchen table. She walked past it once. She didn't let herself read it again until she had sat down at the table, her tea in front of her. When she opened it back up, she discovered that its contents hadn't become more palatable. She tried to shape the information into something that made sense. Could it be Bob was just a roommate? Perhaps Portia and Laney weren't close anymore, and Portia was misinterpreting a simple desire to get out of the dorm. That approach wouldn't work, because Hadel knew the two were close. Portia's Christmas card had contained several photographs of her and Charley at the house in Woodsmere. And if this Bob person were only a roommate, why wouldn't Laney have told Ann? Hadel put the letter back down on the table and stared into space until she heard Michelle's key turn in the lock. "Oh, shit!" Hadel groaned. "It's your Refuge night."

"Forgot again," Michelle said, her hands on her hips.

"I got this letter. . . . Hamburgers?"

"You know I don't eat hamburgers! That was a one-time-only exposure, Hadel, and I suffered the consequences for three days. Forget it. I'll go hungry."

Hadel clicked her tongue against her teeth. "Then how about a scrumptious bowl of brown rice?"

But Michelle was reading the letter. "You have some very strange friends, Hadel," she said, and then she disappeared into the bedroom.

Hadel might have been less puzzled by Laney's behavior if she had understood what had prompted it. In the middle of February, five weeks after she'd moved into the dorm living room, Laney was literally losing her mind, her grasp on sanity eroding before the cacophony around her. The woman upstairs was playing Dylan's "I Threw It All Away" over and over again, occasionally chiming in with a wail a step short of uncontrollable grief. Earlier in the evening, a group had staggered up from town, clutching pints of Irish whiskey. Their raucous laughter and crashing up and down the hall formed a counterpoint to the woman in the room next door, whose two-day acid trip had degenerated into a crying jag. Laney had twisted her body into a defensive knot, pulled her pillow tight against her head, but nothing stopped the noise or the invasive creep of the voices. It was as if a mad scientist had injected the entire dormful of women into her brain, and everywhere she turned, she was banging on the bars, sobbing helplessly, laughing her throat raw, praying for death.

Portia hadn't been around enough to help. In mid-January, a week after Laney arrived at Ridgedale, Portia seemed to have sustained an emotional blow of her own, though she kept insisting that nothing was wrong. A month later, Portia was recovering, but her increased concern about Laney was too late and too little. Laney had needed someone in January, when she was still in shock over Ann's betrayal.

That was how Laney thought of it then. Ann had made a clear choice, her career over the life she and Laney had together. What was Laney supposed to have said when Ann ripped open her job acceptance letter and nearly fainted with joy? No, you can't go? No, I need you here to keep me safe? It was impossible to say such things to Ann's beacon-bright face, especially when Laney knew that Ann would take the job anyway, no matter what Laney forbade or pleaded. To Ann, the timing was wonderful. "You can come with me to Chicago over Christmas to look for an apartment," Ann had told Laney. "Then you can join me when you're finished at Ridgedale. You wouldn't want to be there at first, anyway. I'll probably be going nuts figuring out what I'm supposed to be doing." That was a nice way of saying she wanted to devote every moment to her new job. Ann's definition of going nuts was a passing obsession, a concentration on something that superseded other portions of her life. She had no idea what it really meant.

So Laney had moved into the dorm cursing Ann, cursing the day she'd pinned her all on a woman with other priorities. But now, as the student upstairs repositioned the needle on "I Threw It All Away," Laney understood that *everyone* had other priorities. Most people took continued sanity for granted and were freed to pursue different goals. And the pursuit of these goals, however inappropriate or inexplicable—a chase Laney could never join—was what gave most of humanity the will to continue.

I am simply marking time, she thought. My life consists of trying to make myself comfortable. And now she found herself cursing her brother Ronald, for he had not prepared her for feeling so alien, so apart from the rest of the world. He had not told her that people who attach themselves to other people are doomed to disappointment. But she was not ready to give up, not ready to depart this life which was so difficult for her. She wanted to have more time with Ann, for that was the happiest she had ever been, but she knew that she needed to find something within herself that would make life with Ann possible, would protect her from these times when Ann was forging toward her goal. And yet that inner security she now needed was just what had always been unattainable.

Perhaps she could adopt someone else's goal? Would that

give her a focus that would protect her? She certainly had no wish to be Ann's dream, a newscaster. Nor did she want to devote herself to children or go into the theater or save the world, all of which Portia seemed determined to do in one lifetime. Hadel had been more creative in her choice, being a hero, but Laney knew from her experience at Wilderness that because Hadel was a woman, her goal was the least likely to be realized. So that approach didn't work. But it had given her an idea. If she pretended to have a goal, wasn't that much the same as actually having one? In high school she had been marvelously successful playing Teen Queen. All her energy had gone toward creating that role, living her character. Of course, one couldn't play a role all the time. That had been one of her problems in high school—by the end of four years, she'd been awfully tired of the old school spirit and a date every night. But why couldn't she be someone else for a few months? She could live with Ann the rest of the time. It was a compromise, surely, and not what she wanted, but it was obvious that Ann was incapable of providing her with the enveloping cloak she needed. All right, Laney decided, I'll create my own environment.

The acid-tripper next door finally cried herself to sleep while Laney considered the possibilities for her first role. And when she'd settled on her choice, the drunks in the hall went into a room and slammed the door, reducing the noise factor by half. Laney nodded, pleased with these good omens and with her selection. She had always wondered what it would be like to be married to a man. . . .

Three months after Laney's decision to take on roles, Portia sat in the booth next to Freddie's towering jukebox, glad that she'd told Natalie of Laney's sexual about-face. At least Natalie had reacted with amazement. Portia was feeling a minority of one, carrying her astonishment around with her in face of an air of universal ho-hum. Not only had Laney lost her marbles, but the entire senior class had followed suit. Portia had expected Laney's kidnapping (Portia could think of it in no other way) of Bob Warner would have been pounced on by her gossip-hungry classmates like sharks scenting blood. Instead, the flurry had lasted barely a morning and consisted mostly of headshaking over Laney's betrayal of Jackie. By lunchtime, everyone had moved on to other news: the dean might resign, Angela Dunsfrey was actually going to marry that Scientology creep, and five people (including the old Claire) already had parts in summer stock. In a blink of an eye, Laney had been reclassified as straight—past, present and future. Perhaps, Portia thought, it had never sat well that the most striking woman in the class was a lesbian. But for whatever reason, within twenty-four hours Laney had become "Laney and Bob," the senior who lived with the stockbroker in the city.

Bob Warner had been an easy kidnap victim. Perhaps that was why Jackie, normally so kind and generous, had objected to Laney's coming along on the dinner date. Portia prevailed, however, and the three women had taken off for Manhattan, Jackie driving slowly on the icy roads. When they arrived at the restaurant, Bob stared at Laney in her silk dress and sat back down in his chair looking as if Madame Toussaud had replaced him with a wax replica—plastic eyes, permanently flared nostrils, mouth in the process of forming a greeting. When Jackie's proposal for a toast finally penetrated his fog, his wax arms became clumsily animated, and he clinked his glass with Laney first, and then, nearly jabbing his elbow into Jackie's nose, with Laney last. By the time the steaks came, Portia sensed that Jackie was caving in. Portia drew her attention away from Charley, who was telling a funny story, and focused on Laney. Laney was chatting about stocks with Bob, which was odd in itself, but she was . . . she was flirting, there was no doubt about it. She had a glow to her cheeks, a throatiness in her voice, a tilt to her eyebrow. Bob was emanating extreme pleasure and total bemusement at rapid intervals. Charley had caught on by now. "Tell everybody about that kid at Head Start, Porsh," he suggested in a voice loud enough to jerk Bob away from his contemplation of Laney's white-gold hair and blue eyes.

Portia entertained them with a tale of a four-year-old underachiever confronting the knee-jerk liberals at Head Start, meanwhile gulping down an untasted forkful of dinner the few times she paused. "Get a doggie bag," she directed Charley, and then she poked Laney hard in the ribs. "Off to the ladies' room."

"Oh!" Laney yelped. "I'll come with you."

"You need a Tampax?" Laney asked. "You didn't have to

stab me." She was peering in the mirror, wiping a speck of mascara off her cheekbone.

"What the hell are you doing?"

Laney turned around, startled. "What do you mean?"

"You're practically doing a little dance out there. 'Tell me about your office, Bob. Are you close to downtown?'"

Laney looked hurt. "I'm just being friendly. I never met a stockbroker before."

"Well, be friendly with me and Charley for a while. Jackie's about to commit hara-kiri with her fork."

"Oh. O.K., Portia."

Yet the moment the two returned to the table, Laney stepped up her attack on Bob Warner. By the time they'd gone to a bar and danced a little, Bob was acutely stricken, and Jackie's brooding was getting hard to ignore.

"You'd better do something," Charley advised quietly.

There was nothing really *to* do, but Portia feigned illness, and Charley faked concern so convincingly that the three women were soon in Jackie's car, en route to Ridgedale. The drive back was not pleasant, with Jackie's lip either cement-firm or quivering dangerously. Nor was it pleasant at the dorm, when the quiver finally cracked the cement after Laney went off down the hall whistling. "Portia!" Jackie wailed. It was the heartrending plea of a close friend. Portia spent a few moments comforting Jackie and then paced after Laney, determined to get an answer. "Laney?" she called at the entrance to the living room.

"Yeah?"

Portia shoved open the door. Laney was all bundled up in her sleeping bag, her arms wrapped around her pillow. Portia stepped over her suitcase and sat on the couch, where Laney would have to look up at her. Psychological tactics. "Jackie's in her room crying her eyes out." Start with guilt.

Laney looked appropriately guilty. "Oh. I—I didn't think she'd be so upset, I—"

"What'd you expect? Why were you flirting with him, anyway?"

"I don't know. I guess I thought if I had to be straight for a few months, it'd be fun to see what it felt like."

For some reason she couldn't understand later, Portia felt relieved by this confession. At least Laney had admitted she *was* flirting. "O.K., except just because you're not sleeping with Ann doesn't mean you're straight. If I'm not sleeping with Charley, it doesn't mean I'm gay."

Laney hugged her pillow tighter. "I'm tired, Portia."

"Right. Hey, Laney, one of the first things about being straight is you don't flirt with someone's boyfriend right in front of her."

Laney nodded, and Portia patted her shoulder, telling her she was sorry Laney missed Ann so much. "It's only a few more months," she remembered saying to Laney.

Dumb, Portia told herself now. Why had she been taken in for even one minute by this explanation? Portia gathered from Ann that Laney had planned her kidnap in advance of the dinner: apparently she had called Ann in late February, the day before the dinner, telling Ann that she was terribly busy and wouldn't have time to write for a few weeks. When Ann finally called the dorm at the end of March, she sounded confused. "I thought I'd hear from Laney by now," she said to Portia. "I was wondering about Easter vacation. Do you know if she's planning to come to Chicago?"

Portia pleaded ignorance. Easter vacation came and went, and Ann's calls started once a week. During yesterday's conversation, Ann had demanded to know where Laney was. "I don't know, Ann," Portia said, beginning her familiar explanation: she was working at Head Start so much she hardly ever saw Laney—but Ann had slammed down the receiver before Portia could complete her first sentence.

Portia went up to the bar and routed the bartender out of the back room. When she returned to her booth, she decided she finally understood the attraction of places like Freddy's: a person could escape here, slump in a corner and nurse a couple of beers for hours, listening to the drone of the television set and, later in the evening, to the thump-thump of the jukebox. She was pleased that she'd learned something new about human nature until she realized the implications of her knowledge. She had very rarely felt the need to escape. Days were too short to fit in everything she wanted to do with her friends, with Charley, with her politics, with the theater.

She sipped at her beer, thinking about what had gone wrong. In her case, she concluded, her life had become so problematic, so little hinged to reality, that she needed something real to hang on to, something like—she smiled over the rim of her glass—*General Hospital.* Pathetic when watching a television soap made more sense to her than her own life.

She remembered back to the night when Si Akers had tried to strangle her, how afterward she had cursed herself for being a hypocrite, felt her conception of herself as a politically responsible person had been an illusion. It was ironic that making that illusion more of a reality had rendered her life a labyrinth of half lies and half truths, so twisted now she sometimes wondered who she really was.

Almost two years ago she had met Renny and Mark, two men active in radical politics. After a year of talking, they and a few others had taken the big plunge—they had begun fighting back against the military machine, placing bombs timed to detonate at off-hours in the offices of companies whose businesses were war-related. They followed up the bombings with a carefully written communiqué exposing the companies' involvement: their interests were either protected by the war in Southeast Asia, or the companies were producing matériel for the war effort. Portia discovered that her theater training, along with her youth and her chipmunk face, came in handy when buildings had to be scouted. Guards laughed with her when she was on the wrong floor—she put people so quickly at ease in her funny, inoffensive way, they forgot about her the moment she was escorted to the door. Not that it had come even that far more than twice. Portia found it quite simple to pretend to be an employee on an errand, a sandwich girl looking for an office, a friend of a worker. She radiated harmlessness.

Charley didn't know. To think these words made her dizzy with fear, and she thought them five or six times a day. She had mentioned Renny and Mark to him at the beginning and occasionally brought up topics they were arguing, but Charley responded in good, liberal, student fashion: That's wonderful, I'm glad someone's doing something, tell me if you need any flyers printed up, I've got a friend who can do that.

Charley was busy in his senior year of college, and then in his first year of architectural school at Yale. She didn't tell him, except one night when he was asleep. She lay next to him, talking in a soft voice for almost five minutes. When he flipped over on his side, groaning slightly, she put her hand on his shoulder and drew close to him. He wouldn't want to know, she told herself.

She knew one of the reasons she was upset at Laney was she wanted Laney to tell Ann, so as not to do to Ann what she was doing to Charley. They had been together a long time, almost as long as she and Charley. The idea of their breaking up frightened her, though that would surely be the result, once Ann knew. Would it be the same for her? Once Charley knew, would he never see her again? But Charley would never know, Portia thought, leaning her head against the tall booth. The group—she, Mark, Renny and the others—were disbanding in little more than a month, after one final action. She would graduate in three weeks. Her life would change drastically, but she would be out of the labyrinth, able to be herself again.

Portia listened to the television, still unwilling to leave the sanctuary of the bar. It really was unfortunate that Laney had chosen these few months to alter her whole identity. Portia would have enjoyed Laney's easy company, though it would have increased the danger of Laney discovering her political activities. As it was, however, Laney's craziness had added an unwelcome joker to the deck; Portia was lying not only about her own whereabouts but about Laney's as well. Every time Ann called, Portia's stomach bounded into her throat, which was an odd reaction for someone who was hiding enough firepower in her dorm closet to blow up several city blocks. Unreality again. She couldn't be expected to think clearly when everyone around her was going nuts. She laughed at this rationalization and turned her attention to the next soap opera. By swinging around in the booth, she still could see only a quarter of the screen from behind the bulky jukebox. After a couple minutes, her neck was aching. Back to thinking.

She suspected the group had taken more of a toll on her peace of mind than she realized. It was so undercover and Mickey Mouse that half the time she couldn't take it seriously. The FBI surely would not share this view, especially not after what everyone in the group referred to as "the accident," as if the word would somehow separate them from guilt. A man had come back to a building to retrieve a missing file. The bomb went off five minutes later. Luckily, he had been bending down and was shielded by a file cabinet. Had he been standing, the papers said, or nearer to the door, the blast from across the hall would have killed him.

Renny, who had started the group and whose safety precautions sometimes drove the others crazy, went into a tailspin from which he seemed unable to recover. He absorbed so much of the group's attention that Portia felt deadened, as if her own horror had to be suppressed to take care of him. Steady Mark had helped, of course, but Mark's crazy college friend Gary, the new member, was loud and crude, suggesting to Renny that he should have placed the bomb more centrally so the injured man would have died a richly deserved death. After hearing that, Portia was glad that Renny had divided the armory, giving most of it to her. Gary was capable of anything.

The accident had been in mid-January, and they had laid low for several months, not responding to Nixon's invasion of Laos in February. Practically every other group had responded, however, and that was when Portia decided that groups such as theirs should be short-lived. She suggested to Mark in April that they disband, and he had agreed conditionally. One last action, he pleaded, a successful one this time. Renny's emotional state would only worsen if they disbanded now, with the accident so fresh in his mind.

"Kind of like getting back up on the horse after you've been bucked off?" Portia asked him sarcastically.

Mark twinkled at her. He had that talent. "Sort of," he admitted.

Which probably was why, Portia thought, she persisted in calling it Renny's group, even to herself, when she and Mark had done most of the work in the year they'd been active. Renny had started it, and the state of his mind was the rationale for performing the grand finale. She still thought they should stop now, but because she had promised Mark, she would work on the plans and continue to hold the armory until it could be moved back into the city. What she didn't appreciate was the endless arguments the choice of a target entailed, or the squabbles between Gary and everyone else. It was part of why she had ended up in Freddy's this afternoon. The meeting this morning had gone on for four hours, and they had accomplished nothing that she and Mark couldn't have decided during a five-minute phone conversation.

Portia checked the time. The beer had made her sleepy. If she walked up to Ridgedale now, she could take an hour's nap before dinner. She was about to edge out of the booth when the outside door opened and Laney walked in. Portia settled back down, hidden by the jukebox. Laney sat at the vacant bar and poured her change on the polished surface. Hearing the clink of money, the bartender appeared, drew a draft and disappeared again. Portia watched Laney in the mirror. Her eyes were closed. Her face began to soften, as if the muscles holding it together were sagging. She sighed quietly, rubbing the back of her neck with her fingers. Her head began to bob in the direction of her glass, and when she opened her eyes, realizing she was beginning to fall asleep, she met Portia's stare in the mirror. Portia got up and perched on the next stool. "Are you all right?"

Laney seemed to be regrouping, as if she'd spread herself out to dry, but when the rain started, she had to gather herself in, wet and soggy. "Sure. How's Charley?"

"Fine," Portia answered, thinking that she hadn't really talked to Laney since that conversation in the living room. "How's Bob?"

"Fine." Laney propped her chin on her fist and gazed at herself in the mirror.

"Ann's called a few times," Portia said, toying with an ashtray. "I don't know what to say to her."

Laney shrugged. "Say whatever you want."

Portia spun the ashtray in little circles. "That's not fair, Laney. It's not fair to Ann, and it's not fair to me. Why should I have to make the decision either to tell her or lie to her?"

Laney turned sideways, so she faced Portia. "Gee, I don't know. I guess because you've set that responsibility on your own shoulders." She turned away, but she continued. "Don't try to make me feel bad, Porsh. It won't work. I don't feel responsible because I never met the lady."

Portia's hand had frozen over the twirling ashtray. Laney took a sip of her beer and glanced at Portia's still hand. "Why are you so upset?" she asked. "I'm not doing anything so terrible. I'm just dating a nice young man. *You* do it. How come I can't do what you do?"

"Because you're not me," Portia said, starting up the ashtray again. "Lesbians don't date nice young men and get married. They date nice young women and get married. Which you've already done. I was at your wedding, if you'll recall." She took a deep breath and spun the ashtray out of reach. "So we have two problems to your doing what I do. The first is you're a lesbian, and the second is you're married to this woman you say you've never met."

Laney smiled at her. "You'd go far as a lawyer. Why don't you forget this Head Start stuff and—"

Portia shook her head. She wasn't buying interruptions. She stared at Laney until Laney stopped talking and met her eyes. Portia kept staring because there was something odd about Laney's blue gaze, something unfamiliar, yet the slick charm that partially concealed the strangeness was the same. "What's going on?" Portia demanded.

Laney retreated, looking into her beer. "Nothing. I'll tell you the truth, O.K.? Those two things, that I'm a lesbian and I'm married to Ann, they would be big setbacks if I were the same person you knew as Laney. But I'm not. I'm a different person. And this different person I am now is not a lesbian and is not married to Ann. See? So those things aren't a problem."

Laney picked her beer up and sipped at it as if she'd erased any worries Portia could have. Portia was incredulous. What did she mean, a different person? I know about being different people, Laney, more than you'll ever imagine. It's killed me not to tell Charley about the group all this time, but as the group moved from talking to action and I had said so little before, it became less and less possible to tell. "What about Ann?" she asked Laney. "What about love? I know you loved Ann. Has your new persona stopped loving?"

Laney's face was bland, her voice quiet. "Ann doesn't exist for me anymore. That's the truth, Porsh. Take it or leave it."

Portia struggled against a flood of anger. After months of torment over the accident, over being unable to tell Charley what was upsetting her, she wanted Laney to be real. She had an urge to grab Laney by her shoulders and shake her until she stopped this crazy game, whatever it was. "If you're not the Laney I knew, then who are you?"

"I'm making you mad," Laney said sadly. "I'm sorry. Do you really want to know who I am?"

"Yes."

"O.K. I'm twenty-one years old, I'm about to graduate from Ridgedale College and I'm marrying Robert Warner three weeks from now. I love him and he loves me. You want to know more?"

"You're marrying him?" Portia was stunned, though she couldn't fathom why. Marriage was obviously what this had all been leading up to. A sense of urgency replaced Portia's quick anger. "Laney, you can't run from yourself like this. It doesn't work. People struggle for years to find themselves. You always seemed, I don't know—comfortable. More than anybody else I knew. I used to envy you. It was as if you were born knowing which shoes fit right, and everybody else is trying on all the wrong sizes or stubbornly trying to make their feet shrink or grow to fit the size they've got. But now you're throwing all that away, ripping off the right shoes and plunging over the cliff barefoot. Laney, you can't turn your back on yourself and *live.*"

And now it was Laney's turn to look stunned. "Is that what you've thought all this time?"

Portia blinked, confused. "I—" she began, and then the blankness of Laney's shock rolled off her face, and Portia saw the old Laney before her, the Laney whose eyes seemed to look inward and outward at the same time. Laney's lower lip was trembling with tears. "Laney, honey," Portia said, "you don't have to do this. Go back to Ann. You're happy with Ann."

Laney shook her head. "No, Portia, you don't understand. I *do* have to do this." She reached out and hugged Portia tightly, then drew away. "I'm crying because I'm going to miss you. You're my very wonderful friend, and you care about me. I love you, and I know you love me. But we can't be friends at all right now." She got up and left the bar, closing the door quietly behind her. Portia sat there for such a long time that the bartender finally served her a free hamburger and then told her to go home.

C H A P T E R 14

Laney walked slowly down the deserted dorm hall. It was lunch hour, only a few days before graduation. Quite a few of the underclassmen had already taken off for the summer. Laney knocked lightly on Portia's door. Receiving no answer, she went inside and flopped down on Portia's bed. Her eyelids were heavy. She wished Bob hadn't insisted on going out dancing last night. They had been to the same restaurant, the same bar a dozen times already. He couldn't seem to get enough of re-creating the evening they met. He was sweet, she thought fondly, even though he was exhausting her. She had met his family, his friends, everyone at his office, his clients, even his barber and his car mechanic. He introduced her with a blend of awe and pride, clapping his arm around the person's shoulder, as if he wanted to spread his wonderful luck to everyone he knew. A kind of benevolent Typhoid Mary, Laney thought with a smile.

She felt just the tiniest bit chilly, so she reached down and carefully drew over her the quilt folded at the foot of Portia's bed. Portia wouldn't mind. It was so pleasant lying here, not a care in the world, except, of course, for the three hundred things she had to do before the wedding. Bob had been so sorry her parents couldn't make it. No, sorry didn't quite describe his state of mind. "But you have to have *someone* there!" he had yelped, imagining his relatives looking around for the other side of the family to meet and, failing to find anyone, glancing at his exquisite bride with the beginnings of suspicion. Laney had come up with four Ridgedale faculty members. "What about Portia?" Bob had pressed. "I thought you and Portia were best friends."

Portia. Of course. Laney would invite Jackie if it weren't in such terrible taste. But it had been clever of her to separate out the invitation to her parents and toss it down the trash chute. One could only go so far with this role business. She had written to her parents about Ann, and there was no point in confusing them.

An almost nauseating wave of longing for Ann swept over her, and she gripped the edge of the quilt, willing it to pass. None of this would do any good if she went crawling back to Ann before she'd given her medicine, disappearing into another reality, time to effect a cure. If she joined Ann in Chicago now, nothing would have changed; she would still lack a focus apart from Ann. She needed to know her roles could absorb her totally, that she was capable of consigning Ann to the rumble seat of a very long car—out of sight, out of mind. Once she knew she was the driver of her own life, she could risk returning to Ann.

Laney remembered that lonesome, noisy night in February when she'd huddled in her sleeping bag in the dorm living room and raged at her brother Ronald. He had not prepared her for feeling so utterly alien from the rest of humankind, had not explained to her what she would finally discover herself—that her life would consist of seeking comfort, finding safety, not unlike the wild animals she had understood so well when she had lived in the woods during her Wilderness experience. Yet her solution to her lack of inner security, pretending to be a person with a focus, was much more sensible than the rigid, often hopeless dreams of everyone else. Did Portia really think she could change the world? Did Ann honestly believe she'd find happiness as a newscaster when the show-business side of it was so foreign to her personality? Did Hadel truly ache to be heroic? It was all laughable. Her own disappointment, that Ann could not protect her from the outside world, was minuscule compared to the anguish her three friends would suffer as they saw their life's work collapsing around them, as they, at age thirty or forty, tallied up a midlife evaluation sheet, adding accomplishments and subtracting compromises and coming up red, red, red.

Well, she shouldn't be too smug. One could pretend for only so long, and then it would all be over, for Laney had no intention of ever being as frightened and hopeless as she had been in

January and February. Meanwhile, however, this being someone else was fascinating. She likened her state to what she'd heard about taking LSD. Ann had described a momentary panic during the rush and then a search inside herself for a center unaffected by the drug. Once she had located that stable place, she had been free to forget about it and enjoy her trip. Laney smiled, pulling the quilt up under her chin. How would Ann like living in a perpetual rush, knowing there was no center inside to find and then forget? That had certainly been Laney's condition, post-Ronald and pre-Ann. Now Ann functioned as Laney's unaffected center, and she would remain so for the rest of Laney's life. It was going to be hard to explain this to Ann who, no doubt, believed that Laney had left her in spite of the reassuring telegram Laney had sent her last week. Laney could do nothing more. Her intense longing for Ann had convinced her that Ann was still too close or, rather, that she was too attached to Ann. It was time to forget Ann, to enjoy her trip outside herself.

Laney awoke with a start at five-thirty. She sat up, blinking, wishing she hadn't fallen asleep, wishing more that she hadn't been thinking of Ann. She couldn't make all these unnecessary pilgrimages to herself; if she was playing a role, she should stay in it. Perhaps it would be best just to write out an invitation to Portia and leave it on her desk. Portia was sure to mention Ann. And where was Portia, anyway? Probably at her stupid Head Start program. Portia was obsessed by children.

Headache. When Laney stood up, she felt it pounding. She should go home and make Bob's dinner. Instead, she puttered in the tiny bathroom Portia shared with the woman next door. She searched through the cabinet, finding makeup, toothpaste, a diaphragm, birth-control pills, but no aspirin. Portia's drawers held nothing but neatly folded clothes. Laney was pretty certain Portia would have aspirin. She wasn't one of those natural freaks who were coming out of the woodwork these days. Her overnight case. That was it. Laney wrestled open the sticky sliding door of the closet and began rooting around. The overnight case was next to a big cardboard box. Laney shoved the box and something metallic crashed inside. What the hell did Portia keep in her closet? Skipping thoughtlessly across waves of irritability, Laney pried open the top of the box, peered inside and immediately wished she hadn't. She sat back on her heels. What Portia had in her closet were a couple of broken-down rifles and some revolvers. She tilted forward and looked again. No mistake. Guns plus ammunition of various kinds, arranged on top of sticks of dynamite, timers, wire and stuff in plastic bags. Things, Laney assumed, to build bombs with. She rocked back again and discovered her headache had disappeared. Magic headache remedy! Discover your friend's a terrorist! She heard the door open behind her, but she stayed on her heels. It was too late to move.

"So," Portia said after a long moment, "now you know."

Laney waved at the box, looking at Portia over her shoulder. "This is Head Start?"

Portia sat down on the bed. "That's right. I knew no one would question Head Start or show much interest. Talk about a couple of mythical kids now and then, everybody says that's nice and changes the subject. It's a perfect cover if you ever want one."

Laney remained on the floor, though she turned so she could see Portia. Portia was finding a lot to interest her on the walls of her room. Her foot was tapping nervously. "What are you going to do?" she asked finally.

"Do? What should I do?"

"I don't know," Portia snapped. "Phone the FBI."

"I've never made their acquaintance. Have you . . . used these? Ever?"

Portia hesitated, then nodded.

"And you will again?"

Portia kept her eyes on a Modigliani print. She couldn't look at Laney, nor could she look at the closet. She kept wanting to get up, push the box back into limbo and close the sliding door. She didn't move. She wanted to tell Laney they hadn't used the guns. The guns were ridiculous, boys' games. Gary owned the rifles, Renny the revolvers. They were registered in their names. The guns stayed in the closet so they could be counted as part of the armory. Portia shifted her eyes to an old theater poster. "What's with all the questions?"

"Yes, you will use them again," Laney concluded. "Is this a safe place to keep them? I suppose it is. Arms cache at

Ridgedale. It doesn't compute." She wrapped her arms around her knees. "Well, here we both are, graduating on Saturday, each of us already light-years beyond college. Why are you still here?"

Portia shifted on the bed. Her lips were compressed, as if the answer to this would open reservoirs of unhappiness. "One person kept asking why I stayed. He says it's elitist, classist—well, he's right. I can't deny that." She thought for a moment, her eyes blinking rapidly until she was able to focus on Laney's face. "It has something to do with flexibility. Our group is constantly arguing, constantly questioning, but the questioning ends up in a shift from one rigid position to another. Each month we solve the dilemma of the human race, and each solution is right for all time—or at least until the next month. I've been able to learn here. I've learned there's a kind of death in rigidity, and a joy in the search for questions that lead to more questions. That's why I stayed." She nodded to herself. She had never been forced to explain before, and she had gained from the effort. If only she could have talked with somebody all this time, with Charley especially.

"And Charley doesn't know. He asks about the kids at Head Start."

"Only you," Portia said tightly.

"How did you start?"

Portia wanted to tell her. "Remember the summer after sophomore year? I stayed in New York to work backstage in that little theater in the Village. . . ."

That summer, on the last weekend of June, the Village had exploded with a riot that marked the birth of the gay liberation movement. During a routine gay bar raid, the patrons acted anything but routinely, fighting back until the police locked themselves in the bar. Men armed with garbage cans tried to batter down the door to the Stonewall Inn, yelling, "Police and Mafia out of the bars!" When reinforcements arrived, a full-scale battle raged between the crowd and the riot cops. The riots continued for three nights, beginning again each evening when the bars closed and gay people gathered in the streets.

"You were at the Stonewall?" Laney asked.

"No. But I passed out leaflets and talked to people. The Left was interested, of course, but also dubious. Someone said it was the only revolution he'd heard of that ran on bar time."

Laney laughed.

"I wanted to help because of Hadel," Portia continued. "I felt so terrible that we'd done nothing, and then that crazy guy tried to strangle me in the dorm and everyone but you stood and watched. Well, I realized I was just one of the watchers. Sure, I'd done a lot of political work, but people were still being killed in Southeast Asia, people were still being killed here because they were black or gay or poor. During Stonewall I met two guys who weren't gay but who were excited by the idea of different groups fighting for their freedom. We decided that eventually all those oppressed groups were going to come together, and when that happened, the criminals running this country would be exposed for who and what they are. What we could do was fight back against the war and meanwhile distract the government's attention from the real source of strength: these groups that were just starting on the road to political awareness. We talked for a year, and then we began to act."

Best of intentions, Portia thought. She hadn't expected the numbing arguments, Gary's violence, an injury. But she was relieved that she still believed in the ideal. She watched Laney carefully, looking for a reaction. Laney reached behind her, pushed the box to the rear of the closet and closed the sliding door. Only then did she look at Portia, and Portia could read nothing in her face. Portia experienced a moment of astonishment before despair rushed in to fill the gap she'd opened with her honesty. How could Laney listen and say nothing, especially when she knew that Portia had talked to no one in two years? Portia was choking on her own loneliness, and she fought back in any way she could. "I've been meaning to tell you that Ann showed up on campus the week before last."

Laney nodded. "I knew she was here."

"Then why didn't you come? Scared?" Ann had arrived at Portia's dorm on a Tuesday evening, knowing Laney had classes on Wednesday. "Who's the new lover?" Ann had asked Portia. Portia saw there was no point in lying any longer. "A man," she answered. Although Ann was shocked by the man revelation, it didn't affect her determination to talk to Laney.

Ann sat at the window overlooking the path up from the train station all the next day, but Laney did not attend her classes.

"I sent a telegram to Chicago," Laney told Portia, "saying we were married same as always and that I'd explain later. It was all I could do."

"That must have been a comfort to her. Why send a telegram? I thought you'd never met her."

Laney shrugged. "A moment of weakness, a flip to another consciousness. It turned out O.K. I survived."

Portia studied her, unable to tell whether Laney was joking.

"Actually," Laney said, waving at the closet, "finding that was a lot more dangerous than sending the telegram. I was prepared for Ann. She was bound to come sometime. I wasn't prepared for this."

Portia shook her head, her anger draining away with the effort to understand. "I don't get it."

"Well, a person like me doesn't have friends like you," Laney stated baldly but with an embarrassed grin, as if she were reiterating a rule of the house to a servant who should have known better.

She's embarrassed for me, Portia thought with amazement. "Laney, I'm beginning to think you're absolutely bonkers."

Laney's grin turned into an easy smile. "That's quite a compliment from Portia the bomber. By the way, the reason I'm here is to invite you to my very normal wedding, so don't plan your insurrection on Sunday. The ceremony's here at one, down the wisteria path. Nice, huh?"

Portia made a gagging sound, and Laney's eyes flashed bright with amusement and then faded again. "See you, Porsh," she said. She was almost to the door before she turned back. "Portia, please be careful. Because I can't be friends with you now says nothing about later. I want there to be a later."

Portia missed going to prison because her crosstown bus hit a pedestrian. While the bus passengers gave statements to the police, the FBI team stationed outside Renny's apartment gave up waiting for Mark and Portia, particularly when Gary, the plant, allowed that he *might* have said something that tipped off the impending bust to his old pal Mark. When the agents broke down the door, Renny just managed to sweep his ceramic horse statue off the windowsill, breaking it into a hundred pieces before a knee in the groin dropped him to the floor.

Portia saw the empty sill at the same time the agent left guarding the front of the building saw her. She ran into an alley, her day pack bouncing on her shoulders, thankful that she and Mark had rehearsed this route. She dashed through a restaurant kitchen, past the startled patrons in the dining room and emerged on the sidewalk again. She walked to the subway station, knowing she would only draw attention to herself by running. What she hadn't counted on was another agent at the bottom of the subway steps, and that agent being able to recognize her. He tipped his hand, however, by bolting after her the moment she stepped out of the glare of light at the top of the stairs. She vaulted by threes the half-dozen steps she'd just come down and ran across four lanes of traffic, leaping around the bumper of a skidding cab. She took off up the block, hearing horns behind her as the agent followed her across the street. She knew she had to stop running, but how could she? He would catch her, but as long as she kept running, he would also catch her. The problem seemed insoluble.

In the middle of the next block, the traffic was even more congested. A bus crawled by. She darted back into the street and ran around the back of the bus, jogging beside it as she watched for her pursuer. When she saw his shoulders break above the sea of surrounding cars, she sped ahead of the bus and regained the side of the street she'd just left. She entered the first open door she saw, that of a bookstore. She could see the agent across the street, looking for her. He began trotting along the sidewalk, peering into doorways. She knew she had bought herself not more than a minute or two. He was looking down an alley when Portia spotted a car festooned with the raised fist of the women's movement. She hesitated for an instant, measuring the three women inside, and then she broke for their car. She opened the rear door and hurled herself in, ducking low. "Please," she said to the woman in the backseat, who had brought her hand to her mouth, "my husband is trying to find me. He wants to kill me! Please get me away from here!"

The driver said nothing but turned at the next corner and

sped several blocks away. "Do you want to go to the police?" she asked, looking over her shoulder.

"No." Portia tried to imagine why she wouldn't. "He's a cop," she said suddenly. "They'd just call him to come get me. I don't know what to do. If I could get out of town . . ."

The three women looked at each other. "We're just going to the zoo," the driver said finally. "Would that help?"

"The Bronx?"

The woman in the back apologized. "No, Central Park."

Anything to get out of the Village, Portia decided. "Fine. Could you let me off at Central Park West?"

They dropped her where she requested, wishing her good luck. Portia walked toward Broadway until she saw a little restaurant opening for lunch. She chose a table near the back and ordered a coffee while she studied the menu. Another cup later, she realized the coffee had not been a good idea. She stammered out an order to the bored waiter. She was sorry she'd come into the restaurant. She would spend six or seven dollars on a lunch she didn't want. She had left Charley's apartment in New Haven early that morning, carrying a change of clothes and fifty dollars in her pack, prepared to spend a couple of days in New York until the final action was completed. Now those fifty dollars would have to last her—she had no idea how long. She had no plan of where to spend the afternoon, much less the next few weeks, when the search for her would be most intense.

The worst part was they knew who she was. Both agents—the one guarding the entrance of Renny's apartment, and the one in the subway station—had taken off after her the instant they'd seen her face. Perhaps they knew her from photographs and not by name? Even as the idea began spreading warm waves of comfort through her, soothing her coffee-queasy stomach, she rejected it as a dangerous delusion. They knew who she was, all right, which meant they also knew about Charley, about her parents and her sister Toni, maybe even about Jackie or Laney. That eliminated a lot of possibilities. She wondered why it had never occurred to her that her identity would be known. Because you never expected to get caught, she told herself. It was true, she admitted, especially in the past few months, after they had decided to disband. She and Mark had practiced the escape route a year ago, more as a way to let off steam after the endless meetings than anything else. And how they had kidded Renny about his horse statue. But seeing the empty sill when she was still a building away was what had saved her. Four steps closer and she would have been in the hands of the FBI.

Her lunch came, and she picked through it slowly. They might not know about Laney, she thought, but she didn't trust Bob. Ann? She probably had enough money to get to Chicago by bus, but they might be watching the bus and train stations. She'd never been to Chicago, and to arrive penniless frightened her. What if Ann refused to help her? Of course she would help, Portia argued, but not for long. Ann's career came first. She would do nothing to risk it.

There were people from her demonstration days at Columbia she could contact—in fact, had to contact—to link up with the underground she knew existed throughout the country, but that would take time. She would have to get numbers from friends of friends. Why hadn't she taken this seriously, carried addresses with her? Because, she answered again, she had never expected to get caught.

She left the restaurant and walked up Broadway, looking in shop windows. She knew she had to disguise herself, so she entered the first drugstore she saw. She read the hair dye labels carefully. She couldn't imagine dyeing her hair. She began thinking of all the other things she had to do: get rid of the day pack, dispose of her I.D., change clothes, cut her hair. She lingered in front of the dyes, the color of her hair becoming monumentally important. How dare they force her to change her hair!

Finally she reached out her hand and picked what seemed like a nice, conservative color. Nothing bold. She didn't want to stand out. She stared at the color patch, a golden brown. The woman in the picture had pretty highlights running through her hair. Muted. Perfect. She brought the box up next to her head and looked in the mirror. Then she jumped back, throwing the box on the counter as if her hand had been stung. She had chosen a dye identical to the color of her own hair. The saleswoman glanced at her sharply.

Portia took a deep breath to steady herself, picked up the box and returned it to the display rack. She pretended to consider the other choices, but the colors all seemed to pile on top of each other. Each time she looked at one, her eyes were inexorably drawn to the next, and the next again. The reason she was standing at the counter was lost in panic; her face and neck were stiff as boards. Then she had an insight that allowed her to move. Since her eyes were brown, she should get a color darker than her hair was now. She reached up for the darkest brown, took it to the register and paid for it. She stepped outside and leaned against the building for a moment until she could trust her legs to carry her again. She had to get off the street.

She sought refuge in a phone booth, hoping no one would want to use it for a while. Should she catch a train and get off in a small town? And what? Stay in a motel? Wake up the next morning to the FBI pounding on the door, and the motel manager buffing his nails, asking about a reward? No. Besides, she had to try to contact the people she knew at Columbia. Connecting with the underground web was the only way she could survive for an extended period of time. She told nerself to calm down, that this was like learning a character for a play. She had to live and breathe as someone else. But who? She was becoming hysterical, she could feel it. Every person who walked by the booth was a potential menace, if only because they might evict her from its protection.

Then she thought of the Claire from her sophomore year theater production of *The Maids*. Claire worshipped Portia, told anyone who would listen that Portia had taught her to act. Better yet, she had pressed her phone number on Portia at graduation, telling her to call if she ever needed anything. Portia had filed the slip of paper in her wallet, never intending to use it. But she would call Claire now, she decided, and tell her the truth. If Claire thought harboring a fugitive was too dangerous, well, then she would just find someone else.

She didn't need to tell Claire anything. "Carol?" she questioned, remembering Claire's real name just in time. "I'm in trouble."

"I'm glad you called," Carol said quickly. "I heard on the radio. Where are you?"

Portia's hand snaked out to grab the little shelf under the phone. She hadn't even thought of the radio.

"Where are you?" Carol repeated.

"In a phone booth at Seventy-second and Broadway."

"Good. That's only a couple of blocks." She paused, thinking. "They know you have a backpack, but I don't think you should dump it so close. See that grocery store on the east side? Go in and buy some stuff, and then stick your pack in the bag. Come up to Seventy-fourth and turn right. I'll be waiting outside."

Carol was a godsend. She asked no questions but took charge immediately, throwing the dye in the trash, saying it was cheap stuff and too dark anyway. At the theater that night, she spirited away a salt-and-pepper wig and glasses that made Portia look fifteen years older. She bought the papers the next morning so Portia could stare at her own picture and read that Mark had escaped also and that Renny had knocked over the horse. The papers made much of the horse and more than much of the group. Renny's carefully drawn plans for the last action, his list of other targets and the accident in mid-January were all described in great detail. The armory, which Portia had moved back to the city following Laney's wedding reception, was exaggerated. Portia had trouble relating the news stories to her own experience as a group member. The group in the paper sounded like a commando team, efficient and deadly, not the real bunch of free spirits who often came to meetings only to argue. But crazy Gary had his own view of things, and he was the informer. Of course. How could they have been so stupid?

Carol loaned her money, bought her a change of clothes and disposed of her backpack. She also managed, with the few pieces of information Portia could give her, to contact an old friend from Columbia, who came up with new I.D. and the address of a safe house in Connecticut, as well as two emergency phone numbers.

After five days, Portia left for Connecticut, unwilling to put Carol in danger any longer. For three mornings after she arrived, she woke with a start, adrenaline pounding through her veins, ready to flee or fight, only to find, once dressed, that there was nothing to do but wait. The people at the house seemed also to be waiting. It took her a week to realize they were waiting for her to leave so they could sleep through a night without expecting the FBI to break down the door. Portia left that afternoon, renting an apartment in the same town, using her new I.D. She got a morning job in a doughnut shop soon afterward. One noontime, unable to stand it any longer, she went to a phone booth and called Charley's apartment. When his roommate answered, she heard the click of a tape machine on the line. She hung up and began walking home, more desolate than ever.

A man was waiting at her apartment. He told her the family at the safe house had been questioned, and she had to leave immediately. He drove her to Vermont, leaving her at a house with other waiting people.

She moved twice more in a month, both times because she felt uncomfortable where she was staying. She had expected living underground would be full of adventure, cadres of soldiers continuing the fight from hidden camps. She had thought, at least, that someone would tell her what to do. Instead, her emergency phone numbers brought her a new set of I.D.s and safe addresses in other cities. She decided to stay in Vermont, at least until the end of the year. It would be no different elsewhere. She got another job, another apartment. It amazed her that she'd been underground only eight weeks. She was exhausted. There was no time to relax, no time to be herself. In fact, she realized, her very existence depended on her never being herself again. She had gone from two lives to none and in the process discovered the ultimate nightmare.

CHAPTER 15

Ann finally managed to get off the phone by promising her caller that she would speak to her news director as soon as he was free. Her caller couldn't know that the news director was standing next to her desk. "Who was that one?" he asked.

"Vice president in charge of personnel," Ann reported. "He had lots of figures about injury rates."

The news director nodded. "Mail's running mostly pro. Keep up the good work."

Ann's good work, at the moment, consisted of answering calls from what seemed like every Jamison Industrial Machines official from foreman on up. Their factory had been targeted as "hazardous" by the KPAT news team. Judging from her callers' statistics, the factory was as safe, or safer, than dozens of similar concerns in the Chicago area. Ann couldn't fathom why Jamison had been singled out as the guilty-until-proven-innocent subject of the news team's three two-minute segments, the last of which would air tonight. The news director hadn't told her, nor had he given her the power to cancel the final segment, no matter how convincing the company's assurances of safe operation. Ann had simply been assigned to answer Jamison's calls.

Yet even this exercise in futility was better than thinking, Ann decided, her hand resting on the phone, waiting for the buzz that would alert her to another call. Laney had married Bob Warner in June. It was now October. She hadn't seen Laney since January. Hopeless. Laney would never return to her. But every day she would sit at her desk, going over and over the same tired "if onlys." If only the job hadn't started until June. If only I had visited her on weekends. If only I had kept in closer contact. And the big one, the only one that really counted, if only I hadn't taken the job in the first place. If she hadn't accepted the job, Laney would not have left her. It was as plain as two plus two equal four. And the opposite, that Laney would leave her if she went to Chicago, had also been glaringly predictable, though Ann, at the time, had done her best to convince herself otherwise.

She had had plenty of help on the convincing end. Portia and Charley had practically begged her to take the job. John Farbus, her editor at the *Register,* had hosted a going-away party three days before she'd written her acceptance letter. Her parents had chimed in with offers of deposit money on an apartment. Everyone, herself included, saw the Chicago offer as the chance that comes once in a lifetime. So she had taken it. She had come to Chicago and, as a result, she had lost Laney.

She had only herself to blame, for only she had known that Laney would find such a separation unendurable. What had Laney said after the Phoenix trip? "I need someone I can depend on." She may as well have added, "I mean that literally." Laney was frightened without Ann's presence. Not a constant physical presence, necessarily—Laney could be surprisingly self-contained—but Ann did represent an emotional lifeline that stretched only so far. After Phoenix, Laney was able to countenance Ann's two- or three-day absences. Five months probably was about four and a half months longer than Laney could tolerate.

The strange part was that none of this had anything to do with Laney loving her. Apparently Laney had used Hadel in the same manner, but she hadn't loved Hadel. Her love for Ann was impossibly pure, a crystal-clear window into a world without self-serving motivation. Ann's love for Laney could never be pure, for Ann was unable to survive without the integrity of her self as her primary responsibility. Which was, of course, why she had taken the job.

Laney's blue eyes had opened into pools of pain when Ann told her. Ann couldn't stand it; she had looked away, over Laney's head of silky white-gold hair. Laney hadn't argued. She had even gone along with Ann's proposal that she come help Ann search for an apartment. Ann had hoped that seeing the apartment, imagining herself in it, would give Laney enough substance to live for five months in the dorm. But when Ann put her on the plane to New York, she had known it hadn't worked: Laney had shaken her head, saying she didn't understand. It wasn't a protest. She truly didn't understand. Laney would need someone else to depend on, a new lifeline. The fact that she loved Ann had nothing to do with it.

So the sum result of all this thinking, Ann thought as her phone buzzed and she punched the intercom button, was that she'd added another "if only." If only I had given it all up then, gotten on the plane with Laney and gone back to my old job at the *Register*. But I didn't. What would I have said to Farbus, to my parents? She shook her head and pressed the blinking button. A man announced himself as the head of Jamison's shipping department. He began talking in a quick monotone, as if he were reading a statement he'd prepared beforehand. Ann tuned him out. It wasn't her parents or Farbus. She had wanted the job. Face facts. She had wanted the job more than she'd wanted Laney. That was the answer, right out in front where she could see it. This job had been her dream forever.

And what a dream it had turned out to be. Her coworkers had snubbed her in January. Used to the friendly work atmosphere at the *Register*, she felt she'd entered a deep freeze. No one welcomed her to the station. No one asked her to lunch. Even the news director was flinty-eyed as he doled out Ann's assignments. She soon discovered that the station manager was an old friend of John Farbus. Ann had been recruited over a dozen in-station people hungering for the next crack at field reporter.

She had known explaining her ignorance wouldn't help. Her only option was to quit, but who would that satisfy? One person out of twelve would be promoted, and she would be back mailing her résumés. Not that the résumés would do her any good. Besides the station employees grappling for advancement, there were the flocks of bright young people besieging the personnel office every week, begging for nonpaid intern positions. It seemed everyone wanted to break into television. Damned if she'd give up her chance for a point of honor.

A residue of guilt remained. She dealt with it by volunteering for the jobs no one else wanted, being extra-nice in the face of resentment but, above all, by becoming indispensable. She often spent fourteen hours a day at the station, coming home only to heat up a can of soup before she collapsed. The news director was the first to wave the white flag. He called her into his office, told her she was due for a raise and complimented her on her dedication. "I can see why Frank wanted to hire you," he said. "You'll be up for some on-camera spots in a few weeks."

Her first spot was an interview with several parents whose children had been shaken up on an amusement park ride. Though the report was neutral in presentation, the ride was closed a day later. Her second and third spots were animal stories, one a poisoned guide dog, the other the annual visit to the city's animal shelters, complete with a list of low-priced spay and neuter clinics. Ann knew these "news" stories would not have made the back pages of the *Register* on the slowest day of the year. Yet on television, these items—called "PP's" by the news director, news with people potential—formed a significant part of the broadcast. Under the pressure of a half hour counted in seconds, the PP's often crowded out stories with greater news value and eliminated analysis of the headline news, particularly if the top stories had no film footage to thrill viewers. Television, the news director said, was a visual medium. No one wanted to look at talking heads.

Disappointing? Well, sure. She had happily *watched* hundreds of PP's without realizing that between driving time, unfindable addresses and broken equipment, it could take an entire day to put together a thirty-second segment. The dream was fraying around the edges, all right, but she wasn't willing to give up, in spite of her disappointment and her regretful "if onlys." Hadn't Farbus always told her that good reporters, capable of judging the importance and impact of stories, were needed in television? She was sure she could be one of the good ones. Besides, the lure of the camera, the sheer excitement of being part of that second-by-second countdown, had snared her. She still wanted to be a newscaster, but she was more realistic about what that meant.

One thing it meant was performing mind- and ear-numbing jobs like this one. The shipping department manager was rambling on. She held the receiver away from her ear and then brought it back in time to hear the tail end of a question. "Pardon me? Sorry, sir, my only supervisor is the news director, and he's in conference. I'll be talking to him shortly, however, and I'll be sure to relay your concerns." He hung up in a huff. No sooner had she leaned back in her chair than the secretary buzzed her for another call. Who would it be this time? She hadn't heard from the accounting department yet. They would tell her how safe their adding machines were. "Hello?" No one answered. A new tactic. "Hello?" The call sounded long-distance.

"Don't say my name," a voice cautioned.

It took Ann a moment, and then she whispered "Jesus Christ" into the receiver.

"Not quite," Portia said. "Ann, I—"

"Are you all right?" Ann interrupted. "Charley came to see me, and he'd already seen Laney in Connecticut, and he was going to see Hadel—"

"Stop it!" Portia said sharply. "I can't stay on the phone long. I don't know how to tell you this. I called because . . . because—" Her voice almost broke, and she finished in a rush. "Get *The New York Times* and look on page thirty-three."

"Today's *Times*?" It was a silly question designed to buy a couple of seconds of grace before she allowed herself to imagine a circumstance dire enough for Portia to risk a phone call. She didn't hear Portia's "Yes" because the seconds expired and Ann's mouth was suddenly cotton-dry with fear. She swallowed to unstick her tongue. "Is this about Laney?"

"Just read it."

"Will you call back?" Ann was beginning to feel light-headed. She steadied herself with a hand pressed against her desk.

Portia hesitated and then softened. "Give me another number."

Ann rattled off the film editing department's private line. The phone clicked in her ear. She stood up, sleepwalking, ignored Pat Monahan's jibe about personal calls and went to the secretary's desk. "Gale, have you seen the *Times* around?"

The secretary nodded and got it for her. Ann retreated to the ladies' room and opened up the paper to page thirty-three. "Mrs. Laney Villano Warner, age twenty-two, recent bride of Mr. Robert Warner, account executive for the brokerage firm of Hampton and Smith, is missing and presumed dead. Authorities found her abandoned car yesterday on Davies Drive, a road bordering the beach near Trayner, seventeen miles from the Warner home in Clingford. A note was pinned to the seat. Contents of the note were not divulged, but authorities stated that Mrs. Warner intended to commit suicide by drowning. Her body has not been recovered."

Ann read it twice, sitting on the toilet. Then she turned around and vomited into the bowl, hacking and spitting until nothing was left. She stood by the sink for a minute, catching her breath, and then she headed for the film editing department. The room was empty, since the crew for the evening news had not come in yet. She waited only a few moments before the phone rang. "I want to see you," Ann said. "I have to find out what happened."

"But I don't know anything."

"Please—" Ann stopped herself in time. She had almost said Portia's name. She glanced around the room, as if she expected agents to pop out of the cabinets. Could this phone be tapped? They wouldn't tap every line coming into the station, and she never used this phone. It had to be safe.

"All right," Portia decided. "Tomorrow afternoon at two at Fitzray's bar in Kennerly. That's an hour outside of New Haven."

"I know," Ann said. She had grown up in Connecticut and knew Trayner and Clingford also. Just small towns when she was a teenager; now they would assume importance as the places Laney had lived and died. Laney dead. It was impossible. If she hadn't been able to accept Laney leaving her when she had known it was almost a certainty, how was she ever going to accept this? Or make peace with the devastating consequences of her decision to take the job? If what she believed were true, if Laney would have stayed on quite happily with Ann had Ann not gone to Chicago, then surely, working from the same scenario, Laney would not have taken her own life. This was a burden Ann was not prepared to handle.

The dial tone began, and she set down the phone. She had to call an airline, fly to Kennedy and rent a car. She was grateful that Portia had agreed to see her, whether she knew anything or not. It gave her a reason to move, to do something. And she would tell Portia that Charley was searching for her everywhere and give her his message number. She remained standing a moment, gathering strength. Then she went to find the news director.

Ann arrived at Fitzray's ten minutes early. Twenty minutes later, Portia walked in and touched Ann's shoulder. "Hi," she said. Ann turned, beginning to smile a greeting. The smile faded. Portia looked fifteen years older than she had when Ann came to Ridgedale in her unsuccessful attempt to see Laney. The early graying was an effective disguise. "Two beers, please," Portia was saying to the bartender. She slid a dollar across the bar and handed Ann her beer. "C'mon, let's move to a booth."

"Is this dangerous for you?" Ann asked once they were sitting down. Portia's straight brown hair was now dark and springy, flecked with streaks of white. Ann was confused by this until she realized it was an extremely well-made wig. The glasses Portia wore partially hid the exhaustion in her eyes, but her face was gaunt, her skin pasty. Ann saw she was functioning very close to the edge. She held the beer bottle too tightly, her fingers white-tipped from pressure. Did she live in this town? Did she actually hang out at this awful place? Fitzray's was small and dumpy, worse than the horrible bars they used to go to across the New York State line when they were too young to buy a drink legally in Connecticut. It had two booths and eight stools, a jukebox that was either broken or not plugged in and an old bowling machine with empty bottles stacked on the wooden lane. It was seedy, all right, but Ann couldn't imagine how it could be dangerous.

"To buy food is dangerous," Portia said finally. "To do laundry is dangerous. To live is dangerous." She unleashed her hold on the bottle and dropped her hands in her lap. "I can't drink anymore. I can't afford to. And I don't know anything, Ann. She hadn't talked to me for months."

"Since when?"

"Long before you came to Ridgedale. Since that dinner with Jackie and Bob. You know she moved out of the dorm the next day. We talked once at Freddy's. She told me she was no longer the person I knew as Laney. Because she was no longer that person, she wasn't a lesbian anymore. Then she discovered me.

Who I am. She told me to be careful because she wanted there to be a later when we could be friends again."

"You went to the wedding?"

Portia nodded. "It was nothing. A game. A play. They stood there and got married. Rice. Champagne. Laney was beautiful, of course. She always is. She looked radiant. But underneath—it was a dry-eyed radiance, Ann. She was acting a role."

"I wonder," Ann said. Of course it was gratifying to think Bob was just a substitute, but that made little sense in light of Laney's suicide. Why hadn't Laney come back? Perhaps Laney had felt that Ann, by taking the job, had committed an offense so unforgivable it killed the possibility of their ever again being together. Laney was a loyal lover—in fact, her lover was her world. How could she understand that what she expected in return was impossible for anyone to meet? Maybe she *had* loved Bob, and he had disappointed her also. Spreading the guilt? Ann asked herself. She looked across the table at Portia, who had been waiting patiently, sipping at her beer. "What about the driving? She drove to the beach."

Portia nodded. "I know. Laney and her terror of driving. That's what I'm trying to tell you, Ann. It was as though she were another person, not Laney driving or marrying Bob, but someone else in Laney's body, and you couldn't see the real Laney through the other person. I think she didn't come up to school when you were there because she was afraid you would draw her back to herself."

"But—" Ann stopped. Arguing with Portia wouldn't bring Laney back. Her hands began shaking, and she copied Portia's trick, tightening her hold on the bottle. She would never know why Laney had killed herself.

"I'm sorry, Ann," Portia said. "I have to leave now. I can't stay places." She stood up and walked around to Ann's side of the table.

"Right now? I—"

"Finish your beer and then take off. It's been wonderful seeing you. You can't imagine how important it is for me." She caught Ann's hand in her own and then turned away. Ann had obediently raised the glass of beer to her lips. She set it down with a thunk. "Wait—" she called, but Portia had already closed the door.

I didn't tell her anything! I didn't tell her about Charley or his message phone or the FBI's visits. Ann put down her glass and dashed outside, blinking in the sunlight. She looked up and down the street, then headed to the grocery store next door. The narrow aisles held no one but a couple of kids staring at the Halloween candy. The cafe across the street was serving coffee to a few people who were talking about the new shows on TV. Ann paused by the cash register, mentally kicking herself. She hadn't thought to bring Portia money or clothes or food. She'd even let Portia pay for her beer! But the absolute worst was not giving her Charley's number.

"Can I help you, dear?" the waitress said.

"What? Oh, no, I'm sorry." Ann escaped from the cafe and walked to her rented car. She searched the streets for a while until she finally realized it was hopeless. Now she had several hours to kill. She had assumed she would spend the afternoon with Portia. Her plane didn't leave until nine-thirty.

She drove to the small newspaper office in Trayner, where she learned that Laney's body still hadn't been found. "Depends on the currents," the old guy who ran the paper told her. "That night she went in, there'd been heavy fog for three days. You couldn't see two feet in front of you. Happens a few times every year, people go in when it's foggy, lose sight of the beach." He shrugged. "'Course, she left a note, but what I mean is, if she changed her mind, she might not have been able to find her way back."

Ann thanked him and then drove inland to Clingford. The driveway of Bob's house was crowded with cars, mourners rallying around the bereaved spouse. Ann sat outside in her rented car for a half hour, thinking how different it was for her. There was no acknowledgment of her relationship with Laney, no notice in the *Times,* no one to comfort her, no clothes to clear away, no jewelry to give to friends. It was as if Laney had not existed for Ann, and Ann had never existed at all. Laney had lived the final three months of her life here, and that life took precedence over all that had come before.

And how was it, she wondered, for Charley? She knew he had come here to talk to Laney about Portia. Laney had been short with him and left after a few minutes to go shopping. Ann shook her head. She would never forget the pain on Charley's face when he admitted to her he had known nothing of Portia's secret life. At least he knew Portia was alive, or he would as soon as Ann left a message for him. But wasn't that worse? She'd forgotten to tell Portia about Charley, but why hadn't Portia asked about him? It was too painful, Ann decided. Portia didn't want to talk to Charley, because then she'd want to see him. It would be ripping open a healing wound.

Ann watched as a middle-aged couple left the house, their faces solemn. Bob's parents? Ann wanted to tell them to be solemn for her. What if Portia was right? What if Laney had become someone else? If seeing Ann would have drawn Laney back to herself, would she be alive if Ann had come here, to this house? She rested her head on the steering wheel.

Ann started the car and drove back to Trayner, turning left on Davies Drive to get out to the sound. The beach was desolate in late October, windswept and uninviting. It was hard to imagine how it must have looked during the summer, crowded with Frisbee players, beach umbrellas, romping children and dogs. A few empty trash cans in the parking lot were the only reminders of summer pleasures. As Ann walked down to the water's edge, she was filled with another image: the beach at night, enveloped in fog as thick as a wool cloak. Fog dampened sound, Ann remembered; Laney might not have even heard the gentle lapping of the water. Creeping carefully across the sand, her hand held out in front of her checking for obstacles, Laney wouldn't have known she'd reached the water until she was standing in it. And then what had she done? Had she thought about turning back? Or had she marched resolutely forward into the wall of gray, welcoming the cold water that inched past her shoulders?

Ann sank down in the sand, overcome with the loneliness of Laney's death. She closed her eyes, shutting out the pale afternoon light. She had talked to Portia. She had seen the beach. She had imagined how Laney had died. Yet even here, or perhaps especially here, she could not believe Laney had walked into the water to die. Acceptance would be a long time coming, and all she could do now was wait.

CHAPTER 16

Ann spent New Year's Eve in her apartment, reading the beat poets who were popular when she was an adolescent: Diana DiPrima, Gregory Corso, Lawrence Ferlinghetti. The poems, angry and cynical, nonetheless reminded her of a time in her life when all things seemed possible. Children, she thought, are peculiarly attracted to the disillusionment of adults; a child was capable of sucking up the bitter nectar and transforming it to honey. How eager the children, how marvelous the miracle! How impossible to imagine that one day the bitter would claim squatters' rights and take up permanent residence inside, unchanged and unchangeable.

Her mind was full of such observations. She told herself that grief had made her reflective, but she knew Laney flitted through her thoughts only at brief intervals, as insubstantial as a ghost. What obsessed her were these poems, or the long novels she'd read in November, or the images of past Christmases when she and Karen had joined her parents and her brother Jonathan for Christmas Eve and Karen's parents for Christmas Day. Ann lacked personal involvement in the present, and it had finally begun to bother her.

She had realized as early as Thanksgiving that accepting Laney's death also meant that she must create a life for herself without Laney. It was this task of creation that she found so impossible, for she was instantly confronted by her own aimlessness. She had made no friends in Chicago, had no social life. At work she was rising faster than she'd ever dreamed—her on-camera spots now numbered twenty-two—but she took no pleasure in her success. Her big coup in November, a four-part series on underground fugitives, was simply a reworking for television of pieces she'd written for the *Register* a year and a half earlier. When the series aired, she'd been disturbed by the compliments she received for her out-of-date story; now, on this last night of the year, she saw her greatest success as nothing more than further evidence that she'd been subsisting on past accomplishments.

Her separation from herself was so severe that she hadn't yet been able to think seriously about the proposal she'd received last week, one that might be a lifesaver. The news director from an independent station in San Francisco had called her at work, telling that he had an opening for a field reporter. His station, he said, catered to an older audience. He was looking for a young woman who was serious and sensitive, attractive and refined, who had escaped drugs and radicalism and a hippie lifestyle. In short, he told her, the daughter the viewers wished they had. He had searched high and low for such a person and had nearly given up until he'd seen some of her film clips. She was perfect. She would, he promised, be a local celebrity in a couple of years.

Ann had laughed. The daughter they wished they had? God help them. She hadn't voluntarily communicated with her own parents for months. She told the news director she would get back to him on Monday, which now gave her only three days to make up her mind.

Two days, she corrected herself, as people began honking their horns outside and someone set off a string of firecrackers. Welcome to 1972. Ann thrust aside her volume of poetry and went to her window. People were hugging each other on the sidewalk. Kids pelted up and down the block on squat bikes, cards stuck in the spokes of the wheels. When she turned away from the window, she had made her decision. She would never, she realized, be able to move forward until she had dealt with Laney's death. Keeping thoughts of Laney at bay had just delayed the adjustment she would eventually have to make. Who better to talk with than Hadel, who not only lived near San Francisco, but who also had been Laney's lover and had, presumably, experienced her dependency? Tomorrow, Ann decided, she would give her month's notice at the station.

Ann put off submitting her resignation until late in the afternoon. The news director was sharp; he'd certainly noticed her retreat from the world. She went into his office expecting a lecture, and he didn't disappoint her. He glanced at the typed sheet she handed him and shrugged. "You think you'll be happier in San Francisco?"

"I have friends there," she said.

He tapped her resignation with one finger. "I was referring to work. You've changed, Ann. You don't give a damn anymore." He watched her for a moment, and when she said nothing, he continued. "It's a shame, because you could have been good. But lately you've been about as animated as a piece of wallboard. If you don't care about a story, why should the viewer?" She didn't answer him. "Look," he said, leaning forward, his voice softer, "the life of a story is in the reporter's delivery. You can convey disgust, despair, compassion, joy, warmth, humor. Your delivery gives the viewer an inkling of why he should be interested in the story. We're not telling them what to think," he said, brushing aside an objection Ann hadn't made. "The viewers might react with you or against you. But our first job is to *make them react.*"

"I thought our first job was to keep them informed," Ann snapped.

He smiled. "Good. I was just about to give up on you entirely. You're right. But any politician, any advertiser, any salesman knows that pure facts die on unprepared ground. The emotions you generate are our plows, our fertilizers."

"But can't the viewer react to the story itself? Why does an emotion have to be keyed in by the newscaster?"

"There are two answers to that. The first is that real villains don't wear black hats. The reporter has to interpret the news. The second is there are too many of us. Why should we care if fifty people die in a train wreck? It means fifty less people on our overcrowded earth. But viewers are uncomfortable with not caring. It makes them feel inhuman. They want to nod along with the sad eyes and the downturned mouth of the newscaster. If the reporter doesn't feel, it's too close to the viewer's own reaction. They switch the channel, and that's what we *really* don't want. *Capice?*"

Ann left work that evening by the back entrance, avoiding another person who wanted something from her she couldn't give. As the days had grown shorter, Ann had occasionally opted for the ease of a taxi, but the same driver had started waiting out front for her almost every night. She thought it was odd, and perhaps even sinister, until he told her he had a son who was missing as Portia was missing—part of the underground network that stretched across the country. He complimented her on her four-part series and then began asking questions: how had she gotten her information? Did she have means of reaching those who were underground? She could hardly tell him her "inside knowledge" was completely useless, more than a year old. She put him off with the need to protect her sources, and he told her of his anguish and his own clumsy search. Ann knew soon he would ask her to contact his son. He imagined her making a few phone calls to the right people, the people he would never know, and his son phoning within the hour to speak to Dad. He might even believe she could fail, but he would surely despise her for not trying. Walking home through the dark, slushy streets was infinitely preferable to enduring the driver's disappointment.

Three blocks from her apartment, she stopped, mesmerized by the song coming from an open window above her. A man was belting out "Alice Blue Gown" in a strong baritone; it would have been laughable were it not for the memories it unlocked. Rivers of people on their way home flowed around Ann while she was lost in the garden at Woodsmere, lazing on her bench under dappled pinpoints of May bright sunlight. As the man came to the end of his song, Ann's vision of Laney's dancing eyes dissolved to red for blood and white for bones and blue-green for the quantities of ocean Laney had embraced. Ann clenched her hands into fists, her body taut as a drawn bow. She ran for a taxi and hopped in the rear seat. Dimly she realized the driver was asking her where she wanted to go.

A bar, she told him, not knowing the answer to his question. A minute later, as he was under way, she expanded her request. "A lesbian bar," she said clearly. She had never been to a lesbian bar. But after months of withdrawing from everyone, she needed more than alcohol. She needed people to watch who could drive away the wonder of Laney, of her eyes, of her hair, of her gentle touch. She would have to confront Laney's death someday, she told herself, if she ever wanted to feel again. But since she'd thought of Hadel, she wanted to do it slowly, over a period of weeks, meeting Hadel for dinner and conversation. She couldn't do it in Chicago, not in the apartment Laney had helped her find, which now contained only cans of soup and a few volumes of poetry, the by-products of loneliness and isolation.

She realized the driver was looking in the rearview mirror, cataloguing her expensive clothes, her soft leather shoulder bag, her styled hair. "You need money?" Ann snarled.

He lifted one shoulder in an elaborate shrug. "I'll take you there."

He dropped her in front of the Queen of Hearts. Aretha Franklin's "Chain of Fools" was too insistent to be contained within the walls of the building. Ann pushed open the door, her hands still trembling. Thirty pairs of eyes swept over her, then turned away. Ann crept to a table in the dim light, sat down and ordered a vodka tonic. She didn't care if anyone talked to her. She disappeared in the music, far from Laney and the house in Woodsmere. She watched women dance to Patsy Cline, Otis Redding, Marvin Gaye, the Miracles. She felt safe.

At midnight, a woman in a ripped brown jacket sat down at her table. Her name was Cheryl, she said, and she was a graduate student at the University of Chicago. She talked about her plans to open a combination bookstore and coffeehouse. Cheryl was expansive but nervous; she tapped the corner of her cigarette pack on the table as she talked. After only a few minutes, she asked Ann to come home with her. Ann was surprised. Was this how it was done? She didn't hesitate. If she didn't want to be Ann-who-couldn't-feel, or Ann-who-felt-too-much, she could be Ann-taking-her-life-in-her-own-hands. Perhaps the job offer, this woman, even hearing "Alice Blue Gown" were portents of change. She could, she thought, end her terrible withdrawal from the world. She followed Cheryl outside into the cold. Cheryl led the way to an old Ford. "Sorry it's so dirty. Let me put down a towel. You must have come right from work."

"No, no," Ann protested. She slipped into the passenger seat. The back of the car, all the way to the roof, was packed solidly with books. "Are you moving?"

"Moving? Oh, no, I carry them around. . . ." She drove to an apartment on the South Side, near the university. They walked up the two flights of stairs in silence, didn't speak as Cheryl unlocked the door or as they walked across the paper-strewn living room to the bedroom. Suddenly Ann wanted it to be over with. To take her life into her own hands meant living as herself, not her fantasy of how someone else would act. She didn't like this experience, this not talking, this tense march to the bedroom. It had been a mistake coming to Cheryl's apartment. A typewriter with a gooseneck lamp rigged to the back stood on a chair, a bookmark stuck out two thirds of the way through *Return of the Native,* a museum poster announced a showing of twentieth-century Japanese prints. This life spread out in front of her demanded a reaction. She turned around and removed her clothes when she heard Cheryl throw her ripped jacket on the floor.

Ann crawled under the sleeping bag resting on the foam pad, intensely aware of how thin she'd become, almost skeletal. Cheryl lay next to her, reached out her arms and gathered Ann in. "I never did this before," she said.

"Did what?" Ann asked, horrified.

"Picked up someone. You're cold."

Ann was shaking. She felt Cheryl's hand on her breast and sat up abruptly. "I can't do this. I'm sorry, but I just can't."

Cheryl drew away, lighting a cigarette. "Is this your first time? I don't care if it is, I know a lot of people won't bring someone out—"

"No, it's not. That's not what's wrong. And it's not you, either. I'm sorry." Ann threw off the sleeping bag and began getting back into her clothes.

Cheryl watched her dress, the smoke from her cigarette gathering around her in a blue haze. "Did your girlfriend leave you for someone else?"

Ann didn't answer. What was she supposed to say? She ripped her panty hose in her haste to pull them up.

"I'm sorry too," Cheryl said. Her voice was sincere.

That had been three weeks ago. Ann was astonished at her own blindness, at not understanding that she would never be able to accept her lover's death without grieving for her first. Now that she was letting herself feel, she was healing, and bits and pieces of her life had to be retrieved and polished. Yesterday the news director had stopped her in the hall and told her he was sorry she was leaving now, just when she was showing him she could care again. Then there was Charley. Ann had contacted him shortly after her October trip to tell him she'd seen Portia; she had used the code they'd devised when Charley had visited Chicago the summer before. He was happy she hadn't passed the number on to Portia—it turned out the FBI was tapping his message phone also. He would, he told her, get back to her soon. Ann, deep in her novels and her dreams of the past, had ignored call after call until finally, just before Christmas, Charley had sent a Chicago-based friend to talk to Ann at work. Ann had told the friend Portia hadn't asked about Charley, but she hadn't added her own supposition about the pain that Portia felt over the separation. Now Ann could remedy that situation and also reassure the other people who had tried to reach her during her period of withdrawal—her parents, Natalie, John Farbus at the *Register.* She was also looking forward to contacting Hadel for the first time in years. Ann felt certain that Hadel, with her common sense and her experience of Laney's dependency, could help Ann clarify what her responsibility to Laney really had been.

Her phone buzzed. Gayle told her her sister-in-law was waiting downstairs in the reception area. Her sister-in-law? Had she been so divorced from life that she'd missed notice of her brother's wedding? No, it couldn't be. Portia! Or someone from Portia. Ann hurried down the back steps, too impatient to wait for the elevator. The receptionist waved her to the waiting room off the lobby. At first she could see nothing through the wall of glass. It *had* been Portia, and she had become frightened. But then Ann saw the white-gold hair against the glare of the windows facing the street, the figure that could be coiled and lithe at the same time, the cool blue eyes. Ann took four steps forward while the air sprung open all around her. She didn't know what she would do. She startled herself by slapping Laney hard across the face.

Laney touched her cheek with two fingertips. "I really hurt you, didn't I?"

The rage paralyzed Ann's lungs, but with the air crackling and her pores tingling, she didn't seem to need to breathe.

"You can slap me or beat me or even kill me," Laney said quietly. "I'm not going away again. I'll trail after you like a puppy dog my whole life if I have to. I'd never leave you, Ann. I know you thought I did, but I didn't. I was someone else, and I'll be someone else again. Last time was the hardest because I had to be with another person. And you need to help me with the next one. But after that I promise it'll be easy."

"Wait," Ann had said at the puppy-dog part. Now she said it again, more forcefully. Laney balanced on the balls of her feet as if she expected another blow. Ann backed off a step, and Laney followed her with her eyes. "Ann, I'm sorry."

"Do you think that's enough?" Ann's voice was so low she could barely hear herself, but Laney was listening, her head cocked forward. "How do you think it was for me knowing you were dead?" A blackness came into her vision, and she had to sit down. She couldn't understand what Laney had said, and her own words sounded insane. Laney was at her side instantly, guiding her to a sofa next to a bank of windows.

"You must have died, too," Laney said. "That's what I would do if you were dead."

"But that's just it, I didn't, I—" Ann stopped, her thoughts too confused to untangle. Laney took her hand, and Ann pulled it back, out of Laney's reach.

"Ann, please try to hear me. I didn't leave you. I chose the only way available to me to stay *with* you."

"I'm going to San Francisco," Ann said. "I have a new job." That much she knew. The job was something that made sense.

She could feel Laney nod beside her. "Fine. I'll go with you."

Ann didn't respond. What Laney said echoed in her ears until she became aware she was moving without moving, her skin, her muscles, her toes, every part of her migrating toward Laney's warmth. Ann clasped her hands more rocklike in her lap. Unbendable, stationary, static. She listened to Laney's steady breathing. What would she have given to have heard that sound during all the months she'd believed Laney was gone from her forever? Laney was living next to her. Ann was dying now. She turned toward Laney, searched her eyes, and found a love and a wanting that matched the strength of her own. She loosened her hands, and Laney enclosed her in her arms. The pressure of Laney's body against hers was as reassuring as her own heartbeat.

A knock at the front door interrupted Hadel in midthought. She remained bent over her typewriter, unwilling to interrupt the climax of her latest boys' adventure story. Shortly after Charley had visited her in July, she decided she needed the creative stimulation of something less repetitive than pornography. A try at *True Confessions* netted nothing. She found it hard to identify with her characters, who got pregnant, lost their fiancés in Vietnam, took diet pills, accidentally slept with their long-lost brothers, had babies and were contacted by the dead, all in astonishing rapidity. One day at the newsstand, she picked up a copy of *Boys' World.* She leafed through it with growing excitement, returned her two new confessions magazines to the rack and drove home quickly, eager to start. By Christmas she had sold the second and fourth of four stories, and this, her fifth, was a real nail-biter, describing the nighttime adventures of two boys lost in a Louisiana bayou, surrounded by alligators, snakes and, most deadly of all, poachers. Hadel had promised herself that if this story sold, she would quit her job at the porno magazine and see if she could survive writing adventure stories full time.

Hadel had just finished the sentence she was struggling with when the knocking became too insistent to ignore. She grumbled all the way to the door and threw it open to confront Laney, her fist raised for another assault. "My God!" Hadel said, though somehow she wasn't surprised. Then she was surprised she wasn't surprised. "I didn't think you were dead," she said tentatively.

"Of course not," Laney said with a laugh, hugging her. "How did you hear?"

"Natalie. She sent the clipping."

"Well, here I am, alive and well. Ann's getting our stuff out of the car. Can we take a shower?"

"A shower? Sure, go ahead, it's . . ." Hadel's voice trailed away as Laney moved competently through the house, finding the bathroom, snapping open a small suitcase and laying out clothes for Ann and herself. Hadel greeted Ann in a fog and waved good-bye as they both disappeared into the bathroom. Their laughter pealed into the kitchen as Hadel hurriedly dumped beans and canned tomatoes into a pot, fried onions and garlic and called Michelle at the Women's Law Project to tell her to pick up a can of peeled green chiles and some Monterey jack on her way home.

Laney emerged from the bedroom moments before Michelle arrived with the chiles and cheese. Laney seemed strange, Hadel thought. Maybe it was because she was wearing skinny blue jeans with sharp, narrow bells and sandals with half-inch heels. Or perhaps it was because she was talking nonstop, her eyes flashing. The only break in the barrage of questions she threw at Hadel was when Michelle was introduced. Laney clasped Michelle's hands in hers, smiled dazzlingly and said nothing. The brief span of quiet was unbearable after the previous hyperactivity; though Michelle was blushing with surprise and pleasure, she tried to pull away, intimidated by Laney's direct gaze. Suddenly it was over: Laney squeezed Michelle's hands and then turned back to Hadel to resume her interrogation. How was Natalie? Was she still going with that law student? Fine and yes, Hadel answered, but he was a full-fledged attorney now and had joined an established firm in New York. "How amazing both of you chose lawyers!" Laney cried. "Hadel, do you realize it's been three years?" Hadel tried to frame a question of her own, but Laney interrupted. Was Hadel still at the porno place? But writing her own things! And publishing! Wonderful! Ann drifted in on the tail end of that discussion, said hello to Michelle and asked if she could read one of Hadel's stories. Hadel handed her the new February issue of *Boys' World,* and Ann retreated to a stool by the window. "Have you heard from Portia?" Laney asked.

Hadel said that she hadn't heard a word and neither had Natalie.

"Ann hasn't either. She would have had a helluva time finding me, of course. Damn, I thought for sure she would have gotten in touch with one of us by now."

Hadel hesitated. She wanted to ask Laney about the past year, but it all seemed so bizarre she didn't know where to begin. Instead, she told Laney about the news she'd received from Natalie a few days earlier. Natalie had run into Charley at a restaurant. He was there with a date, a senior from Barnard. That was enough to snap Ann's head up from the magazine, but her eyes locked on the page again a moment later.

"Why didn't you tell me?" Michelle demanded, setting aside the bowl of egg whites she'd been furiously beating.

Hadel tore the plastic wrap off the cheese. "I forgot." She'd actually thought of little else since she'd gotten the letter, but she hadn't wanted to expose Charley, even *in absentia,* to Michelle's barbs. Michelle had used Charley's July visit as a chance to demonstrate her rejection of all things male; she had suffered his presence with such martyrdom that Hadel had finally thrown up her hands and bunked Charley at the University Hotel for the final night. Though Charley professed to be relieved, the memory of her betrayal of him continued to sting. Teeth clenched, she cut the cheese into inch-thick spears and inserted them into the chiles.

"Loyal, wonderful Charley," Michelle sighed. She turned on the oven and started dividing the tortillas.

Hadel was carefully rolling each flour-dusted chile in the egg whites. She paused, holding a wooden spoon aloft, as if she planned to brain Michelle with it as soon as she was finished with the chiles. "How come you want it both ways? How come marriage is a patriarchal trap, but Charley's a rotten bastard if he doesn't wait forever for Portia to surface?"

Laney defused the situation with a charming smile. "You're against marriage?" she asked Michelle.

"Oh, well," Michelle said with a shrug, matching Laney's smile with one of her own. She must be terribly impressed with Laney, Hadel thought, to set aside that issue. But now Hadel had an opening for her own question. "Laney, did you really marry that guy?"

"Bob Warner? Sure."

Hadel laid the coated chiles in a pan of simmering oil and spooned a little oil on top. Laney didn't miss a step. "This is fascinating, Ann. We have to learn all these California things." Ann grunted something from her stool. She was still absorbed in Hadel's story.

Hadel had been about to explain that chile rellenos weren't California things, but the meaning of Laney's remark stopped her. "You're going to live here?"

Laney nodded, helping Michelle set the table. "That's right. Tomorrow we start house-hunting."

"That's wonderful," Hadel said, hoping it would be. She wished Laney didn't seem so mysterious. And why was Ann acting like a bump on a log? Had she just fallen gratefully back into Laney's arms? "I don't quite see—"

"About Bob? Well, of course you know I'm married to Ann." She aimed an apologetic grin in Michelle's direction. "But you must have noticed they don't really let us queers get married. To me, I'm married to Ann; to the people on the street, Ann's my roommate or my friend or my sister. I wanted to see what a marriage recognized by the outside world was like."

Hadel directed Michelle to take the tortillas out of the oven while she loaded plates with the puffed-up chiles and beans. "Yes," she said slowly, trying to figure it out as they sat down to eat. "But—"

Apparently Michelle had been thinking, too. "She wanted to experience firsthand the degradation of marriage to a man, Hadel," she said, buttering a tortilla. "It makes perfect sense to me."

"Exactly," Laney said, smiling cherubically. "Clever of you to understand."

Hadel poked a bean with her fork. She wished Michelle had kept her mouth shut. Now she would never know why Laney had married Bob Warner.

"And I wanted to experience the true heroism in wifehood," Laney added, winking at Hadel. "You know all about heroism."

"Oh, she does," Michelle chimed in, her voice sharpened by a dollop of acid. "You should read her stories." Michelle rated *Boys' World* the barest millimeter above the porno magazine on her scale of political acceptability. She was forever after Hadel to write for the various women's journals and newspapers that had hit the Bay Area like rabbits let loose in fields of alfalfa. Every month, four or five new titles appeared. The argument that these periodicals paid only in contributor's copies didn't sway Michelle.

"Oh, I intend to," Laney assured her.

"Good," Ann muttered, though it was unclear if she was referring to reading Hadel's stories or the dinner.

Hadel hadn't given up yet in her search for answers. "But

what about Bob? And your parents? Have you contacted them yet?"

Laney waved airily. "I wrote a letter to Bob telling him I wouldn't contest a divorce. With no return address, of course. And my parents never heard a thing. I was writing them all along, anyway."

Hadel was no further enlightened, but she pressed on. "What did you do in between? I mean, after you left Bob"—Hadel couldn't bring herself to say "died," it was so insane already—"and before you came back to Ann?"

"Oh, I worked in a factory. Factories are rather interesting. There's a lot of noise and music and gossip. You can sort of disappear." She paused over a forkful of relleno. "Anyway, I needed more time."

"Time for what?" Hadel flashed back, scenting a clue.

"Time for it all to mean something," Laney said thoughtfully. "It doesn't do just to rush back to one's lover, does it? I needed to know I could live without Ann."

Michelle threw down her tortilla in her eagerness to chime in; the terrible dangers of coupledom to the self-determination of each of the partners was her favorite subject. Her theories were always packed full of examples of her own sacrifices to an insensitive and demanding Hadel. Once started, Michelle could rattle on for hours.

Hadel turned quickly to Ann, who was hunched over her plate, stolidly eating. "Are you planning to look for work?"

"She already has a job," Laney said. "That's why we came out here. You probably haven't heard how well Ann's done in television. She's been offered a field reporter job for Channel Eight." She leaned forward confidentially. "Ann was having trouble at KPAT in Chicago, but it was mostly because of me. They didn't mind her leaving, and Channel Eight was glad to get her. I'm tagging along to keep the home fires burning. Once a housewife, always a housewife." She wrapped her arm around Ann's shoulder and laughed, while Michelle kicked Hadel under the table. Laney had finally overstepped Michelle's boundaries. "It's funny," Laney continued. "For years I thought I was a butch."

Hadel was unable to resist sarcasm. "Really? I don't recall noticing." This time the kick came from the other side. Ann was shaking her head ever so slightly. Hadel wondered if Laney had gone bonkers, and this delusion about roles was the outward manifestation. Or maybe she was tripping, though she didn't act like it. Instead, she was looking at Hadel fondly. "I won't ask," she promised, "but marriage or not, I'm sure you two have worked *that* part out. Boy! Dinner's made me so sleepy I can hardly keep my eyes open. I'm going to head off for bed. Did you bring in the sleeping bags?"

Ann nodded, and Laney kissed her cheek. "Come soon," she said. She vanished into the living room, and they could hear her humming as she laid out the sleeping bags. Hadel got up to put on water for coffee. When she sat back down, Ann said quietly, "Don't mind Laney. She's pretending she's a femme."

"And you're pretending to be a butch?"

Ann nodded ruefully. "I'm not very good at it. What do butches do besides keep their mouths shut and glower?"

Hadel smiled. "Well, you haven't got the glowering part down yet. Is this a permanent arrangement?"

"God, no! I told her I'd do it for two weeks. It's kind of fun. It's an experiment. I think she's trying to learn something."

Michelle had been listening closely, nodding her head as Ann spoke. "It's like marrying that guy," she concluded. "That was an experiment, too. Isn't that great, Hadel? Laney's a social pioneer!"

1974–75

CHAPTER 17

Hadel came home from the grocery store to find Michelle waving a sheet of paper at her. "I can't believe it!" Michelle fumed. "If someone as intelligent as Natalie doesn't understand about Laney, who will? 'That nutty Laney'! I suppose *you* haven't bothered to explain to Natalie what Laney's doing."

It took Hadel a moment to realize the sheet of paper Michelle was flinging around was a letter from Natalie. "Michelle!" she protested. "That letter is to me, not to us. Why'd you open it?"

"Oh, Hadel. You left the letter you wrote to her lying on the kitchen table for three days before *I* mailed it. I asked her on the envelope for information about the new women's studies department at Ridgedale. I just wanted to see if she'd answered, which she hadn't."

"Why did you open my mail?" Hadel asked again, unable to budge from this intrusion.

"I already told you." Michelle stormed into the kitchen. Hadel followed her a few minutes later. Although Michelle's back was turned, she seemed to know when Hadel entered, because she started talking the moment Hadel passed the stove. "The point is Natalie's obtuseness about Laney's genius. It really upsets me." Michelle had been Laney's biggest champion since she'd decided she was the first to discover Laney's mission in life, which was none other than to expose the shallowness and humiliation of the few options open to women in American society. "Laney is truly brilliant, Hadel. Unfortunately, her work, being a *social* experiment, is continuing on unrecorded. It's up to her friends, you, me, Natalie to compose an oral herstory about Laney so it can be passed down to generations of women. I'm serious," Michelle said, seeing the look on Hadel's face. "It's a privilege to know her, and it carries with it a responsibility to the women who come after us."

"And where will these herstories be spoken? Around the campfire in front of women's hogans in 2040? Get off it, Michelle."

Michelle stood still for a moment, staring at Hadel. Then her dark eyebrows, so expressive against her nearly translucent skin, seemed to tangle together in a logjam above her nose. "I don't know why I even try talking to you, Hadel. All you do is write those patriarchal stories for boys. It really is disgusting."

"You generally don't talk to me," Hadel countered. "You come in, demand dinner and then tell me you have to study. You might talk to me long enough to tell me what to buy for your mother's birthday."

"Well, you're home all day!" Michelle shot back. "Law school hasn't been easy, you know."

"Oh, do I know. I'm home all day, yes, but I'm working. W-O-R-K-I-N-G. Writing my patriarchal stories." Hadel had finally kept her promise to herself to quit the porno magazine, but she'd done it a few months later than she'd planned, wanting to save up enough money to make the venture of writing full time unlikely rather than impossible.

"If this continues, I may have to leave," Michelle said slowly.

"Leave soon," Hadel shot back, "before you're done with law school. The resentment might kill me otherwise." She stalked into the living room and sat on the couch, her hands shaking. She hated these arguments, absolutely hated them. As far as she was concerned, she was married to Michelle for life, but lately it had occurred to her that death might really be preferable. She snatched Natalie's letter off the floor where it had fallen. The sentence that had offended Michelle was simple: "How's that nutty Laney and her lives? Is she around, or is she in the netherworld? Speaking of netherworlds, I walked by Megan when I was up at Ridgedale the other day for an alumnae luncheon. She had the nerve to say hello to me. Out of sheer habit, I said hello back. Woe be to Ridgedale with Megan there, controlling the incoming classes."

Everyone, Hadel thought, was full of woe.

Megan stared at herself in the mirror. She absolutely had to find someone else to cut her hair. The woman at the shop downtown couldn't seem to understand the concept of layering. "You want it fuller, right?" she had said last time. "Not fuller," Megan explained. "Softer."

"Ah-h-h!" And she proceeded to cut it exactly the same way she had the three times before, which ended up making the back of Megan's head look like a shingled roof.

Megan rubbed cream on her cheeks in steady, circular motions. She supposed she would have to go into New York and find a gay man to get a decent cut. Well, so what? If her hair was her major problem, she should sing hallelujahs to the heavens. Instead of doing anything so melodramatic, she smiled at her mirror image. What she saw, excepting her hair, of course, pleased her immensely. Her twice-a-week exercise class and her morning meditation had erased the last hints of what she called her "college-years manic stage." She had become . . . beautiful. Yes, no doubt about it. Call a spade a spade.

Her manic stage had been useful, though. It had forced her to take action: go to the dean about Hadel, get out of Ridgedale, get the job at Anna Parkins and then become bored to death. Nothing happened at Anna Parkins. When there were cries of rage echoing through every ivied hall in the nation following Nixon's resumption of bombing in 1972, Anna Parkins students were silent. Even if they had been in *favor* of Nixon, Megan might have stayed. But their silence came from lack of interest, and Megan had emerged from the Ridgedale crucible believing that one had to open one's eyes occasionally, if only to avoid stumbling over a tree trunk.

Megan began casting around in May of 1972. And strangely enough, she immediately heard of a big fish in a pond up north: Ridgedale. The director of admissions of twenty-three years was retiring, the equally ancient associate director was moving up, and the associate job was open to a "young woman of superior intellect, innovative and creative in her approach to problem solving; a risk-taker committed to the ideals of Ridgedale's unique educational goals." No experience requirement, but that was Ridgedale's way; diamonds in the rough are the best of all. In fact, Megan thought, her biggest problem might be overqualification—that and the dean, who would file Megan's application in the wastebasket before the Selection Committee ever met. Discreet inquiries revealed the dean had left the year before for a more lucrative position at Radcliffe. Obstacle one had been removed; now Megan had to convince the administration that she had the talent, but had not been rigidified by her exposure to another "educational ideal." She worked up a series of campaign speeches, emphasizing different abilities to different parties—her idealism to the faculty ("Every promising student will be considered, regardless of her life circumstances"), her goals to the administration ("Admissions standards exist hand-in-glove with the success we can expect to attain as an institution that seeks to *educate*") and her consciousness of Ridgedale's unspoken real problem, money, to the board of directors, which every year staved off bankruptcy proceedings by inches.

It had begun as a game for her, a marvel of manipulation to stave off the doldrums at Anna Parkins. By the end, when she was pitted against two other "qualified" applicants, it took on all the trappings of a holy war. And when she had won, she felt vindicated, miraculously resurrected: she had been redeemed. She had returned in triumph to the battleground of her adolescence; once a lonely excommunicant, she was now an archbishop-soon-to-be-cardinal. The new director stayed only one year before she too retired. Megan immediately eliminated the associate's job, replacing it with an unpaid committee of two faculty members and two students, a move that was hailed from every quarter. Despite the problems inherent in this system (committee meetings extending into the wee hours of the morning for two to three months on end), Megan enjoyed it—she had an audience to play to. While the others soared to fanciful heights, Megan sat like a revered elder at the end of the sofa, her feet planted firmly on a yellow cushion that was always in place. One student sat behind Megan's desk, one in front of it, while the faculty members took turns occupying the vacant seat on the sofa and an uncomfortable but impressive oak rocking chair that graced the "Cancer Corner," so called because the smoke from everyone's cigarettes seemed to gather there, sometimes almost obliterating the unlucky professor.

Megan rarely spoke during her committee meetings, and then it was often only to sum up what the others had said. She was fond of beginning the meetings by passing out mimeographed outlines with titles such as, "Qualities of a Ridgedale

Education," "Ridgedale Perceived by Incoming Freshmen," "A Composite Applicant" and, of course, "Educational Goals: Can We Teach Students to Think?" This last she published as a monograph in a journal for college administrators, with acknowledgments by name to the four members of her committee. The committee responded by conducting its affairs with absolute dedication, sending out acceptances in April as if it were conferring 130 prized Holy Grails to the few in the kingdom found worthy. The admissions office became a showplace of student-faculty-administration cooperation, highlighted in the college catalog, pointed out to visitors with near reverence by the campus guides.

Megan told herself she should go to bed. February was the apex of the late nights for her committee. But she picked up the newspaper and read the front-page story again. Patricia Hearst had been kidnapped from her apartment in Berkeley. Megan laughed out loud. She had met Patty at a wedding reception in New York a couple of years back, and she couldn't think of anyone more irritating to kidnap. Poor whoever they were—Symbionese Liberation Army. Where had they picked that one up? Well, of course people had to have something to do now that the war was over. But Patty? It pleased Megan immensely that Patty had been living in sin with her boyfriend, a fact that even the Hearsts couldn't suppress. Megan, in her role as a liberal and responsive college administrator, thought the kidnapping just desserts for Patty's mother Catherine's voting record as a University of California regent. Catherine was so reactionary she made washed-up actor Ron seem moderate.

That a Hearst daughter was considered a suitable kidnap victim, however, did have its serious side. Despite its image as a radical college, many of Ridgedale's students were wealthy. If kidnappings were going to be the new vogue of the disaffected Left, Megan supposed that some protective security measures should be instituted. Not that Ridgedale students, no matter how wealthy, would feel they needed protection. Far from it: Megan was certain that more than a few of the called-in bomb threats in '70 and '71 originated from the hallowed halls of Ridgedale dormitories, not to mention, of course, the activities of Ridgedale's most famous alumna, Portia Bethany. Things had changed in the past two years—the students had added a feminist tag line to their radical identification—but Megan thought this new trend still bore watching. She might even prepare a memo for the next board meeting. She began composing the memo in her head, but she was really remembering herself as a student. She would have been appalled at the idea she needed protection from the Left. To avoid howls of protest, the stepped-up security would have to be strictly undercover—perhaps a new gardener and a couple of those male dance grad students—fake ones, of course—yes, they would certainly be free to roam around, ostensibly doing nothing. But how would the school pay for these bodyguards? Megan watched herself touch her lip in thought. Here was a good use for her trust fund. Four months of salaries, until school closed for the summer, would only be about six thousand dollars. And for this pittance she'd receive a debt of gratitude from the board and raise her status from an employee, sterling though she was, to a benefactor. Excellent!

Yet she noticed a small cloud hanging over her eyes. Had seeing Natalie bothered her that much? Apparently so. When Natalie was on campus, Megan stuck to her office, but she had forgotten that stupid luncheon. She had said hello to her as a reflex. Natalie had answered back and then continued on her way to the library, where some old crow was donating a collection of rare books. Why didn't they give money? But she had seen Natalie and survived, hadn't she? So what was the problem? One thorn in a bed of roses should be acceptable. Perhaps she could bargain with the board—Natalie off her alumnae committees—for a safe student body. No! That was a plan so far out of perspective it was sick. She had to dump this Natalie/Hadel business once and for all. And she also had to stop sitting in front of this mirror! It was two-thirty in the morning.

She climbed into bed and turned off her little lamp. Sleepless. Why had she ever thought of those two? They were both despicable and always had been. She remembered a horrifying incident on the only vacation the three had taken together, in the spring of their sophomore year. They had journeyed down to St. Thomas, rented a small car and spent an entire week on a deserted beach on the other side of the island. Deserted, that is, but for a few natives wandering here and there.

One lazy afternoon, as Hadel and Natalie snoozed away a lunch of cheese and fruit, Megan stayed awake, reading. She glanced out once or twice at the deep blue waters of the Caribbean. On her third peek away from her book, she saw four men, boys really, standing in the water waist-deep. They were all making a funny motion with their right arms.

Luckily, before Megan could reveal her ignorance in front of her two friends, Hadel awoke and poked Natalie. "We have an adoring audience."

Natalie peered through her sunglasses. "Very adoring."

"Wanta take bets on who'll shoot first?" Hadel asked.

Megan had by now understood what was happening. She was so repulsed by Hadel's question she wanted to gag in the sand. Natalie, however, raised herself on one elbow and examined their admirers. After a moment's discussion, they found they had no bet—both picked the second from the left, who, almost before the conversation was concluded, came to his own conclusion, jerking forward for an instant, his mouth open. Megan wondered how they had known.

But now they'd decided on a better wager: who would come last? "Much more important," Hadel said, and Natalie winked at her. Megan was lost again. They settled on two challengers, sticking five-dollar bills under their beach blankets. As Megan watched the men intently, as if she could see under the water, the unbacked contestant stared directly into her eyes and then raised his chin in the air, his body shuddering. It was a moment she would never forget; she felt he had looked directly into her soul.

"Good," Hadel said callously. "Get the little fellas off the stage."

Hadel lost her bet because she made the mistake of turning over. The instant her behind was in the air, her boy had had enough. "You lose, kiddo," Natalie cheered. "Not only that, it was all your fault!"

Hadel hrumphed and handed over the bill. Her sulk didn't last long. "Maybe you oughta go introduce yourself to the winner, Natalie," she suggested.

"Maybe," Natalie said thoughtfully. Now that the contest was over, Natalie felt safe in applying some suntan oil to her breasts, which necessitated lowering her bikini top an important inch or two. The deed done, the four men were soon on their way, swimming north. They got out of the water a hundred yards up the beach and looked at the women, who looked back at them.

"The trouble is," Natalie said, "I don't fancy more than mine, and I don't see how to separate him off without the possibility of the others cutting in. Now, if you two were interested . . ." She glanced at them expectantly.

"Sorry, Nats. Not my type."

"Ah, I forgot. You go for blonds." The Swedish guy on the bed full of coats had been only a month or two earlier. "Megan?"

It was, Megan knew, a courtesy question. What would Natalie have done if she had said yes? She would never know. "Too bad," Natalie muttered regretfully. She flipped on her back, and within a few moments she and Hadel were fast asleep. Megan stayed awake through the long afternoon, unable even to read. She didn't relax until the four men rose to their feet and walked up the beach, finally disappearing from sight.

Now here she was, bleary-eyed again. She tossed around in her bed, rearranging her pillows. Why did the two of them weigh on her so? Unfortunately, she had to think about them to get rid of them. Sighing, she switched on her bedside lamp.

All right, take Hadel, for instance. She hadn't seen Hadel for more than five years, and in all that time she hadn't heard a thing about her. Obviously Hadel had done nothing worth mentioning. She probably spent her days at some lowly job and her nights at a bar full of pathetic lesbians. Natalie, of course, had had her success with the Kent State film, but what had happened afterward? The film about nontraditional jobs for women had shown only at feminist coffeehouses, and the one she'd done last year, on child-care alternatives—well, what did she expect? *Child-care alternatives?* Natalie had been gobbled up in the maw of the feminist imperative. And that sorry little accounting summed up the exploits of the Dynamic Duo. The power brokers, indeed! Compared to her—well, it was clear she had nothing to worry about. Megan the third wheel had become Megan the success. She would look at Natalie a bit differently the next time they ran into each other on campus. It just proved Megan's mother's maxim: those who are least beautiful as children are often most beautiful as adults. Her mother had not said this in reference to Megan; Megan had always been pretty. She had impressed it upon Megan (along with a slap in the face) when she caught Megan teasing a little friend about her pug nose. Megan had taken the point and ignored the rebuke. She shook her head now, thinking about it. Children were cruel. Did her mother expect a saint?

My God, first Natalie and Hadel, now her mother! She switched off the lamp again, determined to get some sleep. Hadn't she started this evening rejoicing that her only problem was her hair? As she began to drift away, she smiled, remembering Patty Hearst. She hoped Patty wouldn't be rescued right away. It had all the earmarks of a wonderful story, and Megan wanted it to go on and on.

CHAPTER 18

Ann's Channel 8 crew was the last to arrive at the Hearst kidnapping site, an apartment close to campus. In Ann's case, however, last was undeniably best. Her viewers wanted the in-depth report that only she could bring to this event, which had captured the imaginations of Hearst-haters and Hearst-sympathizers alike. Ann's audience, most of them fifty or over, sat squarely in the sympathizers' camp, even though Patty had shown poor judgment in living, first, with her boyfriend, and second, in South Berkeley. Hadel and Michelle ate dinner in front of the television, watching as Ann demonstrated that Patty, even though defying her parents' wishes (both the wishes and the defiance were taken for granted), had at least had enough sense to live above Telegraph Avenue, on tree-lined streets jammed with churches and apartment buildings, rather than below Telegraph, where the streets were more likely to be lined with falling-down communal houses and bulletin boards posted with notices describing the physical characteristics of narcotics officers. Patty had not, Ann seemed to maintain, been quite *that* rebellious. And yet, compared to the scruffy neighbors she interviewed, Ann appeared as out of place as a cube of pristine sweet butter inexplicably dumped into a vat of foul-smelling, pig-hair-matted lard. She glided around the neighborhood in her soft gray suit and pale blue scarf, a brave smile on her face, and she occasionally stared directly into the camera, her big gray eyes growing even wider in a combination of astonishment and sadness. One could well imagine Patty, younger and unprotected by Ann's grace and competency, wandering these same streets, an innocent abroad in the wilds of the universe. By the time Ann was finished talking to the neighbors, Hadel was amazed that Patty had gotten up enough nerve to go to the grocery store.

"What *is* the point of this?" Michelle asked irritably. Her ire was kindled by any current happening that tempted her away from her law books.

Hadel assumed Michelle was questioning the point of the kidnapping, not Ann's slant on Berkeley, Terror Town. "Eat the rich," Hadel answered, referring to a popular tune by gay singer Blackberri, who suggested snacking on a Rockefeller when the money was low and the stomach was empty.

"I doubt it. Ransom, probably."

Hadel phoned Laney at their house a few blocks away. "Ann, the voice of the people."

"Ann, with her significant looks at her audience of thousands," Laney replied. "She's becoming so popular it's frightening. You should see her fan mail."

"Are the Hearsts going to interrupt our camping trip?"

"Absolutely not. I told Ann I'd brain her. Are you ready?"

"Ready or not—are you yourself?"

"Yes, yes. I promised you I would be."

"Fine," Hadel said, hanging up the receiver. She had been relieved when Laney had stopped being a femme and Ann a butch, though it had gone on about six weeks longer than the short time Laney had initially requested. It went on, Hadel thought wryly, long enough for Ann to have to deal with the entire process of buying a house, and ended just before femme Laney would have to think about furnishing it. Laney could, of course, have worked on the house in her own right, but just as it was time to begin, she announced that she was completely exhausted—triumphant, she added quickly—but exhausted nevertheless. Hadel, who had bumbled into the middle of Laney's announcement bearing a rhododendron as a housewarming present, listened to what followed with astonishment; it was the first time she'd truly believed there was more madness than method to Laney's alter egos. Laney explained, mostly for Hadel's benefit, since Ann was angrily washing the plates she'd bought that morning, that through her roles as Bob's wife, factory worker and femme, she had demonstrated that she could fashion her own environment. The femme business had been the acid test; she had maintained a separate identity while she was actually in Ann's presence. Now, however, Laney needed both to relax and to become acclimated to the Bay Area. "I hadn't realized everybody would be so busy all the time," Laney told Hadel. "Lucky I found a vocation."

"Busy!" Ann growled, crumpling up a brown paper bag. "Exactly! I work ten hours a day. What are *you* doing?"

"Ann," Laney said as Hadel jumped up, grabbing for her jacket and thrusting the planting instructions at Laney, "remember when I told you I needed somebody I could depend on?" Ann continued washing plates, having evidently heard all this before, so Laney shouted above the water. "Don't you see? Before you were the sun, the stars, the moon, the planets! You're too busy to be all those things. Now you're home. My home."

"Then why can't you help with *our* house?" Ann insisted.

"I've just created a universe," Laney said, splaying out her hands. "Three, to be exact. Don't I deserve a day of rest?"

Perhaps considering Hadel to be an informed observer, Ann called her a few days later. "Laney says she has to 'adjust,'" Ann complained. "Then she tells me she wants to build herself up physically while she's adjusting. So she's joined the YMCA!"

Hadel didn't think joining the YMCA was necessarily a heinous act, but she did sympathize with Ann, who reported she had finally hired a group of women to paint the interior and refinish the floors of the new house. "Laney never tried to beg off work when we lived in Woodsmere," Ann told Hadel. "In fact, she made me feel guilty. And she practically lived in the garden. You'd think that since we have a yard again, and it's a gorgeous spring . . . but no. All she wants to do is hang out at that smelly exercise place."

Hadel had no answers, but after what she'd heard when she'd brought the rhododendron, she suspected that Laney could never be accused of the usual sins, simply because her behavior could not be judged by normal standards. She as Laney's friend, and Ann as Laney's lover, were going to have to take Laney's statements seriously, crazy-sounding or not. "If it's so important for her to maintain distance from you," Hadel theorized to Ann, "maybe she needs mental distance from the house as well . . . just until she's claimed a few territories of her own," Hadel said hastily, because Ann was starting to grumble.

"Maybe," Ann admitted after a moment. "Well, if she wants sole rights to the weight room at the Y, she's welcome to it."

Hadel rarely saw Ann that first spring, but she often chauffeured Laney around on what Laney called her "familiarizing expeditions." One day they drove to San Francisco, and instead of meandering as they usually did, Laney searched for an address, saying she had to run an errand. She directed Hadel to park in front of *Common Bond,* a tiny newspaper that claimed to be "The Voice of the People." Hadel pocketed her keys and followed Laney inside. The office was small and dingy, the walls covered with a million political flyers advertising marches and rallies all over the country. A reprint of a communiqué only a couple of days old about the Weather Underground's attack on New York's 103rd Precinct to protest the police killing of a ten-year-old boy was festooned with streamers. "They Live!" shouted a hand-lettered sign pinned above the reprint. The office's only occupant was a man in his thirties who looked as if he'd been working too many late nights for too many years. He didn't move his pencil from the piece of copy he was editing as Laney marched up to his desk, fanned out five one-hundred-dollar bills and said, "I'd like this money to be delivered to Portia Bethany."

"Where'd you get that?" Hadel squawked, staring at the bills.

"Factory," Laney answered shortly.

The man, meanwhile, had broken the point on his pencil. "Of course I've heard of Portia Bethany," he allowed. "But I have no way of sending money to her. I would have to know where she was first." He awarded himself a thin smile for this quip.

Laney leaned over his desk. "Look at it as a challenge," she suggested. "Psychologists have come up with a method to determine your social quotient in our classless society. You see how many phone calls it would take you to reach the President. You might be interested in your radical quotient."

The man's smile died halfway through Laney's proposal. He straightened purposefully in his chair and looked back at the copy he was editing. Then, as if he couldn't help himself, his eyes strayed upward to discover Laney, now silent but still leaning close enough to plant a kiss on top of his tumbleweed hair. His voice, when it emerged, had as much strength as a duck quacking underwater. "Are you an agent? You're supposed to identify yourself."

Laney didn't take pity on him. If anything, she tilted farther forward. "I'm not an agent. My name's Laney Villano. I live at Twenty-one thirty-seven Eighth Street in Berkeley. I'm afraid you'll have to take me at face value. Portia's an old friend of mine, and I want her to have this money." She plunked the five green bills on his desk and turned away. "Let's go, Hadel."

"Wait!" the man wailed. Suddenly freed from the spell of Laney's dangerous beauty an inch from his nose, he tried to do everything at once. His chair rolled back against a filing cabinet, and two of the bills he was trying to scoop up fell to the floor. "Lady!"

"Thanks," Laney said, steering Hadel outside and closing his door.

"That was asinine," Hadel complained on the way across the bridge. "Once he gets his burned-out mind together, he'll realize you just paid his next printing bill."

"Maybe," Laney said. "Would you drop me off at the Y?"

"What's this obsession with physical fitness?" Hadel asked irritably.

Her question was answered a couple of weeks later when Laney informed her friends that she had decided to become a sports hero. She chose tennis, which she'd played a great deal as a teenager. After a few months of intensive practice, she was amazingly good. She was advancing up a string of local tournaments when she chucked it, claiming sports were insufferably boring. "I don't mean the game," she explained to Hadel. "I mean the people around the game. It's the worst of both worlds. You're treated like a woman and expected to act like a man." Hadel noted, however, that Laney retained enough interest to end her next role, as a woman business executive, just in time to watch Billie Jean King defeat Bobby Riggs.

Laney's businesswoman role was the first time she used another identity, which also allowed her to fabricate a résumé of some half truths and many whole lies. She applied at a private telecommunications company, a new firm finding its way in uncharted territory. Laney evidently convinced them of her navigation skills, because they hired her on the spot, with the vice presidents of both sales and customer relations pleading for her services within the week. By that time Laney had got her hair styled, bought a wardrobe and moved into an apartment overlooking Oakland's Lake Merritt.

Hadel visited Ann several times during that period, mostly as a listener. "I don't understand," Ann said. "Why does she have to take this so seriously? She told me I can't contact her under any circumstances. She wouldn't tell me how long she'll be gone, though she did promise she'd come back." Ann picked at a tuna casserole that was supposed to last her all week. "I didn't mind the tennis thing at first. I thought it was odd that she'd never mentioned tennis, but then—well, why shouldn't she be a tennis star? But then I realized she didn't care about tennis, not in that high-pressured tournament sense, anyway. She doesn't care about this private phone stuff, either. What I can't figure out is why she can't find something to do that she likes."

"Because it's not really she that's doing these things, Ann, or at least she's not doing them as herself. What'd she say? She's creating universes?"

"Yes, but—well, what does she think the rest of us are doing? Does she imagine I emerged from the womb as a field reporter? Does she think Joe Blow knew he would be a murderer when he was three? Things happen to people, and people make do. Sometimes I feel as if I'm playing a role when I'm interviewing people. I *am,* damn it. Everybody's like that. Women give birth and suddenly they're mothers, with all the responsibilities that role implies. I think she's expecting too much. She's too strict with how a real life is lived. If only she'd find what she really wants to do . . ."

But both knew Laney's apparent aimlessness was not the problem. Ann pushed aside the casserole, which would last all month at this rate. "I guess," she said, "it's all my fault."

This assertion was nearly as boggling as Laney's mental state. "How do you figure that?" Hadel asked carefully.

"When we lived in Woodsmere, I realized she needed me to be her anchor. No, more than an anchor. I was her protective shield, guarding her from all the ills of the world. When I went to Chicago, I knew she wouldn't be able to survive without someone else functioning as a shield. That's what I thought she was doing with Bob. But she wasn't. She said that after she met me, she knew there couldn't be anyone else for her. So she came up with her roles as a substitute shield. The roles guard her now. She would never have started doing this if I hadn't left her."

"But you're back. You're together. Why does she have to play her roles now?"

Ann considered. "Because she saw I would always fail. She saw no one was really capable of protecting her in the way she needed. She had to find something for herself."

"Then why are *you* at fault? If no one can do it, why should you? Besides, you can't be responsible for someone else's life." Hadel continued on this line for a few minutes, but she saw that Ann wasn't listening. "Ann?" she prodded gently.

"Oh, I don't know, Hadel. I guess you're right. It's all so confusing. She says she's never left me, that she's found the one way we can stay together. But where is she? And even when she is here, I'm not sure where to find the *real* her. Where's that woman who clung to me? She hasn't needed me in the same way since she started her roles. Maybe I should be glad—her dependence frightened me—but I still miss her."

Laney returned from her corporate career with eight thousand dollars, a car and a case of mono that felled her for three months. Hadel had proposed the camping trip over Christmas, and Laney had asked for one additional month of recuperation. Now it was on, in spite of the station's efforts to entice Ann to work over the weekend on the Hearst kidnapping. Hadel was relieved Ann had stood her ground. Hadel was pinning a lot of hope on this trip. Michelle had multiplied her household tyranny in the past month, insisting she had to be two weeks ahead in her law school study schedule, because somehow, in between a lost Saturday and Sunday, she would fall two weeks behind. Hadel recognized obsession when she saw it. It was just possible that the weekend would break the cycle and allow Michelle to be a human being again.

"This is the first political kidnapping in the United States," Ann said, boiling with excitement. Hadel smoothly guided the car up the first incline into the foothills. "Great car," she told

Laney. They had taken Laney's new Malibu, which, since the demise of her business career and her resumption of being Laney, she no longer drove. It was doubtful that either Hadel or Michelle's old clunkers would have made it as far as Sacramento.

"The strange part is they didn't mention Remiro and Little in their communiqué," Ann continued. The communiqué had arrived on Thursday, explaining that the kidnapping was an action of the Symbionese Liberation Army. The SLA had killed Marcus Foster, Oakland's superintendent of schools, the year before. Little and Remiro had been arrested for that crime, and the assumption of the media was that Patty Hearst would be traded for the two men.

"More FBI," Michelle predicted. "Do they still come around to your place?"

Ann nodded. "Not so often, though. Last time was . . . October. Boy, that is long."

"They were racing around then because the Weather Underground bombed ITT," Hadel said.

"Maybe they've given up," Michelle said hopefully. "This might be a good time for Portia to surface. They've dropped charges against a lot of other people. They even took Bernardine Dohrn's name off the Ten Most Wanted list."

"Well, look what's happened," Ann said. "Agnew resigning and Cox getting fired and the tapes and the whole Watergate mess in general—the government, or Nixon's cronies, at least, should all be committed en masse to the Atascadero Facility for the Criminally Insane. The Justice Department's already lost several conspiracy cases. The last thing they need is something to make them look even more foolish. Besides, they're concentrating on Tricky. He's trying to squirm out of the net, but he's going to get it in the end. Did you watch the hearings last summer?"

"Me?" Michelle gasped. "No! I was at the Women's Law Project twelve or fourteen hours a day! I didn't have time to do anything. Hadel was home, though."

"I was working," Hadel said. She curbed her impulse to spell it. W-O-R . . . Stop it, she told herself. If Michelle's going to relax, I have to meet her halfway and drop all my old garbage, too.

"And I was training companies to use our systems after cutover," Laney said. "It was a good job, I suppose, if you don't mind doing all the work and letting your male partner, who's paid half again as much, accept all the credit. They did it like that in customer relations, you know. A pretty woman was coupled with a soothing guy, who'd have ten martini lunches with the upper management while I trained the people who were actually going to handle the system."

"Ain't it the truth," Michelle sighed, leaning back in the front seat. She closed her eyes and promptly fell asleep. Hadel was ecstatic. Michelle *was* relaxing, the conversation was fine and the weather was lovely, refuting the argument that going on a camping trip in February was silly. They talked quietly until they reached Auburn, where they had to stop to consult maps. When they pulled away again, Michelle woke up and stretched. "That was wonderful!" She squeezed Hadel's hand. "Are we close to the river yet?"

"Yeah, I think if we just follow this county road . . ." She drove until she found a suitable parking place on a dirt turnoff hidden under a mantle of trees. They got out of the car and heard the American River roaring below them. "This is exciting!" Michelle said. She strapped on her backpack and peered over the edge of the road into the canyon. Although the river sounded as if it were about to rise up and wash them away, it wasn't visible. "It looks awfully steep," Ann remarked. Laney and Hadel had joined them at the turnoff's lip. "I think we should walk along the road and look for a trail," Laney said. "There's even supposed to be a dirt road that fishermen use to get down to the river."

"Oh, come on," Michelle said, plunging over the edge. "How far can it be?"

Damn far, Hadel thought when they finally reached the bottom of the canyon and slumped exhausted next to the river. They'd been slipping and sliding down deer trails for more than two hours. "Do we have to go back up that?" Michelle asked. The river was so loud they could hardly hear each other, but Michelle's question was understandable because of her horrified look at the cliff behind them. Laney shook her head. "We'll try to find the road tomorrow!" she hollered.

Hadel dropped her pack among the fallen bodies of her

friends and wandered downstream until she was hidden by a massive boulder. Then she threw back her head and sucked in a great breath of air. She'd thought of this trip as an R&R break for Michelle, or maybe even as a new beginning for their relationship, but she hadn't once considered how she herself might be affected by it. Now she crouched forward over a pool, the river roaring behind her back, and she watched a few minnows gliding warily around the edge of the shadow she cast on the water's surface. She wanted to see the pool in each season: low and green in the summer, nearly empty by fall, then replenished by the winter rains and filled to overflowing again in spring, when the snow melted in the mountains. Years she'd spent in offices, either her own or someone else's, staring at typewriter keys. Years listening to Michelle's time paranoia—time was escaping, every hour must be packed full, we'll be late, we'll be late for life! And yet, according to Michelle, nothing they did in their own lifetimes would change anything; they could, at most, position a couple of foundation stones. But here! Here in the wilderness, Hadel could breathe and be whoever she was right now, let the future generations of women for whom they were chiseling the foundation stones take care of the structure of their own lives. Did it even make sense for a whole lifetime of women to devote themselves to a future they couldn't predict? Hadn't their very own mothers done the same thing, but on a more individual level, sacrificing themselves for their children? It was still the female life-denial syndrome, now retooled and modernized to appeal to a generation suspicious of individual achievement, a generation that sought world solutions instead. Hadel idly threw a stone into the pool and then started back upstream.

Laney was alone on the tiny spit of sand they'd chosen as a campsite. "They're off getting firewood," she told Hadel. "I dug a pit. You want to lay out the sleeping bags? I'll start arranging the food." By the time Ann and Michelle had carried in two loads of wood, however, the weather had turned. They looked at each other apprehensively as the wind picked up with the approach of darkness. Laney began repacking the food, Hadel rolling the bags, while Michelle coaxed a fire into a blaze that was reduced to a sputtering, smoking gray mess as soon as the rain started. "It's pouring!" Ann shouted, stuffing a library book into her backpack. It was more than pouring. Sheets of rain plummeted down upon the four women. They had no tent. Their combined outer gear was jackets and two tarps.

"Never fear!" Laney yelled through the drenching rain. "Remember Wilderness!" She proceeded to chop the bottom branches out of a section of dense brush. After she'd roped the tarps over the remaining branches, it was surprisingly dry inside their dark cave, though the prospect of spending an entire evening and night cramped up together was daunting. Laney managed a small fire, but it took up too much room and closed off their view of the storm outside. She finally put it out after Ann brushed her leg against it trying to shift position.

"I don't like this," Michelle said some hours later.

"No," Hadel agreed. She was relieved at Michelle's good temper. This had been her first comment, and she sounded more scared than angry. Hadel put her arm around her and changed the conversation to the coming baseball season. No wonder Michelle was scared. Ann and Laney had been talking about hypothermia for the past twenty minutes.

They dozed off at intervals. Hadel awoke once to see Laney staring out at the river. "We'll have to move soon," she said. Hadel crawled out of her bag and checked the river. It had crept from twelve feet away to within eight, and the rain showed no signs of letting up.

Hadel retreated back into the bush and shrugged her sleeping bag around her shoulders. "In a half hour," she told Laney. "Let them sleep as long as they can."

Laney nodded. She seemed far away.

"What are you thinking?" Hadel asked softly.

"I was remembering Wilderness," Laney said. "How it was living outdoors. I never told you about it, did I?"

Hadel shook her head, and Laney began to talk in a voice just loud enough to be heard over the muffled pounding of the rain and the surge of the river. "I felt safe in the woods," Laney said. "Safer than I ever have. I knew the dangers; they were identifiable, from sources I could see and hear around me. Like tonight, with the river." She tilted her head toward the opening in the bush. "I was handicapped, of course. I hadn't been born in the woods as the animals had, but we were all handicapped—

we humans, I mean. I know how to overcome that kind of handicap."

As opposed to her being unable to live in society without what Ann called a protective shield? Hadel pulled her knees up to her chest to keep warm. Laney probably did have an advantage over her fellows: she would have approached the wilderness as an eager-to-learn neophyte, not needing to prove something either to herself or to her instructors.

"I found out more from the animals than I did from the teachers," Laney continued. While others huddled around the campfire at night, Laney explained, she had been far beyond the light of the flames, tracking by feel, ranging down animal trails, her fingertips brushing the earth and the calf-high brush. She learned the value of climbing trees for shelter and escape; she learned to sit still for hours, her mind alert for any sound. Her instructors disapproved of women alone in the woods. They tried to keep her close by, but she escaped again and again.

Hadel had been slipping into a reverie, imagining it. Now Laney startled her with a direct question: "Do you know what a solo survival test is?"

"Well, I guess it's where you go out by yourself, huh? For some period of time?"

Laney nodded. "There're different kinds. Some you stay where they drop you until you're retrieved. On ours, we were supposed to find our way back to camp. We had a knife, a compass, a pack of waterproof matches and the clothes we were wearing." As the day of the test approached, Laney said, only she was serene. Most of the men were full of bravado and bluster, and the two other women in the camp chose not to take the test at all. The instructors complimented those women on their good sense while they forced the one man who also tried to renege to climb on the truck that would drop them off at isolated points across the countryside. Once on the road, their blindfolds securely fastened, the nine students kept up a patter of nervous conversation, occasionally making jokes: "I'll have coffee ready when you guys come in." Laney was quiet, scrunched against the cab wall of the pickup. She understood the truck was making a wide circle about twenty-five miles from the nucleus of the camp. When she was helped to disembark, one of the last to be let off, the instructor tried to convince her to come back with them. "There're crazies around here," he insisted. Laney refused. She didn't remove her blindfold until the truck rattled away. She looked around her, taking her bearings, and then she set off. She came in five hours ahead of her nearest competition.

"That's great!" Hadel enthused, but Laney held up a cautioning hand. "Wait. There's more."

The top three finishers, she said, were sent to an instructors' training camp in a remote area. The material they covered was a great deal more comprehensive, and the solo survival test at the end was correspondingly rougher. The staff again tried to convince her not to take the test, telling her she could be an instructor anyway. She insisted, and she came back into camp, fresh and well rested, in the best time ever.

Hadel had learned her lesson. She wrapped her sleeping bag tight around her and waited.

"Around the campfire that evening," Laney continued, "the staff talked about women. They said women were clever, sort of an *animal* cunning. They talked about endurance. They said women spies caught by the enemy didn't feel pain and that women who saved lives acted instinctively. They all agreed that women had stamina. But to call a woman courageous or even competent was similar to saying camels on a long desert crossing were heroic. Silly. They were built for it. No one said a word about me." The other competitors, straggling in over a four-day period, avoided Laney. On the night of the fifth day, as she lay sleeping under a thin blanket, a big hand clamped over her eyes and her mouth, and she was raped.

Hadel felt her breath knocked out of her, as if someone had kicked her hard in the chest. She dropped her head and struggled to make her lungs work again.

"So that's why women can't be heroes, Hadel. When the act is instinctual, when the human element of choice in the face of danger is absent, heroism doesn't apply."

Hadel had recovered her breath. She looked up to see Laney smiling at her easily. "Do you see what I mean?" Laney asked.

Hadel's words came haltingly. "Laney, I'm sorry—it's terrible—but . . . you can't go by what others think about you. You have to judge your own actions."

Laney's eyes brightened. "Would that really satisfy you?"

"Me?" Hadel stammered, bewildered. "I—"

But Laney, who had leaned forward to hear, was now listening intently to something else. Hadel stopped talking. In a moment she heard it, too. The river was closer, much closer. When they stepped outside their shelter of tarps, they saw that the river had edged to within four feet. They used flashlights and stumbled away from their bush, staying close together, helping each other over the slick rocks. Hadel found a niche bounded by the trunk and branch of a fallen tree. The ground was soaking wet, but it would have to do. They moved the packs, their own sleeping bags, and strung one of the tarps before they returned to wake Ann and Michelle. Michelle was already sitting up. "It was raining on me," she said. Then she looked at the river and tried to get to her feet and out of her sleeping bag in one motion. "My God," she cried. Hadel steadied her with an outflung arm. Laney untied the other tarp and woke Ann. "Can't we just go now?" Michelle asked as they began to pick their way across the slippery rocks.

"We have to wait until it gets light," Hadel explained. "Anyway, maybe it'll stop raining."

Hadel lay awake long after the others were settled, lying stiffly in her sodden sleeping bag, thinking about Laney's Wilderness experience. Was Laney capable of separating what others said about her from what she thought about herself? Separating what others did to her? Hadel shivered. Once started, she couldn't stop the convulsive waves of shuddering. It took her a long time to fall asleep.

Morning was better only because they could see the pelting rain, and beyond it, the swollen river. Their bush was awash in a foot of rushing water. "Good thing we moved," Ann said. She held up the accordioned library book. "Guess I'll have to pay for this." Michelle was trying to roll up her wringing-wet sleeping bag. Everything was pounds heavier—their bags, their packs, the clothes they were wearing. Laney dug out a bag of dry granola and insisted everyone eat a few handfuls before they got started. Then they began walking downstream, trying to keep to the narrow stretch between the cliff on their right and the rocks that bordered the river on their left. They came to a dirt road an hour later. "But how do we know it goes where we want it to go?" Michelle asked, taking the opportunity to sit down on a pile of stones.

"It goes up," Hadel said. "That's all we care about." They started on the road. The mud was ankle-deep, overflowing their shoes. After experimenting, they found the mud was less than at shoe height if they performed a sort of tightrope act against the bank that had been gouged out of the cliff. Between the beach and the road they'd been walking a balance beam all morning. "What about going through the forest?" Hadel suggested after an hour of slogging.

Laney vetoed the idea. The trees were too thick, the ground too uneven, and there were several gullies that they would have to work their way back down and then climb out again. "It would take more energy, I think."

As the day wore on, in spite of Laney's nighttime story, Hadel retreated into her fantasies. First she had been a Kurd, feverish with typhus yet staggering on under the rich European's load of nonessentials. Now she was a corporal in the gay army, the only survivor of a recon squad. Straights were moving artillery into Camptree Canyon; she had to tell the command as soon as possible. She unconsciously picked up her pace as the ramifications of the coming battle at Camptree assailed her imagination. Five strides later, she realized she couldn't hear Michelle creaking and huffing behind her. She turned back. Michelle was facedown in the mud in the middle of the road. "Michelle!" Hadel called. "Michelle!" No use. She retraced her hard-fought steps and knelt down as Michelle moved her head to one side. The rain chopped clear trails through the mud on her cheeks. "Leave me," she gasped. "I can't go on."

Hadel reached under Michelle and unhooked the pack, tossing it against the steep bank, out of the mud. "I'll carry your pack. You can't stay here."

Michelle dug her head deeper into the mud. "Just let me sleep."

Laney called through the curtain of rain. "The main road's just two more turns!" Hadel could hardly see her. Ann was sitting on a shelf of the bank some twenty feet ahead, her body bowed forward by the weight of her pack. Apparently she'd been too exhausted to shrug it off.

"Two more turns," Hadel encouraged Michelle. "Come on, that's nothing. It'll be dry in the car. We can turn on the heater."

The promise of heat lured Michelle from the mud. They lurched forward, Hadel carrying Michelle's pack in her arms. Once on the main road, they turned north and found the car in ten minutes. Just as they thankfully yanked open the doors, a huge wind sprang up, whipping their hair and their packs, then cracking an overhanging limb too heavy with water to resist. Hadel stifled a cry as they all fought to get in the car at once. The limb seemed to take a long time to fall, the wind rocking it back and forth as the wood splintered with tortured shrieks. Hadel had just gotten the car started and was reaching for the emergency brake when the branch plummeted down on the hood.

"Smash," Laney said from the backseat after the car stopped reverberating. Hadel got out and pulled off the branch. It didn't seem to have done much damage. When she climbed into the car, Laney was talking about her next role.

"I think I'll be a rock star," she said. "A feminist rock star."

"That's great!" Michelle said. She had recovered from her terminal fatigue. "Did you just think of that?"

"Oh, no. I know what the next one will be before the old one is over."

Hadel turned around and looked at Laney. Her face was coated with drying mud, her corn-silk hair matted and tangled, her jeans ripped at the knees. A feminist rock star. Well, why not?

"I don't know, Laney," Ann said mildly. "I would think many women with real talent would like to be feminist rock stars, and very few of them make it. You can't play any instruments, and we both know you can't sing."

Michelle rolled her eyes to the ceiling, as if these were mere technicalities to a genius like Laney Villano, whose canvases encompassed all of society, whose brights were the fortitude and self-searching of women everywhere, whose darks were the stunted lives of more than half the population of the planet.

"Oh, but I can sing," Laney said, revealing that she was more practical than Michelle. She proceeded to prove this assertion, using a song Hadel considered markedly appropriate, Janis Joplin's "Trust in Me." Her delivery had none of Joplin's rasp. Laney pleaded for more time in a voice reminiscent of Dusty Springfield but with an eerie, Yma Sumac quality on the higher notes. Laney stared directly at Ann as she sang of the toll her love exacted on each of them, and she begged Ann not to lose faith in her. Hadel could see Ann in the rearview mirror. Ann's mouth was open in a sort of horrified astonishment, as if she had leaned over to kiss a baby in its crib only to discover it had vampire teeth. Michelle's mouth was open in simple admiration. Hadel rolled her eyes upward à la Michelle and then shifted the car into gear and started home.

CHAPTER 19

Laney and Hadel often went to Gables on Tuesday evenings. Though listed in the gay guidebooks as a men's bar, it was usually mixed, particularly on Tuesday, which was unofficially designated "Ladies' Night." The bar had two large rooms, one in back with a "dancing" jukebox and the dance floor, and one in front with a "quiet" jukebox and old red leather chairs surrounding a gas fire in a circular brick structure that resembled a well. Just over the Oakland line on Telegraph Avenue, Gables had become a refuge for "hippie queers"—men with long hair and beards, women with long hair and patched jeans. The smell of dope was always strong in the back room, and the straight management checked people's jackets for contraband booze; a common trick was to hide a quart of cheap beer under the table, order one fifty-cent draft and replenish it from the quart before the waiter made his rounds. As was true of nearly every establishment that catered to those in their twenties in Berkeley and North Oakland, flyers were plastered everywhere: inside on the walls, outside on the telephone pole and the trash barrel. At Gables the posters had a gay slant—the Gay Students' Union at Cal was hosting a dance, the Women's Refuge needed money, volunteers who wanted to help with the gay parade should contact the Parade Committee. Hadel had once asked her mother's hairdresser if he wanted to come with her to a gay liberation dance. He shook his head vigorously. "Unh, unh! Those people are *weird*!" For similar reasons, he avoided Gables.

Once Hadel and Laney had gotten their beers, they wandered into the back room, where a mix of men and women were dancing to Stevie Wonder. "Too noisy," Hadel complained. It was only two days after the camping trip, and the sight of people leaping up and down to pounding music while clothed in a gray haze of choking dope fumes was more than she could stand. They returned to the fireplace and the leather chairs. "Did you hear the tape?" Laney asked. A local radio station had found a tape from the SLA in the morning's mail. It contained a diatribe against the Hearsts, a brief message from Patty and a written demand for "a good-faith gesture"—seventy dollars' worth of food for every Californian. It ended with the SLA's sign-off: "Death to the fascist insect that preys upon the life of the people."

"I heard it," Hadel said flatly. She and Michelle had already argued about it, Michelle contending that the food request proved the SLA were "good guys," Hadel saying that a group that had killed Marcus Foster and taken potshots at curious neighbors during the kidnapping didn't qualify for Robin Hood status. As she sipped her beer, she realized how depressed she was. The camping trip had not worked—not at its most optimistic level, of changing their relationship, nor at its least, of relaxing Michelle. Michelle acted as if she'd forgotten the whole trip, except for Laney's announcement of her next role. Michelle had mentioned Laney's coming splash into the music world several times in her mad rush from school to the Women's Law Project to home to school again.

"How will you go about becoming a feminist rock star?" Hadel asked, anxious to abandon the subject of the tapes. Whenever she described her reaction to a political event, Laney always asked what Michelle had thought. Laney would listen to their inevitable difference of opinion, nodding gravely, staring at Hadel all the while, as if she expected Hadel to glimpse some great truth. Hadel suspected Laney didn't like Michelle, though she'd never said so. But the suspicion upset Hadel; Michelle so championed Laney it seemed cruel of Laney not to like her.

"Find a band," Laney said. "Bands advertise in the classified section of the newspaper."

"Oh." Hadel was disappointed. She'd expected something less pedestrian.

They noticed a collegiate-looking young man showing something to two women at the bar. They shook their heads, and the man retreated. He scanned faces around the room, and his eyes lighted when he caught sight of Laney and Hadel. He started toward them. "We look like soft touches," Laney said.

"I hate to bother you," he said, sitting on the brick fireplace in front of them. "I'm trying to find my sister. She came out to our parents' over Christmas, and they threw a fit. A horrible fit. My sister left. Now they feel bad, and they sent me out to Berkeley to find her. I went to her old address, but she's moved, and no one there knew her."

Hadel and Laney nodded sympathetically. Civil wars were common these days as gay newspapers trumpeted at everyone to "come out"—on the job, with friends and above all, with relatives. The papers provided hints on how to approach the ticklish subject: "Don't beat around the bush. Don't be defensive. Encourage them to discuss their stereotypes of gays and then describe your own life. Be sure you let them know you love them." Despite the most careful handling, however, many parents responded with either fury or grief. The reasons for coming out were obvious—remaining hidden encouraged the stereotypes (Hadel had heard people at parties state they'd never met a homosexual in their lives, when half the partygoers listening to them were gay), and it also put an intolerable burden of alienation on anyone who tried, day after day, to live a lie. But the majority of homosexuals still clung to her mother's hairdresser's view: "Why should I tell my parents? They're in their late sixties. They wouldn't understand, and they don't *want* to know. Why throw it in their faces?"

The man in front of the fireplace dug in his jacket pocket for a photograph of his missing sister. Hadel and Laney glanced at each other. If he were telling the truth, it would be nice to help him, but it was also an unspoken law that you kept your mouth shut when faced with a straight person asking questions about a gay person. He passed over the picture. They leaned forward in the firelight and looked at the woman, who was pretty, with a long, slender face and a wide smile. "Her name's Pat," he explained. "Patricia, but she's been calling herself Mizmoon."

"Sorry," Hadel said, handing it back. Neither recognized the picture or the name. The man put it back in his pocket. "I'll be around awhile," he said. "If you run into her, or anyone who knows her, you can call me at the Shattuck Hotel, under Robert Soltysik. O.K.?"

They nodded, Hadel thinking he was a little too businesslike for someone looking for his sister. His eyes had already dismissed them, and he was scanning the room again.

"*You* look familiar," Laney said suddenly. He turned back, startled. Hadel nodded. She remembered the man's slight widow's peak and how the lines at the corners of his eyes and his rounded cheeks signaled two different ages. "You were at my house last fall," Laney told him.

He must have recognized them then too, for he jumped to his feet and walked quickly out of the bar. "He's nobody's brother," Laney said. "He's FBI, and I bet he's working on the Hearst kidnapping."

"Lesbians in the SLA?" No reason why not, Hadel supposed. One of the kidnappers was a woman.

"What'd he say his last name was?"

"I can't remember. Something with an 'S.'"

"The FBI keeps saying they don't know anything about the kidnappers, but Ann thinks they know a lot. Come on, we've got to go tell her about this Mizmoon person."

Ann scored a coup with the Mizmoon revelation, as did a fellow newswoman with her announcement that the leader of the SLA was escaped convict Donald DeFreeze. But more important, Ann was able to exact a form of revenge for the FBI's harassment over the years. During the following weeks she filmed several sequences of the FBI clumsily underfoot in the lesbian community. Their search for Mizmoon and her ex-lover Camilla Hall was similar to a crowd of drunken hunters alerting the deer for miles around. Viewers bored with the media camp-out on the Hearsts' lawn were amused by shots of signs hanging in the bathrooms of lesbian bars: "Camilla, I've got your camera. Leave message here so I can return it to you." Ann interviewed several blond women inches shorter and pounds lighter than Camilla Hall who had nonetheless been routed out of their homes and questioned extensively until they'd proven their identities. Ann managed to maintain her "good girl" image on her sojourns into the Bay Area's hidden world. Dressed as always in her good-taste layerings of wool and silk, she swept into communal apartments, bars and coffeehouses, approaching with grave dignity anyone who was willing to talk on camera. She seemed, Laney said, not to know where she was. Although the station received a few letters decrying the need to "send Ann Bailor into such places," far more were appreciative of the inside look at the FBI's hopeless attempts, and many pledged to write letters demanding a more intelligent and sensitive operation. "If their tactics with the Left are anything like what you've shown us tonight," one viewer wrote, "it's no wonder they haven't caught the underground fugitives yet. I pray for Patty, with her only hope such an inefficient force."

The FBI, of course, responded in their own way. Besides their personal grudge against Ann, they honestly seemed to think that finding Portia would help them find the SLA, as if every dissident were part of a countrywide conspiracy, carefully organized and coordinated. Agents dropped by every few days. Once they came when Hadel was sitting in the kitchen, listening to a talk show on the radio. She answered the door, the radio voices continuing behind her. The agents glanced at each other, shoved Hadel aside and bolted to the kitchen, one hanging back to cover the other, who raced in, his gun drawn, ready to confront the entire SLA, or at least half the Weather Underground. Hadel followed the point man in and laughed at his look of fury as he discovered all he had to arrest was the radio. That day they left without a question.

The FBI grated on Michelle's fragile nerves. So, it seemed, did everything else, including Hadel's refusal to join the food lines. The seventy-dollars-per-Californian demand for "a good-faith gesture" from the Hearsts had been negotiated down to a series of food handouts. The first three distributions had been inadequate, one ending in rioting in East Oakland. But apparently the fourth, near the end of March, had been worth going to. Everyone got a load of food in a huge carton, which was emblazoned with a sticker of the SLA's seven-headed cobra, courtesy of the Hearsts. "I haven't had time to stand in line," Hadel told Michelle. "It takes hours."

"You're not making any money from your stories," Michelle said. "You might as well do something constructive if you're so determined to be downwardly mobile."

"I *am* making money," Hadel insisted. "I'm actually earning enough to live on." This was almost true. They ate a lot of beans and rice and oatmeal, and the rent was always a struggle to gather together. Hadel had, in fact, secretly asked Natalie to visit the New York offices of *Boy's Adventure,* a magazine that paid twice as much as *Boys' World.* Hadel had written twice to *Boy's Adventure*'s editor, but he had not, so far, answered either of her letters. She was keeping it a secret from Michelle because if Michelle had any inkling that Hadel, too, was dissatisfied with her income, all hell would break loose. Michelle was already reading her the ads for copywriters from the classifieds every Sunday.

Michelle's dark eyebrows etched V's of frustration across her moonstone forehead. "The point is you should be making pots of money. You went to Ridgedale. You have advantages. You speak and write the ruler's tongue."

"The ruler's tongue? You went to Radcliffe."

"Exactly. And I'm using my advantages for the good of the movement. The money I make will be funneled right back to women who don't have the class break I have. Look at Patty Hearst, Hadel. Two days ago she announced she was joining the revolutionary cause of her captors. *Patty Hearst* is a million times more politically conscious than you are."

"But isn't that contradictory? She already has pots of money. Shouldn't she be sucking up to her parents, pretending to be a good little Hearst, so everything she gets from them can be shoveled into the revolution? That's what Rita Mae Brown thinks every child of upper- and upper-middle-class parents should be doing." Hadel paused briefly so she could assume a disgusted look at the mere mention of Rita Mae Brown, but this satisfying exercise of contempt had to be cut short because Michelle was opening her mouth. "Anyway," Hadel continued quickly, "I would be miserable making pots of money. I don't see how my being miserable aids a movement that is supposed to free me to be myself."

"Even when you wish to be male-identified? Look at what you've done, Hadel. First it was pornography, and now it's these stupid boys' stories with all their male values of courage and bravery!"

"Michelle, I am willing to fight for every woman's right to be who she chooses. I will fight for women's rights to be childless. I'll fight for child-care in industry so women can work, and I'll picket to open up jobs closed to women. I will lay my life down for any woman assaulted by a man. What I will not do is allow guilt to eliminate my own right to choose. That's just exchanging one tyranny for another." Hadel thought it was a stirring speech, but Michelle's only comment was her eyebrows shooting clear up to the top of her forehead. Then she spun around and left the room.

They didn't speak for several days, during which Hadel alternately shook off and stoked up a load of resentment. She was furious at herself for doing nearly four years of laundry, cooking, shopping and much of the bill-paying just so Michelle could make her big sacrifice to the movement and be self-righteous about it besides. When the FBI came again, the fight boiled over.

"I don't have a clue," Hadel told the agent. She shut the front door and went into the kitchen, where she began cutting up a chicken. Michelle hung around the stove, watching. "That's the third time this month," she said. "I really can't stand this much longer."

"There's nothing to stand," Hadel said, angry that Michelle's first remark in days had been a complaint. And not just a general-malaise complaint, either, but a grievance—Michelle had, after all, never even met Portia, and yet the FBI was forever at Michelle's door.

"They've started going through the garbage. Mrs. Nicasio saw them out her window."

Hadel shrugged.

"In case you've forgotten, I'm taking the bar exam in six months. The bar!"

"Michelle, what can I do about it? Beg them not to come here? I can't control them." Hadel began dipping the pieces of chicken in melted butter and then rolling them in crumbs and parmesan cheese. She had just gotten a check from *Boys' World* and had hoped a good dinner might cool the tension between them. It might even have worked, she thought, if the dumb FBI hadn't picked today to come. But what was the use? What was she trying so hard to save? All this smoothing things over was beginning to resemble darning a nonexistent sock.

"I can't take it, Hadel. I'm serious."

"What can't you take? Us or the FBI? I don't think you give a shit about them." Hadel's ears were ringing while she arranged the chicken in a baking pan and brushed by Michelle to get to the stove. "Dinner will be ready in an hour."

Michelle's face had gone death-white. When Hadel surged past with her baking pan, the blood flowed back into Michelle's lips, and she screamed: "Eat it yourself!" Before the chicken was out of the oven, Michelle was out of the house, taking two suitcases and all of her law books.

During one of the law book trips, when Hadel finally understood Michelle was leaving, she stopped her in the hall. "But where will you go?" she asked, her voice miserable and frightened.

"To the Refuge. That's what it's for, you know."

"But—"

"Move, Hadel! This is heavy!"

Hadel stepped out of the way, and Michelle clattered down the front steps with a grocery store bag full of books. Hadel could see from the porch that Michelle had already packed a lot in her old car. "Michelle—" she started as Michelle came back up the stairs.

Michelle shook her head. "I don't want to talk to you."

Hadel watched her disappear down the hall to the bedroom. Hadel knew this wasn't supposed to be happening. When people had fights, they didn't leave each other. Her parents would have fights and threaten separation and divorce, but no one actually left. Or even if one of them did storm out of the house, it was only to walk around the block a few times to calm down. Michelle came back down the hall with another bag of books. "This isn't right," Hadel said.

Michelle leaned against the porch rail, balancing her bag on her knee. "The idea of you telling anyone what's right or wrong is too ludicrous for words. I already said I didn't want to talk. If you continue to bother me, I'll call for a police escort."

Boggled, Hadel stared at her.

"I mean it. Don't try to start anything."

"Start anything?" Hadel shouted. "You're stopping everything!"

"And you're making a scene." Michelle went down the steps with her bag.

Hadel was shaking too much to stay on the porch. Retreating to the backyard, she followed the path of redwood chips until she stood under the tree she'd planted the first month she'd moved into her house. She wrapped her arms around the trunk, holding on tight. The bark was starting to roughen with age. It felt good against her cheek. The tree's roots anchored her to solid ground. She didn't go back inside until she heard the timer on the stove buzz. The chicken was ready, but the house was empty and silent. Hadel was looking at the chicken in its pan when the doorbell rang. Michelle had come back. She had reconsidered. They would work it out. She rushed to the door and opened it to a smiling Laney, who asked if she wanted to go to a movie.

Hadel returned to the kitchen and sat down in front of the chicken. Laney leaned over, stabbed a piece with a fork and began nibbling at the chicken, dangling it above a napkin. "This is delicious," she said. "What's wrong with you? Where's Michelle?"

Hadel didn't answer for a moment. Then she said, "She's left."

"Left? For where?"

"Left me. This moment, right before you came."

"Really?" Laney yelped with delight. "That's marvelous! You two were never meant to be together."

Hadel didn't look up from her contemplation of the chicken.

"Come on, Hadel," Laney scolded. "You can't possibly think everything was hunky-dory."

"No, I don't think that. I've been miserable. I kept hoping when she got out of school . . ." She sighed. "We had a lot of disagreements. She didn't like—"

"She didn't like anything about you except the fact that you took care of her. Who needs it? You should be rejoicing!"

"Rejoicing about what? Chucking out four years of trying to make it work? That's a long time."

"It sure is. Would you rather waste two or three more years? Face it, Hadel, your intentions were great, but you picked the wrong person."

Hadel was tired of hearing about her mistakes. "I think I want to be alone."

"Sure, fine," Laney said, snagging another piece of chicken and marching off with it triumphantly. "You really oughta eat some of this, Hadel," she hollered from the doorway. "It does wonders for your peace of mind."

Natalie called Hadel on a Tuesday, a month after Michelle left. She sounded terrible, choked up and hoarse. "Are you sick?" Hadel asked. Silence. Then Natalie began crying. Hadel paced around the living room, the receiver tucked between her jaw and her shoulder. Hadel hated it when people cried on the phone. There were no bodies to hug, no hands to hold, no Kleenexes to fetch. It was infuriating. "Do you have any money?" she asked suddenly.

This question startled Natalie so much she began hiccuping instead of sobbing. "Why?" she managed.

"Because I don't have any money or I'd come back there. If you have some money, why don't you fly out?"

"Oh. Oh . . . just a minute." When Natalie returned to the phone, her hiccups had been squelched, but the tune remained the same. "Oh, Hadel. Oh, I don't know. I'd have to be back on Friday or Saturday, at least. . . . All right. I'll do it. I should call you back."

"No. Just take American's night flight. I'll come down and meet you."

The terminal was quiet except for the Hare Krishnas banging their tambourines and chanting. Hadel stalked impatiently as the plane taxied up to the gate. Natalie was first off the ramp. She had changed in three years. Her hair was longer, more disheveled, and lines of strain had begun to crisscross the skin around her eyes. Her cheeks were flushed, however, which at least gave the illusion of good cheer. "You look wonderful," Hadel told her, wishing it were true.

"So do you." Hadel knew it wasn't true, either. Her face had seemed bruised and tired in the harsh light of the airport's bathroom.

"I thought we were going to land in the water," Natalie bubbled. "They let me fly standby, and then they put me in first class. I had champagne all the way!"

Hadel smiled. That explained the pink cheeks. She led Natalie to the car, and an hour later they were sitting in Hadel's living room, sipping tall glasses of orange juice. "I'm really sorry about Michelle," Natalie said. She had turned the tables on Hadel's questions, refusing to say anything about herself until she heard all about Hadel's breakup with Michelle.

"There's a way I can't help but feel a sort of relief," Hadel said slowly. "I know that's wrong—"

Natalie was shaking her head hard enough to stop Hadel's tentative words. "It's not wrong. She must have been an incredibly difficult person to live with. I don't know how you did it this long."

"Still." Hadel rubbed her forehead. "Tell me what's going on with you."

"A duplicate story, except that I was the one to actually move my crap out of what is now Harrison's apartment."

"Oh, Natalie. What a rotten bummer."

"I don't care," Natalie said. She lit a cigarette with shaking fingers.

"What happened?"

"It started over Christmas. I went to Pennsylvania and he stayed in New York. When I got back, he was furious at his parents." Natalie paused to puff violently at her cigarette, raising clouds of blue smoke. "His parents told him it was time to think about marriage. The old fogies at his law firm had a chat with Harrison's father, all very old-boy-drop-a-hint at the club. Surely Harrison wasn't planning to shack up forever!"

"You didn't want to get married," Hadel concluded.

Natalie had just swallowed a gulp of orange juice so all she could do was wave off this theory with her free hand while she hummed "Um-um" through tightly pressed lips. "No," she said a moment later. "It was clear to everyone involved that I was not an appropriate candidate."

"Huh?"

"Being a member of the Chosen People." Natalie waited for comprehension to dawn. When it didn't, she said, "Being Jewish, dummy. Harrison was supposed to stop wasting time with me and get on with the buzz-buzz-buzz world of WASPdom."

Hadel had rarely been rendered speechless. She was now.

Natalie watched the shock give way to horror and disbelief. "Are you serious?"

Natalie nodded, stabbing out her cigarette.

"My God," Hadel breathed.

"Precisely 'my God.' Anyway—"

"Hold it," Hadel interrupted. "His parents actually said these things to him? Had they met you? They must have in five years. Did they act like that with you?"

"Oh, no. They were endlessly cordial. His mother loved to talk to me about sewing. We used to go pattern-hunting together."

"Sewing!"

"There's a lot about me you don't know anymore, Hadel. But the point is Harrison was outraged. He ranted and raved and refused to answer their calls until I was put in the ridiculous position of mediating. It was awful, Hadel."

Hadel nodded at how awful. She waited for more.

"Then he asked me if maybe I couldn't rest on my laurels. I'm still getting checks for the Kent State film. They dust it off every May and college classes rent it. The women's films didn't go over so hot. They're shown occasionally, but they never made it past the coffeehouse stage."

Hadel wiggled her fingers to signify they were getting off the track.

"No, no," Natalie said. "This all has a purpose. Harrison was pissed off because I was sending résumés to ad agencies."

"Advertising?"

"Uhm-hmmm. He said he was making enough money for both of us, so why couldn't I stay home and clean the apartment or something?"

A horrible suspicion was forming in Hadel's mind. "Natalie," she began, her voice ominous.

"Wait!" Natalie insisted, holding up her hand as if she were directing traffic. "Let me tell you. He started criticizing the way I dress. If we went out, couldn't I do more than throw on a skirt? Listen, I thought that was a big concession. After a month or two of this, I realized he was searching for reasons to break up with me. If he couldn't bear to obey his parents, he'd work it around to where he was making his own decision, which just happened to be the same thing they'd asked him to do. When I figured it out, I confronted him with it."

"What'd he say?"

Hadel had been intrigued by the drama, but Harrison's answer killed the illusion that the story might have a happy ending. "He told me I was right," Natalie said softly. "He said he wasn't cut out to be a rebel. He thought we should split up before he hurt me more."

"That low-life piece of shit," Hadel hissed. She wanted to rip him to shreds with her bare hands.

Natalie's eyes brimmed with tears. "He just couldn't deal with it. My Greek athlete."

Natalie stayed for three days. It was a break for both of them, a time of long walks and talking endlessly. They had a lot to talk about. In the midst of her disaster with Harrison, Natalie had found time to visit the offices of *Boy's Adventure,* the magazine that paid twice as much as *Boys' World.* "It's no wonder they didn't answer your letters," Natalie said. "They don't accept unagented material until 'you establish a working relationship' with the editor."

"I have to get an agent?" Hadel groaned.

"I argued my way past the receptionist," Natalie continued, ignoring Hadel's lament. "I saw the editor's assistant. She said she didn't know any agents who were taking on new authors, especially for short fiction."

"For God's sake—"

"However, I persevered. I showed her *Boys' World.* I told her you lived in California, so you couldn't be haunting agents' doors day and night. She finally agreed to look at a couple of stories, and if she liked them, she'd pass them on to the editor. I was still getting the runaround, but a contact's been made."

"Well—"

"Except I'm going to hand-carry those stories in personally. Mailing them is hopeless. The moment I'm back, I'll storm in there like a starving tiger. That assistant will think you're the Messiah of adventure writing. And at least I'll know that the stories got to her, if not to the big muckety-muck himself."

"Oh, I don't want you to have to do all that garbage!"

"It's the only way, Hadel. Honestly. Either that or forget *Boy's*

Adventure. They don't open their mail unless it's got an agent's return address."

Hadel nodded. She hated people to do favors for her, but she didn't see any way around it. "All right," she agreed. "But now I want to hear about this advertising job you're starting Monday. I can't believe it."

"Neither can I. When they called me in for an interview, I was horrified. It was right before I moved, too. I was packing stuff. . . ." Natalie stopped to watch a bearded man deal out a tarot spread on a battered card table. They were strolling along Telegraph Avenue, dipping into a head shop or a record store occasionally. The question must have been a personal one, because the young woman receiving the reading flung her hands over the laid-out cards, meanwhile shooting a zap look at Natalie over her shoulder.

"Pardon me," Natalie said, grinning. The two moved on toward the campus and its creek and towering trees.

"Let me backtrack a minute," Natalie said when they'd reached Sproul Plaza and began edging through the noontime crowd. "Remember when I showed the Kent State film up here, and you said you were jealous? I knew what you meant, but I didn't know how to answer you. You thought I was a big success. Well, now I'm a bigger failure. Dead at age twenty-five. You know how much I lost on my two women's films? The money doesn't matter; I had grants for most of it anyway. It's more my self-esteem. I don't feel I can be successful anymore. And the grant money's dried up." Natalie laughed soundlessly. "Now I'm jealous of you."

Hadel waited to respond until they'd sunk down on a bench by the creek. "You're jealous of me because I haven't done anything? That doesn't make sense."

"You *have* done stuff. You've been plugging away at your stories, and you've built yourself a foundation, while I, on the other hand, already had my day in the sun. I found out you can't succeed at something once. It won't work, not for me or for anyone—well, *judging* me. A success four years ago means I'm a has-been. Once you do it, you've got to do it again and again, an endless treadmill of successes. I'm serious, Hadel. Two months ago I felt like blowing my head off so I wouldn't have to look at myself anymore."

"But don't you think this has a lot to do with Harrison?" Hadel argued. "A sort of watercolor wash of depression over your whole life?"

"No. I admit, Harrison hasn't helped. But this has been building for a long time."

They were silent for a while, watching the water flow across the brown and red stones that lined the creekbed. "So what will you do on your new job?" Hadel asked finally.

Natalie shrugged. "Who knows? Ads about soaps and deodorants, I guess. One thing good—they already told me they're sending me out here for a convention next June. A convention of brainstormers. They described my job as providing 'creative input' for advertising that will appeal to our generation. Isn't that a gas?"

Hadel made a face. "I don't know, sweetie. I can't understand why this film business is so ego-threatening. You made the Kent State movie because you were furious. Politics was the motivator. It isn't as if film is the be-all and end-all of your life."

"As writing is for you? That's true in a way. But I need *something*. I need a challenge, a jungle gym to climb. Advertising is the most cutthroat game in town."

Hadel started. "Cutthroat? Yes. That's what I don't get. Throwing kidney punches on Madison Avenue is a helluva jump from making feminist films. You could join a juice bar collective instead."

The tense muscles in Natalie's face let loose as she laughed. Hadel thought the sound of it was delightful over the rushing of the creek. "I knew you wouldn't be satisfied with the palatable explanation." Natalie rapped herself across the knuckles. "I can't help being power-mad, I've been that way all my life. You were so odd to me back in school. You never cared about the power. I couldn't even give up the school version, what with serving on the alumnae board."

"So the success-failure syndrome is only—"

"Partially correct," Natalie finished for her. "Unfortunately, I seem to need the kidney punching. I'm not happy being just a wonderful, noncompetitive feminist. That's the part I was afraid to tell you."

"Natalie, you're not going to shock *me*. Old porno-writer, war novel-reader Hadel? Michelle couldn't turn around without accusing me of condoning the patriarchy. Damn! There really are times I'm glad she's gone."

"I bet," Natalie said, poking Hadel in the ribs. "C'mon, let's do something really decadent. Let's go see a movie in the middle of the day."

"And not come out until it's dark? And litter with impunity? Natalie, next I hear you'll be moving to Los Angeles."

"Oh, no," Natalie vowed. "Not that."

The night Natalie left, they ate dinner in front of the television news. They settled down with their food in time to watch a cop scream through a bullhorn. Men with semiautomatics were crisscrossing in front and to the side of a dumpy stucco bungalow. Helicopters swept overhead, billowing the clothes of those who prepared for the fight below. Hadel set her plate on the floor. "What the hell?"

"They've found the SLA," Natalie said.

The reporter told them the police had been massing for hours at a staging area several blocks from the yellow building in Watts. Five hundred "crowd control" police backed up three eight-man SWAT teams. After the man with the bullhorn stopped yelling, tear-gas grenades were lobbed into the house, and the SWAT members began shooting. They didn't stop for an hour, one man ducking back to reload as another took his place.

"Do you suppose they're televising this all over the country?" Natalie asked. The food congealed on the plates as they watched. "It's a mock fire fight," she continued. "War games with live targets." Later: "Why didn't they try to talk to them?"

Hadel said nothing, her face growing more masklike as round after round slammed into the house. Finally the tear-gas grenades started a fire. By seven o'clock it was over. The house had burned to the ground, and everyone inside was dead.

Hadel turned off the TV and carried the dishes into the kitchen. She didn't want to listen to the reporters guessing who had perished in the fire. It was enough that anyone had. She covered the full plates with aluminum foil and stuck them in the refrigerator. When she came back to the living room, Natalie was crying. "I can't stand this shit," she said. "Why didn't they let them surrender? They were sitting ducks. Five or six people against a whole arsenal manned by hundreds of cops."

"First they kill off all our leaders," Hadel said. "Then they beat us. Then they kill us."

"What?"

"I thought about that after People's Park and Kent State. King and the Kennedys are assassinated, and people are beaten in Chicago and trampled by horses in Washington and busted on the head in New York. And then they started killing people, just opened up and shot them."

"Yes, that's how it's gone, hasn't it? So what's next? They round us all up and stick us in concentration camps? Kill off everyone you don't like every thirty-odd years? I'm so angry! They've killed hope, don't they see? We're turning into a police state, and I'm going into advertising! I don't understand it, any of it." She wrapped her arms around her knees and drew them up to her chest. They sat in silence until it was time to leave for the airport.

At the gate, Natalie hugged her quickly. Her eyes were still red. "Maybe things will get better," she said unconvincingly. "Maybe by the time I come back for the convention, we'll both be in love."

Hadel wasn't about to abandon her funk for something as ephemeral as love. Who needed it?

CHAPTER 20

The Berkeley-Oakland area was a Disneyland of delights for an "Architectural Styles" walking tour. Even those who wished to confine their exercise to a minimum were rewarded, since it was possible to find Victorians of several vintages (tall and slender Italianates, rambling Queen Annes and the more demure Queen Anne cottages), brown shingles, neoclassic rowhouses, stuccos and even contemporaries clustered within a single block. In Ann's West Berkeley neighborhood, the Victorians ruled, many of them edging into stately disintegration. Though the modified Italianate Ann purchased in 1972 towered a narrow upstairs over its immediate cottage neighbors, providing Ann with a study, most appealing had been two other features: a glassed-in back porch and a large yard bathed in afternoon sunlight. Laney ignored these gardening enticements during her "acclimatization period" and was engaged in her businesswoman role during most of the spring and summer of 1973. This year had, at least, started out differently. Laney spent much of January poring over seed catalogs and drawing scale maps of the backyard, complete with seeds to be sowed per square foot and harvest dates. The seed orders arrived in March, and Laney quickly converted the unused back porch to a greenhouse packed with flats full of seedlings and bags of planting mix, bought during a February "Get a Head Start" sale. As late as early May, Ann loved to step from the kitchen to the porch, where the smells of dirt and green shoots erased the heady excitement and the burden of being one of the Bay Area's known television personalities. Ann could be herself on the back porch—plain Ann Bailor, a mite rigid, a tad conventional, but very solid. That she felt more stable on Laney's back porch than in her own study worried her occasionally, but she consoled herself with rationalizations; lovers were supposed to create a space of serenity for their mates. Hadn't she done the same for Laney in their early years? Although Laney had apparently outstripped her need to be "attached" to Ann, Ann still prided herself on supplying affection, good food and a pleasant house for her wayward lover.

Worries about the source of her serenity, however, were several weeks in the past. Ann now avoided the back porch as if it were about to rise up and engulf her. Which wasn't, Ann thought, far wrong. Laney was getting that in-another-world look in her eyes. She had begun disappearing three nights a week, Tuesdays, Thursdays, and Fridays. Two weeks ago she had chopped her lovely corn-silk hair down to a crew cut. It was then that Ann understood the seedlings' true nature: the ultimate guilt-inducers, they would fold up and die the moment Laney left for her life as a feminist rock star. "What am I supposed to do with all of these?" Ann asked peevishly on the last day of May, waving at the deceptively green stalks.

"Tomorrow we plant," Laney said, walking into the living room while Ann followed. "Saturday, Sunday and then I'll continue until it's done." She settled down in a rocker Ann had picked up at a garage sale and opened a book she'd bought on Telegraph Avenue, a guide to growing sensemilla, the seedless super dope, famous for its resinous buds studded with tiny brown hairs.

Ann collapsed on the couch, sighing. This timetable suggested that Laney would leave before the next weekend. "But don't you want to enjoy them once they're in the ground? Harvest the vegetables?" Ann translated these querulous questions to herself: she was angry Laney was leaving, and she wanted a clue as to when Laney planned to return. Ann got what she expected: no answer. Laney didn't even look up from her book. But she did say, a few minutes later, "It's easy. All you have to do is water."

Ann had heard that one before. The first spring, after the painters and the floor refinishers had left, Ann had contemplated the jungle of weeds in the front yard, got nowhere mentioning it to Laney and finally hired a woman who promised a nearly self-sustaining garden system for $150. The woman arrived on a Monday, rototilled the ground, waited a week and then rototilled again, killing, she said, any burgeoning weed seeds. She then planted ground cover and annuals ("No mowing," she told a grateful Ann) and even sunk posts into the earth, strategically placed to protect the plants from trailing hoses. "All you have to do is water," the woman said as Ann handed her a check.

What the woman and Ann hadn't counted on was Ann's inexperience with California summers. Though days were often overcast, foggy and even quite chilly, rain didn't fall for months at a time. Used to summer showers, Ann hadn't known she should water every second or third day. Each morning on her way to work, she would stare disconsolately at the yard, thinking that today, surely, an afternoon rain would perk up the drying leaves, the drooping stems. Turning on a tap was wasteful when the sky above would release its load of cleansing rain. By mid-August, when Laney was tennis-bumming from tournament to tournament, the ground cover was patchy and brown, the annuals withered. On weekends Ann would stand outside, spraying the top layer of soil with a mist of water. Why, then, did the plants look so terrible by Wednesday? The sky finally broke its pattern of sun and overcast in October, but the damage was done. The yard had looked better as a jungle than a desert. "Great going," Laney commented when she surfaced from her sports career.

Ann hadn't answered. She still had nightmares of plants dying of thirst while the hose tap dripped maddeningly five feet away. "You remember what happened last time someone told me all I have to do is water?" she now snapped, irritated that Laney would dare to resurrect this ugly memory.

Unruffled, Laney turned a page of her book. "Now you know," she said. "Watering becomes a habit."

"Like mowing the lawn," Ann replied hotly. Laney had solved the front-yard disaster by plowing under the on-its-last-legs ground cover and replacing it with a winter lawn. Laney usually took care of its monthly shave, but now Ann would be stuck with that task, too.

Laney didn't rise to the bait. She stretched, yawning. "Big day tomorrow," she said, and went off to bed.

* * *

By Tuesday, all the flats had been emptied and stacked neatly under the shelves. A brave new world of gently waving seedlings was putting down roots in the groomed soil of the backyard. Laney then turned her attention to the house, piling rugs, curtains and bedding in the supermarket cart she'd borrowed from the family across the street. While everything was washing and drying at the corner laundromat, Laney scrubbed woodwork and vacuumed. The next day she paid bills and answered correspondence while the street mechanic she'd hired tuned up the car. Friday found her in the backyard again, this time planting corn and bean seeds. She had waited until the last day for the seed part of the operation: the earth had to be as warm as possible. She was mounding soil for the last hill of beans when a dark shadow fell across her hands. She glanced up and fell backward against the hill she'd just planted.

Portia hauled Laney to her feet. "You cut your hair!" Portia accused, throwing her arms around Laney. They held each other tight, reluctant to let go. "I wasn't even sure it was you," Portia said. "But then you made a little motion with your hand, and it was so familiar. . . . It's wonderful to see you!"

"You look almost the same," Laney said, standing away from her. "I expected—"

"You wouldn't have recognized me the first six months. Gray-streaked hair, pancake makeup and dark circles. The circles were real. When I moved to New Mexico after seeing Ann, I threw away the wig. I couldn't stand it anymore."

"Seeing *Ann*?"

Portia laughed, her brown eyes twinkling. "We met in Connecticut after you'd supposedly died. I knew you were alive when I got the five hundred dollars you sent me. How'd the FBI take the news of your resurrection?"

Laney didn't answer for a minute. Portia in the garden and Ann hiding the Connecticut meeting all this time were too much to comprehend at once. "They kept insisting my 'death' had a connection to your being underground," she said finally. "Ann and I talked to them over and over. . . . In the end they couldn't do anything. There was no insurance money involved."

"What about your parents?"

"Oh, I was writing to them all along." Laney smiled. "Parents receive special consideration. But how did you know where to find me?"

Portia laughed again, her elfin face mischievous. "Well, I knew from the money business that you were in Berkeley. You mean your address? Easy as pie. You're in the book. What an amazing luxury to be listed in the telephone book."

Laney was struck by the pain behind the laughter. "It's been terrible, hasn't it?"

"Yes. Boring, awful, petty and frightening. Deadly to my career, besides. The theaters never know where to call."

"And it's made you bitter."

Portia exhaled, feeling she was letting out the breath she'd been holding during her three years underground. Even seeing her mother hadn't given her this much relief, this solace of being with someone who knew who she was and who she had been. "There's been good and bad," she said. "There have been things that are hard to accept. And yes, you're right. It's made me bitter."

"Come in," Laney invited, reaching for Portia's elbow. "I'll give you tea and anything else you want. You tell me how it's been."

Sometimes she wanted to scream at people, "I'm Portia Bethany!" She understood why murderers left clues to their crimes. They didn't unconsciously want to be stopped; they wanted to sign their names to their work. Portia had first encountered this need for self-recognition when she was eleven, living in a small midwestern farming town. Religious values were hammered into the citizens relentlessly, perhaps because of the town's proximity to the godless army base at which Portia's father was stationed. Portia and Toni, as the major's daughters and representatives, were bundled off to Sunday school each week. The teacher impressed upon them the necessity of paying into a spiritual insurance policy; as children, their currency could be good deeds. They were supposed to perform a good deed every day, but it didn't count unless it was done in strict secrecy, with not even the recipient of the kindness knowing the author. Portia found this homework well-nigh impossible. She wanted acknowledgment of her acts, good or bad. She saw no reason, also, why good works had to be secret while bad ones were supposed to be announced and apologized for and wailed over. Her attempt to explain this to the teacher resulted in both daughters being banished from Sunday school, Toni's first experience at being tarred with the brush meant for her sister. Portia was sent to her room in disgrace, and while she sat looking out her window at acres of heavy-headed wheat, she concluded that nothing was more important to a person than his or her own identity.

This belief, several years later in Texas, led her into political protest: she could not bear to see people's lives squashed by an uncaring government agency or private corporation. Later, during the Vietnam conflict, U.S. military might had sought to prevent an entire nation from defining itself. Portia's attempts at rectifying that injustice had paradoxically returned her to what had been asked of her when she was a child: performing secret acts. She doubted, of course, that either her Sunday school teacher or the U.S. government would agree with her contemporary definition of "good deeds."

So she had, in a sense, traveled full circle back to that little farming town, and during the journey she had lost the chance ever to sign her works again. She suspected that if she were a different person, less concerned with self-definition, living underground would be less onerous. She could accept her other identity, make new friends, begin another life. But being Portia hiding was her only way of still being Portia, no matter how lonely and miserable she was clinging to herself.

The day after she met Ann in Kennerly, Portia left Vermont and moved to New Mexico. She worked as a waitress in a small-town cafe and rented a shack in the back field of an elderly couple who regaled her with their health problems when they came to collect the weekly rent. About once every two months she met with Dooley, her contact.

When she first spotted him at the town park, she looked past him, searching for someone closer to her image. He was *too* innocuous, with his wide-open face and his springy, red-blond hair. He reminded her of a million other young men just out of college: moderately intelligent, somewhat serious, but cheerful above all.

"Hey," he said.

She thought he was trying to pick her up. "Sorry," she told him. "I'm waiting for my boyfriend."

"You'd do better waiting for the devil," he said. "I'm Dooley, by the way, so you can stop pretending I'm not talking to you. Your boyfriend is making things difficult. He's led the FBI to every one of your friends' places, and they're being questioned. He didn't do it purposely," he amended, seeing she was about to leap to Charley's defense, "but he's made a helluva lot of people very nervous."

Poor Charley, Portia thought. She might have been able to call him by now if he'd accepted the situation calmly. But calmness was far too much to expect. Four months ago he had discovered, probably via the morning paper, that she was a fugitive. She remembered how insecure and hurt she had felt when he'd hidden from her his dream of becoming an architect. She gritted her teeth. If only I had told him everything right from the beginning!

"He's set up a message phone," Dooley went on. "It's tapped. His own phone's tapped, and so are all your friends' phones. So you're on your own."

She had known that already. She was furious at him for rubbing it in.

"I was told to watch for someone with graying hair," he said, watching her eyes shut him out. "Your own hair being longer isn't much of a disguise. But you're lucky having a lively face. People with animated faces never look like they do in a photograph."

If the old men a few benches down hadn't been watching, she would have kicked him in the shins. He was examining her as if she were the chief exhibit in a freak show. If she could do without her own face, with its weak chin and too-small mouth, she would consign it to the reject pile. She didn't like standing inspection for this clown. "I'll come every two months," he continued, "so I'll see you again in December. If you need help, call this number." He handed her a slip of paper. "Call from a phone booth and give two times when you'll be at another phone booth, one time a day later than the other. I'll get back to you. If you have to leave here, do the same wherever you end up. Understand?" He made her repeat it, and she did, imagining she was humoring him. How would he like to be stuck in this godforsaken town with a phone number for company, her big excitement anticipating his six visits a year? She couldn't bring herself to look at him. She wanted him to leave. "I know it's awful," he said. "I know you'll get frightened and feel as if you're going nuts. If you need to surface, do it. Forget what anybody else thinks. But I'm here to help for as long as you stay under." Portia finally met his brown eyes, and she nodded, blinking back a sudden rush of tears. Then she wanted him to stay, but he left, whistling as he walked across the park toward an old Chevrolet with California plates.

Dooley lived up to his promise. Every two months he had pulled in front of her little cottage in his rattletrap Chevy. By spring Portia had begun to appreciate his optimism and sensitivity. He had endured her initial bad humor, seeming to realize it was not meant for him. He became serious when he performed his job, for which Portia was thankful—all the rules were for her protection. But after he'd imparted the gossip and the instructions, he always smiled with relief and began joking with her, jokes that often shot to the heart of her misery and left her smiling at herself. On his last visit, in April, he had brought her a kitten.

Then he missed his date in June, calling her at the cafe to tell her he would come at the end of July. He had received some money, he said, and he needed time to gather information about the donor. She had no idea what he was talking about. All she heard was the visit was postponed, a seemingly small change that sent her into a large funk. She was so desperately lonely by the middle of July that she took a chance and called Charley, intending only to listen to his voice answering the phone. A woman picked up the line. "Charley?" Portia blurted.

"He's not in right now," the woman said. "Could I tell him who called?"

Portia hung up. So Charley had abandoned her, too. She couldn't blame him, any more than she blamed him for turning the country upside down during his search for her. But knowing Charley had found someone else affected her more than she'd expected. She hadn't thought about him much since she'd left; enduring torture was not her strong point. But apparently he'd lurked in the background of her mind, providing a pocket of strength, a stageful of props with which she interacted. Now she truly was alone, forlorn on a bare stage, conducting a monologue with herself. Dooley had become her only contact with reality.

Dooley arrived on the afternoon of the twenty-ninth, carrying with him five one-hundred-dollar bills. Portia met him at the door of her cabin. She had taken off from work, hoping he would come in today. Saturdays were always slow at the cafe, anyway. "Crazy," he said, handing her the crisp bills. "There's this paper in San Francisco called *Common Bond.* This beautiful woman waltzed in, announced she was a friend of yours and left the money. The editor told her he couldn't get it to you, of course."

Portia stared at the money. Her sister? No way.

"The editor figured she was an agent. She gave him an address in Berkeley, and it turns out she lives there with a newswoman for one of the Bay Area TV stations. Then we thought it was a stunt, except she actually is a friend of yours."

"Laney Villano," Portia laughed. "She rises from the dead." But then she had to sit down and drop her head to clear the dizziness. Laney was alive!

Dooley sat down next to her on the bed. "I guess it caused a stir, her reappearance. This guy, the editor, he said she acted like he was Western Union. Radical Mail Service. When he found out she was supposed to be dead, he said he hoped some more ghosts would drop by his office."

"So Laney's alive and back with Ann," Portia marveled. "That's very good news." Knowing Laney was thinking of her eased the sting of Charley a little.

Dooley looked around her cramped hut, spic and span as she could make it. Even the bed they were sitting on could pass military inspection. "I have some bad news, too."

"I think I can guess," Portia said. She was afraid to tell him she'd called Charley and, worse, spoken on the phone. He might ask her to move to another part of the country. If the FBI had not descended on her by now, they knew nothing more than that she was alive.

"Charley's getting married next month. A Barnard girl. I guess all of you people travel in rarefied circles, huh? Yale and Ridgedale and Barnard?" It was the first time he'd lost his all's-right-with-me-and-mine expression. Portia reached out and touched his shoulder. "Stay for dinner this time," she suggested.

He recovered quickly from his narrow brush with anger, running his freckle-dusted hands through his springy hair. "You sure? O.K. I'd like that."

Portia had made lasagne that morning, and now she added a salad and a basket of garlic bread. She had even bought a bottle of decent wine from her meager tips. "You never did this before," he said when he'd finished eating. "You did it before you knew about the money."

She was embarrassed. She brought the dishes to the sink and showed him how the water ran red. "You can't really drink it." She told him about buying six-packs of Coke and bottled water. In the middle of an increasingly garbled explanation of how her parents never allowed her to drink Coke, a solitary tear dripped down her right cheek. She wiped it off and went on talking while another tear came down, and another, until there were too many tears to wipe away. She stared at him helplessly, thinking he would leave and never come back. He crossed to her and drew her head against his shoulder, and she liked the smell of him. When she understood he wasn't going to run from her despair, she wanted him, wanted him inside her, wanted the rough of his cheek against the smooth of hers. She led him to her bed, and they kissed and caressed and nuzzled without a sound. She bit her lower lip once, and then she couldn't stand it anymore, she yelled out, splitting the silence with cries that arched upward in her pure joy at being herself, at sharing herself at her deepest with another human being.

"You're lonely," he said later, running his fingertips along the line of her jaw.

The words hung in the air, waiting for her to catch them. She liked how he listened with his hands, laying a comforting arm across her when he sensed the tension in her face. "I am more than lonely," she said finally. "I am dying of contradictions. I have no life, but I'm still alive, and I'm always aware of every threat to this life that isn't a life at all."

He waited until he understood. "Does this make it worse?"

She knew he meant their lovemaking. "No. Right now I can only find myself in you." Filled with panic as she heard what she'd said, she tried to backtrack. "I mean, because I don't have anyone who knows—"

He rubbed her shoulder. "It's O.K.," he said. "Let's sleep. I'd like to stay the night."

Dooley returned three weeks later, on Saturday morning. He had, he said, driven all night. This time he told her something about his own life. He lived in Van Nuys, in a small, run-down apartment building. He worked as a maintenance man for a large hospital. "They call me a stationary engineer," he said, smiling. "Actually, all I do is run around fixing plumbing and boilers and air conditioners."

"How'd you learn to do all of that?"

"A little at a time. I took some classes. . . ." He shrugged. "It's a lot of variety."

"It sounds wonderful," she said.

"You don't like waitressing much."

It was Portia's turn to shrug. She was only marking time—but for what? Until she was caught? Until the nightmare ended and she could go on with theater?

"Why don't you come out to L.A. with me? I could get you another set of I.D. You could find a better job."

Her stomach seized with fear. She hadn't been in a big city since those last days in New York. L.A. was full of people, full of cops, full of agents, all searching for her. Rationally, she knew a city was perhaps safer than a little town—she stuck out here if only because she was young and rootless. But she had proved she could survive in the backwaters, and she had no such assurance about the cities.

"I'm not saying this right," he continued. "I'm asking you for myself. I'm lonely, and I like you."

"Loneliness is no reason for being together," she said sharply, her stomach still churning.

He twisted his big hands in frustration. "God, I'm so bad at talking. When they suggested I be your contact, I was furious. The drive itself . . . Anyway, from the first day I could see you were frightened and confused, but you'd been sticking it through, you kept hold of yourself. I thought about what I would do. . . . I need people to like me too much. I don't think I could do it, be another person, never knowing when it would end."

Portia stood up and walked rapidly to her window, staring out at the bare field shimmering in the summer heat. "But that's why I'm afraid," she said, speaking to the window. "You're the only person who knows who I am. I can't separate how I feel about you from what I need from you. If they'd sent another contact, would I be having this conversation with him? If you weren't my contact, would I want you the same way?"

"How will you ever know?" he asked.

The window reflected the kaleidoscope of emotions whirling across her face: shock, anger, despair, then shading into shock again. He was right. How would she ever know? She was glad he had stayed on the other side of the room, letting her see it by herself. "I have to think," she told him finally.

He nodded. "I'll be back in October, as usual. That won't change, no matter what you decide."

When he returned, she was packed and ready to go. She had lived in New Mexico exactly one year.

"Then what?" Laney urged. In spite of offering Portia anything she wanted, there was almost nothing in the house to eat. They had snacked on tea and oranges, and the bright peels littered the kitchen table. A key turned in the front door, and Portia jumped. "It's just Ann," Laney said.

"Laney?" Ann hollered from the entryway. The shimmer of fear in Ann's voice sent an answering bolt through Portia; she jumped to her feet and began edging toward the porch, not sure what to think. Did Ann know she was here? Had her two friends somehow alerted the FBI?

"I'm in the kitchen!" Laney shouted quickly as she laid a reassuring hand on Portia's arm. "It's all right," she told Portia. "I'm leaving soon, and Ann was afraid I'd already gone."

Portia halted her crabwalk. Ann entered the kitchen, stopping short when she saw Portia. "I can't believe it," Ann said.

Portia couldn't believe it either. Laney was leaving Ann again? Portia and Ann sank into chairs and stared at each other. "You look all right," Ann said. "You look . . . normal."

Portia smiled. "No more wig." Ann reminded Portia of an excessively airbrushed illustration: all her hard edges had been smoothed over for the benefit of her television audience. Her skin was satiny, her hair beautifully scissored into soft brown waves, and even in the midst of being surprised by Portia, her walk was graceful and flowing, her voice low and modulated.

"The all-American dream girl," Laney said, guessing Portia's thoughts.

Ann lifted a warning eyebrow at Laney, and Laney laughed. They don't seem angry at one another, Portia thought. Why is Laney leaving?

Laney wanted to get back to the story. "Please go on," she told Portia. Ann, of course, demanded an update first, so Laney called in a pizza order from a delivery service while Portia ran through a quick version of what she'd spent all afternoon telling Laney. The pizza came as she had once again decided to accept Dooley's offer. "Hadel will love to know you got the five hundred dollars," Ann said.

"How is Hadel?" Portia asked. "I want to see her, too."

Laney waved away Hadel. "We'll call her tomorrow," she promised. "What happened in L.A.?"

"Van Nuys," Portia corrected. "The five hundred was wonderful, because it gave me a breathing space. I got a job—this is funny, Laney—at a children's center. Remember all those lies about Head Start? I guess they rubbed off somehow. I really enjoy working with kids."

"You're still there?" Ann asked.

Portia nodded. She and Laney were fighting for the sausage bits Ann was carefully excising from her pizza. Portia had to surrender so she could finish her story. "I'm on a month's vacation. I wanted to visit people. Dooley wasn't too pleased about it, but he finally gave in."

"So that's still going?" After winning the sausage fight, Laney graciously divided up the rest of Ann's sausage and piled half on Portia's plate.

"Going strong," Portia answered. "We spend a lot of evenings on the beach, just walking around, at least we did before I started helping with this street theater collective. Now I translate crazy scripts to crazier theater a couple nights a week—behind the scenes, of course." She leaned back, her face relaxed. "I'm happy, happier than I ever thought I could be after going underground. Sometimes for days at a time I don't think about being under. Dooley's wonderful. Imagine driving all that way for months just to see if I was all right."

Laney sniffed. "Well, that was his assignment, wasn't it?"

Portia smiled. "They're not military orders. He was active in draft counseling, and then he helped a couple of draft evaders. That's how he got into it. He could have stopped any time he wanted to."

"Have you seen your parents?" Ann asked.

"I just came from there. I dropped in on them, too. They don't live on base, so it was easy. They were so excited! So was I. I know everybody complains about having to see their parents, but when you can't see them, you really miss them. Toni was the only sour note," Portia added, her face darkening.

"She was there?" Laney paused en route to the kitchen sink.

"No. She's living in New York. She stuck it out at Ridgedale. She told my parents she hated it, but after all the stuff about me, she had to stay because she was embarrassed to go anywhere else. . . . That's all crap because, by then, it was the summer between her junior and senior year. Anyway, she was going with some guy who had a house on Martha's Vineyard—"

"Oh, him," Laney said. "I saw him a few times in the dining room."

"He supposedly broke up with her because of me. Since the transferring stuff isn't true, I don't know about the other, but according to her, I've wrecked her life."

"Have you talked to her?"

Portia shook her head. "I didn't want to risk calling her, and then my parents made it clear I wouldn't get a good reception." She shrugged, but it didn't quite come off. Toni's rejection hurt. "Now tell me about you," she demanded, hoping to discover why Laney was leaving. She had perhaps stumbled into the middle of a domestic crisis, and it might be best for everyone if she bunked over at Hadel's house.

The ensuing discussion focused mainly on Ann's career: interesting, but never close to what Portia wanted to know. There were, however, several disturbances as they talked: Laney made a few phone calls, and Ann watched her out of the room and then lost track of what she was saying as she strained to hear Laney's half of the call. Later, Laney broke into a story to announce she had to split; it was almost ten. "I'll be back around two or three," she told Ann, whose facial muscles had tightened into a mask. After Laney left, Ann explained the mystery, beginning with Laney showing up at KPAT two and a half years earlier. Whether it was the late hour or too much conversation, Portia was having a hard time absorbing the sense of Ann's monologue. "Is there a purpose in Laney assuming these roles?" she asked finally.

"A purpose?" Ann echoed. "For her? For me? Yes, I suppose there's a purpose. She says the roles enable her to stay with me. But it's more than that, a lot more."

"She's trying to prove something," Portia said.

Ann shook her head. "No. She's trying to stay alive."

This conclusion shocked both of them. Ann bit her lower lip as Portia stared at her. "I avoid knowing that all the time," Ann said. "I keep thinking each new role is her life. And when they end, I wish she could find what she really wants to do . . . but she never will. What she's doing now is what she will continue to do. It's hard to remember how lost she is because she's so determined about everything. She's never been a person who cares what others think of her." Ann lifted a shoulder. "Even that isn't true. She doesn't care in an individual, self-conscious way, but what other people do and think defines her generally, because she has nothing else."

Portia was trying to talk. "But Laney's so contained, so self-sufficient—"

"She's not self-sufficient," Ann interrupted. She pondered for a moment. "She can't take care of herself. I don't mean that the way it's usually understood."

"You mean psychically," Portia put in.

Ann smiled. "California living. You're right. But that's what's changed since the roles. She is now able to maintain herself. She knows what the next role is before the old one is over. When she's here, she's resting, preparing. . . . That's what I mean about the roles keeping her alive."

It was still shocking the second time around. Ann got up and busied herself with make-work, transferring dishes from the rack to the cupboard, scouring out the teapot, while Portia continued sitting at the table. "I still think she's trying to accomplish something," Portia demurred when Ann had turned off the water.

Ann didn't respond to Portia's quiet challenge. "You can

sleep in my study," she told Portia instead. "I have a bed in there."

Portia swiveled around as Ann was about to point the way upstairs. "I'd prefer the couch, if you don't mind. I have a thing now about needing to be on the ground floor. Easier to get out."

Ann nodded, chilled. She had to force herself not to shiver. "Of course," she said. "That's fine."

The first night of Portia's visit, Ann collapsed in bed, falling asleep instantly. She woke up when Laney came in smelling of smoke and cheap wine. "Yuck," Ann mumbled, moving away.

"Big night in the big city," Laney said, staying on her own side but reaching out an exploratory hand. Ann caught the hand and squeezed, and they fell asleep clasped together.

The next night, Hadel arrived with another pizza. She and Portia hadn't seen each other for more than five years, and it was a pleasure to watch them slip into a smooth mesh again, as if the cogs of their friendship would never grow rusty. Hadel seemed better, Ann thought; the stunned, hurt look she'd worn since Michelle left had been transformed into an endearing hint of bemusement, belied, however, by the searing intensity of her eyes. She had lost weight, and her face had thinned almost to the point of gauntness. "You're going to be skin and bones soon," Laney said.

Hadel laughed. "Hardly. I don't know why I don't lose it off my torso."

"Because you're the sturdy type," Laney said. "What are all those things? Ectomorphic and endomorphic and mesomorphic?"

"I got pepperoni and mushroom for you, Ann," Hadel said. "I know you hate Italian sausage."

"You do?" Laney said, surprised.

Ann furrowed her eyebrows at her. "What did you think? I pick off the little greasy things for fun?"

Laney tilted her head comically. "Yes. I guess that is what I thought."

"Laney!" Portia protested.

But then Hadel caught on. "Oh, shit," she moaned. "You all

had pizza yesterday, didn't you? And here you were all so polite when I showed up with my big box. . . ."

The next day was beautiful. Laney took Portia on a tour of the surrounding area, while Ann stayed home, reading. When Laney and Portia got back, they retired to the backyard for a talk, which turned into an argument. Ann couldn't hear most of it, but it was about Laney's roles, she was sure of that much. Dinner that night was quiet, and they all went to bed early.

Ann woke with a raging thirst at two in the morning. She crept out of bed and padded past Portia's couch to the kitchen, where she drank half a glass of milk while she stared blearily into the refrigerator. It was only on the way back, as she halted for a moment, arrested by the peacefulness of Portia's sleeping face, that the reprehensible idea invaded her sleepy mind and awoke it instantly, so she was sharp and clear, poised above Portia like a bird of prey. If the station only knew . . . if anyone only knew. She was amazed it hadn't occurred to her before. Perhaps because it was Sunday night, and she was already slipping into her work mode. It didn't really matter what had prompted it. Her mind was racing. Portia might know where Patty Hearst was. It was possible. Patty had been in L.A., and Dooley and Portia must certainly be trusted members of the hiding and the hiders. . . . Finding Portia could put Ann on the map. Find Patty and Ann would *own* the map. Portia muttered in her sleep, perhaps sensing the menace above her. Ann looked into Portia's face, and her heart sank. She couldn't do it. She would despise herself forever. When the lamb comes trustingly into the den of the lion, the lion stays its teeth. . . . She could feel herself moving away from the idea, looking at it in its terrible ugliness. By the time she'd reached the door to the bedroom, she no longer knew how close she'd come to enacting it.

Laney's eyes were open in the dark. "Where were you?" she asked. There was a tremor of fear in her question. So Laney had considered the possibility that Ann would find the temptation too great.

"I was getting something to drink."

Laney relaxed. "I thought you might have been making a phone call."

Ann was glad Laney had not skirted the issue. She sat down on the bed. "No. I wasn't. I thought about it, but I rejected it."

"Good," Laney said. She closed her eyes.

"What would you have done, Laney, if I had made that call?" Ann watched her unseeing lover's face. "Divorce me?"

Laney moved her head back and forth against the pillow. "Nope. We're married 'til death do us part. But I might never have spoken to you again. You would've gotten tired of that pretty quick."

Ann crawled under the covers, wondering if it ever occurred to Laney that she got tired of Laney's absences. Probably not. It was like the sausage; Laney interpreted things to her own advantage. If she realized Ann didn't care for sausage, she would have to stop ordering sausage pizzas. Much better to pretend Ann loved to pick off the pieces.

Ann lay awake, her eyes fixed on the dark ceiling. She knew Laney had delayed her future as a feminist rock star because of Portia's arrival. That's what all the frantic phone calls had been about on Friday night. Maybe Portia would stay awhile. And maybe, Ann thought, beginning to sink into dreams, Laney would never leave.

CHAPTER 21

From the air, Ridgedale's auditorium/concert hall/theater looked like a monster field mushroom, growing out to encompass the language arts building, cowering in innocent wood-frame simplicity to the immediate east of the sprawling giant. Megan supposed the famous architect who designed it had intended the inside to be reminiscent of a cathedral—St. Peter's, perhaps. Instead, it most resembled a very large municipal swimming facility, without, unfortunately, the pool, but with, even more unfortunately, all the supporting columns that generations of screaming children slam into when they're illegally running on the wet concrete floors. There were no children at Ridgedale, and the floors were dry, but there was concrete in abundance, enough concrete above- and belowground to qualify the structure as a bomb shelter. Early spaceship, Portia's Charley had called it. Of course, he was no longer Portia's Charley. The Barnard girl he had married had even provided him with a son, according to Robert, who knew the girl's brother.

Megan had been conned into spending this crisp, clear November night in the underheated expanse of the concert hall. Not conned, exactly—Ridgedale prided itself on being a big, happy family, and when a student wanted you to do something with her, you did it. So when one of her student pals insisted she come see the new feminist rock band from California, Megan gave up *All the President's Men* for an evening of cracked eardrums.

In spite of her complaints, Megan was flattered by these invitations. Few administrators had as much contact with their charges as Megan, whose youth, status as an alumna and sympathetic ear convinced the most suspicious of her goodwill. Her office door was always open to a distraught student, and since Megan lived on campus, she was the cool head called in emergencies, especially the kind that had to be kept from the rest of the administration, such as drunken revelers discovered half frozen in snowbanks, or asthma attacks brought on by sucking up clouds of hash smoke. "Ms. Franklin knows how to keep her mouth shut," the students said. And they came to her just to talk, about their love lives, their parents, their fumbling attempts to discover a political, a spiritual or, more rarely, a personal identity. Even the powers-that-be dropped by her office, the Hadels and Natalies of the present student body. She was especially interested in them, girls such as Nancy Linger and Faro Cutman. Megan could see Nancy up front, sandwiched in the middle of the three rows of lesbians who had staked out their seats early. It was easy to identify the lesbians these days, Megan thought. Besides belonging to their club, the Lesbian Students' Alliance, they were firmly "out," and they didn't care who knew it.

The band had finally finished checking plugs and leads and sound levels and all the other minutiae that delayed the start of any rock concert by an hour or so. "We are the Whens!" the guitarist shouted into a mike. The drummer, who looked as if she'd be more at home in a circus, with her bleached-blond Afro, her blue sunglasses balanced on her nose, and her puffed-sleeve blouse dotted with red and purple sequins, began pounding out a beat that the others hooked into on the second go-round. The guitarist and the keyboards player were hollering something into the microphones, but it was impossible to distinguish words over the chain-saw whine of the guitars and the eerie sobbing of the single horn, a sax that probably outweighed the corpse-white, stringy-haired freak sword-swallowing its mouthpiece.

"I love this one," Megan's student friend said. "It's too bad the acoustics in here are so rotten. It's about menstruation. When I saw them in Boston last month, you could hear better."

Megan choked back an incredulous snort. Menstruation? This screaming frenzy? Who would write a song about menstruation? She leaned to the left, away from her friend, and clutched the chair arm in a spasm of repressed merriment.

The band zoomed into its next number, a clanging and banging instrumental. In spite of the crazy song and the rejects-from-an-asylum dress, it was nice to see women up on stage instead of in the audience screaming their heads off. Megan had always hated that image, the girls in *A Hard Day's Night,* howling and tearing their hair out by the roots. In terms of general hysteria, though, the lesbians up front weren't doing too badly. Why were they so agitated? Was this a lesbian band? Everyone said it was a feminist band, but sometimes the words seemed synonymous. What did her student pal think about Ridgedale's lesbian minority laying such noisy claim to her favorite band? Did she feel her heterosexuality was a handicap? Megan couldn't imagine what the student thought. It was disconcerting, as young as Megan was, already to feel at sea with women five years younger. She had somehow stopped listening. . . .

No, that wasn't it. She was being too hard on herself again. These students were formless visionaries, chasing dreams like so many bright butterflies. To understand them she would have to backtrack to her own larval state, eschew her toughly won independence and realism.

Her friend elbowed her, cutting off her self-analysis. The lead singer was ambling on stage, and the audience broke into a pitch octaves above the previous hoopla. Megan couldn't quite see what all the fuss was about, except the lead singer was the very essence of cool, with cropped hair and gold halter top, dust-green paratrooper pants and lace-up jungle boots. Like the drummer, she was wearing sunglasses, though these were the mirrored variety. She began singing in an unexpectedly sweet voice about her lost love, and for once the band played in whispering shreds, so Megan could distinguish the words. The lost love was addressed as a nongender "you," but the chorus contained references to smooth thighs and long hair. The lesbian students went wild to the point of obliterating the chorus each time it was sung.

Megan's student friend was raving on and on. "She always wears her sunglasses. I waited for hours outside the stage door in Boston, and she came out with them on at three in the morning. Oh, isn't she wonderful?" She was clutching her hands together spasmodically, and Megan began questioning her assumption of the woman's heterosexuality, though God knows she had heard enough tear-stained confidences to feel fairly sure of it.

Megan obediently fixed her gaze on Ms. Superstar. There was something familiar about her. Megan squeezed back into her seat, suddenly uncomfortable. Even the outfit was similar. She cast back in rooms whose doors had nearly rusted shut. Halter top and fatigue pants, though something was different. Short hair and boots should be long hair and sandals. . . . Yes! No, it couldn't be. "What's the singer's name?" Megan asked.

Her friend stared at her. "Nina When."

"Nina Win?"

"No! *When!*" She obviously didn't want to cater to Megan's ignorance now that Nina was in charge of the show. "That's why they're called the Whens," she continued hurriedly. "Nina When means when are women going to be free?" She turned back to the stage.

Megan pressed her arm. "But what's her real name?"

"I don't know! No one has a real name. Names mean ownership by a man."

"Yes, of course," Megan answered. She watched. It couldn't be. But after two or three minutes, she knew it was. She pitched from her seat and stumbled up the aisle, aware of heads swiveling to mark her departure from the concert hall. Fell apart. Ms. Franklin fell apart. No, she hadn't fallen apart. She just had to get out into the cold, crackling air. She tried to think while she paced through the darkness. The sound of the Whens followed her, the high piano chords and the thump of the drums. Out, out, they seemed to say. But why out? She was very happy working at Ridgedale, two years of quiet contentment. She was terribly popular. Everyone loved her. No. As a student, she'd endured three and a half years of misery. She was a castoff, a third wheel. Everyone despised her. I thought I was past all that! she screamed at herself, but she knew she wasn't. She hadn't even started. Fear scrambled up her insides. The thumping and screeching of the band mocked every thought, every step. She began running, dashed across the campus drive and into the apple orchard, careening blindly from tree to tree until she found the path to the music building, her retreat from all that assailed her. The door was still unlocked, six years hadn't changed that, and she raced inside and began flipping on the lights until she reached the rehearsal room and the grand piano. Her grand piano. Her fingers were stiff on the keys, it had been so long, and for a horrifying moment she wondered if she could still play, but she began slowly, picking out the notes, and she was back. Back at Ridgedale, and her father was driving her crazy.

The stir Megan's exit created in her section of the auditorium was forgotten as soon as Nina swung into her "Warrior Woman" song, a high-tempo rush of prebattle nerves: "Momma said it was wrong to kill/But Momma, they been killin' me/Thousands of women have had their fill/Now we will die so they can be free." Nina's voice arched up on "die," curling the word around her tongue until it sounded as if the sky had split open and the angels were singing, and then she plummeted back down to earth and graveled out "free," punching the air with her fist. The crowd was delirious.

The band began another intro, slow this time, another love song. But Nina When glared out at the lights, her mouth grim, ignoring her cue. The band tried twice more before it ground to a confused halt. "I didn't want to play this gig," Nina whispered into the microphone when the reverberation from the last chords died away. The audience craned forward to catch every word. "*White privilege!*" Nina screamed at them. As one, they slammed back against their seats, Jacks going back into the box. "How many black women go to this fancy school?" People blinked at each other. No one knew, except one black woman near the stage. "Twelve!" she called out.

"You know why she knows and the rest of you don't?" Nina growled in a deadly undertone. "Because when you're in a war, you know who your sisters are. But don't think she has eleven other buddies. Oh, no. There are fifteen scholarships for poor women at this place. Three of those scholarships go to black women. So we've got three sisters here, not twelve. Know why?" She looked up at the swooping ceiling as if the answer were written there. When she found it, she bellowed so loud several people in the front grabbed their ears. "*Class privilege!* Except for those three women, ninety-eight percent of you are double winners, and the rest of you hit the jackpot once. Now do you understand why it made me puke to play here tonight? I grew up in the alleys. I didn't have a daddy to foot the bill at a finishing school. I'm not *overbred* and *overfed*." Her voice dripped with disgust. "The only reason I agreed to do this gig was for the money to go to the Black Women's Brigade in Watts. They're the real warriors. Their lives are on the line every day." A few people tried to clap, but the sound died quickly. Nina stepped away from the microphone, coming right to the edge of the stage. People faded farther back into their seats, as if she were going to leap at them, a vengeful wolf. Instead her body relaxed with a shudder, and she tilted up her mirror sunglasses, straining to see the crowd beyond the bank of lights. Her face without the sunglasses was a surprise. Laugh lines appeared, seeming to etch themselves in her skin as the audience gaped. Her jaw unclenched. Those lucky enough to be in the first few rows could see her eyes were soft and clear, and the smile in them was now seconded by her lips, drawing upward across her teeth in a quizzical, charming grin, full of wonder, as if she had just awakened to find herself in an enchanted garden. The crowd eased its own tension in turn, beginning to scoot forward again; she seemed to be *with them*. But just as quickly as they'd shifted, Nina shut them out, flipping the mirrored lenses back down, her chin hard as ice. She reached the microphone in two large strides. "You're not fit to hear about *real* warriors," she snarled. She spat on the floor and spun backstage in stiff fury.

She left behind her the eerie silence that befalls a crowd in shock. The silence lasted until she reached the backstage room. Then two hands started clapping, six hands picked it up and within a minute the whole audience was clapping rhythmically, the sound bouncing in waves off the concrete walls. Nina curled up on the freezing floor and wrapped her arms around herself, trying to stay whole, but the Nina part of her had already faded there on the stage, when she'd raised her sunglasses, and the other part of her was coming on full force, grinning and tickling and showing her teeth. The ironies of this evening were too delicious to miss. Laney threw her head back and laughed, thinking she had to tell Hadel this story as soon as possible.

The band began again out front, cutting into the clapping, playing the long instrumental number that was a lead-in for Nina When. Laney barely heard. She got up off the floor and looked in the full-length mirror. She would have to grow out her hair. She should never have risked playing here; starting to come back to herself in front of several hundred people, while rather miraculous at the time, now seemed frightening and disorienting, even from this short distance of a few minutes. Laney was never far beneath the surface in any case, and it had been silly to expect that Nina could survive a gig at Ridgedale. Well, not entirely silly, perhaps, because Laney had had remarkable success staying within the boundaries of her roles in the Bay Area. Of course, she smiled, Nina might have remained solvent if the element of humor hadn't forced Laney to consciousness, but she doubted it. College memories were just too ingrained. Portia, for instance, had spent days in this very room, still as sterile and cold as ever. "The theaters never know where to call," Portia had said. Poor Portia. And poor me. Laney was sorry she had to stop being Nina. She had enjoyed it tremendously.

She left by the side entrance and began walking down the familiar paths, hearing the band behind her. A nice group of women. She would miss them, even the sax player, who was, face facts, decidedly bizarre, with her fetish for hanging around the amusement park of every city they played, stuffing her mouth full of cotton candy and flirting with the kids who ran the rifle ranges until they gave her free shots. What would they do now that Nina When had disappeared into the Great Beyond? Rename themselves first and then put together another tour, she supposed. If they were smart, they'd hang out in New York until they found Nina the Second. Cindy, the guitar ace, she'd think of that. She handled all the bookings. A very smart cookie.

She'd gotten far enough away from the sound of the band to hear the crickets and the hum of the cars on the highway a half mile distant. And now that she'd left the band behind, her mind turned, as it always did when she came out of a role, to the events of the days before she left to assume her new life. It was as if she were half another person during those days; now that she was back, she could properly assimilate the past.

Ann had tried so hard to wheedle information about the band out of her. "There's a rehearsal space I know about in the City," she'd say, or, "Are you playing on Friday nights? You must be, you get home so late," or worse, "I met Martin Goodman the other day. Want me to introduce you?" If Cindy had ever heard Laney turned down a meeting with Martin Goodman, Regal Records' impresario, she would have collapsed kicking and screaming on the rat-shit-splattered floor of the Emeryville warehouse they shared with the Fitz, a black R&B band that had fallen on lean times. The Nina When role had certainly been the hardest to keep from Ann's meddlesome fingers, because they were functioning in areas with a degree of overlap. In spite of Ann's "Who, me? I'm just a reporter" exterior, she *was* in show biz, she went to the fund-raisers and the cocktail parties and she was on nodding terms with people such as Martin Goodman. And she insisted on pretending Laney's roles were legitimate career changes, as if Laney had a career to change in the first place. Ann put on a hurt face when Laney rejected all her offers to help. There had also been the problem of being a public figure—Laney could hardly ask the people on the door to turn away Ann or Hadel if they wanted to come in. Luckily, most of the Whens' early gigs had been at women's dances in the City, which neither Hadel nor Ann attended, and then they'd gotten a steady date at a spot on Broadway; like some Village bars, it seemed to exist solely so conventioneers from Kansas could come and look at some real lesbians. Nevertheless, Laney had breathed more easily when Cindy had promoted an eastern tour.

Portia's arrival had also thrown a fly into the Nina ointment. It had been Laney's fault, really; she had delayed the full-time assumption of her role because, crazily enough, she couldn't bear to leave her seedlings to Ann's brown thumb. She was, however, supposed to have moved in with Jessica Steele, the drummer, the same Friday Portia showed up. Portia ended up staying until Thursday morning, and Laney even missed a rehearsal. Jessica was furious, the band was screaming but Laney wouldn't have skipped one second of Portia's visit, even the argument they'd had Sunday, while Ann was upstairs working. Portia was so . . . righteous. But could she help it? Her whole life (or nonlife) was constructed around I'm right and you're wrong. She'd sacrificed her name, the theater, Charley and the freedom to move around like a normal citizen just to prove a point. It would be nearly impossible to be nonjudgmental under those circumstances.

Laney pushed open the door of the empty dining hall (open twenty-four hours a day for coffee or milk out of a machine, one of Hadel's junior year accomplishments) and got a cup of coffee. She carried it to a table and stirred the brown gook (that hadn't changed) while she thought of the Sunday argument.

Laney had unwittingly started it. She had asked Portia to explain how Portia had made the leap from observer to actor, from protester to revolutionary. Portia had answered as Laney had suspected: with a recounting of her conversation with herself the night of the strangling, when she had realized she, too, was watching, not lifting a finger while thousands of people were being killed in Southeast Asia. "We hadn't even helped Hadel," she finished. "We let her go."

Laney had waited years to say it. "I told you then not to feel guilty, Portia. I told you getting tossed out fit right into Hadel's hero image. Remember? Natalie the politico, Hadel the hero? So for guilt, you erase your past, your life."

"Damn you!" Portia exploded. "It was a lot more than Hadel, and that was enough! You sound like my parents. They spent my whole time with them searching for answers. Where did we go wrong? My life experiences had an effect on my political awakening, but it's the waking that's important, not the catalyst. Because you don't understand the importance of the upheaval of this society, you search for psychological reasons for my actions when the real reason is staring you in the face: I believe what I'm doing is right."

"Spoken like a zealot," Laney said sadly. She was drawing circles and squares in her manicured earth with a gardening fork; when she looked up, she raised the fork instinctively. Portia's eyes were red with the broken blood vessels of rage. "And you? What of you and your roles? How are you benefiting our wonderful earth?"

Laney had lowered the fork when Portia began talking. Her hands were shaking too much to hold it, so she laid it down carefully by her side. It frightened her that she had lifted it, even more so that she'd jutted it in Portia's direction without a thought in her mind. "My roles mean nothing," she said, her voice heavy. "They're a way of passing the time." She didn't know why she'd said that, except she was afraid, both of herself and of Portia, and she didn't know why they were fighting. Why had Portia's face hardened? A segment of Laney wouldn't admit that Portia believed in the revolution, because then she'd have to peg Portia as either remarkably stupid or dangerously deluded. But if Portia was going to insist upon playing Miss Guevara *cum* Fidel instead of saying something about her red eyes or Laney's gardening fork, then Laney could sling shit, too, especially when the shit she'd slung was largely true.

"Passing time," Portia repeated. "You've managed to convince Ann it's the only thing keeping you alive."

That startled Laney enough to look back down to the dirt. So Ann knew, in spite of her pretenses of careers and second chances. And she had shared it with Portia. Ann's real self was a hill shrouded in shadow. Laney had scaled the peak to share her public personality and her private life, but would she ever light up the slope? She put her hand to her forehead. "I can't lose myself in a movement," she told Portia. "It won't work. Movements are locked in time."

Portia's eyes gleamed. "And you're not locked in time? Aren't you a feminist, Laney, really? Don't you believe women are treated as second-class citizens? I know you do. So don't you subscribe to a philosophy that's become a movement? Philosophies aren't time-locked."

"I suppose most women our age would buy that, but I can't. You can't have a philosophy whose sole purpose for existence is fighting the oppression of someone by someone else. That's a movement, not a philosophy. And movements don't have the slightest thing to do with living one's life."

"But that's just the point! Oppression halts people from living their own lives, from fulfilling whatever their potential is."

Laney suddenly felt as depressed and alien as she had that winter back in the dorm, when Ann had gone off for her job in Chicago. What did she know about living one's own life? Look at Hadel, with her hopeless hero dreams. Wasn't she doomed to failure because of oppression? In fact, hadn't Laney thought that Hadel and Portia and Ann would someday tally up their accomplishments and their compromises and come out in the red?

"Look," Laney said, her voice heavy, "maybe I think it's sad that a kid who's supposed to be a doctor becomes an activist instead. Maybe I want a perfect world where no one has to postpone what they ought to be doing, just so they can stop someone from oppressing someone else." She held up her hand, because Portia was about to jump in. "I'm a perfectionist in an imperfect world. So I can't live the life I want either. The difference with me is, I've given up looking for that perfect world or trying to live as I want. Since I've given up, I have to fill in the time some way, so I lead other people's lives."

"That's insane!" Portia exploded. "I don't believe that for a minute, Laney. You're trying to do something, I don't know what, but . . . None of this makes sense. Don't you see that?"

Laney shook her head. She stood up and retrieved the gardening fork, walking with it over to the tool shed under the porch. She wiped the fork with an oily cloth and hung it on its hook, then closed the door to the shed and clicked the padlock in place. Portia remained in the same position, her eyes burning for answers. "You don't make sense to me," Laney said finally. "How can you expect I would make sense to you?" She climbed the steps and went into the house to make dinner.

They made up after dinner. Portia stopped Laney in the hall. "I didn't come here to attack you," she said. "You're right. There are parts of each other we probably won't ever understand."

"I'm worried about the way I grabbed that goddamn fork," Laney told her. She'd been able to think of nothing else since. "I may not have much of a philosophy, but the one thing I never want to do is hurt someone."

"You weren't going to hurt me," Portia said, squeezing Laney's arm. As they went into the living room, Laney noticed a quizzical expression on Portia's face. "What?" she asked.

Portia begged off. "I don't want us to start arguing again."

"If we can't talk to each other, we can't do anything," Laney insisted. "Tell me."

"Well, I knew you didn't want to hurt people. But Bob—you married him, and then you dumped him. And Hadel. Don't you think you hurt her?"

"No. Both of them needed something, and I was able to give them that something. But it wasn't me, Laney Villano, they needed. It could have been someone else. I see it as a fair exchange. Hadel needed to find herself, and Bob needed a way to bridge college and adulthood. And though Jackie was upset at the time, aren't you glad she was rid of him? He's a shallow person. Jackie deserves better than that."

Portia thought about it. Looking at it from this distance, Laney probably was right. But how had she been so sure at the time? "I guess," Portia hedged. Laney accepted the equivocation with a quick smile.

Laney was smiling now, remembering. But then she heard voices outside, coming up the walk. She scampered to the side door and let herself out. The concert must be over, and students would be going back to dorms, to the bar downtown, to the dining room for coffee. Laney didn't want to see anyone who knew her as Nina When. She cut around the mailroom and walked outside the campus grounds. Keeping to the shadows opposite the fence, she trudged up the street that circled the school. She should head directly for the taxi office, but there was one thing left she wanted to do. For three years, since her first night as a sophomore transfer student, she'd skirted that damn music building. Laying the music building superstition to rest would partially compensate for killing off Nina prematurely.

She cautiously crossed the road and disappeared into the apple orchard. The leaf pile was enormous. Did people still play in the leaves? She stopped at the fork. Previously, she always went straight ahead, past the old swing. Now she resolutely turned left and headed up the gravel path toward the music building. As she got closer, she heard the piano, the discordant slamming and banging on the keys. She told herself she was hallucinating, having an acid flashback without ever dropping acid. A contact acid flashback, she thought, a generational disease. She reached the door before her mind accepted that someone really was in there, massacring the piano, playing exactly the same tortured, deranged music she had heard in 1968. It was impossible. A student would have graduated long before. A faculty member? An administrator? Had the person been playing for six long years? She couldn't keep standing here outside the door; that funny feeling was taking over her stomach, she was absorbing the chaos of the music. She pushed open the door and walked quickly past the dark practice rooms until she reached the lighted section, bulbs ablaze everywhere. She turned the corner and looked into the rehearsal area. There was her nemesis, her profile sharply defined against the white walls, hunched over the keyboard of the grand, her hair hanging in sheaves across her wet face. "You!" Laney yelped. She should have guessed. She had forgotten that Megan was employed at Ridgedale. She had never really thought about Megan, even during the Hadel business.

The fingers paused in their crash downward as Megan turned toward Laney. Megan kept her hands above the keys, claws poised to strike while she blinked at the intruder, trying to comprehend. "All this time it was you," Laney said. It was almost laughable.

Megan's eyes had brightened with the sharpness of the hunted. She rose from the bench and sidestepped past the piano, away from Laney. Laney stepped forward, her hand outstretched. "Don't go. I was just surprised. When I first came here—" she took another step, and Megan backpedaled two.

"Stay away from me!" Megan hissed. "Stay away!"

Laney stopped her creep forward. She had never seen anyone so frightened, never seen anyone's skin quiver with fear. And Laney knew again why she had avoided the music building—Megan's terror was contagious. Laney turned her back on Megan and spoke soothingly, "I'm leaving now. I didn't mean to scare you. I'm sorry. Now I'm leaving." She walked toward the door, hearing Megan's whistling breath behind her. "It's all right," Laney said as she turned into the hall. She kept repeating her assurances until she was out of the music building and all the way back to the apple orchard, until she realized she was talking to herself.

CHAPTER 22

Hadel spent New Year's Day in bed with a woman she didn't know, her slamming headache pierced regularly by the "Ooohs" and "Ahhhs" of the Rose Bowl parade announcers, Betty White, Bob Barker and Ted Knight. Would anyone notice if they broadcast the same parade each and every year? Hadel would have thought not, but the woman, whose name Hadel couldn't recall, insisted that the uniforms of the Glendale Marching Band had last year been blue with gold braid, rather than this year's gold with blue braid.

That night was the third, and hopefully last, of the one-night stands. Hadel decided she had to be more selective and more alert. Her selectiveness tacked a week on to the two flirtations that followed. It was hard to see this as a success. Hadel backed off from the romance sweepstakes, comforting herself with an old pearl: You find someone when you stop looking. This old pearl had lost its luster, but pretending it worked was considerably cheaper. A person alone can sit home and watch television or read a book. Two lovers can entertain each other. Two dating, it seemed, had to be entertained, which meant going out to dinner, going out to movies, going out to bars and dances, all of which cost money.

Hadel's bank balance, in fact, was the one area where things were looking up. Natalie's persistence with the staff of *Boy's Adventure* had paid off. Hadel was now selling an average of one story a month to the magazine, and they paid on acceptance rather than on publication. Her income had effectively tripled. Hadel had added two hundred dollars to the proceeds of the sale of her old car and bought one a year older, but with thirty-five thousand less miles on the odometer and a pristine body that had never been exposed to the Rust Monster of the East

Coast. She had Laney and Ann to dinner on Sundays and included Portia when she appeared, about once every three months. There was only one problem with *Boy's Adventure,* and that was the salutation of every letter: "Dear Mr. Farnon." Hadel had written that a number of alternatives were acceptable: Ms. Farnon, Hester, Hadel. She had turned to humor: "Dear Mr. Cromwell, Mr. Farnon is sadly, and permanently, deceased. Ms. Farnon has taken his place. Please address all correspondence to her." The next letter, as usual, began, "Dear Mr. Farnon, many thanks for your letter. Your story, 'Bright Falls,' surpassed even your usual standard of excellence. The editorial board has asked me to inform you that we are raising your per-word payment." This last held her for some time, but finally she sent a plea: "Dear Mr. Cromwell, I know you mean well, but I cannot continue to be addressed as a man. Please, please call me Ms. Farnon." In response, she received a telegram addressed to Hester Dale. "Please, please stop writing letters to Mr. Cromwell," it said. "Sam." Hadel fired back a return telegram: "Sam. Who are you? Hester Dale." To this she received no answer.

She was mulling all this over (even the lusterless pearl) on a fine afternoon in March. She heard the mailman flip up the metal lid of her mailbox, and she went out to greet him. "How's it going, Jason?"

"Super," he said. He was forever debating with himself (and her) whether he should get his Ph.D. It seemed silly, he said, except to add to the statistics of the Berkeley-Oakland postal system: more graduate degrees per square inch than on the Berkeley campus itself.

"How's Big Brother?" Big Brother was the unit supervisor. He would periodically sit down each of his charges and impress upon them the wonders to be reaped by a lifelong commitment to the U.S. Postal Service. Jason did marvelous impersonations. Now he pulled her mail back out of the box and handed it to her. "Nothing for Mr. Farnon today," he announced. "Instead we have the phone bill, the garbage bill—"

"Always addressed to 'Occupant,'" Hadel interrupted. "My mother's neighbor got so pissed they didn't bill her by name that she signed her checks 'Occupant.' The bank sent them right through, of course"

"Of course. And the last—a plea for funds from Ridgedale College."

"The perpetual tap," Hadel sighed. She had actually sent the alumnae fund ten dollars in response to a particularly moving appeal. Laney had chided her—"How could you think of giving them anything after they threw you out of school?"—but Hadel had argued that President Pattison had basically acted alone in her case, and there was no sense in punishing the entire college for the behavior of one lamebrain, even if he did happen to be the president. Hadel's meager contribution had resulted, unfortunately, in an additional flurry of letters, with every third one now reminding her to include Ridgedale in her will. "Graduating from a college," she told Jason, "is the same as having a kid in college. Please send money."

This was another familiar topic between them, but Jason wasn't warming up to anything today. "Hey, Hadel," he said, looking off down the street as if he weren't speaking to her, "I'm having a little party this Sunday, and I was wondering if you'd like to come."

"Oh. I'm sorry, Jason. I have a standing date on Sunday. Some people come over for dinner."

"I see. Sure. Well, next time, huh?"

"Right," she said, waving her mail at him as he turned away toward Mrs. Nicasio's house.

Rats, she thought, pausing halfway up her front stairs. If only I were straight. He was sweet, he was cute—what was the matter with straight women? Why weren't they running after him in droves? She sat down on the step she'd reached and opened the dun letter from Ridgedale. It was, instead, a photocopy from President Pattison, telling her, as well as every other alumna and parent, that Ridgedale had no lesbian problem. "Huh?" Hadel muttered. The man had truly gone bonkers this time. A closer reading of the letter revealed that Ridgedale had been the subject of a television documentary that strongly implied that the college was overrun with radical lesbians who subjected the straight women there to political harassment and *worse.* No student was safe as more and more women bowed to the pressure of the lesbian leadership. Pattison was trying to reassure "everyone in our little community, past and present, that these charges are utterly false." "My, my," Hadel laughed.

She bounced into the house to call Natalie. "What a wonderful rumor!" Hadel exclaimed when she reached Natalie at work. "Why didn't you tell me?"

"I haven't had time," Natalie said. "I tried to call once, but you were gone. It all happened so fast, no one knew what hit them."

"Pretty funny."

"It's not funny at all. Don't you know how broke Ridgedale is?"

"Sure. I was just telling my mailman about the perpetual tap. Once they've got your address, they never let up. Ridgedale probably could move into the black by cutting out their printing and mailing costs."

"Don't be silly," Natalie said sharply. "Contributions are the only way the school survives at all, that and tuition. Parents have been swooping down all week, spiriting away their daughters. We've lost a third of the freshman class! It's a disaster. And Megan's admissions committee is sending out their acceptances next week. How many of those high school seniors are going to come next year? This could be the end. Really the end." Natalie sounded as if she were going to cry.

"I'm sorry," Hadel said, considerably sobered. "I didn't realize . . ." What hadn't she realized? That anyone would take this seriously? That parents would actually withdraw their children? She still couldn't quite believe it. Maybe she'd been living in a ghetto mentality too long. "Is there any way I can help?"

"I hate to sound like the letters, but send money. Another thing: find out who the applicants from the Bay Area are and go talk to them. They'll have a million questions, and being able to talk to a real, live Ridgedale grad might allay their fears. . . . Oh, although I suppose that might present some difficulties for you."

"Me being one of the perpetrators of terror? Perhaps."

"But Hadel, you know lesbians aren't attacking people—"

"I don't know a goddamn thing," Hadel said. "I haven't been there for years. I would *assume* lesbians aren't attacking people. Where'd this TV show get that idea, anyway?"

"They interviewed those students who are, well, sort of aggressively out. They have an organization now, the Lesbian Students' Alliance. It's not like when we were there. People walk around holding hands, and they showed that, but then the students have this governing board with a revolving chair, and most of the people on the board are also members of the alliance, so they drew their own conclusions about lesbians being in control of everything. But you know what the board does—they raise money for scholarships, and they try to get smaller classes and better food in the dining hall. We already did everything that could be done—overthrew the parietal laws and got the liquor license and stuff. They've been reduced to demanding impossibilities and booking entertainment for the concert hall. But they're *not* running around attacking straight women." Hadel heard Natalie gasp for breath.

"All right, I'll see what I can do. If you see Megan, give her my undying love. Poor girl. Here she is again, faced with the lesbian menace."

As it developed, Megan had tried every trick in the book to head off the television show. She had even, when things looked hopeless, again tapped her trust fund to bribe one of the programmers at the network. He had assured her the show wouldn't air, at least in the New York area. Megan returned to Ridgedale to report to the board that the threat had been squelched. Three evenings later, the program was run—a replacement for a sputtering series. Although it was unadvertised, it seemed that everyone in the universe had watched it. Megan was so outraged at the duplicity of the programmer that she had to ask the school physician for something to reduce her blood pressure.

But in a way, the whole escalating panic about the show (the contents of which the administration had known as early as December) had been a relief to Megan personally. Everyone—board, faculty, Pattison, the dean and even the students—had looked to Megan to solve the crisis. That she hadn't was not held against her. Everyone knew she had done all she could.

At least the crisis had gotten her off the "My God, do I need to see a psychiatrist?" kick she'd been on ever since the Whens' concert. She still couldn't quite believe the way she had acted, dashing out of the auditorium in front of the whole student body, racing madly around the apple orchard and then ending up at the music building, which she hadn't even thought of for years. A cover story had been duck's soup, of course. All she had to mention was the fact that she'd eaten in the dining room that night, and her stomach seemed turbulent. The students all laughed and winked at her. "See what we mean?" they pressed. "The food's poisoned, we swear."

Explaining her freak-out (there was no other word) to herself was more difficult. What did That Woman mean to her? Examined in the cold light of day, absolutely nothing. But Megan knew instinctively that if Laney had taken one step closer to her, she would have been so terrified her fingers would have hit the "eject" button, the way out of the rational world we all can use when things get too tough. She had not, luckily, pushed that button: there was no guarantee one could return to the land of what passes for sane. But how could Laney have driven her to such an extreme? The obvious answer, she supposed, was unresolved guilt—she had, after all, been responsible for separating Laney and Hadel. But hard as Megan tried, she couldn't locate a microgram of guilt in her entire body, except, perhaps, a shred about Hadel, who had taken her seriously and had hardly ever treated her with the disdain that was, for instance, Natalie's *modus operandi* when it came to Megan. Laney, however, was not Hadel, and Megan didn't think guilt in Laney's case was warranted; Laney had moved in almost instantly with that Ann Bailor person, the one everyone had gossiped about when they were freshmen and whom Natalie and Hadel had befriended in the first indication of their intended journey toward the state of Great Liberal Splendor. (Hadel's journey didn't count anymore, Megan realized; she had become an Oppressed Minority and therefore one of the unwashed millions, not a potential Benefactor.)

Megan tried to imagine what a psychiatrist would say. They were always linking everything to one's parents. Did Laney remind her of her mother or her father? That was too silly. How could this crew-cut, falsely named probable lunatic bear any resemblance to either her mother or her father? Megan had got no farther in her quest for truth when the anonymous caller from the network informed the dean that Ridgedale might not be happy with the documentary scheduled to air over Christmas. The school had requested and received a tape of the show, and the administration, the board and certain trusted members of the faculty viewed it one evening. Megan had gone to bat the next morning. She had stalled its showing three separate times—all this before her wasted bribe—and now she wished it had been on when it was originally scheduled. Fewer people would have seen it in the holiday rush, and there was a psychological factor to this year/last year, even if last year was only two months earlier. The administration had also had so long to discuss it that their own hysteria had mellowed, and although they were prepared for the flood of phone calls, they were shocked by the irrationality of those calls in spite of their own similar reactions in December. What no one had expected was that parents would actually withdraw their daughters from school, especially not in March, when the second semester was halfway finished. Few if any of those withdrawn could be counted on to return, so they would have to bolster that class with sophomore transfers. Then there was the matter of the incoming freshmen. The letters had been sent out and a trickle of acceptances had come in, but the largest response so far had been silence, as if daughters were arguing with their parents, or the parents had adopted a wait-and-see attitude.

Last week the word had come down from the board: get rid of those students who appeared on the show. We don't care how you do it, what you have to give them, just get them out. The board was formulating a letter to be sent to those parents whose daughters had received a favorable answer to their entrance application. The letter, it was hoped, would turn the wait-and-sees into the proud parents of a Ridgedale freshman. Megan, who had already performed so splendidly, was chosen as the cohatchet man, along with the dean, who quickly awarded the two seniors with early diplomas, transferred the one sophomore, who was about to flunk out, with glowing recommendations and handed the four juniors to Megan.

Thanks heaps, Megan thought. The four juniors were all members of the Lesbian Students' Alliance, three of them were on the governing board and none of them had the slightest intention of leaving Ridgedale. No one had failed to notice the purge of those who had appeared on the program, and faculty members had already appeared in Megan's office to plead the case of the Ridgedale Four: Surely we will not bow to public opinion, they insisted righteously. Megan tried to point out to them that there might not be a "we" to bow if the school went bankrupt, but this seemed to go in one ear and out the other—better to be unemployed and principled, it seemed. She got farther with the four juniors than with the faculty; instead of taking them one by one, she called them in for a group conference in her office, described the school's financial plight, told them the board was writing a letter and gave them a choice: they could be noble, even though everyone knew the request was grossly unfair, or they could stay and fight while the school collapsed around them. The terms of their leave-taking were not onerous, Megan emphasized. They would graduate from Ridgedale, and if any of them chose to go on to graduate school, she personally promised the highest recommendations. All they had to do to save the school was vacate by the weekend.

Megan listened to them argue among themselves. It was clear Nancy Linger was the ringleader; if she gave in, the rest would follow. They left her office without a decision, but Jody Drafmore called her up that night at Megan's apartment in the back of the Chemistry Building and accepted the offer: as a late-decision premed student, she could spend a year taking science and math courses at Michigan and then cash in on the recommendations promise. Megan was pleased. One down, one to go. The other two would follow Nancy's lead. That had been four days ago, the weekend had passed and Megan hadn't heard a word. She was beginning to think about Plan B, reprehensible as it seemed. But she'd give it a few more days. The students, less principled, apparently, than the faculty, had begun to glimpse the awful truth. Nancy Linger's car had been trashed and spray-painted the night before, huge red letters dripping across her hood: "Get Out Before We All Have To."

Someone knocked politely on Megan's open office door. "Come in," Megan called. When Natalie stuck her head in and smiled, Megan smiled back, remembering that the emergency alumnae board meeting was held today. Ever since Megan had realized the bite of the formerly Dynamic Duo had lost its teeth, she had stopped avoiding Natalie. Today, however, was the first day she'd actually run into her, if Natalie purposely coming to see her could be deemed anything so casual. Megan was now able to look at Natalie with objectivity—and objectively speaking, Natalie looked like shit—dissipated, as if she'd been partying without letup, and desiccated, as if the partying had been sucking the vital fluids from her cells. Megan patted her own correctly shorn hair and smiled again. She herself, in spite of the almost Herculean demands on her time and her psyche, appeared competently serene, rather like Florence Nightingale in a state of siege: quiet, beautiful and thoroughly capable. She wasn't even concerned about Nancy Linger, she realized. Nancy would fall, one way or another. It would be easier on everyone if she accepted Plan A, but B would do quite nicely. "How are you, Natalie?" Megan asked warmly. No harm in renewing old ties. Natalie wielded some power with her alumnae board position.

Natalie didn't answer. She stalked around, examining every inch of the office. "Charming," she said, indicating a miniature watercolor gradually browning in the Cancer Corner.

"Yes, my aunt painted that. It really is good, isn't it? She had a show once in New York. The highlight of her life . . ." Her voice died away as she saw that Natalie's office safari had brought her smack against the couch, where she seemed transfixed by Megan's yellow footcushion, the pillow that was never moved an inch, even when the office was being vacuumed. Natalie prodded it with her toe. "What's this doing here?" she demanded. She swept down her hand imperiously, snatched the pillow by its corner and tossed it on the sofa so it draped over one carved wooden arm. "Much better," she said. Then she flung herself on the sofa, as if she intended to stay for a long chat.

Megan's heart had stopped when Natalie kicked her pillow. It reengaged with a hitch and pumped its whole load of blood directly to Megan's face. She could feel her cheeks blistering with rage.

"I trust someone is doing something about that student's car in the parking lot," Natalie said. "If any parents come to find out the real story, they're not going to be calmed by seeing a hulk on four slashed tires with 'dyke cunt-lapper' written all over it." Natalie stared at the watercolor across the room. "Lesbians again. They seem to rise like locusts every seven years to plague you, don't they?"

"They are scarcely just plaguing me," Megan said. She was glad to hear her voice so controlled. "This time they might close down the school."

Natalie shook her head. "That's what I came to talk to you about. The dean says you're responsible for the four juniors"—she consulted a list—"Susan, Jody, Nancy and Micah. What are you doing to them?"

Megan restrained an impulse to shout "Nothing!" at Natalie and throw her out of the office. "I'm explaining the financial situation," she said.

"You're telling them to get out or their asses are in slings," Natalie corrected. "What good is that going to do? Whatever damage those four have wreaked is old news."

"Old news can still bring bad tidings," Megan snapped. She continually had to force her eyes away from her yellow cushion, lying so disconsolately on the sofa. "Besides, it's not my decision. The board is writing a letter to the parents of incoming freshmen."

"I heard. We're reacting in the worst possible fashion. We should be standing behind those students, banding together as a college for the free expression of ideas. Meanwhile, the alumnae board has assigned alumnae to go talk to the parents of students who were withdrawn and those accepted as incoming freshmen. I have a list of the withdrawals from the dean. What I need from you is a list by area, hopefully, of the high school seniors."

Megan rose to get a copy from her files. She had to pass the cushion on the way. It took all her concentration not to return it to its rightful place on the floor.

"What if the four decide not to leave?" Natalie asked.

"Jody has already left," Megan said, handing Natalie the list. "I think the others will follow soon enough."

"After their cars have been burned and their rooms wrecked? We both want the school to survive, Megan. But we differ on one point: I want the end result to be worth the effort." Natalie rose from the couch and left the office. Megan slammed the door behind her. She retrieved the yellow cushion from the sofa and hugged it against her chest. Damn Natalie! Megan was not pleased to find herself blinking back tears.

Plan B never had to be initiated. Nancy Linger showed up in Megan's office that afternoon, her clothes and her hair sopping wet. Her sorry state was not aided, Megan noted, by the hot tears pouring down her cheeks. Megan directed her to the one wooden chair. She didn't want great, moist circles on her upholstered furniture. "My car is wrecked, my clothes are torn to shreds and people poured spaghetti on me at lunch," Nancy cried by way of greeting.

Plan C, Megan thought. A student-conceived plot that implicated no one, except, perhaps, the spaghetti-pourers. "I see," she said, making her voice sympathetic. Actually, she couldn't imagine how she had ever found this girl the slightest bit interesting or congenial. She had about as much appeal as a drowned dog fished out of a lake.

"If I got another car," the wet one said, "it would be wrecked. If I buy more clothes, they'll be ruined, and any schoolwork I manage to produce in the midst of all of this would be destroyed. They stole my notebooks. So you've won. We'll go, Susan and Micah, too."

Megan said nothing.

"They don't hate me because I'm a lesbian," Nancy continued with a note of wonder in her voice. "They elected me to the governing board after I'd been head of the alliance for a year."

"Economic realities," Megan postulated. She was, however, thinking that Nancy assigned too much importance to the liberal pose: the other students had, of course, hated Nancy all along, but now they had a good reason to express their hidden contempt. The image of pus rupturing a scarred-over abscess made Megan duck her head to hide a smirk.

"I thought you were my friend," Nancy said suddenly, and her face turned ten years old. "You've always been so willing to talk to me. I thought you would help us. . . ."

"I did all I could for you when I tried to keep the program off the air," Megan answered sharply. "Once it was on, it became you versus the survival of the school. End of choices, end of help." She began straightening things on her desk. "I'm really rather busy. . . ."

"Of course," Nancy Linger said. When Nancy trailed down the hall, Megan closed her always-open door for the second time that day. Had Hadel looked like Nancy when she had left Ridgedale? If so, Megan deeply regretted missing the sight of proud, sturdy Hadel reduced to a stunned animal. Megan's own years of misery would have been erased then and there. And yet, couldn't she imagine it? Couldn't she now see the disintegration of Natalie's shopworn face? Wouldn't Hadel look even worse?

Megan crossed to her closet and opened it up to reveal the full-length mirror hung on the inside of the door. She examined herself critically and could find no flaws. But under the skin? Had she not herself appeared animallike in front of Laney? She had, she admitted, but she had challenged the beast and survived. She had reenacted the Hadel battle with these young gladiators, and this time she had won. She closed the closet door and went to call the board. They could, she told a grateful chairman, mail out their letters.

CHAPTER 23

Somewhere in the middle of June, close to Natalie's arrival for her brainstorming convention, Hadel realized that the world had lockstepped its way right up to the mid-seventies. For an entire futile day, she tried to identify one salient feature of the decade. There were a dozen new dance steps, of course, among them an interest in natural foods, in astrology, in mysticism, in radical psychology and psychiatry, in born-again religions of all types, in finding one's roots, in ESP and *est.* But what was the point of all this self-examination? Hadel began to think of the sixties as a massive compost heap, a time when everyone shoveled tons of information into their brains, heated up the heap with acid and speed and periodically stirred the contents by questioning every damn thing that had seemed sacrosanct the week before. That the unbelievably rich soil created by this monumental effort was now spawning thousands of mutant plants, all bloomless, all growing from the outside in so no one could touch them or be delighted by them, was unbearably disappointing. It was as if everyone had shouted a collective "Nyah, nyah!" at society, gathered their toys together and shut themselves up in separate cells to indulge in a few years of solitary masturbation.

Not that the generation of the sixties had run out of energy. Energy abounded, especially as people noticed, one by one, that in spite of all predictions to the contrary, they were still alive and even approaching their thirties. What happened? The revolution didn't come, the stock market hadn't crashed, the bombs never fell. *Nothing had happened.* What *seemed* to be happening was the last thing in the world anyone could have expected: they might live out their entire lives on this planet. The composting process had already disintegrated the careful road maps parents hand down to their children: this is the way to a nuclear family, this is the way we worship God, this is how we make money, this is why we want the money, this is how women behave, this is how men behave, this is what the past has taught us. It was very unsettling to find that the book you'd years ago decided ended at page sixteen had fifty-nine more blank pages, and here you were, already on page twenty-seven, and you didn't even know the *plot.*

Some people quickly disappeared into the karmic residue of a dozen past lives to figure out what they were supposed to be doing in this one. Some people decided that if they had to live with themselves that long, they should get their heads screwed on better. And some people decided that if their bodies were going to have to last them fifty more years, they should cut out the drugs and start eating right.

None of which, Hadel argued with herself, should be particularly depressing. Any army worth its rations had to halt the advance occasionally to take stock, look at the larger picture. An unexamined life was not worth living. But why, by God, or Goddess, or Seth, or the hanged man, or ten Indian gurus, or even fifteen Berkeley feminist therapists, did everybody have to whine about it so much?

Hadel was beginning to think of this Natalie visit as Natalie in chains. She had been in San Francisco for three entire days, and Hadel hadn't seen her yet. "Two more hours," Natalie moaned over the phone. "Another conference, but everybody else is getting tired, too. I've already checked out of the hotel. There's no reason for you to come all the way over here. I'll take a cab."

When the cab pulled up, Hadel expected it to disgorge a broken woman. Instead, Natalie burst out whistling, shrieked when she saw Hadel, shoveled money at the driver and ran up Hadel's front steps, carrying a huge suitcase as if it weighed no more than a purse. "My goodness," Hadel said, taking and then nearly dropping the suitcase, "here I was wishing I'd stocked up on chicken soup and rented a hospital bed. You don't look like you need taking care of."

"Hah!" Natalie shouted. "They accepted my concept! Can you believe it, Hadel? It was so late, and they hadn't discussed it at all, and I was getting paranoid about proposing it in the first place, I haven't been there *that* long, and my main area is creativity in *execution* of an idea, but when we'd finished and gone back to our little room, they told me they thought it was terrific and I should start mapping it out the moment I got back!"

"I see," Hadel said with an owl's seriousness.

Natalie grinned at her expectantly.

"But how about a translation?" Hadel appended weakly.

Natalie clapped her arm around Hadel's shoulder. "One of our clients is Juliana Jeans, pants and tops and jackets and stuff. My idea is, picture this, you have a bunch of young people in various situations, on campus the day before a concert, for instance. You have a before photo through a blue filter; the kids look like the usual grungy loser types hanging around wasting time. The photo underneath is intermission at the concert. The kids are in *exactly* the same positions, even to the way they have their hands, except now they're all dressed in Juliana Jeans clothes, and they look animated and romantic and absolutely super! This is for magazines, of course, but it can be adapted to anything."

Hadel imagined thousands of people in magazine land, poring over the twin photos, examining each transformed kid in turn, meanwhile getting an intense eyeful of Juliana Jeans. "Is there a caption?"

"Very discreet, in light italics. 'Juliana Jeans—Clothes for the night you.' Then underneath, 'Clothes for the new you.'"

"Get 'em out of those old torn groddies and into fame time," Hadel concluded, glancing down involuntarily at her own untorn but strictly utilitarian Levi's. Time marches on. "It really is brilliant, Natalie. Champagne?"

Natalie looked at her. "You *have* champagne?"

"Of course not," Hadel admitted. "But we could go to the liquor store and get some."

"I have a better idea. You and I are going out to dinner on my expense account. Pick a restaurant, preferably French."

"Japanese," Hadel countered.

Natalie threw up her hands. "Japanese! And you with your Guadalcanal books. You still read those things?"

"Occasionally."

Natalie shook her head. "Come on, trooper. I hope we don't have to wait. I'm starving!"

"After I change. If I'm going out with the new fashion czarina, I don't want to look like a slob."

They did have to wait, but not long. Over sashimi, tempura, chicken teriyaki and two flasks of saki, they discussed how they would spend the rest of the evening. "We didn't get out of the hotel once," Natalie complained. "I want to play! Listen, Hadel, what are you doing about sex?"

Hadel choked on a prawn. "Sex?"

"You know, fuckee-fuckee, in and out? No, I suppose it's not in and out for you."

"Could be," Hadel said, reaching for a fat green bean puffed with batter. She noticed that the two men at the next table were watching them. "We have an audience," she muttered through her bean.

Natalie swung around in her chair and contemplated the men, who stared back at her frankly. "Well, hello," Natalie said. Hadel groaned to herself.

"And how are you ladies?" one of the men asked. They moved their chairs closer. Pertinent information was exchanged quickly: their names were Raymond and John, Raymond with the smooth look, John a bit more hip with a handlebar moustache. They both worked, they said, for U.C. Extension, the adult-education arm of the university. "Your eyes are incredible," John said to Hadel. "I've never seen anything like them."

"Aren't they?" Natalie beamed proudly.

"We were just out running around," Raymond said, smiling at Natalie.

"Really! So were we."

Hadel groaned again, this time more audibly. Natalie turned her shoulder, cutting out the two men and whispered to Hadel: "I thought you said 'Could be.'"

Hadel rolled her eyes. "That was not at all what I meant by that unfortunate remark."

Natalie nodded at her. "All right," she said. She pulled out her credit card and waved it at the waitress. "It's been wonderful talking to you," she said to Raymond and John, who looked very unhappy. They had enough sense, however, to turn back to their dinners.

"What was that all about?" Hadel demanded once they were on the road.

"I want to have some fun," Natalie said.

"But you don't know them!"

"So what?"

There was no answer to this. They drove along in silence for a minute, and then Hadel swung down Ashby toward the freeway. "Where are we going?" Natalie asked.

"You want to have fun, we'll go to Union Street."

"Oh, come on, Hadel. We don't have to do this. We don't even have to go out."

"No, it's really all right, I swear. I'd like to go out. I've spent weeks sitting around the house."

"O.K., then let's go to a gay bar."

"No, no. I am perfectly comfortable in straight bars, Natalie."

"But I've never been to a gay bar! I want to see!"

Hadel sighed. "All right. First we'll go to a gay bar, and then we'll hit the singles scene. Just don't pick up a twosome. I'm the silent observer."

The evening passed in a kaleidoscope of images: Maud's, with its incessant pool game, which at first glance seemed to be the center of everyone's attention until one noticed the quick looks, the twitches of hands and eyebrows, the brushes of fingers against forearms. Maud's had been the first "hippie" lesbian bar—close to Golden Gate Park and Kezar Stadium, it attracted the same crowd it had in the late sixties—though now everyone was getting longer in the tooth and complaining about the new bar downtown: too loud, too young, too dressy. "These people need Juliana Jeans," Natalie remarked, observing the standard uniform of Levi's, boots, flannel shirt and shredded Levi's jacket, with a few vests thrown in for spice. "Why don't you go talk to *her*?" Natalie suggested with a casual flip of her hand after her third Scotch and water.

Hadel peered through the darkness and smoke at the indicated victim: a woman with short, curly hair and big brown eyes, sitting at a table by herself, watching the pool game.

"She's cute," Natalie pressed, "and she looks intelligent."

"Not my type," Hadel said, though she actually agreed with Natalie's appraisal. But how could she walk up to someone in a bar and have a decent conversation, particularly when she didn't want to pick someone up? "Hi, you look interesting. I've discovered I hate one-night stands, so would you like to come to the museum with me next Sunday?" It was a stupid way to meet people.

Once they'd gotten to Union Street, Hadel found straight society didn't have it any better. The same covert glances, the same "accidental" bumps combined for a spider's web of ambivalent thoughts: I hope no one talks to me. I hope that guy on the end talks to me. I never come to places like this. Only rejects come to places like this. Why is he looking at her? Is she prettier than I am? It's my personality, I know it. Rotten, and it's written all over my face! It must have been even worse for the men. Hadel wondered how they could bear being rejected ten or twelve times in the course of an evening. Why didn't they all go home and stick their heads in the oven? At least lesbians shared the burden of the approach and the resulting approval or disapproval.

"Welcome to the sexual revolution," Natalie said, ordering another round of drinks. She proceeded to discard two suitors and eventually settled on another, a man their own age with a Star of David barely visible in the curls of black hair on his chest. His other adornments were a chunky graduation ring and a Phi Beta Kappa key hung on his watch pocket. Hadel was surprised his income tax return wasn't stapled to his back, but she supposed a steady income was meant to be evident by his casual, insouciant stance and the suede jacket he wore perched over his shoulder, even while he was sitting. He smelled of some sort of men's cologne.

Leaving Natalie to her own funeral, Hadel worked her way toward the bar, where she got into a conversation with a guy who really did seem out of place: he had come with a friend, he said. He published a bimonthly collection of short stories by local authors, so they had something to talk about for fifteen minutes. After that topic was exhausted, he decried the meat market atmosphere of singles bars, the spiritual poverty of a generation without an accepted way to communicate with one another, the promise of sexual freedom versus the reality of sequential monogamy. It all sounded terribly familiar, since she'd heard it from a hundred people, herself included, and she finally realized his version had the spit-and-polish glow of long practice, even to his sipping at his white wine during appropriate pauses for her agreement and applause. "Where's your friend?" she asked him suddenly.

"Hmmm? Oh! I'm not sure. Maybe he got caught in the men's room." He laughed. "Maybe he's decided to switch-hit."

"Maybe," Hadel said. She could see Natalie across the room, leaning close to her gold and suede wonder. "Well, I think my friend's looking for me," she told him, and she edged through the packed bodies until she reached her own table. Natalie instantly stood up, her eyes glazed. "Sweetie—" she began.

"Certainly," Hadel said. She nodded a good-bye to Natalie's swain and left by the side door.

Hadel's expectation of the cab arriving with a broken woman was finally fulfilled the next morning at ten o'clock. Natalie dragged up the steps and collapsed on the sofa. "Why do I do it?" she wailed.

Hadel handed her a cup of coffee laced with a little brandy. Natalie drank it down in three scalding gulps and asked for another. Hadel pleaded for calmness as she fixed Natalie a second cupful.

"But it's disgusting. It's reprehensible. I could puke. I should puke. So why do I do it?"

"Because you want to get laid?" Hadel hazarded.

Natalie shook off this unseemly suggestion.

"You want some warmth and affection."

"Closer, but I never get either. He's what—the eighth or ninth this year? In New York—oh, it's all the same. Maybe I thought I'd meet Prince Charming on Union Street instead of Count Dracula in Manhattan. I feel like I should do a fourteen-hour purification ritual. But what's the alternative? No one wants to go back to the old virgin-whore routine, the double standard, the little woman lighting candles in the window—oh, shit!"

"At least he was Jewish," Hadel said, feeling helpless.

Natalie didn't deign to answer this observation. Instead she dropped her head on her arm and started sobbing. "Oh, Natalie!" Hadel cried, now really distressed.

"It must be better with women," Natalie wept. "Sweet and loving . . . Why wasn't I born gay? Instead I'm condemned to wander in singles bars the rest of my life until I get too old—I'm already over the hill, Hadel! You should see the twenty-year-olds!"

"Are all the women you know paragons of sweetness?" Hadel asked, pressing a Kleenex into Natalie's outstretched hand. "You can't imagine how many times I've heard lesbians say, 'Women! I'd go back to men in a minute if I could.' You think it's a joy to wander in gay bars? It's all the same, Natalie, except probably worse for gay people, because we've got the experimenters, and the closet cases, and the guilt-ridden and fewer places to meet, besides. So it's not all massages and candlelight and soft kisses. In fact, there are special problems because it's two women. Lesbians expect their lovers to intuit every asinine thought that's in their heads. A lot of misunderstandings between straight people can be written off as 'Men!' instead of 'Harry doesn't love me.' I tell you, there're real advantages to the war between the sexes."

"All of this is fascinating, Hadel, but very unconvincing if you've just spent seven hours in bed with Godzilla. At least he didn't wake up before I left." She sighed, wiping her eyes. "I'm going to take a long, hot bath."

"All right," Hadel said. She decided to make a coffee brandy for herself. It was remarkably exhausting trying to prove your own life was worse than someone else's.

That night Laney, Ann and Portia were supposed to come to dinner. Ann, however, showed up that afternoon to say hello. "I've got to have some time to myself," she said, sounding harried. "Laney's driving me nuts. She's taken over part of my study to grow three sensemilla plants. She's upstairs crooning to them all day. And I love it when Portia comes, but all the two of them do is argue and scream at each other."

"Sounds lovely," Natalie said. "What do they scream about?"

"Portia's politics, Laney's roles," Ann singsonged.

"I thought they'd agreed to disagree," Hadel said, remembering Laney's version of the gardening fork incident.

"Oh, they do. Every time. But only after twenty-four hours of arguing."

Apparently they had made up by the time they got to Hadel's that evening, because they were bearing gifts of wine and flowers. Portia's cheeks were flushed with excitement. "Natalie!" she cried, dropping two dozen roses on the floor.

Hadel scooped up the roses while Natalie and Portia hugged each other. "I was so thrilled when I finally figured out what Hadel meant in her letter," Natalie said. "'The antique dresser Laney put five hundred dollars down on has finally arrived.' I thought about it for three hours before I got it. Then I called Hadel, and we had a silly discussion about the antique dresser. Do you think the FBI still has the phones tapped?"

"Let them eat crow," Laney said. "Tonight we party!"

They ate too much. They drank too much. And everyone but Hadel had a long, involved story to tell—first Portia with her reenactment of the past years, and then Natalie with her summation of the television show crisis. "You know how many incoming freshmen responded favorably to the board's letter?" Natalie asked. "Ten. And two people who had already decided to come dropped out *because* of the letter. My alumnae, on the other hand, snagged thirty-eight incoming freshmen and convinced twenty of the withdrawals to return. It looks like the school will survive."

"That's so horrible," Portia said, pouring herself more wine. "They wrecked this student's car?"

"Uh-oh," Laney muttered, holding her index finger in the air. "Don't drive Portia into straight guilt, or she'll start the revolution again, and then where will we be?"

"A lot better off than you are now," Portia contended.

Laney dropped her finger down to tap her chest. "I don't know if I qualify as one of the good guys."

"Gee, I don't know if I do anymore, either," Natalie said, startled.

"Oh, for God's sake," Portia growled.

"It's not like gay people are lauded in Russia or China or Cuba," Laney said. "In fact—"

"Never mind," Hadel cut in. "Natalie and I made cheesecake this afternoon, and it isn't exactly pretty, but—"

"I'm not apologizing," Natalie proclaimed. "Bring it in here."

Dessert turned out to be the high point of the evening, with Laney's description of Nina When's white-privilege, class-privilege speech at Ridgedale's concert hall. Portia tried to maintain a disapproving scowl during Laney's monologue but broke midway through. "I can't help it," she moaned, wiping away tears of laughter with her napkin. "After years of going to those girls' schools, Cathedral and Ridgedale, I just wish I'd seen it. They were stamping on the floor for you to come back and berate them some more?"

"I'm glad to see that your lifelong subscription to the *Trotsky Times* hasn't destroyed your sense of humor, Portia," Laney said archly.

Portia stabbed at her with her dessert fork. "You see, I can be homicidal, too."

Natalie struggled to a sitting position from her Roman lounge on the sofa. "I was thinking today I should be homosexual."

"Don't bother," Laney told her. "It's more fun to imagine the grass is greener. What's life without hope?"

"Speaking of hilarity," Portia said, "I finally got in touch with my sister." This subject was so obviously unhilarious everyone shut up. "Gee, I didn't mean to—"

"What'd she say?"

"She said if she ever saw me again, she'd spit in my face."

"Oh, my." Natalie began clearing up empty plates, waving off Hadel's halfhearted attempt to rise to help. "What's her beef?"

"Me. I've wrecked her life, selfishly and irreparably."

"That's a good excuse for continuing on her present bitchy and unfulfilled path," Hadel remarked.

"It made me feel bad," Portia admitted.

"Well, you gave her what she wanted, so you can stop thinking about it now," Laney said. "Now I have to tell you the tale of Megan and the Music Building, which starts on a warm fall night in 1968. . . ."

"Laney's not the most sensitive person in the world, is she?" Natalie said when the two guests had left. "I wish she hadn't interrupted Portia's thing with her sister. I already knew about the Music Building."

"You did?"

"Not this latest episode, of course, but one night I followed Megan when she went running off—it was junior year, I guess. I was worried about her. No, let's be honest. I was curious. You know how she'd disappear for hours and then come back looking like she'd been crawling around in the river downtown? I thought maybe she was meeting someone or going to séances or covens or something. I trailed her to the Music Building and stood outside. She went from room to room in one section, turning on all the lights. Then she started playing her Scott Joplin stuff, except after a while she *added* things, it got jumbled. And then the mania or whatever it is took over. There were still elements of ragtime, but it was submerged under this crazy pounding." Natalie shivered, remembering. "It was demonic, Hadel. Joplin played in hell."

"Did you ever say anything to her?"

"Are you kidding? I'd sooner pet a tarantula."

They sat in silence for a moment. "You know," Hadel said pensively, "sometimes I'm almost envious of Megan."

"I'm sure I didn't hear that right. You're *envious*? Of *Megan*?"

Hadel started drawing pictures in the air, trying to explain, a habit she'd picked up from Natalie years ago. "She has . . . certainties. She looks at something and knows if it's right or wrong. She's not floundering in all the gray areas of culpability and conviction."

"I can't believe you're saying this. You're right. Megan has certainties. She has a rigid code of behavior that doesn't let in either thought or empathy. She's a robot programmed to protect herself at any cost."

"But aren't you tired of always questioning?" Hadel insisted. "If you're monogamous, you're stale and frightened. If you're nonmonogamous, you're shallow and selfish. Work is oppressive. Living off the land is copping out on the future. Having children is selfish. Not having children is selfish. No one can be free in a capitalist society, but socialism kills initiative. We're stuck in the center of a maze, and every beckoning doorway out comes to a dead end! And it's all future-oriented. It's never concerned with living right this minute." She sighed. "You know, silly as it sounds, Laney is the only person I know who lives from day to day. It may be someone else's present, but at least it's now."

"I hate to disappoint you, Hadel, but I think Laney is a fruitcake. What's the point of these roles?"

"Well, I think they keep her safe. If she's not herself, then she can't be herself being scared, see?"

Natalie clicked her tongue. "Loony tunes. What'd I tell you?"

"But," Hadel overrode, "apart from that, she's exploring all these places a woman can be right now, not ten years or two generations in the future."

Natalie laughed, a sharp bark of sound that snapped Hadel's head up. "Good fucking luck. That project should take her all of a few minutes."

There was an edge in Natalie's eyes that frightened Hadel into anger. "Goddamnit, Natalie," she shouted, "why are you so lost and bitter?" She jumped off the couch in a fury. "You're so excited about your 'concept' that you run off and screw with a gorilla, and then you hate yourself and decide you want to be gay, and New York is horrible and you're ancient and you're not one of the good guys—I can't stand it!" Her voice broke, and she sank back down on the couch. "I can't stand it," she finished, beginning to cry.

"Do you think I can stand it?" Natalie asked, her voice shrill. "You sit in your study writing your stories with the clear-cut life-and-death decisions—that's your reality—"

"You sound like Michelle," Hadel moaned.

"And you're not out in the trenches, fighting for your life—" Natalie stopped short. "Whoops. I shouldn't have said that, not with your war novels syndrome. Protect Hadel at all costs."

"Protect me from what?" Hadel screamed at her.

"From yourself!" Natalie screamed back. "You think you're so strong! We all have to go along with the illusion, or you might break into a million pieces. Laney said it to me once with this little wink, 'Hadel, the hero, Natalie, the politico.' Well, I know now I have no chance to be a fucking politico!"

"Oh, my God," Hadel said, rocking back and forth, tears streaming between her fingers. "Is that what you've believed all this time? I never wanted to be a hero. *Never*." She pulled her hands away from her face and stared at Natalie. "I want to stop thinking!" she hollered passionately. "Kill thought! React! No questions!" She covered her face again and mumbled into her hands, "I'm so tired of thinking."

"Oh, Hadel," Natalie said, "why are we yelling at each other?" She came over to the sofa and sat down next to Hadel. "Please stop crying. Please. It makes me want to die. Remember how you saved everybody at Ridgedale? The one-woman rescue squad?"

Hadel gulped down a sob and started giggling. "Don't mind me, I'm just breaking into a million pieces."

"Hmmm?" Then Natalie laughed and wrapped her arm around Hadel's shoulders. "O.K. Cry all you want. I'll try to keep on breathing."

Hadel watched Natalie in the armchair, failing in her attempt to stay awake. Natalie's hair was wild, her face thinner and more arresting and her eyes more acute than they had been in college or even the year before. Hadel rested her head against the arm of the couch and knew the edge she'd seen in Natalie's eyes tonight was fear. That was the difference between last year and now. Hadel had been afraid for years before college, ever since she'd realized what being gay meant to her as a person. To most of society, she was a freak to be shunned, dismissed, or tolerated at best. The relief of giving in, of saying she'd been defeated before she ever started, was something she would have to guard against her whole life. Natalie had known anxiety, had been frightened, been challenged—in fact, had sought challenge—but it wasn't until now that she'd come upon the stifling fear that her dreams would be stillborn, that she would lose her way in a wilderness of concrete and high rent and broken love affairs, that one day she wouldn't even notice the old Natalie was missing.

Once the edge came into the eyes, Hadel thought, you prayed to God it stayed, because it meant Natalie's dreams were frayed but still remembered. Why else the fear? The only two forks left in the road after the fear were a solution or a blankness. And wasn't that her own hero dream, her yearning to choose the wrong fork, to be blank? But was it the wrong fork? She laughed at herself. Yes, on that point, she could be as sure as Megan.

Natalie's head slipped to one side, and her mouth opened slightly. Hadel covered her with a blanket and tiptoed off to bed.

1977–79

CHAPTER 24

Two parades.

The Gay Freedom Day Parade in 1977 was a solemn occasion, shadowed by the repeal of the gay rights ordinance in Miami by a two-to-one vote early in the month, and the five-day-old slaying of Robert Hillsborough by a knife-wielding man who chanted "Faggot, faggot" as he plunged the blade into the gardener's chest. The defeat in Dade County sparked hurt and angry demonstrations originating from the overwhelmingly gay Castro Street area: Hillsborough's murder substituted fear and a simmering rage for the hurt surprise of two weeks earlier. The gardener's mother said her son's blood was on Anita Bryant's hands; and, indeed, violence against gays had risen dramatically since Bryant had begun her Save Our Children campaign. On the day of the parade, city flags flew at half mast as 250,000 marchers filed along Market Street. A silent contingent carried huge posters of Hitler, Stalin, Idi Amin and Anita Bryant. Marchers placed flowers on the steps of City Hall.

Hadel was uneasy throughout the long day. Participants had been warned to keep an eye out for objects thrown from windows of the tall buildings lining the parade route; as Hadel walked, she kept up a continuous scan of the crowds to the left and to the right and of the throngs watching from balconies and windows. She also cataloged upcoming overhangs, alcoves and trucks, all of them suited to duck into or dive under if necessary. By the time she and Laney got to Civic Center, Hadel was too tired and wound up to enjoy the speeches and the entertainment. She set off immediately for the car, leaving Laney to find Ann and her television crew in the mob.

It was different in 1978, with an almost festive atmosphere.

Hadel didn't know if it was because the fear and rage had matured to a defiant strength, or because Thea marched by her side, but her mood was high, and she was unafraid. She smiled at the small group of Bible-thumpers on a traffic island, shouting at the sinners to repent. The sheer size of the parade was inspiring—375,000 people took to the streets, the largest gathering in San Francisco since the Vietnam Day Moratorium of 1969.

The celebratory spirit, Hadel thought, must come from thousands of individual decisions to stand and fight, for there was nothing to celebrate. A wave of repeals of gay rights laws had followed Miami's: in Wichita, St. Paul, Eugene. A fundamentalist religious fervor was gathering force, and gays were the target, accused of everything from recruiting to being the harbingers of the fall of Western civilization. In California, State Senator John Briggs introduced a measure to bar anyone advocating or promoting private or public homosexuality from teaching in California public schools. Even the most optimistic thought the chances of defeating Briggs' Proposition 6 were slim.

"There's Harvey Milk," Laney called, pointing out the openly gay camera store owner who had been elected to the San Francisco Board of Supervisors last November on his third try for the office.

Hadel poked Thea. "There's your conquering hero."

Thea waved frantically. "Harvey! Harvey!" The band twanging on top of the country-and-western bar's float two contingents ahead took a momentary break to toss Reno-style free drink chips into the colorful army of spectators. *"Harvey!"*

Milk twisted around, his thin face alive to the lure of the crowd. He waved back at Thea, bouncing on the seat of his convertible.

"How come his sign says he's from New York?" Laney asked.

Thea turned to her. "The parade committee wanted everyone to know we're from all over. They wanted people to carry signs saying their hometown."

"Berkeley's not exactly 'all over,'" Hadel said. "Where would you say, Laney?"

Laney thought a moment. "That's a hard one. Ecuador? Madras? Casablanca? I don't know. Come on, let's keep walking."

Since the three of them had started the march at Market and Spear streets, Laney had been alternately pushing them forward and holding them back whenever she wanted to see something. They weren't walking with any particular contingent, which this year seemed to be a requirement; there were no large, unaffiliated groups like the several block-long processions of the past, labeled simply, "East Bay Women." The disattached were either strolling between floats or doing as the three of them were, falling in briefly with a variety of causes and classifications. So far they had marched with Gay Doctors, the Gay Rodeo float, Gay Fathers ("Laney!" Hadel had protested at this point) and the cars bearing those politicians conscious of the voting power of the gay population, now estimated at 20 percent of the total in San Francisco.

Thea asked Laney why Ann wasn't walking with them. "She covered it last year," Laney explained. "The station got all these protest letters. Must they subject wonder girl Ann Bailor to *those* people?"

Thea's curly hair bobbed as she walked. "I saw her story. Hers was the only report that estimated the crowd in the right range, and she gave the best summary—no snide remarks, no snickers. I didn't know then she was gay herself, of course. Harvey liked her, too. He had me call the station to leak her a story, but they said she wasn't available."

Laney nodded. "The station doesn't want her doing gay stuff. The news director gave her a big lecture about her image. I honestly think they had her cover the parade last year because they didn't want her marching in it. She considered marching this year—she thinks she should, with everyone coming out to fight the Briggs thing—but she finally decided against it this morning. Both she and the station are putting a lot of energy into their new gimmick."

"Which is?" Hadel sidestepped a motorcycle cop who was hollering at the spectators to stay on the sidewalk. The moment he rode down a few yards, they all pressed back into the street, crowding the marchers.

"Ann to the rescue." Laney laughed, waving at a friend perched on top of a lamppost. She turned back to Hadel and Thea. "Once a week they do a special story where Ann reunites long-lost relatives or saves an animal or shames a rotten landlord into installing a wheelchair ramp."

Hadel moaned. "All the stations are doing that garbage—inventing their own news or having jolly newscasters or using those damned teaser headlines. One night, in the middle of *Paper Chase,* we're going to hear them say: 'Newsbreak. Missiles headed for Bay Area. One megaton or fifteen? Details at eleven.'"

They were all momentarily distracted by a loud noise up the street, which turned out to be a sound truck backfiring. The last of the politicians' limousines sped closer to their fellows ahead. The drivers had also been startled by the bang and probably thought there was safety in numbers. Thea returned to the issue at hand when they began walking again, this time with Gays of Marin County, who were carrying hot-tub joke placards. "But it's *because* of her image that it would be so wonderful if Ann came out. Her audience is the over-fifty group, the hardest to reach, and they think the world of her. If Ann's viewers voted No on Six, it would make a tremendous difference."

"Look," Hadel said, pointing behind the tag end of Gays of Marin County. "'Gays Against Brunch, Lesbians Against Potlucks.' Let's march with them." They stood off to one side until the twin groups came by. "Is this a real organization?" Hadel asked a woman with dragons painted on her cheeks. The woman shook her head. "No, it's just for fun. But it does illustrate an important socioeconomic point, doesn't it?"

It did indeed. Very few lesbians could afford to host a brunch. Potlucks, where each guest brought something to share, were the bane of the poor. Hadel thought if she had to go to another potluck she would die, and, of course, they were going to one tonight. Not only that, but also it was her turn to produce the communal dish, because Thea had, only on Tuesday, made cherries jubilee, a flaming extravaganza that knocked everybody back a step or two. Hadel was considering a bag of potato chips and a container of onion dip. Her culinary interests did not extend to potlucks.

Laney began asking Thea about her childhood. Neither knew the other well, though Hadel and Thea had been lovers for eight months. Laney had returned from her nurse-role failure shortly after Hadel and Thea met, and then she had traveled down to L.A. to visit Portia for a few weeks. By the time Laney got back, Hadel and Thea had disappeared into what Laney called the "gooey-icky honeymoon stage."

Every so often Hadel spent a day with her mother's hairdresser. She had seen him more frequently during the summer and fall of 1977 because she had truly given up looking for a lover—she had, in fact, decided she was too old, too picky and too set in her ways ever to get along with anyone else. She had been pushed toward this conclusion by a disastrous three-month affair that spring; the affair ended the day the gay rights ordinance was repealed in Miami. Although Hadel had been quite enamored of her quasilover for an entire month, she immediately disqualified her fling as counting as a relationship the moment it was over. She couldn't stand another failure. But mostly she couldn't bear to admit that she had seriously considered moving in with the woman, whom she now categorized as a shallow, materialistic snob. Horrible. Surely it didn't count. But then she admitted to herself that she wouldn't count Michelle if she could possibly get away with it, although it was certainly stretching definitions to call a live-in lover of four years an affair.

"So who's counting?" Tony, her mother's hairdresser, asked as he docked his enormous Cadillac between two Volkswagens in the Castro-area church parking lot.

Hadel sighed. "I suppose I am. I'm afflicted with a fatal mind-set that says I'm supposed to have a partner for life. I think what bothers me about that *thing* is I feel I can't trust myself. How could I ever have been attracted to her in the first place? How could I have been attracted to Michelle? No. That's not fair. There *was* something with Michelle. But Sarah? I must have been on some sort of drug."

"Spring," Tony said confidently. "Spring is a drug. Look, why don't you forget about relationships and have lovers instead? Just screw. No ties, no binds, no nothing."

"Exactly. No nothing. I don't like that, either."

"O.K., I give up. Let's go see Harvey Milk."

Hadel thought Milk was going to address the Sunday afternoon church social hour, but instead he was glad-handing around, gabbing and telling jokes. By the time Hadel got her cup of coffee, he had left—off to another church or a bar or a coffeeshop. Two volunteers stayed behind to answer questions and drum up support, one a serious-faced young man, the other a laughing-eyed young woman whose tightly curled brown hair bounced with every emphatic statement. Hadel drifted over toward her direction, leaving Tony to talk to a clutch of elderly women. The curly-haired volunteer was telling the minister about her visit to the People's Temple to leave off campaign literature. "They have guards posted," she said. "We'd called ahead, but the guards still had to get some kind of authorization for us to go inside."

The minister looked doubtful. "I know, that magazine piece about Jim Jones made me wonder. Still . . ."

"Their paper talks a good line," Hadel interrupted. Her neighborhood was peppered by People's Temple newspapers from time to time, and the concepts of the San Francisco-based church—black and white together; rich and poor together; congregational involvement in the problems of the poor, such as housing and child-care—seemed worthwhile. Hadel had considered sending them money, except she had no money to send. Besides, Natalie had drilled into her that any extra sou had to go posthaste to Ridgedale's alumnae fund-raising effort.

The curly-haired volunteer didn't dismiss Hadel's less-than-incisive entry into the conversation. "Yes," she said, looking at Hadel, "it does. And that's what makes it all so weird. Why the paramilitary business and all the rumors about coercion when they're basically a Robin Hood-type organization? It doesn't add up."

Hadel caught sight of Tony grinning at her, pointing all too blatantly at the volunteer. Hadel whirled around so she wouldn't have to see him. The minister was now describing her own church's various programs. "Of course, we're strictly a neighborhood church, unlike the People's Temple," she explained. The temple was located in the Fillmore district, a ghetto area that had been earmarked for redevelopment and then bypassed. Housing units had been razed and never reconstructed. The temple had area-wide support, however, including large groups from Berkeley and Oakland. "They have a much broader base, so they can afford more programs," the minister continued. "But we do have a child-care facility on

Sundays for those children too young to attend Sunday school, and the number of families using both child-care and the school has increased." She smiled. "I think people have started having babies again." She talked about the new Sunday school teacher, who was a seminary student in Berkeley. "She's magnificent. She's gotten the children involved in dramatizing events, in making prayer a part of their lives. Since she came, we've had families switch to our church."

Hadel had never thought much about Sunday school. She couldn't remember ever knowing anyone who had gone to specific religious training sessions as a child. Now that she had been reminded of the existence of such an institution, she discovered the concept shocked her. When her distress could no longer be contained, she blurted: "Aren't these children you're talking about?"

The minister nodded, perplexed. "Yes. Four- to eleven-year-olds. Why?"

"Uh, well, it seems like brainwashing." Or *real* recruiting, she thought darkly. "I mean, surely they're too young at age four to decide for themselves what they wish to believe in."

The volunteer was unable to muffle entirely a delighted laugh. The minister looked as if she'd awakened in a hospital to find she had no legs: astonishment shading into horror. Several other people on the fringes of the conversation were playing goldfish, their mouths gaping open. "Let's get some cake," the volunteer suggested to Hadel, steering her away from the minister with a firm hand on Hadel's elbow. "What's going on?" Hadel asked. "What happened?"

"My name's Thea," the volunteer said. "Have a piece of cake. Where are you from?"

"Berkeley," Hadel answered. "Born and raised. Why?"

Thea nodded, satisfied. "The only possible answer in the entire country. And here I was afraid you were a fraud. Come on, let's take a walk."

"Don't you have to stay and politick?"

"No. My partner will mend any mendable fences. Anyway," she said, glancing over her shoulder as they climbed the steps, "he's talking to your friend. We'll be back in a few minutes."

Hadel was pleased that Thea had noticed whom she'd come with but she didn't let on. They walked along formerly residential streets that were rapidly being taken over by what seemed like hundreds of gay-oriented boutiques. "I was born and raised here, in this neighborhood," Thea said. "I'm not sure I like what's happening, even though I'm gay. A lot of families sold their places for almost nothing, fearing a gay invasion and a drop in real-estate values. The invasion was worse than anyone expected, but—"

"Housing values went up five hundred percent," Hadel finished. "Now tell me what happened in there."

"You just questioned the principles of practically every religion, that's all. It's like saying people shouldn't be issued citizenship papers until they're old enough to decide what country they want to belong to."

"Oh. Well—"

"But that's fine," Thea said. "Just fine." They looked at each other. Hadel liked Thea's face, liked her open expression and her laughing, gold-brown eyes, her curly hair, her high cheekbones and her beautifully curved lips. Hadel liked her face so much she had to turn away. When she looked again, Thea's lips had opened slightly to expose a tiny chip on one of her front teeth. Hadel could just barely see the tip of Thea's tongue below the chip. Hadel saw the whole of Thea's face with its quizzical, intelligent humor, and all the parts—the eyes, the chip, the tongue and the lips and she thought: the old pearl hasn't lost its luster after all. And then: My God, she likes me, too. I can tell.

Laney spotted a bare-chested man with a twelve-foot boa constrictor wrapped around his shoulders. As Hadel waited on the sidewalk with Thea, leaning against her slightly, Hadel thought about why she liked Harvey Milk. It was more than Thea working for him; Thea had walked into Milk's camera store to ask him what he planned to do for the remaining elderly residents of the Castro. She found she had been preceded by a number of those residents, who were all telling a receptive Milk their troubles. Thea stayed to listen and ended up being drafted as a worker.

Hadel liked Harvey for a far more personal and much less sensible reason: she and Harvey were both given to spouting the same speech to anyone who seemed to be falling off in their duties toward freedom for gays. Both of them conjured up an image of a lonely teenager, isolated and frightened in a small town, feeling as if he or she were a visitor from outer space—and now knowing what that feeling meant. Gay. Queer. Faggot. Dyke. The one hope that teenager had was to turn on the television and see thousands marching for their right to exist and be free, see that the stereotypes were wrong, see there was no reason to be ashamed. And, Hadel and Harvey would rail, if we are all too lazy to march, if we are all too tired to sign a petition, if we are too frightened to fight for a meeting place or a dance hall, then that teenager will see nothing, and everything will go back to what it was when we grew up—loneliness without hope.

Hadel had, in fact, just last night delivered the whole ten-minute harangue to her insurance agent, who had been unlucky enough to be the fourth person in a row to tell Hadel she was too busy to attend the parade. She had listened with great concentration, told Hadel she was absolutely right and pledged that she would see Hadel at the parade. And, indeed, when Laney had finally exhausted all of her snake conversational gambits and the three finally made the turn into Civic Center Plaza, Hadel spotted her insurance agent walking backward through the marchers, handing out business cards. She slapped Hadel on the back. "Got here late," the agent confessed. "I had to find a Quik-Print open on Sunday morning. Sure glad you convinced me, sport. I'm going to get a thousand customers out of this!"

Hadel was about to strangle her from behind, but Thea, who had listened to Hadel's end of last night's conversation, laid a hand on her arm. "To each her own," Thea counseled. "Come on, I want to hear Harvey's speech, and it's nearly time."

They separated from the marchers and crossed the green lawn of the plaza, now covered with bodies in various stages of undress, all soaking up the high early-summer sun. "He's starting," Thea said and they clambered over people, trying to get close to the front. As they circled around a picnic spread on a blanket, Milk was talking about the three hundred thousand gay men and women put to death in concentration camps in Nazi Germany. Many people, Hadel saw, were wearing the pink triangle, the symbol used in the camps to designate homosexuals. By the time they reached the edge of the trees, Milk was shouting about the conspiracy of silence from religious leaders who knew Anita Bryant was wrong, from educators who knew John Briggs was wrong, from Jimmy Carter's White House. By the time they reached the front, the whole crowd, hundreds of thousands of people, were silent themselves, listening to his speech. He called upon all of them to come out, impressing upon them that there were no "safe closets." He ended with a reminder: "On the Statue of Liberty it says: 'Give me your tired, your poor, your huddled masses yearning to breathe free. . . .' In the Declaration of Independence it is written, ' . . . all Men are created equal [and] . . . they are endowed . . . with certain inalienable Rights. . . .' And in our national anthem it says: 'Oh, say does that star-spangled banner yet wave/O'er the land of the free . . . ?' For Mr. Briggs and Mrs. Bryant and all the bigots out there: That's what America is. No matter how hard you try, you cannot erase those words from the Declaration of Independence. No matter how hard you try, you cannot chip those words from the base of the Statue of Liberty. No matter how hard you try, you cannot sing 'The Star-Spangled Banner' without those words. That's what America is. Love it or leave it."

The crowd went mad. Hadel's chest felt too tight, her ribs bruised. She wondered why she became less cynical the older she got. Was that the way of the world? Laney was tugging on her sleeve. "Let's climb that tree!" she shouted. All around them, people were standing and applauding and shouting. The noise was stupefying. Hadel shook her head. "Why not?" Laney mouthed.

Hadel laughed. "I'm afraid of heights!" she bellowed at Laney. Hadel grabbed Thea's hands and kissed her and then turned to watch Laney scale the tree. Several other people were up already, one man hanging off a branch by his hands, swinging back and forth, yelling, "Look at me! Look at me!" at the top of his lungs. Laney waved from way up high, her hair glistening white in the sunlight, the slight breeze lifting her hair in the air, silver floss in a field of green leaves. Hadel grasped Thea around the waist and they spun in circles, waving at Laney as Laney laughed and waved back at them.

CHAPTER 25

Berkeley was changing. The sixties generation's obsession with the body—eating health foods and being in good enough shape to strap on a fifty-pound pack and set off for the Sierras—had taken a quantum leap to gourmet foods and gyms with Nautilus equipment. The city had installed traffic diverters, restricting cars to eight or nine main arteries, so all these superbly in-shape beings spent half their time swearing behind the wheels of their cars. Many things seemed odd to Hadel. Jason, her mailman, who in younger days had spearheaded boycotts of banks with South African interests, had recently confessed to her that he was burying Krugerrands in his house plants. And wasn't it strange that the chief soothsayer in Berkeley, the person everyone looked to for pronouncements on the future, gained her predictive powers by serving on the state board of solid waste management? That one hardly noticed the punks strolling the streets with their purple hair and powder-white faces? That Whole Earth Access, which used to stock overalls, axes, sensible flannel shirts and wood stoves for those going back to the land or, more frequently, those going back to the land in the city, now catered to exactly the same clientele but had added pasta dryers, Cuisinarts and costly Italian pepper grinders along with five different kinds of peppercorns and a gourmet mix? It was enough to make one ponder all the way to the nearest charcuterie.

Hadel was, in fact, pondering Berkeley's transformation while she stared at various meats and pâtés through the polished glass of Pig by the Tail's display case. She was holding a number. One problem with Berkeley's craze for cooking was it took hours longer to shop. After the charcuterie, Hadel planned to visit the cheese store, at which she would take a playing card; the produce store, at which she would wait in line; the coffee bean store, at which she would wait in line; the dessert store, at which she would take a number; and finally, for cat food and paper towels, the supermarket, at which she would endlessly wait in line. Luckily, all these stores were clustered in a three-block radius, so once one was parked in the vicinity of the Gourmet Ghetto, one could embark on the entire shopping expedition by foot. Unless, Hadel thought, considering her very last stop of the afternoon, one wanted the absolutely highest-quality croissants, for which she planned to drive three miles through heavy traffic to Gourmet Ghetto number two. Nothing but the best for her darling Thea.

The Cheese Board was packed, grotesquely packed. Hadel was holding the seven of clubs, which meant she had to wait through the entire run of spades. The man with the two of spades had just been called, and he fought his way to the counter, holding the card above his head, shouting, "Here! Here!" He sounded half crazed. Hadel settled down on the bench to wait. She had plenty of time to mull over the conversation she had heard last night at yet another potluck, an exchange that was surely a sign of the times.

Hadel had been escaping enforced conviviality in the deepening shadows of her hostess's backyard, watching steam rise off the hot tub, when two women who had done a "You first," "No, you," routine at the top of the back stairs finally worked out an order of descent and emerged into the floodlit area around the redwood table. One woman was wearing a tie, and the other was dressed in full leathers. The feminist sisters of the second woman had found much to criticize. Copying gay men, one group cried. Advocating violence, another group charged. Wearing the skins of dead animals, a further group railed. But apparently this prospect of a new breed of Carrie Nations, rising to ax her sexual bed to smithereens, was of passing concern. "What's really been bothering me lately," she told the woman with the tie, "is trying to integrate health and gourmet."

A black woman poked her head over the rim of the hot tub. She made a rapid assessment, decided the house was safer and in short order had disappeared up the stairs, wrapped modestly in a fluffy towel. Hadel, however, wanted to hear how the leathered woman planned to integrate health and gourmet. It seemed she had no plan, but Tie was sympathetic anyway. "Oh, I know," Tie affirmed. "For years I ate brown rice and veggies. Period. Sometimes an egg, but not often. And now—"

"Cheese," Leather mourned.

"Cheese?" Cheese wasn't the worst offender in Tie's book.

"Full of fat, *full* of salt. But God, try to give it up!"

Hadel agreed with that sentiment. She and Thea totaled an average of a pound of cheese a week, usually a Brie and a creamy blue. Hadel had no intention of giving it up.

"Cream sauces," Tie said.

They both paused in obeisance to cream sauces. Then the woman with the tie decided to be bold. "It sounds to me that you've slipped over the edge to gourmet. The problem is you haven't accepted it yet."

Leather nodded glumly. "You're right. But I have to fit all this in to my arthritis diet. I can't eat anything acidic."

"No tomatoes," Tie agreed.

At some point, Hadel thought, What Is Wrong with My Body had become a *de rigueur* topic of conversation. It wasn't unlikely, she supposed, since What Is Right with My Body had occupied everyone's attention for the previous ten years. But spending one quarter of every discussion on the back, the neck, the stomach and "What are they putting in the water?" was dismal, especially since that percentage of talk time was certain to increase. They were, after all, only in their thirties. But she had been missing out on the plan, if one existed. As soon as she focused back in, she sensed an awkward silence. A tilt of her head told her why. Tie had put her hand on a leather-clad knee. "Would you like to go in the hot tub?" she asked.

Leather wasn't sure.

Hadel coughed discreetly, firing up a cigarette as a cover for the cough. Two heads whipped around, complete with baleful glares. It was difficult to tell if the glares were caused by being startled or by the sight of someone smoking. "Pardon me," Hadel said and made what she hoped was a dignified exit.

The army that had hoisted picket signs in the sixties and then gone on leave in the mid-seventies to study the tarot and raise organic vegetables had now regrouped, Hadel thought as she set her charcuterie purchases between her feet. Regrouped along lines unpredictable to its own members, but these new passions were entirely logical outgrowths of the old ones. You are what you eat led to ravioli makers. Living off the land led to down jackets, Vibram soles, and Gore-Tex raingear. Hippie crafts and head shops led to a myriad of boutiques selling everything from uncarded wool to silk-screened greeting cards to handblown glass goblets. And be your own master led to collective businesses, a whole range of self-employed service personnel and small-time real-estate speculators. It was interesting what had survived. The counterculture *was* thriving, though it was perhaps hard to identify it as counter, judging from its wealth. But it was the way they chose to dispose of that wealth that was the clincher. A person who owned an entire set of Le Sabatier knives might drive around in an old clunker with anti-nuke stickers pasted all over the rear window. A woman (even a straight woman!) with an extremely active social life might not own a single dress, nor have been in a department store for more years than she could remember. Few twenty-year-olds or fifty-year-olds shopped at Whole Earth or the boutiques. Four fifths of those eating Thai and Szechuan on any given night had been screaming at the cops ten years earlier. In Berkeley, at least, the counterculture had become the prevailing culture, with its interests satisfied on practically every corner, but there was no doubt it was a generation out of sync with its elders or with youth. It's lucky, Hadel thought, jockeying into position to fight her way to the front (they had just called the five of clubs), that there are so damn many of us.

Laney was standing outside the coffee bean store, along with twenty or so other people, sipping strong French roast out of styrofoam cups. Another odd thing: all the wealth seemed to come from nowhere. The shops were only a little more crowded on Saturday than on any weekday.

"Bad at the Cheese Board?" Laney asked.

"Twenty minutes. At least they have a bench to sit on."

Laney grimaced. "I told Ann I would get some feta. What a torture."

Hadel was eager to carry on. The closer it got to five, the worse the traffic. Apparently some people did work. She began to edge away from Laney, but Laney reached out and caught her arm. "Hey!" she protested. "Sit and talk for a minute. I haven't seen you since the parade."

"All right, but let me get the coffee first." Getting the coffee took only ten minutes. There was always a lull when the coffee-to-go section closed. Hadel carried the last two cups and a pound of beans out to the sidewalk.

Laney had disappeared. Hadel found her at the plant store around the corner, gazing at a large orchid in the window. "Pretty, huh?"

Hadel nodded. Actually she thought its purple blooms were slightly obscene. "How's the sensemilla?"

"Almost ready to harvest," Laney said. "Nice plants this year. I'll wind up with a couple of thousand a plant."

That was even more obscene. Hadel sipped at her coffee, putting her packages next to her on the curb. "And then you'll take off?" Laney had established a pattern in the past couple of years. She would wait until October to slip into a role and then return in March in time to start her new plants. "What's it going to be this time?"

"I'll tell everybody later," Laney said. "This one will cause some problems." Since Laney knew her roles well in advance, she *could* prepare people, but she preferred to spring them on her friends only a week or two ahead. She had, she confided in Hadel, announced her rock-star role far too early. The last three—stewardess, bartender and nurse—had been surprises. The nurse role had also been a surprise for Laney. She realized, after a bare two months of on-the-job training, that she would endanger patients with her ignorance, so she had cut the role short and gone to visit Portia instead.

"How's Portia doing?" Hadel asked. "Has she been rehired?" The day-care center at which Portia worked had been hit by federal funding reductions, and half the staff had been laid off, Portia included.

Laney shook her head. "She's furious. She's mad at the government and mad at herself because she really wants to fight these state and federal budget cuts but she can't expose herself publicly. She's sick of hiding, and she forgets about it half the time. Why shouldn't she? She's been Angela Draborne for years now."

Hadel nodded. "She moved from New Mexico in '73, right?"

"In '72. Six years. No wonder she forgets."

Hadel stretched her legs. Her back hurt from waiting in

lines. She decided to forgo the dessert store and the supermarket. She could buy two cans of cat food at her corner grocery. She might even get the croissants here instead of driving clear across town to College Avenue. It wouldn't kill them, just this once. Then she remembered she had to put gas in the car. "Damn!" she snapped, starting to rise. That was another half-hour project.

Laney pulled her back down. "Come on," she wheedled. "If you leave, I have to go down there and buy feta. Save me for a few more minutes. What's happening with Natalie?"

"Natalie is just fine. Ridgedale has almost recovered from the lesbian scare, and it looks as if she'll be head of the alumnae board by 1980. Her job is wonderful, she's making tons of money and she seems to be falling in love with this guy she just met, an obstetrician who's divorced. They're going away for weekends together, but Natalie says she wants to take it slowly."

"Going away for weekends is slowly?"

"He's asked her to marry him."

Laney nodded. "Ah, so."

"Look, Laney, I really have to leave. Why don't you and Ann come to dinner in a couple of weeks. First Saturday in October?"

"Perfect. I'll make my announcement then."

Hadel frowned. She wished Laney would tell Ann a few days ahead. Hadel always felt so sorry when Ann had to suffer through these public statements of intent. Thank God for Thea, Hadel thought for probably the fourteenth time that day. She stood up and contemplated the various bakeries. Then she headed straight for her car. She could get gas on her way home from Gourmet Ghetto number two. Nothing but the best.

Hadel missed Natalie terribly. They hadn't seen each other since the brainstorming convention of 1975, more than three years ago. So many things had happened. Natalie hadn't even met Thea yet! And it sounded as if Hadel should meet Hank. "Can you come to New York for our ten-year college reunion?" Natalie had written. "I just can't get away right now."

Ten-year reunion? But it was true; they had graduated in 1969. They had turned thirty last year. Hadel had been writing her boys' adventure stories for seven years, and writing had been her sole source of income for six and a half. She found it perfectly possible to imagine herself writing stories in her study for another thirty years. What had begun as a flaky idea ("You can't possibly live on that!" her parents had cried) had now settled into a rather mundane pattern, just as Hadel had unknowingly slipped into adulthood and what some people referred to as a "lifestyle" somewhere along the way.

How settled her life had become was amply illustrated by her continuing fight with *Boy's Adventure* over the "Mr. Farnon" salutations. *Boys' World* sent her "want" letters every three or four months—lists of situational and holiday stories they needed. Early in 1976, Hadel had become so irritated with Mr. Cromwell's inability to see she was a woman that she dashed off a story for *Boys' World.* They responded a week later, welcoming her back to the fold and congratulating her on her status as an established children's writer. For authors of her caliber, they said, they paid slightly more per word. Slightly more was a good deal less than for *Boy's Adventure,* but at least they called her by her name. She continued writing for them, submitting an occasional piece to Mr. Cromwell when times got lean, until the magazine went bimonthly in 1977, which meant the number of stories they published was cut by half. Only then did Hadel step up her contributions to *Boy's Adventure,* prompting another telegram from the mysterious Sam: "Hester Dale. Good news. Glad to have you back. Sam."

Almost immediately afterward, Hadel received an acceptance letter addressed to Ms. Farnon. Could it possibly be? But the signature looked odd. She showed it to Laney. "Not his signature," Laney opined, comparing the new letter with a stack of old ones. "Never once has he made a 'C' like this. What's going on with those people?"

Was Sam retyping Mr. Cromwell's letters? Hadel thought it might be worth going to the tenth reunion if only to drop in unannounced at the *Boy's Adventure* offices. Thea advocated not stirring the soup. "They're paying you enough to live on. Forget it."

Enough was creeping higher and higher. Laney had once joked about the younger generation's mania for work. "As freshmen," she related, "they're already shunting themselves toward M.B.A.s, and they don't want to learn anything off the track. Literature is a dead art written by dead people. On the other hand, they don't have the option of living on two hundred dollars a month like we did, Hadel. It's just not possible anymore."

Hadel thought Laney's observation was uncharacteristically acute. Laney rarely considered money a factor in any scenario. But she was right: Hadel certainly couldn't live on two hundred dollars a month, especially since she'd discovered, just last year, that she was supposed to be paying a self-employment tax. "You're joking," she said when Thea clued her in.

Thea was not joking. She knew all about it because she had her own graphics business, which she had now located in Hadel's refurbished garage. "It's your Social Security payment," she explained. That Social Security would be bankrupt by the time they were old enough to collect meant nothing. "Look at it as a gift to your parents," the accountant Hadel flew to that very week told her. "Look at it as your pledge to society. You might as well, because you're sure not going to get anything else out of it." Hadel started keeping track of expenses. They were, unfortunately, minimal. How much can you spend on postage and typing paper?

She was bemoaning all of this to Laney when she ran into her again outside the coffee bean store, this time shopping for the Saturday dinner, now one day away. Laney listened for a moment and then suddenly growled, "*Why* are you talking to me about *taxes*?" as if the word "taxes" could be replaced by a number of other irrelevant topics, like the best bus routes to Kansas City or how often Muhammad Ali would come out of retirement.

"Well—" Hadel sputtered, feeling slightly silly—why *was* she talking about taxes? Didn't she remember vowing as an idealistic fourteen-year-old never, ever to allow her life to descend to such a state that she would focus one iota of attention on such a blatantly self-involved and lifeless subject? She also felt slightly puzzled.

"Ann is always wanting to talk about her taxes," Laney complained. "You know, she's making quite a substantial income now."

Ann had recently purchased another house, one divided into several apartments. She had intimated that Laney might be interested in managing the apartments for her. "I told her," Laney related with great relish, sucking up her coffee, "that if I had ever wanted to experience life as an apartment manager, I would have included it in my repertoire, and since I hadn't, I *probably didn't*." She flipped her hair away from her face with an emphatic toss of her head. It had rained the day before; the air was fresh and clean. "Besides," Laney continued with a laugh, "I contribute to the family coffers with my dope plants."

"But—" Hadel began, arguing more for Ann than for herself. Poor Ann. Why couldn't Laney manage the apartments? Ann was terribly busy with her version of "happy news."

"I'm what you might call tax-exempt. The plants are illegal. And the rest—false names, temporary addresses, short careers." She shrugged, and the wisps of corn-silk hair fell across her face again. The strands were so fine the slightest breeze could disturb them. In Laney's case, the effect was lovely: pink cheeks; shiny, windblown hair; clear blue eyes. She smiled now, very pleased with herself. "I'm so low-profile, I'm no-profile."

"I see," Hadel said, unable to keep the censure from her voice. "What if you get sick?" This suggestion seemed as unlikely as a volcano arising out of the bay, spewing lava across the Golden Gate Bridge. Hadel, however, doggedly went on painting her grim picture. "You might need emergency care. You don't have health insurance, and you're not covered by Ann's, unless they've started recognizing gay marriages in the past few months."

Laney finished her coffee and wiped out her pottery mug with a napkin. She had graduated to a regular, one who eschewed the styrofoam cups and their inescapable plastic flavor. The regulars carried their mugs with them on their errands, producing the knobby, handmade mugs at the coffee bar with a quiet satisfaction, handing them to the employee to fill from the giant stainless steel urns. "I don't plan to get sick," Laney answered.

"Nobody *plans* to get sick."

Laney smiled. "I do," she said. "I plan everything."

Hadel clicked her tongue against her teeth. Laney could be very trying at times.

* * *

No one had been thrilled a year ago when Laney said she was going to be a nurse. "How?" Ann asked over Hadel's Sunday dinner, an exceptionally delicious chicken curry that Laney, the Indian expert, pronounced "perfect." Hadel rolled some lasi around in her mouth as she watched Ann's face become redder and redder. This was an achievement, since the three of them were already sweating from the hot curry. "Nurses need years of training," Ann pointed out. "You think you can just put on a nurse's uniform and waltz into a hospital?"

"I plan to take some on-the-job instruction," Laney said mysteriously. "I'm aware of the problems."

The mystery was cleared up when a nurse named Evan started hanging around at Laney's house during the day. Evan had been a Nina When groupie during the band's early days, before Laney cut off her hair. Evan had approached Laney at a restaurant a year or two later. Laney generally told these fossils from the past that her name was Laney Villano, that people often told her she looked like so-and-so but she guessed she just had one of those common faces. This statement was so absurd that the questioners would back away, bewildered. Evan stood her ground. She told Laney she didn't believe her and demanded to know what was going on. Laney told her. Evan listened, gave Laney her phone number and hinted strongly that she was interested in Laney as a person, not as a rock star. If Laney ever wanted to call . . .

Laney called because Evan was a night-shift nurse in charge of an orthopedics ward at a local hospital. Apparently Evan was still interested in Laney as a person, because she showed up the day after Laney's call. But Evan was even more dubious about Laney's proposed role than Ann was. "You can come with me to work," Evan conceded. "But you can't pretend to be a nurse. That's impossible."

Laney found out how impossible after a couple months with Evan on orthopedics. Laney had been introduced as a nighttime volunteer, a welcome commodity in any hospital. She was immediately pressed into service, answering bells, cleaning messes in the hall, answering phones, reassuring elderly patients who had had pins placed in hips or knees. One night, however, while Evan was in the bathroom and an assistant had gone to retrieve a missing chart, a patient's bell rang urgently. A woman had begun hemorrhaging in 413. Laney dashed to her side, nearly fainted at the amount of blood the woman was choking on, ran down the hall and pounded on the bathroom door, shouting for Evan, ran upstairs to intensive care, ran downstairs to emergency and arrived with help just in time to see Evan calmly wheeling the woman off. Laney returned home the next day, telling Ann she had forgotten she couldn't bear to see anyone in distress. Ann nodded, remembering Laney refusing to look at the injured raccoon when they lived in Woodsmere. "Even in your roles?" After all, Laney could drive in her roles. Why not look at blood?

"It was too much," Laney confessed, "and too early. I was still training. Now the idea makes me sick. I couldn't possibly do it anymore."

Tonight, when Laney announced over a superb *boeuf bourguignon* that she was going to become a prostitute, Ann dropped the baguette on the floor, Hadel swallowed her wine wrong and Thea was too busy making Hadel keep her arms raised above her head and pounding her on the back to do anything else. Laney smiled sphinxlike, pleased with the commotion she'd produced.

Once Hadel had recovered her breath, she realized that Laney's next role answered one of her years-long unasked questions about Laney's trips to other lives: Was she faithful to Ann *en mise,* or did she abandon her marriage vows with her identity? She had, of course, slept with Bob—she had *married* him—but had she gone to singles bars when she was a businesswoman? Had she taken the groupies up on their offers when she was Nina When? Had she joined the stews on the manhunts she was always talking about? It seemed as if she *had* done all those things, if she was now seriously planning to be a prostitute. How could Ann bear it?

Ann couldn't. She flew off the handle, and the evening disintegrated into a chaotic mess during which Ann stated that if Laney left, she could never, repeat *never* come back to their house. Laney was the picture of indifference at this threat. "I hadn't planned on leaving so soon," she said, "but I doubt we'll have a lot of fun together in the next week." She got up and walked out. Hadel dashed off after her, catching her at the corner. "Sorry I spoiled your dinner," Laney said. "It really was good." She smiled and tapped Hadel on the shoulder. "Don't follow me. It's my life."

"It's dangerous," Hadel said, unable to come up with anything more compelling on the spur of the moment. "Ann's flipped out," she added, seeing that Laney hadn't wavered.

"She'll get over it," Laney said. "And by the time I get back, she'll have forgotten that business with the house. See you in a while."

She began walking again, apparently on her way to the bus stop.

"Laney!" Hadel called.

Laney crossed the street at an angle and turned the next corner, disappearing into the falling darkness.

CHAPTER 26

Hadel thought of time as Before Thea and Now. Now was the way Hadel had dreamed life could be in her most outrageous fantasies. Before Thea was unenlightened, because Hadel, in her late twenties, had briefly switched her allegiance from the hope that her dreams could ever be fulfilled to the cynicism that passes for maturity. She had begun to believe that growing with another person was nothing more than a tantalizing image to test relationships against or a beacon of false hope used to invest the worst relationships with the illusion of love and caring. Hadel didn't consider herself married to Thea as she had to Michelle; life with Michelle had taken on the aspect of running a long-distance marathon, losing badly in the end but completing the distance, even if she had to crawl the last thousand yards. There were no goals with Thea, no finish line. They simply were.

Days passed quietly. Since they both worked at home, weekends were no different from weekdays, and the weeks stretched into months without either noticing. A strange timelessness took hold; each minute counted, but they lost months, lost holidays, forgot entire seasons. They separated before breakfast, hardly talking. Both did their best work in the mornings, and they wandered into the kitchen at intervals, Hadel for tea and cereal, Thea for coffee and toast. Sometime in the middle of the afternoon they would finish for the day and whoever stopped last would find the other reading or cleaning or weeding. Hadel often went off shopping while Thea did political work of one sort or another; she was now involved in the Proposition 6 battle. The first polls, released in September, showed 60 percent for, 30 percent against. It was hopeless, just as everyone had predicted in June.

Thea had given Hadel ten cards to carry with her. Hadel faithfully transferred the cards every time she changed her pants, but she didn't give one out until two days before the election, when she spotted two elderly women standing on the shoulder of Frontage Road, staring at a flat tire. They had known enough to open the trunk of their car, but beyond that, it was a mystery. Hadel pulled over and changed the tire for them in ten minutes. She waved away the five-dollar bill they offered, but as she was walking to her car, she thought about the cards. The cards were made for such a situation, but would the ladies think she had stopped to change their tire just so she could give them a card? Would they be frightened? Would the card turn a pleasant favor into a debt? She wavered on the pavement, the wind off the bay lofting her sweat shirt. Then she pulled a card out of her pocket and walked back a few steps. She handed the card, on which was printed, "You have just been aided by a gay person. Please vote No on Proposition 6," to the driver. Hadel smiled at her encouragingly. My God, what if she screams? The driver smiled back at Hadel and handed the card to the other lady. "Thank you again," the driver told Hadel.

"No problem," Hadel said. As she was getting in her car, the ladies drove by and waved. Hadel was jubilant. She wanted to hop out and click her heels in the air, except she was far too shy for such an expression of public joy, and anyway, she wasn't even sure she could do it. The ladies hadn't screamed. They hadn't fainted. Their faces hadn't fallen. For the next two days, Hadel jetted around looking for people to help, but everyone appeared to be getting along just fine without her.

The pollsters had readjusted their figures, claiming Proposition 6 would squeak by to a narrow victory, but they were still wrong. It was defeated by a two-to-one margin statewide, and a three-to-one margin in the Bay Area. On the same night, Seattle squelched a repeal of its gay rights law. The tides were turning. Hadel and Thea celebrated with a bottle of champagne while they watched the television coverage of the party at the No on Proposition 6 headquarters. "Good job, Thea," Hadel toasted. The same weekend that Hadel changed the tire, Thea had spent hours knocking on people's doors, arguing against 6.

Her feet still were swollen; she had them propped on the sofa, wrapped up, like the rest of her, in a blanket.

"Maybe we should turn on the heat," Hadel suggested. She rarely used the heat, not so much to save energy but because it instantly ascended to hover in a warm cloud along the high ceilings while Hadel and Thea shivered below. It made more sense to be cold and not pay for it, Hadel maintained, than to pay to be cold. But Thea looked so pathetic, all bundled up, her eyes bright as new moons. When Hadel rose to switch on the thermostat, however, Thea stopped her. "Better idea," she said, the whiter tint of her chipped tooth gleaming as she smiled. "Let's warm up in the bedroom. We do have something else to celebrate."

Hadel furrowed her brow. Then she remembered. "But it was yesterday!" she cried.

"I know, but I was too exhausted yesterday to move. And then today, well, I figured I'd see how the voting came out." Thea clambered to her feet, standing bowlegged so she could support her weight on the outer edges of her tender soles. "Happy first anniversary, tiger," she said as Hadel came alongside to help her hobble into the bedroom. "May there be many more."

Amen, Hadel thought. They moved slowly through the kitchen, dark in deference to Jimmy Carter and his energy conservation program. "I'm willing to stumble around without lights in the national interest," Hadel told Thea. "But if we had heat we could feel, I'd use it." The bedroom, however, was no problem. Hadel's sleeping bag and Thea's down comforter combined for a lovely, warm nest. Hadel fell asleep much later, lulled by visions of spending the entire winter in bed.

Hadel's mother did not forget occasions. Often, in fact, she wanted to get them over with by celebrating them ahead of time. When she called on Sunday to propose taking Hadel out the next day to buy her a new pair of Nikes for Christmas, Hadel demurred. She felt rotten. The news from Jonestown, site of the People's Temple mass suicide, was worse and worse. Last week's body count was four hundred, Saturday's 780 and this morning's paper announced a final tally of 910 dead. The deaths were unthinkable, especially of the children. Thea had read all the accounts to Hadel, but Hadel tried not to listen. It was enough to see the black crepe paper strung up in the windows of two houses across the street. One of the neighbors had lost a daughter and two grandchildren, ages five and seven. Cars arrived hourly, disgorging relatives bearing steaming pots wrapped in towels. How could anyone eat?

The procession of cars began again the next morning at eight. Hadel watched from the living-room window. She imagined hearing the hushed voices of the black-jacketed men standing on the sidewalk in front of the houses; they had come outside to smoke, or to get away from the crying, but they were stiff with their own grief. The early morning was unnaturally still, and the smoke clung above the heads of the men, no movement or loud talk to chase it off. When Hadel's mother called to renew her plan, Hadel agreed to go; she couldn't moon around the house all day, enticing Thea to join her either in depression or in denial—Thea had a project to complete, a brochure for the city of Oakland detailing redevelopment procedures for neighborhood groups.

Hadel and her mother were at the second shoe store when a skinny man threw open the door and shrieked: "Moscone and Milk have been killed! They think it was Dan White!"

"That's not funny," Hadel snapped at the man, who was bent over, hands on his knees, wheezing. Hadel had heard too many sick jokes in the ten days since the first reports from Guyana, when they thought a large group had escaped into the jungle, before they found the bodies under bodies under bodies: Kool-Aid jokes, suicide jokes, dead-baby jokes and none of it was funny, not when her whole street was suspended in a pocket of mourning. The man was trying to catch his breath, however, not laughing, and when he looked up at her, his eyes were liquid brown, hurt and serious, and Hadel knew, as her stomach collided head-on with her diaphragm, that he was telling the truth. Dan White, the disgruntled supervisor who had given up his seat and then tried to get it back, had killed Mayor Moscone and Harvey Milk. Hadel heard her mother chanting, "My God, my God," next to her.

Hadel dashed outside to stand by the curb. She was going to vomit, the bile was already rising up her throat, but she didn't—her stomach stopped heaving, and she hung on to a lamppost with one hand. She wiped tears off her chin and saw the skinny guy bolt past her, buttonholing pedestrians with his news. Her mother tapped her on the shoulder. "I'm going to call Tony," she mouthed, or perhaps she spoke the words—Hadel couldn't hear anything through the roaring in her ears. She stood there a moment longer before she went to find her mother and a phone booth—she should call Thea. The booth next to her mother's was empty. Hadel dropped in her dime and stammered "Thea?" when Thea picked up the garage extension.

"I know," Thea said. "Please come home."

Going home meant routing her mother out of the telephone booth and delivering her to her own house, since Hadel had picked her up for the shopping trip. Her mother was motioning at the receiver; she wanted Hadel to talk to Tony. Then she wanted Hadel to buy the shoes she was wearing. Hadel agreed that would be polite—she'd been walking around in them outside for fifteen minutes. They went back in the shoe store to find everyone in the same positions, frozen by the news, except for one college student who kept explaining that Moscone had decided not to give White his seat back. Hadel's mother bought the shoes from a clerk who had forgotten how to write out a sales slip, and then Hadel dropped her mother off at her house. When Hadel finally got home, Thea was in the backyard, her eyes red, throwing bread crumbs to the little sparrows that lived in the fuchsia.

"I'm so furious," Ann said a few days later. "One of the most interesting parts of this is who Feinstein will appoint to succeed Milk—she's going to become mayor, I'm sure of it. Apparently Milk left a tape with instructions. If I could only get hold of that tape! But the station won't even let me try. Damn them. David is assigned to it. David!"

Ann's nemesis on the station. While Ann's wonder-woman-of-the-bay image dovetailed her toward what she called "happy news," David covered the real stories. Hadel didn't tell Ann that Thea had already heard the tape—since there was nothing Hadel could do to help Ann with her story assignment problem, there was no point in dangling out-of-reach carrots in front of her face. "Ann," she asked, "how do you suppose

Laney reacts to this? Do you think it shocks her out of her role and she experiences it as herself, or is she too far under?"

"Damn them!" Ann shouted. "You know what my script is for tomorrow? A monkey trained to help a paraplegic. A monkey!"

Portia arrived the next evening, taxiing down from the bus station on San Pablo, just in time for the monkey interview. She was at loose ends, she explained; the summer had been taken up by her street theater group, but now she was job-hunting again, so far without success. Dooley made enough for both of them—his union saw to that—but Portia didn't like it. "I've been thinking of having a child," Portia told Hadel and Thea later. "Can you imagine me bringing a child into this world? I wonder about my motives—do I want a child to etch my mark in the sand, to send out as my proxy? And because of that motive, real or not, I've thought about surfacing, reclaiming my own life and my past. I've been reflecting a lot lately," she admitted, "instead of living. Of course, it may have something to do with being unemployed. But this thinking has brought up some schisms I need to put back in place. Sometimes I feel like California, with a series of faults tracing my bedrock, and I've been surviving the tremors. It's all connected with the coming quake. Can I hang on for the one that upends society, or will I be devastated first by my own personal misalignments?" But now, at the end of the monkey story, which Ann had milked for every last bit of newsworthiness, connecting the young man and his helper to disabled persons' rights, veterans' rights, veterans' hospitals and state agencies for the handicapped, Portia wanted to know why Ann wasn't covering the assassinations.

Thea switched off the television. "Bad karma," she said. "Liberals and faggots."

Hadel objected to this verbal shorthand. "She did do that thing on Moscone," she pointed out to Thea. "But in a way it's true. The station picks her stories to conform to the image she's supposed to represent, the heartwarming, bright spot in the newscast. Her news director says people identify with her. Her good deeds are theirs, her empathy is their empathy. All they have to do to move a step closer to heaven is watch Ann every night."

"Friday nights especially," Thea added. "They stuck a half hour on the broadcast to fit in Ann's fifteen-minute special."

"The director said 'a step closer to heaven'?" Portia marveled.

"Her advertising line is 'Heaven-Sent,'" Hadel quoted. "'Courageous, committed, compassionate. Our Ann Bailor.' Didn't you notice the billboards coming down San Pablo? Her face is plastered all over."

"I thought this was a little station."

"It is," Thea answered. "Little in everything but the news. They outdraw one of the networks, and all three on Friday nights. It's because of Ann."

"But she did Patty Hearst. She went into the bars and poked fun at the FBI."

"Before," Hadel amended. "Now she's too famous to do the stuff that made her famous."

In spite of her griping to Hadel, Ann knew that David was just as dissatisfied as she. While David was assigned the top stories, Ann received the accolades. She had, in fact, just been presented with a bouquet of roses by the station manager, applauding their ratings during the Nielsen sweep, with a card attached: "Congratulations to our Goliath." Ann wasn't proud of her success, particularly when the consequences of her image-building conflicted with her own ideas of news selection. David, for instance, had been dispatched to Castro Street the night of Milk's death and had brought back a beautiful film of the candlelight march from the Castro area to City Hall, where forty thousand people listened silently to a variety of leaders, gay and straight. David's two-minute story, already cut to the bone, was pruned to a garbled fifty seconds, a helicopter shot of wavering candles along Market Street and a clip from Acting Mayor Dianne Feinstein's speech. Ann's crazy quilt of folksy interviews with old friends of George Moscone was shown full-length. Since Ann felt one of the station's responsibilities was to clue in viewers to the relative importance of stories, it infuriated her that her chitchat with the Moscones' mailman consumed more of the broadcast than thousands marching.

David, too, was the one more likely to be called in at night or on weekends, except for natural disasters, which everyone agreed fell into Ann's province. People whose houses had just slid down cliffs jostled each other for a chance to cry publicly on Ann's much-advertised compassionate shoulder. As the two big stars, however, they were most often undisturbed—the lesser lights did the bulk of the late-night work, scrambling for stories, willingly climbing out of bed at three in the morning to get one more shot for airtime. Much of the news department's energy, David had told Ann when they were still speaking civilly to each other, was due to her success—the spiraling ratings of the little independent's news show had inspired the station manager to loosen his purse strings, hiring more people, covering more stories, even running features: the Money Man, who advised listeners of current money market rates and special senior citizens' privileges at local banks; the Weekly Shopper, who compared food values at chain supermarkets; and Events Around the Bay, a series of quick, clever interviews with museum, opera and symphony personnel, often highlighting amusing problems, such as how half the university's collection of Indian artifacts showed up at an auction house in Seattle, noticed, luckily, by a vacationing curator and quickly removed from the sales lists. Much to David's consternation, the Money Man proved so popular that he became a nightly feature, sometimes halving airtime for whatever assignment David had filmed that day. "Your fault," David had jibed at Ann several times. The jibes had turned bitter, and now the two ignored each other, though their animosity occasionally blew open when they met at the desk of the assignment editor each morning.

David's anger was more likely to flare in the next couple of months, because Ann was on her Laney-less fall-winter schedule, spending hours longer at the station, often arriving at seven in the morning and staying until she'd watched the eleven-o'clock news on the monitors. Since she was around for more than her customary fifty-hour workweeks, the assignment editor took advantage of his star's presence, relaxing some of the strictures handed down to him from on high in the matter of proper subjects for Ann to cover. This pleased Ann but drove husband-and-father David nuts, since he insisted on matching her hour for grim hour. Apart from David, Ann's pattern, less time in the spring and summer and more in the fall and winter, generated humorous comments from the station personnel, including Lorin Hansen, the news director who had hired her and had survived the dizzying climb in the ratings: "What's with your girlfriend, Annie? She hibernate? A little bit of cold and off to the Big Sleep?" Ann laughed with him because she liked him, and she appreciated his early-on acceptance. He had called her into his office a few months after she'd arrived, telling her the FBI had paid him a visit to inform him that Ann was a lesbian. "Just in case I wanted to know," he mimicked. "I told them I didn't think it was a super story, that they'd have to do better than that if they wanted to get on the tube." He laughed, and Ann relaxed. "I don't think they'll be back. I can see advantages and disadvantages to this big revelation. But I hope we both agree on what we've discussed about your image."

Ann simply nodded at Lorin's feeler, knowing that slight tilt of her head consigned her to a life in the closet, especially if she became as well-known as Lorin planned. But what difference did it make? She wasn't a rabble-rouser or a joiner, and she wasn't planning to champion any causes but her own. She hadn't run into problems with her acquiescence until the past two years, when she'd taken Harvey Milk's coming-out trumpetings to heart, when the huge Bay Area gay community was increasingly in the news and when she finally realized, as more and more right-wing groups denied her right to exist, that her own cause and gay rights were inextricably linked. She would never, she saw, achieve personal dignity until gay people as a whole were taken seriously; one way of furthering that common goal was for respected members of the gay community to step forward and declare themselves. Ann deeply admired the ministers and athletes who had come out during the fight against Proposition 6. But so far she had stayed on the leash, rationalizing that as a person with unusual access to the media she still could do more behind the scenes than in the open. This comforting idea became an unbearable cross, however, as the station eliminated her from covering gay news and as her own popularity eclipsed the amount of time allotted to such news, exemplified perfectly by the short shrift given to David's candlelight-march film. Ann's image-building had succeeded beyond either her or Lorin's most incredible fantasies, and the closet she was trapped in collected more and more debris—a great deal of her professional ethics and goals, for instance. Her image-constructing had been pyramidal, and Ann was now confined to the tiny point at the top, hardly able to turn around. She had thought of asking John Farbus, her old editor at the *Register,* for advice, but she was too ashamed to call him. "You're a fighter, Ann," he had told her. "You'll make television news *news.*" Instead, she now refused to legitimize her work by calling herself a reporter, preferring the colloquial term for their profession, streetwalker. It had not escaped her that Laney's present role and her own tiptoeing around the top of the pyramid were not as dissimilar as Ann's admiring public might believe. They were both selling themselves.

Meanwhile, during all of this inner searching, Laney had left, and Ann faced not only her professional problems and her personal anguish, much of which she attributed to Laney, but also an onslaught of duties and errands. Three weeks after Laney's departure, Ann gave up and hired a college girl to come in and do the shopping, the laundry, the cleaning and any chores that required her to go out in public. Her neighbors were used to living next door to a celebrity and didn't stare at her when she was in the front yard, but she was in trouble a block farther afield. A trip to the supermarket or the bank was an ordeal. It seemed contradictory, because she was out on the streets all day when she was working, but she was protected by her job and her three-man crew. In her private dealings with the world, she felt naked.

Shortly after the college girl began working for her, Ann was plagued by the notion that she was forgetting some major task. She went over and over the different layers of her life, ferreting out omissions. She was keeping up with her few friends. She had called her parents and her brother recently. She was paying the bills, saving receipts for her taxes and managing the apartments, which had turned out to be less work than she'd thought. Laney's sensemilla plants were harvested and manicured, ready for sale when she returned in March. Ann couldn't imagine what she was forgetting. It took her two days to discover the answer: herself. She was lonely for Laney and furious at Laney simultaneously; when Portia arrived shortly after the assassinations, she walked into the full brunt of both. Ann was in a terrible state, unable to find where her new employee had hidden the fresh linen. Ann raged that all the money she spent to keep up the house, and all the time she devoted to shoring up Ann Bailor, star of the Channel 8 news team, a person unrelated to herself, were wasted. Why was she doing this? she asked Portia. And how should she deal with Laney?

"Portia thinks I shouldn't throw Laney out of the house," Ann told Hadel and Thea the next weekend.

Thea smiled. She had predicted Ann would change her mind about the eviction before Christmas.

"It's hard to throw out someone who's not around," Hadel said diplomatically.

"Portia thinks there's going to be a revolution," Ann continued. "She says there are going to be massive layoffs and soup lines and no housing, and everyone will rise up and revolt."

"I don't doubt the layoffs," Hadel said, "but I do a revolution. What does that have to do with throwing Laney out of the house?"

Ann thought a moment. Her face was sagging. She had begun to look different on television from the way she did in the flesh, as if they somehow slapped life into her face before they stuck her in front of the camera. "I don't know," she confessed. "And that question you asked me—about whether Laney came back to herself when she heard about Harvey—I don't know that, either." She looked down at her plate. "It bothers me I don't know, Hadel. It really bothers me." She put her hands over her face as her voice broke, and Hadel and Thea sat unmoving, watching the clock on the wall tick off minute after minute.

CHAPTER 27

Things heated up back East after New Year's. Natalie called Hadel two Fridays in a row, bristling with ambivalences. Hank was the most wonderful man in the world, but marriage? Did she really want to be someone's *wife*? "It's not necessary to say 'wife' in that tone," Hadel scolded. "There's nothing wrong with being someone's wife or husband or partner or lover if you *want* to be committed to that person."

"But no one can predict what will happen in the future, so what's the point of being committed? Why can't we just go on as we've been doing?"

"I don't know. Why can't you? There's obviously something missing."

"For him," Natalie barked.

Hadel imagined her terrible scowl, her eyes blazing. She laughed. "Where are you, Natalie? I want to get the full picture."

"In my office . . . Damn it, Hadel, take this seriously. Why are you laughing at me?"

"Because . . . because I've never heard you so happy in the past six months. Because you've been slipping and sliding between ways of looking at yourself and this relationship—Natalie on a madcap adventure, Natalie with a steady lover, Natalie as possible wife—and I think you've run into two views of the future—his optimism and your pessimism—and neither of you is looking at the present. Focus on the day-to-day, and you'll see. Could you stand to live with the guy tomorrow?"

Natalie heaved a sigh that rattled the wires. "Oh, Hadel! You don't understand what this means! It means finding a house and living with him, giving up my apartment and my freedom!"

"Far be it from me to advise anyone to give up her freedom,"

Hadel said, leaning back on the couch and lighting up a cigarette, prepared for a long talk. Instead Natalie wailed, "Oh, you're no help at all!" and slammed down the receiver.

When Natalie called again the next week, Hadel was ready. "I know it's a big decision," she said, continuing the conversation as if nothing had happened. "But since you can't know what will happen, why assume it'll be bad?"

"Why good?" Natalie snapped back.

"That's the point of the day-to-day. Is it good?"

"Yes," Natalie admitted. "It's wonderful. I've never felt so wonderful with anyone."

"And you sound damn miserable about it. It's almost as if you're sorry you met such a terrific guy."

"It's scary, Hadel. I'm frightened. I didn't think things could go so deep."

Hadel paused for a minute, thinking. "It is frightening," she agreed. "It was like that with Thea. Suddenly I couldn't imagine being without her, and yet I knew I hadn't been desperately unhappy before, and I also knew I wouldn't be desperately unhappy if something happened and we couldn't be together."

"Yes!" Natalie cried. "That's it exactly! What does that mean?"

"It means you and I had carved out damn nice existences for ourselves, and we'd settled down into them. And then it means a miracle happened, we received a gift and we're walking on miracle ground. And if it ends, we'll go back to our damn nice existences knowing we've experienced a miracle. What it really means is we're the luckiest people in the world."

This time Natalie's sigh was a soft breath of release. "I'm not mad at you this time," she said. "I just have to think."

"You don't have to think about a miracle," Hadel cautioned even as the receiver hit the cradle. "Oh, well," she said.

Then Hadel heard nothing for a month. "What's going on with them?" she complained to Thea.

"They'll work it out," Thea said.

But Hadel was worried. "Here I've been encouraging her. What if Hank's a creep?"

"Hadel! Don't you trust her judgment? Can't she recognize a creep?"

"Yes, of course she could. I just wonder why I haven't heard anything."

The phone rang early the next morning. Thea buried her head under the blankets. Hadel picked up the receiver groggily to listen to a male voice humming the wedding march. In the background she could hear what sounded like Natalie reciting something. Then the wedding march stopped as Hadel raised herself to one elbow, shaking her head to clear it. She heard the receiver being set down on something. Glass shattered in her ear, and then the receiver was hoisted up again. Hadel was beginning to smile, but she grated into the receiver: "What the fuck is this? The Memorex commercial?"

"You know what the glass means, don't you, sweetie?" Natalie's voice was loud and clear this time. "Go get on the other extension," she told her new husband.

"When?"

"One-half hour ago exactly. A civil ceremony. This was our own little private replay, just for you."

"Hello," Hank said. He sounded gaga, as if he'd won a Nobel prize and the Irish Sweepstakes in one day.

"Hello, Hank," Hadel said. "Congratulations." She was grinning ear to ear now, and Thea was beginning to tunnel out from the blankets.

"Mark your calendar," Natalie said. "February twenty-second. And in exactly three months we are taking a honeymoon out in your direction. Four days of bliss."

"Three months?"

"Big ad campaign now, Hadel, and Hank has many babies to deliver. It cuts into our tenth class reunion, but it's the only time Hank and I can get away. You don't mind not coming back here, do you? We can do the college-reunion thing next year."

"No, I don't care about the reunion. I wanted to *see* you get married, though. I'm never going to see anybody get married! I bet I'm the only person in the world who's never been to a wedding."

"But you *heard* a wedding, and that's even better. Both of us have to get to work now."

"O.K. Congratulations again. Bye, Hank."

"Looking forward to meeting you, Hadel."

The phones clicked. "Nothing to worry about," Thea said, divesting her head of the last blanket.

Hadel leaned over and kissed her, then lay on her back, staring at the bedroom ceiling. "Imagine," she said. "Natalie married. I've gotta call Ann and Portia. And where's that idiot Laney?"

"Back soon," Thea said. "It's nearly March. But I don't suggest you call anyone now. It's six-thirty in the morning. How 'bout some tea?"

"How 'bout going out to breakfast?" Hadel countered.

"Spendthrift. But I guess it could be managed."

The lesbian breakfast place didn't open until seven-thirty, but there were a million others. Berkeley had become a mecca for breakfasters, all of them gathering to linger long over home fries and wheat pancakes while the lines outside waited impatiently. Everyone was, after all, eager to get on with shopping.

At the cafe, amid the smoky voice of Marlene Dietrich singing "Lili Marlene," Hadel and Thea toasted each other, clinking together their mugs steaming with tea and coffee. "To fine days," Hadel said, "and happy marriages."

"Where is Laney?" Ann demanded. "It's the middle of April. Do you think I should start her stupid plants?"

Hadel curled her fingers in the air. "Who knows? I suppose it wouldn't hurt to start a few."

"Do you know how to do it?" Thea asked. She had made dinner this time, a beef stroganoff with sirloin strips. She was piling egg noodles on three plates, special made-that-very-day noodles Hadel had purchased at Gourmet Ghetto number two.

Ann copied Hadel's helpless gesture. "What's to know? You just toss 'em in a pot and water 'em, I guess." She paused for a taste as Thea set the plate in front of her. "Thea! My God! This is heaven."

"I've sworn off cooking forever," Hadel said after her sampling.

Thea flushed with pleasure and sat down at the table. "It *is* good," she agreed.

"Do you suppose Laney's gotten into some kind of trouble?" Ann asked, stating what was uppermost in their thoughts but so far unspoken.

It was certainly inappropriate to say the usual things, Hadel thought, such as, "Oh, she's probably just having too much fun to call." Besides, she was worried, too. What the hell did Laney know about being a prostitute? It was a floating culture with rules all its own, like the circus and the racetrack. Danger from within was only part of it. How many nuts had she run across in seven months? "We don't even know what name she was using," Hadel said with despair. "I don't see what we can do."

"She may be in jail," Thea suggested.

Hadel and Ann nodded, both thinking Laney in jail was safer than Laney on the street. "Can you use some of your connections to find out anything?" Hadel asked Ann.

"I suppose," Ann said, tapping her fingers next to her half-eaten dinner. "She's so adamant about our not getting involved in her other lives. But still—I think I'll wait another week and then see."

Ann ended up waiting three weeks, and then she put out the word to several policemen she knew. One man, with the Oakland P.D., called her back a few days later. "My guys have seen her," he told Ann. "Pretty, huh? I mean, really striking."

"That's right." Ann said.

"She was around awhile, but then she took off. They thought she'd moved on to a house or a call-girl deal. Too good for flagging down cars, you know? And it seemed she wasn't pumping it in her arm. Who is she, anyhow?"

Ann had debated how she would answer this question, formulating involved explanations about story contacts and features on prostitutes. She had finally decided on a simpler answer. "She's a friend of mine."

Her contact took it in stride. "O.K., if I hear anything more, I'll get back to you."

Meanwhile, Hadel was gearing up for Natalie and Hank's arrival. They were staying four days, arriving late Friday night and leaving Tuesday morning. "It's the most we can do," Natalie said, calling again from her office.

"Where do you want to stay?" Hadel asked. She could hardly consign the two of them to her couch for their honeymoon.

"Hank's sister's out there, too. She's gotten us a room at the Claremont in Berkeley. Is that nice?"

"Very nice," Hadel said. "Where's the sister live?"

"Walnut Creek. We're renting a car at the airport. Oh, Hadel, I can't wait until you meet him!"

"I can't wait for you to meet Thea. I guess it's bound to be all different," Hadel said, vaguely disgruntled. "No more sitting up late talking and stuff."

"Wrong, wrong, wrong. Here's the schedule. Saturday we zoom between your place and Walnut Creek. Saturday night we hang out in Walnut Creek. Sunday we spend together. Sunday night we split—I come to your place, and he goes back to his sister's. Monday we spend together. Monday night we spend with you. How's that sound?"

Hadel laughed. "Doesn't sound like much of a honeymoon."

"Well, you can't have it both ways. But honestly, it's O.K. He hasn't seen his sister for a long time, and I haven't seen you either. Besides, we've been honeymooning for months, even before we were married. Weekends, you know. Last week we went sailing on a friend's yacht. Rich doctors. Could you have the gang over Sunday?"

"There's not much of a gang. Ann'll come, I'm sure. I'll try to get Angela—"

"Angela? Oh. All right." They still didn't mention Portia's name on the telephone, though none of them believed the phones were tapped. It had become a habit.

"And Laney's not back yet," Hadel finished.

"Really? It's May."

"I know it's May, and Ann sure as hell knows it's May, but does Laney?"

"Hmmm. I hope she's O.K."

"Me, too," Hadel said, wishing there were some way of finding out for sure.

Hank was that rare sort of man who seemed gawky and uncomfortable when he was restrained—which could mean as little as being compelled to endure fifteen minutes of small talk over a cup of coffee—and beautifully graceful whenever his attention was engaged, particularly if movement was involved. Hadel had seen basketball players like Hank. Standing on the sidelines, their arms and legs seemed too big, and their shiftings from foot to foot uncoordinated and restless. But once they were motioned in by the coach, the gawkiness was revealed as the overcoat of enforced inactivity. Gliding up and down the court, timing jumps perfectly, they invested the sport with the smoothness of a well-choreographed ballet. Hank's hands seemed almost as long as his forearms and were moving constantly, with a raccoon's inquisitiveness, picking up objects, turning them over and over, feeling each plane. He looked at whatever he held only once; he trusted his fingertips more than his eyes. The contrast between Natalie and Hank was instructive: Natalie's semaphoring hands were trying to explain, to weave connections, to sketch in the shape of what she was saying. Hank's hands were testing, gauging, sensing. Their hands spelled out their professions, Hadel admitted to herself. Natalie's advertising career had never sat well with Hadel, but seeing her now in juxtaposition to a more interior Hank, Hadel understood Natalie's greatest joy came from communicating her own excitement to the public. She used the same skills selling Juliana Jeans as she had changing the parietal laws or appearing at showings of her Kent State film.

Both Thea and Hadel saw that Hank was incapable of relaxing in the living room. He was the kind of doctor who would rest from sixteen-hour days by crewing in a race or playing three sets of hard tennis. They took their guests on a tour of the house, ending up in Thea's redone garage. "Graphics," Hank said, trying out the word on his tongue. "I wonder . . . My business card is . . ." He couldn't find the right description.

"Your business card is one of ten million supplied free by a pharmaceutical company. It's the most mundane thing in the world," Natalie supplied tartly.

"I wonder," Hank continued. "Something more interesting?" He nearly stumbled over "interesting." The concept was hard for him. He probably *liked* the one-weight serif type centered on five lines.

"Exotic," Natalie prodded. Natalie craved four-color cards that blared trumpets upon being released from the confines of a wallet. "Best obstetrician east of the Mississippi."

But Thea had caught the drift. "Refined," she suggested.

Hank nodded vigorously.

"Nothing startling, nothing arty," Thea went on. "Simple but tasteful."

"Exactly!" Hank cried, relieved that his entry into such an unknown field had not ended in disaster. They both bent over

Thea's type book, discussing different faces. Within two minutes, Hank was penciling out ideas on scratch paper.

Natalie and Hadel sneaked out the side door of the garage and went back into the house. "Whatcha think, Hadel?" Natalie asked once she had her hand wrapped around a tall glass of orange juice.

"I think brilliant, sensitive, a perfect match and madly in love with you."

Natalie smiled. "Funny. That's just what I was going to say about Thea."

A great wave of exultation engulfed both of them, and though they sat motionless, they were far underwater, rolling and spinning. Natalie poked her head out first. "Ain't life swell?"

Hadel suggested eating out Monday night. "I thought you might be tired of home-cooked meals," Hadel told Natalie on the phone. "It'll be just the three of us, because Thea has a graphics class she teaches once a month. She can't switch it." The truth was, Hadel and Thea had put on quite a big spread for the gang the night before—a gang reduced to Ann, since Laney still wasn't back, and Portia couldn't make it up from L.A., having gotten a job working weekends on a word processor. Hadel didn't want to cook another big dinner.

"Wonderful," Natalie said. "Hank's feeling guilty. He says he's never had so many super meals, and he wants to reciprocate. So off to the City."

"You want to go over there?" Hadel had been thinking of a pasta place on University where the wait on Monday night was under a half hour.

"No! French in the City. Hank insists. Anyway, we haven't even been across the bridge yet. Why don't you meet us downtown around five-thirty, and we'll make it early."

"Sounds good," Hadel agreed.

The exterior of the restaurant boded ill, framed as it was by panhandling winos and scurrying elderly residents of the Tenderloin, their packages clutched to their chests in an attempt to discourage robbers, but once inside the heavy oak doors, quiet and opulence settled like silk snowflakes drifting down to cover satin sheets. Anything above a whisper seemed an affront.

"This is a surprise," Natalie breathed to Hadel.

"I know," Hadel mouthed back. "I thought we'd be mugged before we got in."

"You can talk," Hank told them in a normal voice, which made them both jump away, practically into the path of the maître d', who bore down upon them with the look of a man meeting his beloved in a field of tall grass. "Dr. Rothman!" he cried. "How delightful!"

Hank's explanation had to wait until after they were seated, an operation that demanded much pulling out of chairs and waving of napkins in the air. "Well?" Natalie asked finally.

"He's my sister's husband's boyhood buddy," Hank told them. "Last time I was here, we all went fishing out on the bay."

Hadel tried to imagine the maître d' in spray-drenched old clothes, trailing his fishing line from the stern of a boat. It was impossible. Surely the man had been born in that tux.

Hank arranged courses of escargot, asparagus vinaigrette and entrées for the three of them. Hadel ended up with veal and mushrooms bathed in brown sauce and Madeira. "Oh Lord," she said, "I've got to stop eating this way, but tomorrow is soon enough."

Natalie made her big announcement over fresh blueberries in cream and a bottle of champagne. "I'm pregnant," she told Hadel.

"Already?" Hadel yelped. "When?" When what? she asked herself, scandalized by her own question.

Natalie laughed at Hadel's confusion. "Calm down," she said. "I'm seven weeks pregnant. We found out just before we left for the trip. The only people we've told are Hank's sister and you. I'm going to tell my parents when we get back to New York."

"That's great! You didn't waste any time," Hadel said, counting back to the first of April. "Imagine." She sipped at her champagne. Natalie pregnant. Natalie with a child. Natalie a mother. "You shouldn't be drinking!" she said suddenly.

"I haven't had much," Natalie protested. "Hardly any. And I stopped smoking. Almost, anyway," she amended, remembering she had bummed two cigarettes from Hadel the night before. "And no dope," she added solemnly.

Hadel laughed. "You don't get points for that, Nats. You haven't smoked dope since 1970."

"She knows me too well," Natalie told Hank.

The bill arrived, and Hank paid it off with plastic, always easier, Hadel thought, than everyone discreetly turning one's head as the bills were piled on the tray. Once out on the street, Hank proposed a walk. "Lovely evening."

"Lots of sirens," Hadel said. They ambled toward Civic Center and met up with White Night, the riot that followed the jury bringing back a verdict of voluntary manslaughter against Dan White.

"Manslaughter?" Hadel asked a woman in the crowd. "Both counts?" Since White had reloaded his gun before he shot Harvey Milk, few felt he would receive the lower conviction for Milk's death.

"He got away with murder," the woman said, a sentiment that was echoed by a huge spray-painted sign on a restaurant wall next to the plaza, and by the avengers' chants: "Kill Dan White! Kill Dan White!"

Hadel could see a mob of people on the steps of City Hall, and she edged closer, Natalie and Hank a cautious rear guard. Behind the people on the steps, who seemed to be holding back the rioters, the heavy glass doors to City Hall were broken. As the three moved forward, a cadre of police mounted the steps and began beating the few who had been trying to calm the crowd. Someone lit a police car on fire, and then someone else built a blaze near the steps. The police car's gas tank exploded with a roar. Natalie caught up to Hadel. "Hey!" Natalie shouted.

"I don't want to leave!" Hadel shouted back. Then she spotted a familiar head several inches taller than hers, midway through the crowd. "Ann!" she hollered. "Ann!" Ann turned around, first to the left, then behind. She waved the three of them forward. Glass shattered close by and someone screamed. A man next to Hadel picked up a chunk of concrete and threw it, breaking one of the first-floor windows. Hadel looked at him, a short-haired young guy with the requisite Castro Street moustache. They smiled at each other, and then he disappeared behind two men trying to hoist another man onto their shoulders.

Ann was motioning at them to move to the right. She started moving in that direction herself. Hadel turned and encountered the moustached young man again, this time ripping at the concrete to find more pieces to throw. Natalie caught up to her as Hadel watched the man for a minute, amazed he had enough strength to tear the concrete from the plaza. As if to underline this image of strength, two young musclemen types, incongruously clothed in sweat pants and cutoff tee shirts, abbreviated to show off their washboard stomachs, trotted by with the perfect urban battering rams, a mangled parking meter post apiece, the coins inside the meters jangling as the men ran. Hadel closed her eyes for an instant, finding herself. Had she ever pictured herself in a riot, she would have imagined being among the people at the front, begging the rioters for a return to sanity. Far from it. She would not throw a rock, nor break down a door, but she wouldn't do as the three men next to her were doing either, trying to drag the guy with the moustache away from his pile of concrete ammunition. She would stand here with a wide grin on her face and watch it all night if it went on that long. She would let the cries and chants and breaking glass heal the infected wounds of growing up gay. When she turned at the sound of another hollered "Kill Dan White!" she was startled to see Natalie standing beside her, watching her with the expression she usually reserved for Megan. "What's wrong?" Hadel asked.

"What's wrong with you?" Natalie countered. "Why are you smiling?" Hank hove into view and wrapped his arm around Natalie's shoulder.

"Because it's time, that's why," Hadel told Natalie. "For once we're saying, 'Stop pissing on me.' Because," she gestured at the glass and rocks flying around them, "this makes me feel what I've wanted to feel for years."

Hank tugged at Natalie. "Come on," he insisted, "let's get out of here."

Natalie nodded. She and Hadel looked at each other for a moment, and then Natalie swung around and strode through the crowd after Hank.

Hadel found Ann under a tree. "Where were you?" Ann

asked, her voice too high. She needed no makeup to put life into her face tonight. "Did you see the crew? I've been looking for them. Where's Natalie?"

"Natalie and Hank left," Hadel said. "I'll come with you."

The Channel 8 team was under cover of another tree a dozen yards away. The cameraman grabbed Ann. "Let's hit it," he said. "They've called David down, but he hasn't gotten here yet. We need a stand-up right away." Ann began moving through the crowd, the crew following her, searching for a good place to show the action behind her as she provided commentary. She tagged one rock-thrower for an interview on the way. After less than twenty seconds, the soundman laid his hand on her elbow. Hadel stepped close to hear. "Lorin says for us to get you the hell out of here."

"Why?" Ann sputtered, knowing why.

"No-go. Anyway, here comes David."

David grabbed the microphone out of Ann's limp fingers. He pointed toward a knot of people tossing things, and they moved in that direction. The soundman yelled back, "Lorin says he wants to see you at the station." At the look on Ann's face, he raised his hand waist high. "Messenger boy, right? Not my fault."

David hollered, "Come on!" at him, and the four took off, dragging their equipment with them.

Ann was anchored to the pavement. "Ann," Hadel said. Then something caught her eye and she pointed. "Look!"

A coordinated team of men was systematically firing a block-long line of empty police cars. The upholstery of each car caught fire seconds after the one before, and the flames shot up inside, illuminating the jagged windows through which the men had stuffed burning material. Activated by the heat, each siren clicked on in turn, wailing eerily until the fire ate its way through their wires. As if by signal, as the siren on the last car faded, the gas tank of the first car exploded, and the sound echoed all down the line, staggered booms hollow in the night.

CHAPTER 28

Natalie hadn't called from the hotel before she and Hank had gone back to New York Tuesday morning. A week later, Hadel received a letter. "I guess there are some things I never understood," Natalie wrote. "Years ago, when you told me about yourself, I saw myself strangling the whole world to protect you. I didn't think you were in a position to protect yourself. I suppose I was still protecting you when I tackled Megan over the Ridgedale purge business. What I felt Monday night, seeing you smile at that devastation, was confusion and betrayal. I've thought about it since, as you can see, and now I believe I understand. I suppose I was frightened you may not need me anymore, until I realized you haven't needed me that way for a long time, maybe ever.

"I don't know whether you heard there was a demonstration in New York the next night. Between the flight and gaining three hours, we almost walked into that one, too. The signs the demonstrators carried said, 'We all live in San Francisco,' and 'Who killed Harvey Milk?' When I went to work Wednesday, no one could fathom the second sign. 'Dan White killed him,' they said. 'What are they talking about?' This letter is to tell you I think I know what you're talking about."

"Natalie," Hadel wrote back, "your letter means as much to me as the riot, so that should tell you how much I need you. And I'm thankful that you need me enough to make the effort to understand. P.S. Have you thought about names yet? I'm so excited you're pregnant I raced to the library for a name book. After looking through it, I see I'm tending to Gaelic names, but I suppose that's not on. Anyway, I want to hear every little detail, so keep in touch."

Natalie rejected Gaelic names, but she did write or call once a week. If Hank was home, he got on the line, too. "Easiest pregnancy I've ever seen," he crowed. "She's the absolute picture of health."

"Great! No smoking now, Natalie."

"I should import you back here to watch me at work," Natalie said, "except I have a dozen watchers already. In fact, I was in seeing Mr. Pearson, head honcho, who would probably run over his own grandmother if it resulted in a good campaign, and I was so nervous being called into his office that I reached out for one of the cigarettes on his desk, and he slapped my hand away! I didn't even know he knew!"

"Why were you called in?"

"Praise. Can you believe it? And praise from him means an automatic raise, though he would never mention anything so crass."

"What will you do about work? Are you going to quit?"

"Oh, no! I'm taking four months off starting in December. It's a bad time, but every time is bad. Then it's back to the grindstone. We have to hire someone to take care of little whoever."

"Whoever?"

"You'll be the first to know of names in the running, Hadel. Laney's still not back, huh? You would have said."

"No. Ann is about ready to tear out her hair."

"Being a prostitute may have been Laney's last hurrah. You all should have checked her into a bin when she came up with that one."

"It happened in the space of twenty minutes, and she was out the door. Ann's been going through a lot of changes over it."

"I bet," Natalie said. "I just bet."

Ann had recontacted her policemen friends in June. They had heard nothing. "Maybe it's for the best," Ann told Hadel on one of Hadel's rare visits to Ann's house. "I don't know what to think. When she left that night, I was determined I would never see her again. Period. Determined isn't even strong enough. I *knew*. The thought of her being a prostitute makes me sick. And I started wondering about what she'd done before, as the rock star or the businesswoman or the tennis player. We never talked about that—I just assumed. . . . I don't know *why* I assumed anything. Anything! I mean, this is crazy, Hadel, look at it realistically. It's nuts!"

Hadel noticed Ann didn't say Laney was nuts.

"Seeing you and Thea together makes it worse," Ann continued. "I think, why can't I have that? Why does my lover leave for six months out of each year? And half the time she's around, she's not really there. She's coming out of something and going into something else. Then I feel bad for thinking all that, because I love her. There was a night in Woodsmere when I knew I loved her . . . that hasn't changed. I suppose the knowing then was stronger than the knowing I felt at your house the night she left. But I'm tired, Hadel. I'm tired of it."

Two weeks later, in the middle of July, Ann called Hadel at one in the morning. "Hadel!" she choked.

Hadel juggled the receiver between numb hands, trying to wake up fast. She finally got the receiver back to speaking level. "Ann?"

"I just got home and listened to my answering machine. Evan called sometime today, and she said Laney's at Herrick Hospital and she might die."

"I'll pick you up."

"No!" Ann hollered as Hadel was about to disconnect. "I'll meet you there."

"What's going on?" Thea asked, watching Hadel pull on her pants.

"Laney's at Herrick," Hadel said. "Remember when Laney was being a nurse? Evan, that nurse friend of hers, says Laney may be dying. Do you want to come with me?"

Thea didn't hesitate. "No, I don't. Would you feel terrible?"

"No, honey." Hadel leaned over and kissed her. "I'll be back."

"Is she there as the prostitute?" Thea wondered. "Or as herself?"

Hadel shook her head. "I guess we'll find out."

Hadel dashed to emergency, and they directed her to the third floor. She burst out of the elevator to find Ann standing a few feet away from the nurses' station, holding a small white daisy in her hand, talking to a doctor whose attempt to hide his bald spot by combing his hair forward made him look like Nero. He was beaming at Ann. "I can't believe it's really you," he said, his voice trembling with awe. "Evan didn't tell me she meant *the* Ann Bailor." Hadel stepped into their tiny circle, and the doctor glared at her and moved a few inches closer to Ann, protecting her, it seemed, from her star-struck public.

"She's my friend," Ann explained. "I asked her to come. Hadel, this is Dr. Johnson."

Hadel nodded at him. "How is Laney?"

Hadel thought he was returning her nod, but instead he was bobbing his head to indicate Laney was all right. "The message Evan left on your machine was correct at the time," he told Ann. "I should have had her call you back. But I suppose we all wanted some answers. Apparently this Laney has a dual personality?"

"Well—" Ann began.

"Laney's not dying?" Hadel asked.

"Not now." The doctor swung toward Hadel. "But she *was* in danger this afternoon when she was brought in. Her throat was slashed from ear to ear."

Ann's face went as gray as her eyes, and Hadel caught her elbow.

The doctor swung back. "I'm terribly sorry, Miss Bailor. I didn't mean to shock you like that. Would you like to sit down?" He touched her other elbow, but Ann shook them both off.

"No, please, just tell me what happened."

"She was brought to emergency by the Berkeley police ambulance after a fight with other prostitutes. She was admitted as Dorie Purser." He beckoned to one of the two nurses behind the counter of the nurses' station. She handed him an envelope containing a thin stack of cards. "All I.D. as Dorie Purser," he said, fanning out the cards. "Yet Evan insists her name is Laney Villano. The police don't know that part, but they do have questions for Purser."

"I'll take care of the police," Ann said softly.

"But I would like to understand too, Miss Bailor. This Dorie Purser lives in Florida. If Laney becomes Dorie often, it could get expensive." He smiled.

"No," Ann said. "She's never been this particular person before. It's hard to explain, Doctor. She's, uhm—"

"Disturbed?" the doctor prompted.

"She's not certifiable," Hadel told him. "She'd waltz through an observation period. These things she does are like . . . a hobby."

"A dangerous one then," he told Hadel. He looked back at Ann, who was growing wide-eyed as the shock of thinking Laney dead began to hit. The doctor himself, Hadel thought, was also a little boggled. He was probably wondering why on earth *the* Ann Bailor was mixed up with this nut case who'd happened to have her throat slit. He seemed to think about it for a moment before he chose Ann's well-publicized compassion as the reason. "I must say, Miss Bailor, it's certainly lucky for Laney that she has such a devoted friend—"

"She's my lover," Ann interrupted.

Hadel wondered why she'd said it. Because she felt the doctor was crediting her for something she didn't deserve? Because she couldn't disassociate herself from Laney so blatantly? The nurses behind Hadel had stopped rustling papers to listen.

"Yes . . ." Dr. Johnson said, as if he were about to continue, and then, "Oh," when what Ann had said finally penetrated.

"Could we see Laney now?" Hadel asked.

"Room three-fifteen. I've enjoyed meeting you, Miss Bailor," he told Ann stiffly. His rubber-soled shoes whispered as he strode off down the tiled hallway.

Ann and Hadel walked in the other direction, looking at room numbers. Room 315 was at the end of a long hall. Hadel shoved open the door. Ann stepped in front of her and peered inside. She seemed to collapse. The bed was empty and unmade.

"Maybe she's in the bathroom," Hadel said, moving toward the closed door on the left, knowing that Laney wasn't in the bathroom, that Laney had simply strolled down the stairway next to her room, leaving Ann to deal with questions from the doctor and the police. Hadel turned back from the bathroom in time to see Ann, rooted beside the disheveled bed, snip her wilted daisy in half between two fingernails. She dropped the pieces on the floor. "Damn her."

They left by the same staircase Laney had used, walking up Dwight Way to their cars. "Can you drive?" Hadel asked. "Would you like me to follow you?"

"I'm fine. Anyway, I have to get right to bed. Thank you for coming." She took Hadel's hand and then seemed unsure what to do with it. A squeeze was too human for her robotlike state. She extricated her hand carefully, got in her car and drove away. Hadel followed at a discreet distance and watched Ann into the house. By the time Hadel had arrived home and unlocked her front door, the phone was ringing. She grabbed it an instant before Thea's flailing arm connected with the receiver. "Yes?" One didn't have to be polite at two-thirty in the morning.

"She's here," Ann reported, herself again. "Her face is cut up." Hadel heard her suck in a deep breath. "I'll tell you more tomorrow."

Hadel set the phone down as Thea, still searching, found the bedside lamp switch. She sat up blinking. "What happened?"

Hadel told her. Thea nodded, shielding her eyes from the light. "So. Laney returns with a bang, and Ann comes out. In front of a doctor and what? Two nurses?"

"And me," Hadel reminded her.

"And you. Lordy, what will her public think? Not that anyone is likely to hear." She paused, tilting her head. "Maybe a few rumors."

Hadel was remembering how her own mother had refused to believe Tony was gay for years, because "he's such a nice man." "You know what?" Hadel marveled. "Ann could announce right on her news show that she's a lesbian, say she's been a lesbian for years and I bet not more than a tenth of her viewers would believe it! They'd write in asking why the station was making wonderful Ann tell such horrible lies." She leaned over to untie her shoelaces. "My God," she said, her chin between her knees, "what an awful fix she's in. How can she possibly stand it?"

Hadel waited to hear from Ann for two days, gave up and called their place on Sunday morning. Laney answered. "Hadel! I missed you. How're you doing?"

"Fine," Hadel said. "I hear you're not in the best shape."

"Garbage. I'm super. I may look a little different, but I'm O.K. You weren't calling about one of your Sunday dinners, were you? We'd love to see you, and I certainly wouldn't turn down your cooking."

Hadel hesitated. She hadn't been planning a dinner, but

more than that, she felt she should clear the idea with Ann first. How could she talk to Ann without Laney knowing? Hadel pondered logistics and cover stories for a moment; then she listened to her thoughts and performed the mental gymnastics of jumping back from herself in horror. What's the matter with me? I don't think Laney is competent to make a decision about dinner? "Of course," she said. "Six-thirty?"

"With bells," Laney answered. Hadel thought she heard a smile in her voice.

Thea answered the door while Hadel washed the last of the lettuce. When Thea reentered the kitchen, her eyes were slightly glazed. "Uh—" she began, but Laney sidled in front of her, while Ann hung to the back, trapped in the hallway by the traffic jam at the doorway. Hadel put down the lettuce leaf she was holding. Laney's face was a road map of cuts and sutures; her lips were swollen, and along the joining of her throat and her head, etched strikingly against her pale skin, was an incision the shape of a shark's bite, traveling ear to ear. Black stitches studded the cut. "Frankenstein's monster, huh?" Laney grinned. "Poor Hadel. You're shocked, aren't you?"

Hadel swallowed.

"Honestly, Hadel, two weeks and they'll just be little red lines, and then little white lines, and then"—she snapped her fingers—"nothing. Missed my jugular, missed my windpipe, missed everything. Lucky, of course."

Hadel couldn't imagine that word fitting anything she saw in front of her. She realized Ann was still standing in the hallway. "Come in," Hadel said. "Everybody come in and sit down." Reflex courtesy. She busied herself spinning the lettuce. "How can you talk, Laney? Doesn't it hurt?"

"Oh, I can talk," Laney said, and she proceeded to do so. Later, all Hadel remembered of the dinner was Laney talking on and on, while Ann ate silently and Thea got up frequently to perform little errands, as if she couldn't bear to be at the table. Only one stretch of conversation stood out, and it began when Laney announced, without prompting, that she had no idea what her next role would be. "Odd, huh?" When no one responded, Laney equivocated: "Well, that's not *entirely* true. I do have a last role in mind, but I'm not sure I want to use it. I'll have to see how things go first."

"Last role?" Ann asked after a moment. "Does that mean no more roles?"

Hadel had to force herself to look at Laney, trying to find one unbruised section of Laney's face she could focus on. That the next role might be the last was a far more amazing revelation than Laney's October pronouncement that she was going off to be a prostitute, but this time no one dropped baguettes or choked. The only reaction Laney had provoked was Ann's belated and almost tremulous question. Laney had exhausted all three of them.

But what did this last-role business mean? Hadel knew that Ann felt responsible for Laney's starting the roles, that Laney hadn't been able to depend upon Ann and had developed this bizarre other means to control her environment. Did stopping the roles mean Laney would again look to Ann to keep her safe? Or had Laney somehow cured herself?

Laney didn't answer Ann directly. "Ann, it really is amazing how much you resemble my brother. Sometimes I just can't get over it."

Hadel couldn't stop herself from glancing at Ann. She felt as if she were staring at a car wreck, but Ann seemed normal enough, her index finger angled toward her temple in that sometimes inquiring, sometimes bewildered way she had. Thea chose that moment to check an imagined noise in the backyard. Hadel wished Thea had stuck around when Ann reclaimed her raised hand to join the other in an intertwined knot on the table in front of her, lifted up her chin and said, in a voice as dry as sand, "I shall take that as a compliment."

A smile broke out all over Laney's ravaged face. "But of course! What else?"

"I didn't know you had a brother, Laney," Hadel said. "What does he do?" She hoped he was a computer programmer in Houston, with a wife and two kids, and that they could spend the rest of the evening talking about him.

"He's dead," Laney said. "He died two days before I graduated from high school."

Thea returned in time for this information. She sat down gingerly, probably praying, Hadel thought, for more noises in back or a full-scale assault up the front steps. Laney began to describe racial problems in Miami, where, she said, she had gone for Christmas but stayed six months. Thea remembered a telephone call she had to make. It turned out to be very long and involved, stretching all the way through dessert, coffee and good-byes.

1980

CHAPTER 29

"So where's the kid?" Hadel asked Natalie after she'd finally gotten through to New Rochelle on New Year's Day. Natalie and Hank had recently purchased a three-bedroom house, which they'd moved into over Thanksgiving.

"They don't just pop out after nine months on the button, Hadel. Babies aren't slices of toast."

"But if he-she-it were born today, he-she, et cetera would be exactly twenty years old in the year 2000."

Natalie sighed. "That hadn't occurred to me. I'll try to convey that information by osmosis. Believe me, I'm not the one who's holding up the show. I feel like a hotel that's bursting at the seams."

"Uncomfortable, huh?" Hadel stretched out on the living-room couch. She could tell, by Natalie's wistful tone as opposed to her usual rush-rush, that Natalie would like to talk for a while.

"Just the last few weeks. What's going on out there?"

"Thea's fine," Hadel reported. "We were just talking about her business. She started operating out of the garage about two years ago, and it's just now really taken off. It was difficult at first, because most of her clients were in the City or on the Peninsula, so she lost some people and she had to do pickup and delivery for others. But now she has two monthly papers and a lot of city of Oakland jobs."

"That's good. What about Laney and Ann?"

"Ann's riding high. Channel Eight's Christmas show was the height of something—I don't know what. Treacle and glitter and neon sweetness."

"Ann is a reporter, Hadel, not a one-woman soap opera."

"Tell her. She did animal stories, grandmother stories, Santa stories, a Christmas ham story—on Thanksgiving she went to a turkey farm—and, of course, many children stories, ill, newly born, caught in trees, abandoned, mastering computers at age four—"

"Stop already! I get the idea!"

"Laney is strangely quiescent," Hadel continued. "No one's used to having her around at this time of year, but still, all she's done since she returned in July is play in her yard. I think she's landscaping. I know she's planted two trees. Ann says Laney communes with them during the day."

"Sounds relaxing. I don't suppose work is in her future. Since she's stopped her roles, I mean."

"I don't know that she has stopped. I told you she had a last role in mind. I gathered it was different, something she'd thought of a long time ago. I'm not really sure what she's doing, Natalie. I've seen them only briefly."

"All right," Natalie said, jumping ahead to the next topic. "Angela?"

It always took Hadel a moment to remember Angela was Portia. "Ah. Now we do have news. Something happened to Angela."

"What?"

"She got arrested at an antinuke demonstration."

"*What?* But that means—"

"Oddly enough, it doesn't. They booked her and then they released her immediately. Angela thought one could choose to be arrested, like if she blocked a gate or something. She went to lend peripheral support to those who had planned to be arrested. Except the cops swept everyone up. They dragged them all in on buses, booked them, released them and then dropped the charges two weeks later. The county was screaming about court costs."

"But her fingerprints . . ."

"She says now they know she's alive. She's completely unconcerned about it."

"My God." Hadel imagined Natalie in the bedroom of a house she'd never seen, her belly enormous, shaking her head in astonishment.

"Is Hank there?" Hadel asked.

"He dashed off a couple of hours ago. He should be back by now."

"But what if you go into labor?"

"Hadel, remember women in the fields? I am perfectly capable of calling him or taking a cab. He's at the hospital, which is ten minutes away. There is no danger—repeat, no danger."

"All right," Hadel grumbled. "Phone instantly, day or night."

"I will," Natalie promised. "Now I think I'll try that osmosis business. I'm as eager for this to be over as you are."

Hadel refused to leave the house for more than fifteen minutes during the next two days. She sat at her desk waiting, telling herself she was too excited to write. Laney called once, but Hadel hurried her off the phone. Finally, past dark on the third, just as Hadel and Thea were sitting down to dinner, the phone rang.

"Natalie?" Hadel asked. Then she glanced guiltily at Thea; it might, after all, be one of Thea's graphics clients.

"Yes," came an exhausted voice. "It is me. I. Whatever."

Hadel gave Thea a thumbs-up sign and said, "Well?" into the receiver.

"Boy, eight pounds exactly."

"Boy," Hadel told Thea. "Are you all right?" she asked Natalie.

"Tired as hell, but I'm fine. He's fine, too. I've got him right here in front of me as I talk."

"Is he cute?"

"Oh!" Natalie sounded surprised at this question. "Well, I don't know that I'd go that far. I don't think babies are cute—human babies, anyway. When you think about it, humans aren't very attractive. He's kind of ugly."

"Don't worry, Natalie. After you get to know him, you'll bore everybody to tears with how lovely he is."

"I can't imagine that!" Natalie huffed. "Hank thinks he's magnificent. But I already love him. Isn't that strange? Why do I love this red, shriveled thing that's going to keep me up nights for six months or more? By the way, I've extended my leave from work until June. That's better, don't you think?" Natalie's voice had begun to fade.

"Much. Give baby and Papa a kiss from me and Thea. I'm getting off right now, but tell me his name. David or Paul?"

"At the last moment—now, Hadel—"

"My God," Hadel was muttering. "How long have we pondered these names?"

"There are simply too many Pauls," Natalie said with a new burst of energy. "And I already told you I don't like Dave."

"You don't call him Dave."

"His friends might. Anyway, we named him Michael. Mike's O.K."

"Michael. Mike." Hadel rolled it around on her tongue. "Perfect."

"Oh, good." Natalie heaved a sigh of relief.

"All right, now give Michael a kiss. Give yourself a kiss, and call me when you're home." Hadel broke the connection and stepped around the table to hug Thea, who said through the hug that she thought Michael was a wonderful name. Hadel sat back down and began to dial numbers as she ate. She left a message for Ann at work, talked briefly to Portia in L.A. and then called Laney at home. "Terrific!" Laney said. "Good she had a boy."

"Why?" Hadel was puzzled. "I think Hank wanted a girl, and Natalie didn't care."

"Things aren't getting any better in this cold, cruel world of ours. A boy has a better chance of survival. Listen, when am I going to see you?"

"Oh, I don't know. I'll call you later, O.K.?"

"The truth of the matter," Hadel told Thea after she'd hung up, "is I don't especially want to see Laney."

"Why?" Thea was carefully cutting the fat from her lamb chop into tiny pieces for her elderly orange-and-white cat, who was waiting patiently by the side of her chair.

"I'm not sure. Maybe I'm still suffering from the aftereffects of that horrible dinner in July, when she had those stitches. I keep staring at her throat, looking for scars. And she seems so aimless now, as if she's not sure what to do with herself. In a way, I wish she'd do her last role, whatever the hell it is, and then go on with her life."

"You've always said the roles are her life," Thea reminded her.

"Well, yes, but she must have something more in mind or she wouldn't have a last role, right?"

Thea shook her head. "Nothing is ever simple where Laney's concerned."

When Hadel ran into Laney the following week outside the coffee bean store, she remembered Thea's observation. Their encounter began innocently enough: Laney was, as usual, sitting on one of the wooden benches, sipping coffee out of her pottery mug. The only jarring note was her eyes, which were red and swollen, as if she'd been crying.

"What's wrong?" Hadel asked, checking to make sure the bench was dry before she sat down.

"Nothing," Laney said. "Nice day, huh?"

The perpetual winter rains had taken a break the night before. "That's why I ventured out," Hadel said. "Get away from the house while I can."

Laney fixed her with a watery gaze. "How come you haven't mentioned your stories lately?"

"I haven't been writing much," Hadel admitted. She couldn't help examining Laney's throat. The scars had faded to the barest white lines, probably only noticeable to someone who knew they were there.

"Waving the white flag, eh? Retreating from the battlements of boys' adventure? Get with it, kid. Your audience awaits."

Hadel smiled. Laney must be all right if she were capable of making her snide remarks. Laney handed her the mug of coffee, and Hadel downed a hefty slug of the dark, rich brew.

"So," Laney continued, "the child is born. Portia, too, is thinking of having a kid. How strange that we've forgotten what we knew instinctively in our twenties."

"Which was?"

"That bringing a baby into this world is close to negligence. We killed the conventions, Hadel. But the joke's on us. We're all so idealistic and mannerly we'll never be able to live with the chaos that's rushed in to fill the gap our slaughter of convention created. Our children won't be able to live with that chaos either, because they'll be raised with our values. In twenty years we'll be longing for the fifties, not the sixties."

"What are you babbling about, Laney?" Hadel asked hotly.

"At least she had a boy," Laney concluded. Then she turned away and sneezed at least six times in rapid succession.

"You're sick!" Hadel accused. "You've got that flu, and you let me drink out of your mug. I thought," she added irritably, "that getting sick wasn't part of your life plan."

"I am not sick," Laney insisted. "Are you buying something? Yes? Come on, I'll wait in line with you."

They entered the store and instantly met up with the end of the line. Hadel groaned. "Good God, must everyone buy coffee the same damn day?" Then she turned again to Laney. "Do you hang out here every afternoon?"

Laney smiled. "No, I generally hang out in my backyard every afternoon. I come here in the mornings."

"You know, you could help Ann—"

"With her apartment building," Laney finished. "Funny, Ann was just saying that very thing yesterday. She says it's almost no work. If it's so little work, why does she need help?"

"Because her job takes fifty-five hours a week," Hadel said reasonably, moving forward an inch as the person way at the head of the line was served. "Any extra thing is too much for her."

"She'll need that apartment building soon," Laney said mysteriously.

Hadel bore the silence for another inch of forward movement. "Why?" she finally sighed.

"Because she's getting sick of her job," Laney answered. "'Happy news' is becoming too much for her. It's odd—she's the only one who had a career at the start, when everybody was flailing around for four or five years finding themselves. And now she'll drop her career just as everyone else settles into theirs." She began sneezing again. Hadel touched her hand to Laney's forehead. "You have a fever."

"Nah," Laney said.

"You do, Laney. Look, I'll drive you home after I've finished here. You can show me your trees."

"And my perennials," Laney added. "I'm putting in a big perennial bed."

"Where?" Hadel tried to visualize Laney's backyard.

"Where the vegetable garden used to be. Ann needs something easy and carefree."

Why, Hadel wondered. Was Laney planning to go off again? Hadel faced front, her eyes narrowed with thought.

"You know," Laney said behind her, "I never thanked you for coming to the hospital that night. I had to get out of there. You've probably noticed how it is when someone feels rotten and then someone else does, and pretty soon it's a malaise sweeping through everything and everyone."

"Sure I have," Hadel said. "Like letting me drink out of your mug." But a woman in a red cape had just drifted over from contemplating the timed coffee-maker display to cut in line in front of her. "Pardon me," Hadel said, tapping the woman's shoulder, "I believe my friend and I and"—she glanced over her shoulder at the eight people who'd come in after them—"those people back there are all in front of you."

"My goodness!" the woman exclaimed, feigning amazement. "Is this a line? My goodness!"

She wavered back toward the coffee makers, as if unsure what to do next. Hadel watched her out of the corner of her eye. "Now what were you saying?"

"The hospital," Laney said. "They put in the stitches with a local, but they wanted to check on me later because it was such a big gash. They admitted me. In my wing alone—"

The woman in the red cape was strolling around again. Hadel stepped closer to the man in front of her. Her nose was almost against his spine. "Yes?"

"There were heart problems and kidney disease and who knows what else."

Hadel turned slightly, still watching the woman, who seemed to be tiptoeing toward the front door. "So?"

"So all those things are wafting around. That's why I left. It wasn't because you and Ann were coming. I wanted you to know that."

"Laney! What's wrong with you? You can't catch heart disease!"

But as Laney was looking dismayed, struggling for an answer, the woman in the red cape slid behind her, inserting herself neatly between Laney and a man who had been yelling at his dog to stay out of the store. "Hey, lady," the man said when he'd swiveled around to see the telltale cape in front of his eyes, "this is a line."

The woman studiously ignored him. She stared straight ahead toward the jars of imported jams and jellies.

"Hey, now look," the man complained. He tapped her as Hadel had done, and when she still didn't respond, he gave her a small shove, enough to send her into Laney, who appeared suddenly paralyzed, her limbs immobile, as if she were carved out of marble.

"Laney?" Hadel said.

Two tears gathered in the corners of Laney's eyes.

"Laney?"

The caped woman's jaw was set determinedly. Laney's face was also set, Hadel saw, but it was cemented with panic. Hadel touched her shoulder. "Let's go, Laney. Let's get out of here."

"Goddamnit, you can't cut in on me!" the man shouted. He shoved again, harder, and this time the whole front of the line reacted. The caped woman nearly fell on top of Laney. Hadel caught Laney, who had toppled as stiffly as a tree, and Hadel bumped hard into the man in front of her.

"What's going on here?" one of the employees asked. "Who's doing this?" The answer was apparent, because everyone in back of the aggrieved man was staring at him. "Shame on you," the employee told the man. He began to explain, but she had already swung her attention toward Hadel and the man in front of her. "Now what would you both like?" she asked.

Hadel shook her head helplessly. "Nothing." She gripped Laney's arm. "C'mon, let's go!"

Laney moved slowly, sleepwalking through the crowd, her eyes almost closed. They finally reached the sidewalk. "What's happening?" Hadel asked, but Laney had already come to with a start. "I didn't mean to say that," she said over Hadel's question. "I didn't mean it."

"What?"

"The hospital. I didn't mean you could catch heart disease."

Hadel watched her for a moment. Laney was breathing shallowly, but that might be the effects of the flu. All that mattered to Laney at the moment was that Hadel believed her. "Oh, I know," Hadel said. "Of course that wasn't what you meant. But are you still scared? That guy in back of you—"

"I'm not scared. And I'm not sick!"

Humor her, Hadel told herself. "O.K. Would you like to show me your trees?"

"No," Laney said. She walked away down Walnut, heading toward the plant store.

Hadel stared after her until Laney had turned into the arcade. What the hell? Hadel wondered. What the hell is going on?

When Thea came into the house the next morning for her coffee and toast break, she peeked into the study. Hadel was surrounded by a heap of receipts for copying and stationery supplies. She was so busy punching buttons on her little pocket calculator, she didn't notice Thea. "Aren't you writing?" Thea asked.

"Oh! Well, not exactly. I'm figuring out my taxes."

Thea hesitated, tapping her fingers on the desk. Hadel knew she was working on a brochure that was due the following afternoon. "You don't have to—" Hadel started.

"No," Thea decided. "Come on, let's go for a walk down at the Marina. I've got lots of time."

On the beach, walking amid half-buried tires and broken chunks of concrete, Thea asked, "So why aren't you writing?"

"I'm having a midlife crisis."

"You're too young. You're only thirty-two."

"Nevertheless."

They continued on until they'd crested the knoll and come to the edge of the brick yard, where they sat looking out at the bay and the bridges. "Are you still worried about that Mr. Cromwell not signing his own letters?" Thea had agreed with Laney that the signatures could not possibly be by the same hand.

"No . . . I guess his letters are being retyped by someone. I was thinking just now about Portia getting arrested."

"Yes?"

"Well, maybe she'll have a further charge."

"You said they'd dropped all the charges."

"For her. A further charge for her. Because she's a fugitive." Hadel raised her hands to sketch an explanation in the air, but what she'd said made no sense to her. She dropped her hands into her lap. "Also," she continued doggedly, "Laney tore up the vegetable garden to put in a perennial bed. She said Ann would have an easier time taking care of it. What's that mean?"

"Hadel, you told me that last night. I want to hear why you haven't been writing."

"It just seems like a lot of stuff is going on, and I'm lost in fantasies of honor and courage. I've been writing adventure stories for boys for nine years." She paused. "Maybe the trouble is I'm not lost in them anymore." She didn't continue, but Thea knew there was a lot more.

"You don't want to see Laney because she seems so aimless," Thea said. "Don't you feel aimless, too?"

"No. Yes." Hadel smiled at herself. "But it's more than indecision and aimlessness. I feel as if I'm missing something, that these things that are happening around me would be comprehensible if I could just grab hold of them for one minute."

"You think your stories are somehow related to what's going on, or they're completely irrelevant?"

"Both. Maybe related in a bad way. I don't know. I try to inject some concern for the earth and animals and stuff, and I think I've done it pretty well, but sometimes I wonder if some kid who's grown up on my stories isn't running around looking for ways to be honorable or brave. Seeking avenues of bravery, like the army."

"But you always point up personal courage," Thea argued. She read each of Hadel's stories before they were mailed off to the magazine. "There's nothing wrong with encouraging kids to be courageous enough to think for themselves."

"I know. But it's so much easier to find someone else to think for you, to go along with what people say is the brave and honorable way, to see the action and not the result."

They sat quietly for a time, and then Thea said, "There's money."

Hadel nodded. "That's right. There's the money problem."

"Will you make much from the anthology?" Hadel had received a letter during Christmas week informing her that eight of her stories would be included in a hard-cover collection, along with the stories of two other well-known adventure writers. The book was being published in June.

"That'll be enough for a year, maybe, if I really skimp. We'll see. Come on, let's get you back to your brochure. Thank you for coming out here with me."

Thea kissed her cheek. "My pleasure."

When Thea came in from the garage late that afternoon, she found Hadel sitting in the living room, staring at the telephone. "What's wrong?"

"Ann just called. She said Laney's decided to do her last role. Her deciding had something to do with what happened when we were buying coffee. Or not buying coffee. You know what her last role is?" Hadel waited, but Thea chose not to answer. "Dying," Hadel said. "She's going to die."

Thea nodded. "That's what I figured."

CHAPTER 30

"Laney . . ." Her brother was just ahead, but he was making his voice sound eerie and far away. "Laney-y-y . . ." She loved to play with Ronald. She kept expecting him to disappear into his world of sports and his friends, but he always saved a little time for her. Today, when he'd come home from soccer practice to find her sitting alone in her room, he had initiated this game of catch-me-if-you-can.

"Laney-y-y . . ." She stepped over a low broken-stone wall and traversed a dirt street. They had come too far from their own neighborhood to worry about anyone seeing them. Her mother wouldn't bother to call them before dinnertime; they had another hour, at least. Laney crouched next to a wooden pull-cart and listened for Ronald's footsteps. He had shot up in the few months since his fourteenth birthday, and he hadn't become comfortable with his new height yet. Sometimes he stumbled over his feet, two whole sizes larger. She heard him. She edged around a hut covered with cow dung patties, big pancakes drying in the sunlight. They were used as fuel for cooking fires. Sometimes the burning dung was all she could smell for miles, that and the curry.

"Laney-y-y-y . . ." Damn! Now he was off to her left. He had to be in the little market area, among the stalls covered with bright fabrics and dried spices hanging on strings. Mother had told them never to enter the market alone, saying it was too dangerous. Laney had never understood why it was supposed to be dangerous, and she knew Ronald and his friends came here often.

"Laney!" There was a laugh in Ronald's voice as he was suddenly near enough to touch. She whirled around and saw nothing. She vaulted a box set between the first two stalls and glimpsed him disappearing down the next aisle. He would, she decided, make a circuit and come back to the middle aisle. She had him. She darted behind a crate of vegetables and dashed in back of the line of stalls where the goods were stacked, waiting their turn to be placed on the flat counters for people to finger and haggle over. She ran full-tilt around a strung-up rug and tripped on something. She flew, hitting her head with a crash on a copper pot suspended from a stick. Her head was still ringing when she looked behind to see what she had tripped over. A man flailed in the dust, his white cotton shirt much too long for his legless body, his stump-arms gyrating as he tried to heave himself upright. Laney watched him rocking back and forth until he finally settled, face in profile. He had no nose. He had no ears. Laney's hands were braced under her chest, ready to push her body up. Instead she made a small sound, and the man twisted toward her. The leprosy had eaten away even his lips, and he gargled something through an open hole as he fixed her with sightless, milky eyes. "Laney-y-y . . ." Ronald called.

She screamed. She bucked full-length along the ground, a shrieking centipede, until Ronald snatched her around the waist and slapped her and gave some money to the angry stall-keeper. Ronald stood behind her and force-marched her out of the market, one arm across her chest, his other arm tight against her mouth until she couldn't breathe anymore, and she bit him through the cloth of his shirt. "Stop it!" he shouted at her, letting her go. His eyes were blood-red from the sweat pouring into them.

Laney was panting. She held onto the broken-stone wall for support.

"You can't scream," he told her through gritted teeth. "You can't do that."

She panted, wanting to faint. Her own sweat was ice-old across her shoulders.

"Come on," he said. "Come on!" He grabbed her arm, and she twisted away from him. He stopped grappling, now panting himself. "I know it's hard, but you have to control yourself. You have to be brave."

"Why is it so important not to be frightened?" she asked him furiously. "Why is it so important to hide everything I feel?"

"Because . . . because we've gone through this again and again, Laney, because what you feel isn't what other people feel, and it can get you in trouble."

She was frustrated beyond thought. She didn't know how long she stood on the dusty road, gripping the low wall with tight fingers. What finally broke through was the anguish on Ronald's face and the realization that none of this was his fault. He had tried to keep her safe for as many years as she remembered. "I'm sorry," she told him.

"It's all right," he said, and she was lightened by his relief. "Let's go back home."

Fever memories. Laney twisted her head on her pillow; she still felt weak, though that could be from not eating. Hadel had been right, of course, about her being sick. Laney had gotten the flu the day before she'd met Hadel outside the coffee store, and it was only now waning, four days later.

Ann, shocked at this first illness in the eleven years they'd been together, had actually offered to stay home from work. Laney had squelched that notion, but Ann was determined to spend every available nonwork minute with Laney. She could hardly help noticing that Laney wasn't eating the little treats Ann had prepared. "Is your stomach upset?" she asked.

"No," Laney said truthfully. And she had finally told Ann about her last role, if only to erase the hurt from Ann's eyes when her homemade soup was returned untasted.

Laney began by explaining the circumstances in which she'd created the roles: her terror at living in the dorm after Ann had taken her first television job in Chicago, how Laney had promised herself she need never endure that degree of fear again, how she had realized that asking another person to shield her was demanding the impossible. Laney had told all of this to Ann before, and each time it had the opposite effect she'd intended: Ann responded with defensiveness and guilt, saying television newscasting had been her dream forever, that she could not have lived with herself if she'd let the opportunity pass, while at the same time her eyes filled with tears and she wallowed in apologies and remorse.

Laney cut Ann's protestations short by telling her about Ronald. He had never lived a full life, she said, because he had been so focused on protecting her. Ann asked if Laney blamed herself for Ronald's death, and when Laney shook her head impatiently, Ann seemed confused. "I don't understand," she said.

"The roles are the point," Laney reiterated. "In the past few months I've tried to live without them, and I find I can't. At the coffee store I said something I shouldn't have, and then people started pushing and shoving—I was paralyzed again, Ann. I haven't known that kind of fear since I was back in the dorm."

"But can't you just pick another role?" Ann asked.

"It doesn't work that way. The only two roles I chose were the first and the last, both that night at school. Remember how I always knew the next role before the old one is over? Well, this last time, when I found myself in a hospital, which was bad enough in itself, I also didn't know the next role. I accepted then they were over. All they were, really, was a little game I could control, a game to keep me safe. They gave me time to be with you."

"But you still have time, Laney. You can do the last one and then try living without them again. I could help now that I know what you're doing—"

Laney interrupted Ann to tell her the last role was a dying person.

"How do you plan to die without dying?" Ann asked.

"I don't," Laney said. When Ann continued to look puzzled, Laney added, "I plan to die."

Ann's voice was heavy with sarcasm when she spoke again moments later. "Where are you going for this one? Katmandu? Back to Ecuador? India?"

"I thought I'd stick around here. It's a bit hard to separate from me."

"Yes. You can die as yourself, is that what you mean? Put an end to fear forever?" Tears of utter rage had sprung to Ann's eyes, and their presence seemed to make her even more furious. "Excuse me," she said to Laney and she left the room. She hadn't returned in a night, a day and another night, but Laney had heard her talking on the phone several times, so she expected the cavalry, in the persons of Hadel and Portia, to arrive at any moment. Until that happened, her memories were suitable bed-partners.

What had Ronald expected from a ten-year-old child who'd just banged her head on a cooking pot and tripped over a man with no legs and no face? Wouldn't anyone scream? Poor Ronald. He had trained himself so carefully to downpedal Laney's reactions that he could not allow the smallest break either in herself or himself, since he knew he functioned as her example. That was what she'd meant when she'd told Ann Ronald had never lived a full life.

She stretched her neck and listened to it crack. She reminded herself to write her parents a last letter that would not sound like a good-bye. Any other loose ends? She had, she thought, led a life as divorced from society as she could make it. She had no checking account, no savings account, had never filed a tax return. Her possessions were a few clothes and a few books—she had sold her Malibu three years earlier, when Ann had bought a gas-saving Datsun suited to her bridge commute. The remains of last year's dope money would pay for the cremation. She stretched again. It was a satisfying sound, that cracking, as if another life form with a different language existed beneath her skin. She stared at the ceiling. She supposed she should get up now that her fever had finally broken.

She was just setting her right foot on the floor when she heard a key in the front door. She scampered back under the covers. It was Friday; Ann occasionally came home early if her special segment was complete, though she often returned to the studio that night to watch it on the station's monitors. Ann, however, was not alone. "Look at this!" Laney heard her tell someone. "My letter slot came. Isn't that ducky?" Ann's voice was just short of hysterical. Laney remembered that Ann had ordered a brass letter slot, complete with knocker, from a Victorian house restoration catalog. She'd been excited about it a month ago, though Laney had said at the time she'd thought it ridiculous, a silly affectation. "What shall I do with it?" Ann now demanded of her companion.

Laney couldn't hear Hadel's answer, but she was certain it was Hadel because of the slow, measured way the person spoke. The voices continued in the kitchen for several minutes, and then Laney heard Hadel's footsteps coming toward the bedroom. She quickly arranged herself as if in sleep, burrowing her head halfway between two pillows. The door swung fully open, and Laney sensed Hadel staring at her. Then the door was pulled partially shut again. Hadel was too polite to wake her.

Laney did actually fall asleep later, and when she awoke, the voices began again, but this time Ann's visitor was Portia. Laney tried to duplicate her sleeping trick when Portia entered the bedroom, but Portia simply strode to the bed, grabbed Laney's shoulder and demanded, "What are you trying to pull?" Laney steeled herself for another long evening of explanations.

Hadel had picked up Portia at the Oakland airport. It was, Hadel thought, the least she could do, since she was evidently too cowardly to confront Laney herself. She had suspected Laney was not really asleep as she'd stood in the bedroom doorway, but she hadn't known what to say to her. Please don't die? How can you do this to Ann? She had left Ann and Laney's with delicious, though guilt-tinged, relief.

She had attempted to outline the situation for Portia, but Portia would have none of it. "Laney is not the slightest bit mad," she scolded. "Not one iota. How could you think such a thing?"

Hadel was stumped. If Portia would not admit that Laney's mental state had something to do with her intention to die, Hadel doubted that Portia would get far with Laney. On the other hand, who really knew to what prod Laney might respond? Portia's way, whatever it was, was probably just as good as any other. "What *are* you planning to do?" Hadel asked.

"I'm going to talk," Portia answered. "For hours on end. She'll either die of boredom or eat in self-defense."

Hadel nodded. As good as any, all right.

"What I find interesting," Portia continued, "is her method. Don't you think this starving herself to death has political significance? An act in sympathy with hunger strikers, or the millions starving all over the world?"

"I sincerely doubt it," Hadel snapped. How can we all be such good friends and be so blind to each other? But, she thought with a smile, Portia is undoubtedly thinking I'm the blind one. Portia might be able to make Laney eat again through sheer force of will. She certainly has never lacked commitment.

Portia began talking of her arrest at the antinuclear demonstration. "I felt so stupid," she said. "The whole bus ride in, I kept kicking myself. The only semismart thing I'd done was bring along my emergency set of I.D.—not Angela, but someone different. That would hold them until the fingerprints got typed in Washington, and then they'd know who I really was. My one hope was that Dooley could bail me out before then. I started worrying that they kept track of phone calls made from the jail. I didn't dare call our apartment. I decided I'd call the switchboard at the hospital where Dooley works, but that meant waiting an extra twelve hours for him to be there, and they could figure out who I was in that time. My head was really going around in circles." She laughed. "When we finally got there, it was so funny, Hadel. They booked us and directed us right back out to the parking lot. 'Don't hang around here,' they said, 'or we'll get you for loitering.' They knew almost no one would bail themselves out, so it meant feeding all those people. They wanted to get rid of us as fast as they could."

"The FBI hasn't pounded on my door," Hadel said. "Maybe they never even sent in the prints."

"No, they did. They know I'm alive. We still have sources. But the FBI isn't too interested. Our source said they implied I wouldn't do more than a few months if I surfaced."

Hadel switched to the far right-hand lane, out of the path of the enormous trucks barreling along the Nimitz Freeway. "It'd be nice for you to be able to use your own name."

"It would. I could tell my sister what a moron she is to her face. And that," she shook her head as someone swung onto the freeway ahead of them, causing Hadel to pump her brakes, "is the least of it. I could do more theater stuff, and I could do a lot more political work. Speaking of work, my word-processing gig has turned into a fifty-hour crazy factory. Turns out I'm indispensable. You should have heard the shouts when I announced I was leaving for the weekend." Her eyes twinkled. "Guess what I've gotten interested in lately? You might call it the Great White Collar Rebellion. Half of American workers are now in information handling. Half! And almost none of those people are organized. They're frustrated, isolated, tied to their desks and computers and word processors." She grinned. "A new form of office politics."

Hadel laughed. "Portia moves into the eighties."

"That's right. But first I have to free myself of the sixties. I haven't even come to the main reason for surfacing. I'm still thinking of having a child, especially now with Natalie's kid. If I'm planning a stint in jail, I should do it soon. I'm not getting any younger."

"How do you go about it? You walk into an FBI office and say, 'Here I am'?"

"No, you do it through a lawyer."

"Well, right in beautiful downtown L.A. is Michelle the Great. I'm sure she'd be glad to take you on. It'd get her name in the papers."

"Ah, yes, the ex. That's a thought."

Hadel pulled off at the Ashby exit and traveled north for a few minutes. She made a U-turn on Laney and Ann's street, parked in front of their house and switched off her ignition. The two of them sat in the car for a moment. "I hope your talking to Laney will do some good," Hadel said finally.

"It will. I might call you for a ride back out to the airport."

Hadel nodded and remained in the car while Portia mounted the steps and rang the bell. A light went on upstairs in Ann's study. Ann appeared at the door in her bathrobe. They both waved to her as Hadel started her car. Hadel waved back, waiting until they were safe inside before she pulled away from the curb. "Good luck," she said to the closing door.

Ann retreated to her study shortly after Portia arrived. She sat down at her desk and realized that with all this worry about Laney, she had forgotten to watch her half-hour special. Great, she thought, another black mark added to Laney's ledger. I could write an entire book called *The Things She's Done to Me.* Poor me.

She pushed a pen around the top of the desk aimlessly. Whom, she asked, had she to blame but herself? Ann could hardly fail to recognize the pattern that had ruled her adulthood with an iron fist. The victim mentality, the Berkeley therapists called it, the mentality that coerced her into spending miserable years with a depressed Karen until Laney appeared with fantasies of escape. Escape to another Valhalla, where Laney sucked her dry and then left, only to return to begin the process anew. How many times had it happened? Ten. It could have been as many as ten. And what had emerged from all this was the recurring image of herself standing in the doorway of the empty hospital room, squashing the daisy, staring at the unmade bed. That Laney had not even bothered to pull up the sheets before she'd vanished down the rear stairwell stuck in Ann's brain like a needle delivering electric shocks. Making the bed isn't important! she had cried to herself in these six months since, but her mind insisted on flashing the picture of the rumpled bedding at her again and again, until her memory was awash with the vision of starched white sheets, hospital sheets, *holy* sheets defiled by thoughtlessness. Did she imagine she was the sheets thrown so cavalierly to the bottom of the bed? A woman who loved a woman who loved her illusory lives so much that she must die when they were over? Or did she see herself as a public commodity in a media that daily sucked her as dry as Laney ever had?

After the night in the hospital, Ann had decided to maintain an emotional distance between herself and Laney. And yet—and here Ann slammed a fist on her desk—what had her distance-taking meant except a plea for Laney to respond? For such a punishment to work, one needed a victim, and Laney had not chosen to be a victim. Laney never chose to be the victim. Even now, as she was about to move beyond Ann's reach forever, she was forcing Ann to watch. Damn her!

Ann considered alternatives to her present status of hovering in the wings while Laney acted out her final drama. She could commit Laney, though Hadel had been right about Laney waltzing through an observation period; Laney would start eating, joke with the attendants and come out after seventy-two hours to resume her fast. I could leave, Ann thought. I could stay in a hotel. I could stay at Hadel's. But she continued sitting, listening to Portia's voice downstairs become more shrill and argumentative by the hour.

Portia scorned psychiatric interpretations, believing definitions of mental illness were a tool of the ruling class to enforce conformity. "Think about it," she told Ann the next morning. "Do you realize that if someone didn't wash her hair for three months, she could be called insane and put away? We live in one of the most rigidly codified societies in the history of the world, and yet we call ourselves free." She had said she would approach Laney with an open mind, but she was finding it difficult not to explode with anger. "What good does it do anyone for you to die?" Ann heard her shout that afternoon.

Ann pictured Laney's shrug and then listened to her quiet answer drift from the bedroom: "I told you the roles were just a way of passing the time. They had to end someday. Besides, I thought you were a big one for self-determinism."

"Your ego and your selfishness are limitless! Look past your nose and you might see something worth doing! You've lived in a box, unresponsive to the world. Even Ann," (and here Ann smiled, knowing Portia's opinions of the press) "even Ann is trying to be aware, trying to be responsive."

"Oh, Ann's miles more responsive than I am," Laney agreed.

"Well?"

"Well what?"

Break in the action. Portia came into the kitchen for a glass of juice, saw Ann sitting at the table and managed a weak grin. "Infuriating," Portia said. After a few more hours, the grin had disappeared in favor of hurt confusion. "I suppose I've never understood," she told Ann. "I always thought she was so comfortable, so self-assured. Once I said to her that she couldn't turn her back on herself and live. And now she tells me the only thing she can do as herself is die."

There were facets of Laney that Portia admired, Ann saw, even idolized. Laney was the free spirit, the beautiful being able to slide with charm from triumph to scrape and emerge from both unruffled. Portia was hindered by her sense of fair/unfair, her need to be active in fighting the injustices she saw, her chipmunk face, which had aged to what people would describe as "interesting"—good for a character actress. Portia would never see herself as a leading lady, would, in fact, reject such a role on political grounds were it ever, by some miracle, offered to her, but that did not mean she was not delighted by Laney's embodying the very traits Portia argued against—Laney's outrageousness, her noblesse oblige attitude to her friends and the world around her. It was a cruel cut for Laney to emerge flawed, to insist that her fairy-tale world was ruled by fear, and an escape from that fear demanded death—for it was at death that Portia drew the line. Respect for life had been her downfall, and she could not, would not compromise. She left late Sunday night, drained, her whole posture altered, as if someone had been beating her with a stick. "Will you call in a doctor?" she asked Ann. "Put her on IV's, I mean?"

"No," Ann said.

Portia nodded. "Good. That would only compound the horror. I'm sorry, Ann. You can't imagine how sorry. I'll come back."

Ann knew she meant when it was over.

"She's gone?" Hadel asked Monday morning. "She went back to L.A.?" Ann watched Hadel's face cloud over. Hadel had been counting on Portia's performing a miracle; Hadel would not admit they were waiting for Laney to die. When Portia abandoned the company flag on the field of battle, Hadel was compelled by her sense of honor and loyalty to carry on the fight. She had a problem, however. To be able to do nothing for herself would have been infuriating. To be able to do nothing for someone else, when death was at stake, was the torture of the damned. In that sense, Ann thought, it didn't matter whether Laney was killing herself or dying of cancer. Hadel would have agonized equally.

"You demand too much of yourself, Hadel," Ann told her when she'd returned from work to find Hadel sitting disconsolately in the kitchen. "You demand the power of God."

Hadel's eyes were half shut. She made a curious gesture with her fingers, a little flip to the right, her palm upraised, the essence of hopelessness.

"All we can do is try," Ann continued. "If we can't change the outcome for ourselves, we can't change it for someone else, either."

"I suppose," Hadel said.

When Hadel went in to tell Laney she was leaving for the evening, Laney was more blunt. "How come you haven't been writing your hero stories lately?"

"I'm tired of them," Hadel said.

"I'm sure you're not, really. You'll never tire of making life manageable, because that means you can make death meaningful. Your characters can control their destinies in little staged scenes. It's a good trick as long as you separate your characters from your friends."

"Such as you?"

"Face it, Hadel, you're obsessed by death. Your life is geared to that one final moment, to the time you can be a hero. Hadel the hero, Natalie the politico."

"Yes. You coined that, didn't you? You're wrong about my wanting to be a hero. And how can you say I'm obsessed by death? You're the one who's dying!"

Laney smiled, the tiny white scars around her throat barely visible against the paleness of her skin. Her fine hair formed a filmy curtain of tangles across her shoulders. She looked like the subject of an old print, "Beauty Waning," a consumptive fading away under her coverlets. "This is certainly distressing for you, Hadel. How honorable to save a friend. Methinks your life has been too mundane lately. Too many gourmet dinners and hot sex sessions with Thea."

Hadel went home to her hot sex partner, who told her, "Imagine that Laney is already dead. By some strange quirk, you have a few days with this already dead person to tell her how much she's meant to you. Take advantage of it."

"But she doesn't have to do this!"

"Apparently she does, Hadel. We don't understand why, but she does. Let her live her own life."

"Live her own death?" Hadel countered.

"Yes," Thea said. "Isn't that just as important?"

Hadel dropped her head in her hands. Thea was right. Some of the agony disappeared. In its place, however, rose not acceptance of Laney's decision, but instead a few last-minute schemes to convince her to change her mind.

Ann, meanwhile, had tired of her vigil in the kitchen. Laney looked up from *TV Guide* to find Ann looming in the doorway. "You've driven off all your friends," Ann challenged.

Laney turned back to *TV Guide*. Ann walked into the room and perched on the end of the bed. "Why did you plant the perennials?" she asked. "You put them in long before the business at the coffee store."

"Fall is the time to plant," Laney explained wearily. "I didn't have much faith in my being able to live without the roles."

"You never gave yourself a chance! You'd already made up your mind!" Then Ann switched from belligerence to a studied carelessness. "Anyway, how could you possibly imagine I would care about those perennials? You don't expect me to stay here, do you?"

A brief spasm of hurt closed Laney's eyes, and Ann was glad before she was sorry. "It makes me crazy," she said in an indirect apology, "that your roles meant nothing. If I could think of them as . . . as career changes, or even Michelle's 'experiments,' your leaving all those times had some purpose."

"But they did mean something!" Laney protested. "They kept us together! They kept me alive! Ann, I have always loved you. You must believe that. My loving you has nothing to do with the roles or the fear."

"Doesn't it? Really? Aren't you saying your death is my fault?"

"No!" Laney wailed. "No! How can you think that after all I've told you? My life past the age of twenty is your accomplishment! The only reason I can see that one would cling to life is because of love!"

"Yes? But then love proved not to be enough. You're not clinging to life any longer."

Laney had no answer. She held her fingers to her temples as if to steady herself, while Ann rose and padded lightly to the door, stepping so cautiously it seemed the soles of her feet must be covered with blisters.

CHAPTER 31

When Hadel arrived at Ann's spired Victorian the next morning, brimming with her newly hatched schemes to save Laney from herself, she found Laney on the front porch, screwing the letter slot in the neat hole she'd cut in the door. "It really is cute," Hadel exclaimed. She leaned over and tested out the knocker, which made a satisfying thunk against the plate behind it. "Is it solid brass?"

Laney's sunken cheeks expanded with indignation. "Ann doesn't buy cheap shit," she huffed.

"Pardon me," Hadel smiled.

Laney tried to rise and instead fell backward before Hadel could catch her. "Whoa," Laney said. "Just putting in that slot exhausted me."

She looked terrible, Hadel thought, her weakness progressing geometrically. "What's it been?" Hadel asked. "Eight days?" That didn't seem terribly long to go without eating; Hadel knew of a number of people who went on week-long clean-up fasts. Of course, she reminded herself, Laney had been sick before she'd stopped eating, so she was weak to begin with. And Hadel vaguely remembered that people on fasts drank fruit juice during their cleansing routines. Juices had a lot of natural sugars.

"I'm glad you came over," Laney said, now recovered enough to pick up her tools. "I want you to drive me up to Northside. Ann's filming a segment there today, one of her reunion deals. Long-lost relatives she's reuniting? She told me about it two weeks ago. I thought at the time you might like to come with me, but now that I've discovered you haven't been writing, it's perfect! This guy she's interviewing is a hero, see—"

Hadel wasn't listening. She was eager to try her rescue strategies. She waited until Laney paused for breath and then said, "Did you know that starving people often go blind?"

Laney's forehead furrowed with worry. "Really?"

"It has something to do with lack of protein," Hadel confirmed. "Blindness is common. Of course, that's farther down the road, after cramps and muscles atrophying—"

But now Laney wasn't listening. She had brightened again, thinking of the show Ann would film that day. "This guy she's going to reunite is a bona fide hero, Hadel. You say you're tired of your stories, right? Well, the razor's edge is dulled, know what I mean? Too much happiness lately. So I figured . . ."

Scratch dissuasion, Hadel thought. Next we'll try substitution. She waited until they were on the road up to the north campus area. "Yesterday I was thinking of a very important role you missed, Laney. So important you might feel you have to do it."

Laney moaned. "You won't stop, will you? O.K., let's have it."

"A prisoner. You haven't been in jail, you haven't been in prison."

Laney laughed, clutching the door handle to keep from toppling over. "I don't have to be a prisoner," she gasped. "You all have that one covered just fine."

Hadel restrained an impulse to tell Laney she was being juvenile and thwap her over the bridge of her nose with a backhand. Instead, she turned to her final attempt, which was truly last-ditch, the fighter pilot brought out of a blackout by the shrieking of his engine, seeing nothing but ocean through the spray-drenched glass of his windscreen, and he whips out an arm to yank back on the stick. "Why don't you open an orchid shop? There's a new block of stores building in Gourmet Ghetto number two. Orchids are getting big, and you like playing with plants."

Laney looked at her for a long moment. "After this is all over," she said finally, "you can tell people you were the only one who suggested something that made me think. Does that satisfy you? Now please listen to me about this guy. Ann was telling me last week . . ."

The subject of Ann's show, Laney explained, really was a hero. He had saved six members of his company from a Cong patrol by going back into a swampy area no one else would enter. He found the six and covered them as they made their way out. He was, however, unable to adjust to life back in the States. He slept on rooftops around the north campus area, a different roof every few days, and he parked his old Chevy blocks away, so no one would know where he was. He carried a revolver and a knife, and he wore his fatigues on his eternal stakeouts on the roofs.

"What does he eat?" Hadel asked, distracted. She was ransacking her brain for other save-Laney tactics and drawing a blank.

Laney shrugged. "From garbage cans, I guess. There are a lot of restaurants up there. Anyway, the station heard about him from the cops, and Ann located his sister. He hasn't seen any of his family since he got back in '71."

Hadel was now distracted because she had reached Euclid Avenue and was engaged in a concerted hunt for a parking space, which demanded watching for lounging students, suicidal dogs and other cars while keeping a further eagle eye peeled for anyone walking purposely, anyone digging keys out of pockets, anyone giving the slightest hint that he or she not only owned a car but also would be departing in it within a few minutes. Nevertheless, as she turned off Euclid onto a side street, Hadel couldn't help noticing the bright yellow Channel 8 truck jockeyed up to a red zone outside a delicatessen. "I'll let you off here," Hadel told Laney.

"You'll come back?" Laney suddenly sounded frightened and pathetic.

Hadel stared at her. "Of course. I'm just going to park."

By the time Hadel returned five minutes later, a small crowd had gathered. Laney was deep in conversation with an older, red-haired woman who lived in one of the buildings the man frequented. "I don't really mind him," she was telling Laney. "He keeps the burglars away." Most of the rest of the crowd were students of either U.C. Berkeley or the Pacific School of Religion, one block north. "There's Ann Bailor," a kid in cowboy boots said.

Ann had just hopped out of the truck. She was dressed in a pale yellow blouse, an attractive muting of the truck's garish color. "She's already tried to talk to him," the older woman said knowledgeably.

"Who?" the booted kid asked.

"The man who lives on the roof. He doesn't hurt anyone," the woman told the kid. "She's calling him Gary."

"Gary?" Ann was now saying, shading her eyes as she searched the roof ledge. "I just want to ask you one question. You don't have to come down here."

"Must be a hard job dealing with nuts all the time," the woman muttered.

Hadel turned away from the nonaction on the delicatessen roof to see great beads of sweat standing on Laney's forehead. She was supporting herself on a car, her hands splayed across the hood. "Sit down," Hadel told her.

"I want to see."

"You can see sitting down." Hadel helped her to a space between two parked cars, and Laney collapsed in a heap at the curb. Just as she sat down, the delicatessen owner, a disagreeable, pudgy little man Hadel remembered from her student days, darted from his shop doorway. "Hey!" he said to the crowd. "Hey! Get away from here!"

"Is she all right?" the woman asked Hadel.

"Dizzy," Hadel said.

"Oh, I know, that happens to me all the time. I'll be walking along and—" She whirled back to the scene above them. Ann had continued her quiet assurances to the unseen Gary while they were talking. The crowd stirred when a khaki-covered man with a bearded face peered over the edge.

"Get off my roof!" the delicatessen owner shouted. "He's on my roof!"

Ann motioned to her crew to get in position, and then she spoke softly to the pudgy man. He opened his mouth to protest, but he stepped back a foot or so, his eyes straying to the bright yellow truck. Ann returned her attention to the bearded figure above her. "Just one question," she promised Gary. "Could you explain to us, in your own words, exactly what kind of statement you're making here?" The soundman was hopping up and down frantically. "Speak clearly," Ann told Gary.

Gary's face slipped from neutral into hyperintelligent, and then, with a monumental effort that included gritting his teeth back into dumb neutral. "Huh?" he said.

The soundman shook his head and tapped Ann on the shoulder. The cameraman grinned. Ann ignored both of them. "Huh?" Gary said again. Ann still waited. She had seen the comprehension in his eyes. "Why should I talk to you?" he asked.

"Because if you're making a statement, you should communicate it. And the best way to do that is through me."

"Ann, the pipeline to God," Laney mumbled from the curb. The older woman turned and skewered Laney with the most baleful glare Hadel had ever seen.

"We're not gonna hear him unless he comes down off that roof," the soundman warned.

Ann was smiling at Gary. "How 'bout explaining to all of us what you're saying?"

"I'm not making a statement," Gary said.

The crowd moaned like a punctured tire.

"If he's not making a statement, then why's he allowed to hang around on the roof?" the older woman asked no one in particular. The red blinking light focused on their little group. Hadel could hear the camera whirring. She wanted to crawl under the car next to Laney. The camera moved away because the deli owner was demanding to make his own statement. The older woman punched Hadel on the arm. "I got on TV! Gee, I hope I look all right! Will it be on tonight? I just love Ann Bailor, and I got on her show!"

"News," Hadel reminded her. "You got on the news. But why did you say that?"

"What? What'd I say? Oh, about his being on the roof? I don't care. He doesn't bother me. He's just another nut. We got plenty of those in Berkeley."

"He's a veteran, actually," Hadel said. "He saved six people in Vietnam."

"Oh?" The woman looked worried. "I hated that war. It wasn't like World War II. We didn't have half the country running off to Sweden and Canada." She looked at Hadel, who was trying to bite back a rush of anger. Her generation had been hammered out on the anvil of that war. It didn't matter anymore which of them had protested it and which had fought it. What mattered was not sweeping it under the rug as if it were a ball of dust one didn't want the neighbors to see.

Laney was tapping Hadel's knee. She wanted an arm-up.

Hadel hoisted her around so she could lean on the bumper. "Maybe I should go home," Laney said.

But Hadel, in spite of herself, had become interested in the show. She wanted to see the reunion. "Wait just a minute," she pleaded. She had always loved the part in *Truth or Consequences* when Bob Barker would drag some old lady up on the stage, dress her in a funny costume and trick her into knocking on a door. Lo and behold, out would step her long-lost son, gone for three, four years in the ice and mud of Korea. Another forgotten war, Hadel thought, except for *M*A*S*H*. Now Hadel wondered how the loved ones hadn't known beforehand they were to be reunited. The son knew, of course, but how'd the network get the old lady to Hollywood, to the *Truth or Consequences* studio without letting her in on the surprise? The whole thing was very suspicious.

Ann was doing a good imitation of Bob Barker. She had a toothy grin and a softness in her eyes, which proved to anyone watching that she really cared. "Gary? There's someone in the truck you haven't seen for a long time."

"He's gotta come down off that roof," the soundman warned again.

Hadel felt the intake of breath all around her, the sudden quickening of interest. Laney stood up straighter against her car bumper. The delicatessen owner finally shut his mouth, sensing the change in mood. The kid in cowboy boots craned his head toward the Channel 8 truck. "Mother," he said confidently.

"Sister," Laney corrected.

Ann squired a red-faced twenty-two-year-old out of the truck. The man on the roof looked stricken, not at all like the people on *Truth or Consequences* who would fall sobbing into each other's arms, causing the entire audience to reach hastily for their handkerchiefs. The girl said, "I didn't want to come," as if this incantation would make her disappear.

"Come down!" Cowboy Boots shouted at Gary. All hostility had vanished. Everyone was festive. The deli owner smiled benevolently. This was something they could understand. This was what "happy news" was all about, and for one afternoon, they could all be actors. Reuniting loved ones carried a lot of good-guy points, warmed the cockles of a lot of hearts. Besides, if the dumb guy would only climb out of his soldier suit and go get a job, the war would never have happened, or at least everybody could forget about the damn thing. Who wanted to be reminded all the time? No war if only the kid would come off that roof. "Come down!" they shouted in a great cheer.

Gary pulled his revolver out of his jacket, leaned over the ledge, shot, and splattered his brains across half the crowd. He hit the sidewalk with a squishy thunk that sounded as if the Channel 8 truck had run over a crate of oranges.

Ann came home two hours later. Laney was sitting outside in the backyard, watching the reflected sunlight glint off the windows of the neighbor's house beyond the fence. "I saw you there," Ann said. "When that woman yelled something, I saw you and Hadel."

Laney said nothing.

"You know what Lorin told me? He said not to let it bother me, these things happen. I said he was right, it was a story waiting to happen. If you spend enough time creating the news, you have to figure one of your creations is going to turn into Frankenstein's monster. . . . I asked him, 'If my good deeds are their good deeds, are my murders their murders?' He said I was overreacting. I wish you would say something, Laney."

Laney was gazing at the high red on the windows across the fence. Her mouth remained stubbornly closed.

"First no eat, then no talk? You think I *liked* what happened? Let me put it this way, Laney: I need you to speak. I want you to talk to me. Do you hear me? My job is destroying me, and I need help from *you*."

Laney turned toward her, but she was still silent.

"All these years," Ann said, "I imagined myself a victim of your roles, of your absences, of your goddamn self-containment. When I saw Hadel and Thea together, I wondered why you wouldn't stay with me through one entire year, why you wouldn't give me what I needed. I thought I deserved more. I thought you weren't enough for me." She paused. "And now I see I wasn't enough for you. *You never needed me*."

Laney gave one violent shake of her head, and then an odd sort of tic surfaced at the corners of her eyes, a wordless protest.

"If you think I'm wrong," Ann challenged, "then say so."

She watched Laney's eyes, the clear blue that she had lost herself in the first evening they'd met, at the alumnae fund-raiser in Boston. She thought of her own eyes, gray as a shepherd's sweater. She remembered how the colors melded together, how they had fallen into each other that night in the cocktail lounge. Laney was confident then. She was confident now. The tic had slipped away, and a steady plane of calm remained, as if Laney were a sea captain gazing out at the horizon. Her eyes were no longer protesting, nor were they censuring. They were kind, compassionate. That made Ann angrier than blankness or coldness. "Say so," she demanded. She slapped Laney hard across the face. Laney flinched in pain, but she didn't try to get away, so Ann hit her again and again and Laney sat there, her head flinging back with the force of Ann's blows, but she said nothing.

Ann wasn't sure why she stopped, perhaps because of the utter unreality of the scene, the only sound the slaps, the only light the feathery softness of dusk. It was growing cold, and a wind was beginning to rustle the leaves in the oak tree.

Ann could still see enough to make out Laney's face, to watch the tears begin to pour out in a stream, coursing down her cheeks and mouth, dripping from her jaw to splash on her hands folded in her lap. Her tears were riveting—it seemed incredible she could cry such a quantity without moving her face. Ann found herself following the progress of individual tears. And then the position of Laney's hands struck Ann with the same stinging shock as had the tangled sheets on Laney's bed at the hospital. Laney hadn't unclasped her hands once while Ann hit her, and she hadn't cried until Ann stopped. That unutterable sadness in Laney's eyes, now faded blue in the darkness, was meant for Ann alone. "No one loves a saint, Laney," Ann told her, and she climbed the steps and went into the house.

CHAPTER 32

Hadel was floating, her body sensitive its full length to Thea's body pressed against hers, Thea's leg draped over her leg. Thea's heel fit like a jigsaw puzzle piece in the hollow of Hadel's ankle. Every bit of it felt good. They made love often these days, rediscovering little pieces of each other, sinking deeper under layers until, magically, they burst free in a flash of sweat and heat and humming between the ears: pleasure so pervasive nothing else existed.

The phone rang. Thea snaked a hand over the edge of the bed and answered; she had waited since dinnertime for a woman to call with her choice of a headline type for her brochure. It was now eleven. Thea listened for a second and wordlessly handed the receiver to Hadel. "Hello?" Hadel tested. She wasn't sure her voice hadn't floated away with the rest of her.

"You're the only one left who might care, so I thought I should tell you." Ann sounded as if she were drowning.

Fear slapped Hadel upright. "Oh, God!" she moaned.

"No," Ann said. "But when I came home, she'd left the house. She hasn't come back."

"But how? She can hardly walk."

Ann didn't care about the mechanics of Laney's departure. She hung up the receiver.

"What?" Thea asked, touching Hadel's arm.

"Somehow Laney has left the house."

"Will Ann look for her?"

"No." Hadel struggled against a pounding wave of exhaustion at the thought of going out into the freezing, dark night. "No, I'll go look for her." And what, she wondered in a panic, will I do if I find her? She got out of bed and started dressing. Thea padded into the kitchen on bare feet and fixed a Thermos of tea. "It'll be cold," she said, handing it to Hadel, who smiled and nipped Thea's neck gratefully. "I hope that job calls," Hadel said.

Thea was shifting from foot to foot, her arms wrapped around her ribs. "Be careful."

"I will," Hadel promised and kissed her again. You're lucky, she told herself as she clattered down the front steps. Lucky Hadel.

The next few minutes eroded her thankfulness. A layer of frost and ice coated the windshield, so Hadel climbed under the rose bush to turn on the garden hose. The hose end sprayed one sneakered foot before she directed it at the car, and then her hands got wet and stuck tackily to the steering wheel. She grumbled as the car warmed up. Laney was probably fine, while she would die of pneumonia. Where would Laney go? A bar? That seemed unlikely. But where else?

Gables was quiet. A few people glanced at her curiously. She didn't recognize anyone, and no one was old enough to recognize her. The women looked sleazier, the men trimmer. Hadel stayed for one beer and a brief warm-up at the fireplace, and then she went back out into the cold.

She drove next to a bar she hadn't been to for years, since before Michelle. It was a sexless bar in the style of the sixties—equal parts men and women of all persuasions—with loud rock music, pitchers of beer, people standing outside huddled over joints. Not one thing had changed, except everyone had aged ten years. Same hippie clothes, same hippie people, probably even the same long-haired band. Hadel got a beer and nursed it in a corner, waving at acquaintances from the past. No one was doing much talking; the band was too loud. Instead, people danced like jumping jacks, wide grins on their faces, sweat trickling from under their headbands. No one, apparently, had heard of disco or punk. Hadel was enjoying herself tremendously until duty forced her out the door.

All right, she thought, Laney's probably not in a bar—the two Hadel had visited were the likeliest. Too late for restaurants. Laney never wanted to go to the movies. That meant she was out wandering the streets, barely able to stand up, which was impossible, so she had to be holed up somewhere. Had she gone to L.A. to be with Portia? That was conceivable. But how would she get there? She couldn't have taken a bus either to the Greyhound station or to the airport in her condition. Hadel started the car and drove around aimlessly, curving up and down streets between Shattuck and Telegraph. No special reason, but it was as good as anything else.

While she drove, she found herself thinking of Laney's assertion that she'd been postponing her death for years, that she'd simply clung to life a little longer so she could be with Ann. One could say that all life is a postponement of death, Hadel argued. But more narrowly, if Laney could not separate herself from the society around her, if she was unable to tell where she ended and the rest of the world began, how could she have kept at bay the overriding assumption of her generation, that all of them would die before they had reached adulthood, that they were living on borrowed time? How could she tell the difference between thinking *she* was supposed to die and thinking everyone would die or should have died? After all, Hadel thought, she herself considered the past twenty years an unexpected bonus. And that led her to remembering the dog tags.

Starting in the second grade, all the students were required to wear the dog tags on little chains around their necks. Those who came to school without their tags were sent home immediately to fetch them. Spot checks usually uncovered only a few miscreants. Parents were as responsible as the school system when it came to the tags.

The tags gave the child's name, birth date and an address outside the Bay Area where each of them was to be taken in the event of a nuclear attack. That was for yellow alerts, of course. Once a week they practiced diving under the desk and covering their necks with their hands for the red ones.

Hadel's address was that of an old school buddy of her father's who lived on a ranch near Stockton. Her friend Sally's address was in the Sierra foothills, between Sutter Creek and Jackson. They promised to try to outwit the school bus driver so they could stay together. That was in the second grade. By the third grade, all the kids realized the plan was ridiculous. The bus drivers, who were paid to remain at the school for the entire day, liked the extra money, but they could hardly be expected to ferry kids all over Northern California in the midst of World War III. They had said as much several times, as if they thought it was only fair to warn the kids. "I'll take you as far as my girlfriend's," the driver told them. "Least as many of you as can get on the bus in thirty seconds flat."

In their infinite wisdom, the kids decided the school and their parents had to pretend a system existed to save the children. They were good at pretend games; they would humor their parents. The pretense took on an added irony when they discovered, early in the fourth grade, that the funny structure a half mile from the playground was a Nike site.

They weren't so good at pretend games in junior high, and anyway, much of the pretense had been dropped. Bus drivers weren't paid to stay for the day. It seemed less and less likely that anyone would receive more than a few minutes' warning. Nonetheless, they were still supposed to wear their tags.

The tags were abandoned in the midst of the Cuban missile crisis. The teachers were too nervous to hold classes; they herded the kids into the cafeteria and patrolled the perimeters, as if they were keeping lions in cages. The lions were surprisingly quiet. Everyone's attention was focused on the minute-by-minute account piped through the loudspeaker. Suddenly, however, a scared young voice broke into the news station's broadcast. "Please go home," the voice said. "There are no buses. No one will come to pick you up. We have no food or water stored at the school. Please leave now. Go home as quickly as you can." It struck Hadel as odd that she still remembered the voice as young. The woman was some sort of school administrator and therefore had to be at least twice as old as any of them. Her voice had sounded much younger.

The teachers scrammed at the first squawk of the loudspeaker, leaving the lions to fend for themselves. The lions stretched, hesitated and finally began walking home, most of them alone. No school official ever mentioned the dog tags again, and their parents took the laconic "We don't have to wear them anymore" as gospel. Perhaps they too had tired of playing pretend.

Hadel discovered the real reason for the tags a year later. In a Telegraph Avenue coffeehouse, her mind bent by too much dope and too many espressos, she told a girl whose father was in the Navy about the dog tags. "They're body-count tags," the girl corrected, "so they can identify you."

"Really," Hadel said. But what about the buses all through elementary school? Had her parents known why they had to wear the tags? She didn't think so. She didn't think so now, either. Apparently the pretend game had gone several levels higher than parents and kids, and school and parents.

She wondered if she still had her dog tag. Was it lurking in a drawer at her parents' house, along with her diary and those pictures of lines of children, one boy holding a sign that said: "Miss Sanders, Fourth Grade"? She switched the radio on to the oldies station, which was playing "Duke of Earl," a song she'd always hated but that now had at least gained her finger-tapping-on-the-dash approval by virtue of its age and the memories it unlocked inside her head. But when her mind, a stern taskmaster, demanded that she focus for just one moment on the here and now, she was amazed to see that she had somehow ferried herself up to Tilden Park. How could Laney have gotten up here? She had to admit it: she wasn't even looking for Laney anymore, if she ever had been.

The oldies station was juxtaposing fast and slow. They put on a great song to sing to, Johnny Mathis's "Twelfth of Never." Hadel barreled along, nearly drowning out poor Johnny, remembering yet another nuke-before-they-were-fondly-called-nukes story: the saying *adiós*. Hadel hung out with four other girls through the last two grades of elementary school and into junior high, until the ninth grade, when all of them splintered off into migraine headaches, boyfriends, pot and suicide threats. But before that, on at least five occasions she could recall, they had solemnly said good-bye to each other as they separated to go home. One time stood out. Hadel saw them again, standing on a hill overlooking the flatlands, wearing skirts and sweaters and carrying purses awkwardly—they had just gotten their first purses—all of them in that ugly eleven-year-old phase, when you stare in the mirror and want God to strike you dead. But not *truly* dead, they had thought that day, and life and friends became unbearably sweet. They didn't speak as they stood there, overlooking the whole Bay Area, the bridges silver and orange against gray-blue water, Alcatraz a big round rock in the middle. They sniffed the air and gloried in the leaves greening up on the trees and the daffodils blooming in the yard next to them. Every day the three who lived on the hill walked Hadel and Vicky to this shortcut down to the beginning of the flats. Usually they all sat down, if it wasn't too wet, and gossiped all the gossip they hadn't been able to impart during lunch hour, during recess or during the walk to the shortcut. Sometimes it took an hour before Hadel and Vicky started down the hill. But today they paused for no more than five minutes, and then, in a parody of hearty good fellows, or courage, they shook hands, favored each other with sharp nods and separated with quick good-byes, off to flaming death. Hadel couldn't remember what crisis it had been, pre-Cuba, of course, since they were still in elementary school. The military was on alert, she knew that much. All the air-raid sirens had been tested the day before, getting ready.

It hadn't mattered when they appeared the next day at school, and the next time and the next. No sheepish grins. They'd been granted a reprieve, and who could be ashamed of that? A few more months of life. If they were lucky, they'd reach sweet sixteen. If they were really lucky, they might have a chance to see themselves grow into prettiness before they died. If they were super lucky, they might lose their virginity and die as full-fledged women instead of girls. And if they were lucky beyond the bounds of reality, they might find someone to love. But no, that was going too far. Think about sixteen. Even that was a chance in a hundred. College was years away, unimaginable. Hadel had been so conditioned not to think of it that she didn't really start considering colleges until she was seventeen, almost too late, and then only because her parents were pressing her. A dream world. In all those years, midnight hadn't struck, and they hadn't turned into pumpkins.

The oldies station overstepped its limits by playing "The Elusive Butterfly," a song incapable of being aided by the passage of time. Hadel switched it off and started back down the hill. She even turned on the car heater. So what if she got sleepy? Fifteen minutes and she'd be home. Twenty and she'd be in bed lying next to Thea. Lucky, lucky Hadel had hit the jackpot.

The kids of the late fifties, the early sixties were so serious. If the bombs didn't get them, DDT would. *Silent Spring* was a big hit. They watched doomsday reports on the educational channel. From ten to fifteen is a serious age. They hadn't lived long enough to learn that emergencies have a way of being bridged.

And, Hadel thought, they hadn't lived long enough to delude themselves that all emergencies have a way of being bridged. Some emergencies were final, and kids take emergencies seriously.

There was more. Although they sometimes pictured themselves trapped inside a soap bubble that was rising toward its eventual extinction on the ceiling ("Pop," they told each other softly), and the question was not "if" but "when"—for all that, they were still the coddled generation, the ones for whom the world had been made safe, tomorrow's bearers of freedom's banner, the nation's hope. They were to be scientists and engineers (Sputnik still grated), they were to be doctors and teachers, they were to be physically fit. (Hadel remembered the hours of testing and training they endured during Kennedy's physical fitness program; the PE teacher exhorting the lines of red-faced, straining girls, "Come on, don't ya wanta beat the Russians? Come on, don't ya wanta beat the Russians?" in a mindless chant that lasted until one of her students either threw up or fainted.) That was, of course, during the days of Camelot, when we had a national purpose, when everyone dashed home from school to watch Kennedy's televised press conferences, when the Peace Corps and VISTA were far more beckoning than science or engineering, when—yet that soap bubble was still floating. Hadel thought now, from a perspective of seventeen years, that the bubble had burst the day Kennedy was shot, but everyone had been in too much pain to notice, and anyway, they weren't dead.

The fifties, thank God, were. The children born in the middle and late forties had grown up on what they considered spoon-fed hypocrisy. Eisenhower, they were told, was a good President because "he did nothing." (That a great deal had actually occurred during his administration, from the landmark school desegregation decision to the McCarthy witch-hunts, was simply another instance of duplicity.) They raged against the illusion of safety, the thin veneer of respectability laid over the tranquilizer-popping, the ulcers and the heart attacks; the worship of security as a god, with the accumulation of material goods a divinely inspired insurance policy; the stultifying sameness of it all. One could say that they had not understood their parents were products of the years before they were born, not felt the war-induced fear that led their parents to seek safety, not participated in the depression-bred struggle that made job, money and family the triumvirate of security. Many of their generation had been born late to older parents whose lives had been interrupted by the war. Their parents had settled in at last, and fears of a nuclear holocaust were just something we had to live with. If it happened, it happened. Relax, don't worry about it.

And their children had raged at them: how could anyone relax when the greatest slaughter in human history had occurred just fifteen years earlier? How could anyone relax when dogs were set on people wanting to go to school down South? Now. Today. How could anyone relax when we were killing off everything around us, the oceans, the air, the soil, and ourselves next? And you call us civilized! You call us safe!

The parents were disturbed by their children's anger. Hadn't they given them everything? One could say that the coddled generation had plenty of time to worry about the world's survival because they weren't concerned with the roof over their heads or the food on the table. They hadn't seen the backbiting fight for the security they took for granted. The social relevance of a job was far more important than the pay or the benefits. Materialism was shallow and criminal in a country where many still starved. They didn't want to be safe. They wanted to be *saved.* It was, Hadel recalled, like standing on the deck of an ocean liner that was listing badly to one side, shouting that the ship was sinking, and all around you people played shuffleboard and bridge and asked when the bar opened. It was infuriating. It was crazy-making. The frustration of those unheard shouts created a generation determined to kill the vampire of war and disease and prejudice and starvation. When John Kennedy was shot and the national purpose exploded into so much rubble, their determination intensified. And why not? Hadel thought as she turned down University Avenue, heading toward the bay. They had nothing to lose but the overwhelming powerlessness to save their own lives.

So they embarked on their holy crusade of vampire-killing. They took drugs so they could root out their private vampires and see the promise of a new future, but that backfired—they ended up spawning so much misery that a lot of them died from it. They listened to black-magic rock 'n' roll, an army of countervampires to challenge the big one, and white-magic rock 'n' roll, to convince themselves that what they were doing was working. They broke off into dozens of splinter groups, each claiming their struggle was more murderous to the vampire than any of the others. They took to the streets with signs and slogans, and some of them sat in buildings, and some of them bombed them. Some of them died protesting, and a lot of them died overseas, and some of the survivors came home to die.

Hadel pulled to the curb and let the engine idle. Their crusade had caused a societal upheaval on some fronts, while on others they had accomplished virtually nothing. And now, when so much had failed, had they lost their vision? Had they learned their lesson, accepted their powerlessness? Hadel shook her head. She could never believe they were completely powerless, just as she would never believe her parents had known the real purpose of the dog tags.

Laney, she reminded herself as the engine purred. You are looking for Laney, who has no holy or personal goals to sustain her, who lives cheek-by-jowl with the vampire, unshielded and alone. No, she argued, you are on your way home, having given up your search. Except she drove around the block and headed up to Northside. Since Laney could not escape the vampire, Hadel decided, she had gone to his last known lair.

The north campus area was deserted, as if no one had been there in months. A few scraps of paper blew in the wind, scuttering across the street with a raspy noise. A fog had begun rolling off the bay, and the air was heavy with moisture, opaque droplets that misted the surface layer of Hadel's hair. Hadel walked across the street to the delicatessen and looked up at the ledge. Nothing. "Laney?" she called quietly. "Laney?" A little louder this time.

"I thought you might come," Laney said. Hadel had to strain to hear her. A dog began barking in the next block, not at them, but the solitary, staccato bark of a dog shut outside in wet weather. Hadel stepped back into the gutter so she could at least see where Laney was speaking from, but then she realized she wouldn't be able to hear her, so she crossed the sidewalk and leaned against the building. "How'd you get here?" she asked.

"Taxi," Laney said. "Then I walked up the steps to the apartments next door. There's a landing that opens right on this roof, with a door that can be locked from the outside."

"And did you lock the door?" Of course she had. Why ask? "So what's the deal?" Hadel knew that too.

"You're afraid of heights. Here's your big chance. Rescue me and be a hero."

"That's absurd," Hadel protested. "Why play games?"

"Why not?" Laney answered, her voice thready. "A little harmless entertainment."

"Well, you can entertain yourself without me."

"Oh, Hadel! Here I set this up for you—if you came, that is—and now you've taken all the trouble to figure out where I was, and you can't accept a simple gift of gratitude."

Hadel stepped back into the gutter and looked up, shading her eyes from the mist. She couldn't see any sign of life on the ledge. Laney must be lying behind it, talking into the fog, which was settling over everything like a huge gray manta ray coming to rest on the ocean floor. "What makes you think I want to climb up there and rescue you?" Hadel asked evenly.

She couldn't hear Laney at first, so she had to scamper back across the sidewalk. ". . . showed you who you were at Ridgedale, Hadel, when we made love. Now I can show you who you've always wanted to be."

Hadel shook her head, and then she laughed. "What I wanted was a way to make horror manageable," she said, still caught in her memories of the dog tags. "A way to imagine individuals could still function with honor instead of being added up on a tally sheet of obscenities. But the only person you can be a hero for is yourself, because you're the only person who understands what it took." Hadel leaned against the wall, waiting. She had stopped being cold.

"I've been pretending all my life I'm not scared," Laney said finally. "But you're really not, are you?"

"Of course I'm scared," Hadel said. "I'm often scared."

"But you can choose when to act on it. You see when it's right to be frightened."

Hadel didn't know how to answer this.

"I don't see how I can be anything for myself," Laney concluded, "if I don't know when it's right to be frightened."

What am I to do? Hadel wondered. Laney's perpetual shoring up of her battlements has taken her nowhere. But Laney was growing impatient with Hadel's silence. "Come on!" Laney insisted. "It's not that hard. Don't you want to overcome your fear of heights?"

"You've put me in a no-win position here," Hadel said. "If I climb up and rescue you, I'll be letting you manipulate me. If I walk away, I'm a rat leaving a sinking ship." She thought a moment. "I think I'd rather be a rat, Laney. At least it's my own life. I spent a long time with Michelle living her life, and I'm tired of it."

"You weren't very good at it," Laney said.

"No. I wasn't very good at it. I don't think I'd be very good at rescuing you, either. I'd probably fall down and break my neck."

"So you do know," Laney said. "You know about living your life. You're lucky, Hadel."

The wistfulness in her voice pulled Hadel up short. "Laney, I'm going to find the building manager and get the door unlocked."

"No!" Laney cried, her voice strong. "Talk about manipulation. I know what's wrong here. I'm not making this exciting enough for you. How 'bout if I pretend I'm a machine gun? Ack-ack, ack-ack!"

Hadel smiled, relieved. Even if Laney thought she could be nothing for herself, her competitive spirit had not been dented. Her attempt at coercion had to triumph. "If you got up there, you can get back down. There's a phone booth where you can call a cab right on the corner. See ya."

Hadel walked across the street, and as she walked, Laney stopped making machine gun noises and started making chicken noises. "Bruk, bruk, bruk . . ." Hadel laughed out loud. When she reached her car, she turned back. "You got a dime, Laney?" The response was a louder "Bruk!" Hadel got in her car and drove away.

Thea was wandering around the kitchen when Hadel got home. "What are you doing?" Hadel cried.

"Oh, that woman with the headlines called right after you

left. I lay awake thinking about doing it in the morning, and I finally just got up and finished the damn thing. Want some tea?"

Hadel slapped her forehead. "Tea!" She ran outside to the car for the thermos.

Thea had arranged herself into the essence of complaint in time for Hadel's entrance. Her arms were folded across her chest, her eyes fiery, her mouth downturned. "Here I get up to make you a nice Thermos of tea, and you forget!"

Hadel was to remember this picture in the days ahead: Thea ramrod straight in her old jeans with the cutoff legs fraying around her ankles, her blue and orange flannel shirt, the one Hadel loved to rub, with its contrast of soft cloth draped loosely over Thea's smooth firmness; Thea's eyes unable to hold the star's cold fire but now twinkling with the warm light of the sun, here in their kitchen, at three-thirty in the morning.

When the phone rang at five, they had been asleep for maybe a half hour after talking awhile over mugs of Hadel's still-hot tea. Ann's voice was sodden, as if she were speaking through wet cotton. "Laney jumped off that same building up on Northside, Hadel. She died in the ambulance."

Hadel lay her head back on the pillow, the receiver next to her ear. "I have to call Portia," Ann said. She hung up.

"You must have known," Thea said quietly as Hadel replaced the receiver. "Inside, you must have known she was planning to die tonight. Did she jump?"

"Yes. If I did know, I should have stopped her. I should have gotten the manager. I should have called the cops. I should have climbed up on that damned roof!"

"She would have jumped the moment you got up there and thought she was teaching you a lesson," Thea said.

"I just hopped in my car and drove away. . . ."

"It was Laney's production, Hadel. She wrote it, she directed it and she starred in it. If you want to kid yourself you were anything more than a member of the audience, you can, but I don't recommend it."

Hadel lay on her back, staring at the ceiling, her eyes unblinking, moving past the fantasy of control and responsibility that evoked guilt, to acceptance. Her face suddenly crumpled, her mouth moving soundlessly. "Laney's dead!" she wailed when she could speak, and Thea, who had carefully remained on her side of the bed while Hadel struggled to escape the demons of her own imagined power, now reached over her arm and pulled Hadel close.

CHAPTER 33

Ann arranged a simple memorial service at the North Berkeley Episcopal Church. "Why Episcopal?" Hadel wondered.

"Ann probably knows the minister," Thea surmised.

They pushed open the heavy doors and walked into the tall, beamed chapel. There weren't many people; Evan, the nurse, sat by herself at the end of a pew, and Hadel saw Portia off to one side, reading a metal plaque beneath the stained-glass windows. Ann was setting flower arrangements on a card table in front of the altar. She worked mechanically, her features static, as if the muscles of her face feared being overwhelmed by conflicting emotions and had chosen paralysis as a cover until it was safe to come out of hiding. The young minister glanced at his watch. Hadel moved to help Ann, but Portia intercepted her. "Let her do it herself," Portia cautioned.

Hadel hugged her. "Did you bring Dooley with you?"

Portia shook her head. "I would have, but I had something else I needed to do." She inclined her head toward a gray-suited man leaning against the wall closest to the street. Hadel looked at him, and then she understood. "I forget, I'm so used to seeing you . . . But you said you'd do it through a lawyer."

Portia winked. "Michelle sends her regards. And she was able to insist on this rather unusual meeting place."

At Hadel's look, the man had begun walking toward them. He arrived just as Ann, finished with the flowers, joined them from behind. "Portia Bethany?" he asked.

"Yes," Portia said.

"The car's outside."

All very polite, Hadel thought.

"She'll stay for the service," Ann told the FBI man in a quiet voice.

"She'll stay," Hadel agreed. They moved closer to Portia, as if to prevent him from snatching her and dashing out the door.

"Of course," he said. "Already settled. However, Miss Bailor, I would appreciate it if you would tell me if you're planning to alert your station. If a lot of newspeople—"

"I don't plan to alert anyone," Ann said. "I didn't call my station when it might have meant something. Why should I call them now?"

He nodded. "I'm sorry for your loss."

"Thank you," Ann said, tears springing to her eyes. She turned away abruptly and sat down. Portia sat next to her, and Hadel and Thea moved to Ann's other side. Hadel could hear the FBI man take the seat behind them. She was aware of him throughout the short service, though he was absolutely silent. Ann sat with her hands folded in her lap, her lips slightly apart, as if she were meditating, while both Portia and Hadel wiped away tears with their fingers. Ann finally leaned over, opened her purse and handed them each a tissue. The clasp of her purse closed with a snap, and she sat back again, refolding her hands.

The minister hadn't known Laney; he made general remarks about death and grieving, referring to those in his small audience as "loved ones" and finished by asking them to reflect on the gift of love Laney had brought all of them. After a moment of quiet, he left his station in front of the flower arrangements and disappeared through a side doorway. Evan got up and walked down the aisle, stopping for a moment to reach over Portia and touch Ann on the shoulder. The four of them—Portia, Ann, Hadel and Thea—continued sitting in silence. Hadel wondered if she would be able to stand. She hadn't expected these bolts of pain, nor her strange, isolated images: Ann competently handing them the tissues, Portia reading the plaque while she waited for the gray-suited man to approach her, Ann placing the flower arrangements on the card table. No one moved until Ann stood, and then Portia stepped into the aisle. Hadel and Thea got to their feet as the FBI man joined Portia. "I'm parked in front," he told her. They all filed down the row of pews and walked outside to stand on the steps, the bamboo hedge growing close around them. Portia hugged them all and then followed the FBI man down, meeting him on the sidewalk as he held the door open for her. She waved when the car pulled away from the curb.

Ann began to go back in, and Hadel moved to accompany her. "I'm leaving the flowers," Ann told her, squeezing Hadel's hand. "I'll call you in a few days."

"All right," Hadel said, but she stood on the steps until Thea took her elbow and led her away.

Hadel waited five days, and then she drove by Ann's house. Two advertising circulars stood against the door. All the drapes were drawn. It was amazing to Hadel how houses radiated desertion. Houses whose owners are on vacation seemed to be waiting. Ann's house already looked abandoned, cold and seedy. Hadel climbed the steps and stood on the porch for a moment, noting that Ann had left behind her expensive brass letter slot. How Laney had laughed at it, but Ann had gotten it for them. It meant nothing without Laney, just as the house meant nothing.

"She moved," a neighbor said, pausing with a bag of groceries as Hadel came back down to the sidewalk. "Two days ago. A U-Haul truck and a guy to load it. Figured she was moving to a better neighborhood, big star like her, but then they had her good-bye show that night."

"Good-bye show?" Hadel echoed. She had been unable to watch Ann's program since Ann's attempt to reunite Gary and his sister.

"Everybody was on it," the neighbor said, putting up a knee to balance the groceries. "You know that David Meyers? He kissed her on the cheek. They had the guys who run the cameras, too. Everybody was crying. I bet there wasn't a dry eye in half the Bay Area."

"I bet," Hadel said. "Did they say where she was going?"

"Nope. That was odd. But I figure New York. She's a pretty big star, you know. We'll see her on some network show soon, maybe some interview thing."

Hadel nodded. "She'd be good at that. Thanks for the information."

"Say, what happened to her friend? The beautiful one. She sure kept up the yard nice."

"She left too," Hadel answered.

"Well, sure hope whoever moves in does half as good a job as she did. Bye."

Hadel waved good-bye and went home to call Natalie. Perhaps Ann would go to New York. It wasn't so farfetched. Natalie could keep an ear to the ground.

"Any news?" Natalie asked her several months later, in May, as they sat in the backyard of Natalie and Hank's home in New Rochelle, eating breakfast while they watched little Michael trying to grab at a butterfly skimming above his head.

"I called Ann's parents at the beginning of April, and they said she was taking a long trip. They'd gotten a postcard from Italy. I guess she's running around Europe."

"Maybe she went to see Laney's parents in Morocco."

Hadel nodded. She had thought of this before. As far as she knew, Ann hadn't scattered Laney's ashes. It was possible she had decided to bring them to Laney's parents.

"I'm sorry, Hadel. It must have been horrible for you."

"It was pretty awful for everyone," Hadel agreed. She finished her roll and stretched out on the grass. The morning sun shone on the pale green of new leaves. She closed her eyes and said, "I'm not sure I even want to go to the class reunion. Can't we just stay here?" Once she had finally arrived at Natalie's house, she would have been perfectly happy lying on the lawn all day rather than tramping around at Ridgedale. She was amused that while the reunion had served as her excuse to come to New York, now it seemed the least important thing in the world. But would she have allowed herself to come simply to lie on the lawn? She admitted sadly that the idea would never have occurred to her.

She had arrived yesterday afternoon and headed directly for the offices of *Boy's Adventure* instead of meeting Natalie at her office as they had planned. "I can't stand this unsolved mystery any longer," she had explained to Natalie from a pay phone.

Boy's Adventure was easy to find, located in an old midtown building. Hadel walked into the editorial offices and asked to see Mr. Cromwell. "Do you have an appointment?" the woman at the desk asked frostily.

"No."

"Well, it's quarter to five, and—"

"I see. Could you possibly leave a message that Hester Farnon is in town for the next few days and would like to meet with him?"

The woman was in the act of rising—Hadel realized then that this was not her desk—but she sat back down with a thump. "You're Hadel?"

Hadel nodded.

"Oh, dear," the woman said.

Hadel waited, trying to smother the smile itching on her lips. She couldn't help but be satisfied with the effect her name had produced.

"I'm Sarah Mitchell," the woman said. "Sarah Anne Mitchell."

It took Hadel a moment, but then she had it. "You're Sam."

"That's right. You see, when—" She tapped her fingers on the desk. "Come into my office. The receptionist left at four, that's why I'm here." She walked around the desk, and Hadel followed her down a hall and into an office with an abbreviated view of the building across the street. "When your friend came in, I tried to head her off, but she was very insistent. Mr. Cromwell does not—I mean, absolutely does not—accept any stories from women writers. That I'm his editorial assistant occurred through a minor miracle, and as it is, he thinks of me as a glorified secretary. Anyway," she sighed, "your friend—"

"Natalie."

"When Natalie came in, she got past the receptionist, and she badgered me into reading your stories. I read them at home one night. You were good! I mean, you are good. That's when it came to me. Since you just put 'Farnon' on your pages, it was easy to retype the title page as Harold each time. I told Mr. Cromwell you insisted on using 'H. Farnon' in the magazine." She took a deep breath. "Of course, the accounting department knew, but they thought it was wonderful. Everyone ended up knowing but Mr. Cromwell. Then you started writing the letters."

The endless series of letters demanding that Mr. Cromwell stop addressing her as "Mr. Farnon." Hadel remembered them well.

"Luckily, I open his mail. I started retyping your letters, leaving out, well, those parts. But then I got worried. What if I was sick for a couple of days, and he opened one of your letters? I sent you that telegram asking you to stop writing the letters, and the next thing I know, I see your stories in *Boys' World.* I meant the telegram to be funny, but then I realized you must be terribly offended. You see, by then I felt we were all playing a game, conspiring against Mr. Cromwell, and I'd forgotten you had no idea what was happening. After all, that's why you were writing the letters! Mr. Cromwell also noticed your stories in *Boys' World.* He mentioned it each time a new issue came out. Weren't we paying you enough? What was the problem? I could hardly tell him the real problem. Then, when you started sending us stories again, I began retyping Mr. Cromwell's letters. He signed one, I signed the one addressed to 'Ms.,' and his went in the trash."

Hadel felt like an idiot. She'd suspected something like this all along, yet she'd persisted with her affronted letters for months. "I'm sorry I put you through so much trouble."

"Oh, no, please don't apologize! I'm sorry I didn't think of retyping his letters sooner, at the very beginning."

Hadel thought a moment. "I'm afraid I'm going to cause you more trouble."

Sarah nodded. "The anthology. Photographs of all three authors. It's coming out next month, isn't it? Truth will out. I've been trying to figure out a way to tell him."

"Sarah! Where are you?" A big, bluff man, who looked the prototype of Agatha Christie's home-from-India colonels, burst into the room. "I thought you were on recep—oh, pardon me!"

Sarah plunged ahead. "Mr. Cromwell, this is Hadel Farnon."

"Uhm, glad to meet you." He stuck out his hand, which Hadel duly shook.

"H. Farnon, Mr. Cromwell," Sarah persisted.

"Hmm? Oh!" He stared at Hadel, then turned to Sarah with a worried face. "But you know—women writing for boys, lets down the standards, almost like women writing pornography . . ." This thought got twisted in his mind, and he ended up looking at the ceiling. "But"—he stuck out his hand once more, and Hadel shook it again—"fine writing, young lady. Keep it up. Haven't seen much from you lately. With that anthology coming out, we'll need a few of your things for the summer issues. Good for the magazine, two of our authors picked like that."

"Sure," Hadel said, bemused. What harm would it do to write three or four more stories? She owed it to Sarah, not to mention her own pocketbook, slimmer now by the cost of her trip to New York.

"Fine," he said. "Well, I'm off. See you tomorrow."

Hadel and Sarah sat quietly for a moment after he'd left. "You must think I'm batty," Sarah said.

Hadel smiled. "Not one bit." By the time they'd had a couple of drinks and Hadel boarded the train to New Rochelle, she counted the trip worthwhile just for this one contact with the shadowy source of her livelihood. The rest of the evening, with Natalie and Hank, had been spent meeting Michael and exchanging quick updates of news, so this lazy outdoor breakfast was the first time she'd had a chance to talk to Natalie.

"Of course we have to go to the reunion," Natalie scolded. "You'll find it strange being at Ridgedale, though, very different from when we were there. The students are superstraight. They all look neat and tidy and homogenized." Natalie made a face. "At first I blamed Megan's admissions policies, but then I realized it was the same all over."

"True," Hadel said. "You should see Berkeley. The old nuts like us are the scruffy ones, while the kids are out buying kegs for their frat parties and swallowing goldfish, for all I know."

"Frats. My God. Well, kiddo, it's about that time. Aren't you going to change?"

"Already?" She groaned as she hoisted herself up to a sitting position. "What am I supposed to wear?"

Natalie shrugged. "Whatever."

"Jeans are a no-go on the current campus scene, I gather. What if they're Juliana Jeans?"

"Juliana Jeans are perfect anywhere," Natalie said loyally.

"Well, the best I can do is cords. Will you still be my date?"

"Sure. Hop upstairs. We'll drop Michael off at the babysitter's on the way."

Hadel was disappointed. "Can't we bring him? Won't everyone want to bill and coo? He's certainly cooable." She demonstrated by dangling her fingers in front of him, laughing as he had better luck capturing her finger in his pudgy hands than the butterfly.

"No, no, no!" Natalie insisted. "You haven't been keeping up on your feminist reading lately: 'The Isolation of the Single Mother.'"

"You're not a single mother!"

"Anyone married to an obstetrician is a single mother."

Hadel gathered the mugs and plates from their breakfast, and Natalie picked up Michael. They moved slowly toward the house. "He's gone a lot, huh?"

"Yeah, but it's all right. Things will slow down by next year. He's getting a partner in his practice, and he's a sailing freak, not a workaholic. I've gotten to like sailing, too." She smiled shyly while Hadel grinned at her. "It's wonderful being with him. We're planning a trip to the Caribbean in February."

Hadel was pleased. When Natalie was happy, all seemed right with the world.

"Come on, Hadel!" Natalie yelped, looking at the kitchen clock. "We're going to be late!"

The campus was much the same, though the school had somehow scraped up enough money to put in a swimming pool below the post office area, a pool that was now filled with boisterous students taking advantage of warm weather and sparkling air. "They're so young!" Hadel said.

"I know. It's amazing, isn't it? We have to register up at the administration building."

They were disappointed to find only two or three people from their class, none of whom they knew well. "Everybody came last year, I heard," Natalie said. "We'll have to wait 'til the fifteenth."

But there was one familiar face. "There's Portia's sister," Hadel said, pointing her out. "What's her name? I can't remember."

"Me neither. You gonna talk to her?"

"Sure. I'll go over and say hello." Hadel threaded her way through groups of women, some dressed up, some not, some elderly, some barely out of college. Everyone seemed to be talking at a volume loud enough to project to the rear seats of an auditorium. "Hi," Hadel said. "I'm sorry, I don't remember your name. . . ."

Toni pulled back a shank of hair to reveal her name tag, with the words printed on it in black Magic Marker: "Toni Bethany,

'72." Then she barked, a short breath of sound that had no connection with enjoyment. "My name's Portia Bethany's sister. It has been for years. I either announce it at the start, or I don't let on, and then people get angry, as if I'd kept something from them. 'Why didn't you tell me you're Portia Bethany's sister?' As if I'd lied. As if I said my name was Sally when it was Sue." She lit a cigarette with a flourish, but Hadel knew she was only trying to calm down. "You're Hadel, aren't you? You were there at the funeral."

"I was there," Hadel said tonelessly.

"Well, I'm glad," Toni said. "Now that she's in jail, at least it's starting to be over. Maybe when I'm fifty I can be Toni. Maybe they'll keep her for a long time."

"They won't," Hadel said. "She's getting out next month."

"Five months? Since I was nineteen I've been Portia Bethany's sister, and she only gets five months?"

"It hasn't been easy for her either," Hadel said, "but she can tell you that herself. I think you're one of the first people she wants to see."

Toni looked at her and then wheeled around and left the reception area.

Natalie had been hovering nearby, watching the interchange. "I don't think you made a very good impression."

"No, I certainly didn't." Hadel was shocked by the depth of Toni's bitterness. "Portia doesn't know what she's getting into. Maybe I should write her a letter of warning."

"She can handle it," Natalie said. "Portia's a survivor. And so is Ann, you know? They're doing just fine. What workshops do you want to go to?"

Hadel dragged herself back to the reunion with an effort. "Oh, I don't know. How about this one?" She pointed to a title at random: "Pirandello: Worlds Within Worlds." Natalie clicked her tongue. The other choices, however, were "Film as Art," "The English Country House" and "Manners: Are They Disappearing?"

Natalie sighted ceilingward to express her disapproval. "Give me a break."

"Don't you work on this?"

"No. I'm a money gofer and a communications network

among ten committees. The head honcho who makes no decisions. All right, Pirandello it is."

Pirandello was fascinating, but they took no further chances, opting for the softball game during the afternoon. Cocktails were cocktails, with desultory chitchat with their few classmates. Dinner was boring, complete with the requisite money pitches at the end. Natalie tapped Hadel's elbow at the close of the speeches. "I have to go talk to a wealthy alumna for a bit. Duty calls."

"Fine," Hadel said, waving her away. "I'd kinda like to wander around a bit, indulge myself in old memories."

"All right. We'll meet at the car in forty-five minutes." Natalie made a beeline across the crowded dining room, adjusting her scarf, her eyes fixed on her prey. Hadel watched her, smiling. Natalie had become more impatient, more efficient and more eccentric all at the same time. Hadel suspected her underlings at the advertising agency adored her, even if she made life difficult for them with her quick switches of attention. She had grown into herself, and she fit well.

Hadel went outside, skirted the new swimming pool and walked up the road outside the grounds. She crossed over at the apple orchard and turned left up the path to the music building. No demonic music tonight. Someone was sawing industriously at a cello. She startled a couple in the orchard on her way back; the boy leaped away from his girlfriend as if he had been slapped. "Just walking," Hadel assured them. They stared after her as if she were a Martian. Do I look so old? she wondered. Have I become such a symbol of authority they quake in their boots as I pass?

Eventually, as she'd known she would, she meandered up to the third floor of Simpson, her home as a senior, scene of Laney's grand seduction, of the revising of the parietal laws, of Megan's marathon Clue game. The hall looked the same—dim light and peeling paint, though this had to be at least a second peeling paint job—but something was indefinably different. No life in the hall, for one thing. Maybe people dated in this day and age, or actually went to the library to study. The hall was deserted, true, but Hadel had the impression that it would seem deserted even if its inhabitants were home Ageist, she accused. You've become a crotchety old lady. Just think what you'll be like at sixty.

When the bathroom door at the end of the hall opened right in front of her, Hadel jumped. She hadn't noticed it was closed, or if she had, she'd attached no importance to the fact, assuming she was alone. She found herself looking into Megan's face.

"I use this bathroom sometimes," Megan said.

"Really." And so this would not be the sum total of their first conversation in twelve years, Hadel said, and meant it, "You look wonderful, Megan." In fact, Hadel thought, if the ice around her face melted and she actually broke free with a smile, Megan could be called beautiful. Her old air of frantic preoccupation had vanished, though she was now managing to look anywhere but at Hadel. Hadel sensed Megan mentally drawing a deep breath to steady herself. She was going to say something more.

"Are you working?" Megan asked.

"Well, yes and no. More no at the moment, though I have some projects in the wind." Hadel smiled at her. "Do you like your job?"

Megan nodded, apparently not trusting herself to speak again. Her eyes darted everywhere around Hadel's periphery, as if she were measuring Hadel's aura for a costume. Hadel herself was rendered speechless by an immense wave of sadness. Though Megan had guarded her front door so assiduously, so faultlessly, thieves had broken in the rear and stolen all her valuables from under her nose. Worse, she hadn't noticed anything missing yet. "The things you're frightened of," Hadel said gently, finding her voice now that she had something to say, "aren't really so important. They really aren't."

Megan seemed to be staring way back into herself, doing a quick tally. She came forward with an effort. "You always did have beautiful eyes, Hadel." Then she stepped around Hadel and walked down the hall. Her footsteps echoed on the wooden stairs until she reached the carpeted section below.

The heavy outside door on the first level had clanged shut minutes before Hadel moved forward to stand in front of her old room. She reached out one finger and pushed at the partially open door until she could see inside. The bed was against the wall instead of under the window and was covered by a tasseled bedspread instead of a navy-blue sleeping bag. A stuffed Snoopy sat on top of a nonstandard desk of drawers, and the walls were hung with three-foot-high skiing posters—Aspen, St. Moritz, Squaw Valley. Hadel stepped into the room and saw what had been there: the Salvation Army armchairs grouped in one corner around a Navajo rug, the trunk with leather straps, the standing wooden ashtray full of butts, the walls a riot of color with posters from the Fillmore—the Grateful Dead, Jefferson Airplane, Country Joe, Joplin. And she heard the music, Indian ragas, eerie acid rock, Mimi and Richard Farina. She heard it so intensely that she was knocked off balance by sheets of pulsating energy, and she reached out for the coatrack that wasn't there to root herself to one time and one place. Then the smells came back, the sweet incense, the heavy musty odor of a whole floor of smokers, the summer scent of marijuana clinging to everyone's clothes, the tarriness of hash and the resinous empty beer can hookas, with their brown-stained swatches of aluminum foil pressed carefully into the open triangles at the top. The energy reached such a point that Hadel had to move into the room, had to stride to the window and look out upon the lawn and the arbor, as she had so often in that past that was now claiming her by its urgency. She stared out at the dark lawn and recognized a figure, just as she had that day of Thanksgiving vacation when she had returned early from Megan's. Hadel had turned from the window, barely able to contain her excitement, and said to Natalie: "Look, Laney's back!" Laney had been sporting on the lawn, tossing her football up and down, throwing it ahead a few yards and running underneath to catch it. Hadel could see her, the small, lithe figure with the white-gold hair, so happy playing by herself. She had played by herself her whole life, Hadel thought.

But the figure on the lawn was not Laney. It was Natalie, peering around her anxiously. The promised forty-five minutes, Hadel realized, had been more like an hour or more. She rapped on the window with her knuckles. Natalie raised her head, and her eyes lit up when she saw Hadel waving at her behind the panes of glass. Hadel smiled as she watched the puzzle being solved on Natalie's face, the comprehension dawn that Hadel was standing in a student's room. Natalie's mouth twisted in a combination of disapproval and delighted wickedness, and she beckoned Hadel with exaggerated ferocity, sneaking glances to the side as if they were robbing a bank. Hadel laughed out loud, giving Natalie a thumbs-up sign. She reclosed the room door three quarters of the way and bounded down the steps. Tomorrow, she told herself, she could have her day on the lawn.